ADVICE FROM PIGEONS
A Royal Academy At Osyth Novel

Patricia S. Bowne

ADVICE FROM PIGEONS

DOUBLE DRAGON

Dedication

This book is dedicated to all the people who made my college and university experiences so much fun that I wanted to spend my fictional time in a university.

The good points of my characters are drawn from life.

I only made up their flaws.

Many thanks to all who read and commented on the manuscript.

It could not have been written without insightful and detailed critiques from Milwaukee Area Writers' Guild, particularly Sue Blom, Emory Churness, Kate Martin, Jill Maier, and Sue Burke.

They've kept their interest and their tempers through endless pages of Osyth fiction, and now know more about the world than I do.

Thank you!

Chapter One

Within the next half-hour, Warren Oldham thought, he would either be successful or dismembered. At the thought, all the worries that had romped through his mind ever since he opened his eyes that morning froze or dove for cover, and Warren stood up taller. He felt his bones balancing on each other and the muscles that held them in place, the nerves that sent messages to them with pinpoint accuracy, the brain that generated the messages, the mind that thought them up, the soul that determined what the mind would come up with, what defined him as Warren and nobody else. Warren had called up a demon every weekday morning for almost twenty-eight years, and every time he did the preparatory inventory he felt this satisfaction and confidence. It was a sign of having chosen the right career.

He shut his eyes for a moment, swaying backwards and forwards a little, and thought that anyone who looked at him would have seen a stout pink-and-white man with a little tonsure and a large mustache-a man with no worries.

"Well?" James Kalin said.

"Ready," Warren answered, opening his eyes, and took a half-step forward toward the golden chain inside the pentarium.

"Too far!" James warned, from his left.

"Not far enough," Russell Cinea said, from his right.

Warren concluded that he was just right. He raised his voice in the first syllables of the summoning charm, and the rest of the Demonology Department joined in.

"Inquiring spirit," they intoned. "Adventurer in the arcane realms, Lord of Darkness, seeker of knowledge, hear us! Teach us!"

Warren was invoking his colleagues as much as the demons with these epithets, and he mentally divided them into those who knew this and those who didn't. The senior faculty nearest him-Russell Cinea, James Kalin, the herbalist Anders Regan and Cham Ligalla the exorcist-knew it. Their powers, more subtle and self-aware than their colleagues', made the foundation of the circle of magic beginning to fill the pentarium.

The pentarium at the Royal Academy of the Arcane Arts and Sciences lay belowground in a cavern under the Magic Building, dug into the ley-line itself and humming with power. A circular room, plated with gold and almost featureless except for the door and the safety switch in the wall behind Warren, it shone with a pale yellow light. The thirteen magicians of the Demonology Department stood outside a gold safety chain that stretched, knee-height, between five gold posts set a meter in from the chamber's edge. Within the chain lay the pentacle itself, drawn in blood.

Warren stood at the side furthest from the pentarium door, where he could look across at the junior faculty who stood by it. That was the only perk of heading the Demonology Department. He got to stand furthest from the door, so if anything went wrong the demon would have more time to

8

dismember him. That was how one got out of heading the department, Warren had said, but it wasn't true. Only two administrators had left that way.

The demonologists wore blue paper smocks, belted with gold chains from which hung the Academy's ward and other protective charms, and all had gold chains around their necks. Warren's chain was a gift from his wife Lilian and his mother Bosie, made of square medallions so heavy they needed a counterweight at the back of his neck. James Kalin wore a thinner necklace, decorated with gold roses. Some of the roses had fallen off, leaving unsightly lumps of solder, but it was a gift from Kalin's daughter and he wore it, nevertheless. Cinea, a bachelor, wore the standard chain available from any lab supplies catalog.

When they began the second verse of the charm, Warren always took what might be a last look at his colleagues. They stood in a lopsided circle and a row of reflected magicians stood behind them, with their backs to the circle as if they were uninterested in their fellows.

"Spirit of knowledge, enlighten us," they chanted, flattering the demons and themselves. "Join our discourse. We open our minds to your wisdom; we invite you."

This was Theodora Whin's language, and her magic glowed warmer with every word. Even though she had pulled back to lean casually against the wall, and Warren could only see her nail-bitten hand reaching around the curve of the circle, her power stretched across the room as if she were willing to define the entire project, if invited to.

9

The same language enraged Linus Ukadnian, the geomancer who towered over the other side of the circle. Linus was the only person wearing anything around his neck except a gold chain; he had on a bow tie, but he was so fierce that nobody dared smile at it. The next clauses were more to his taste. "Sages of the nether realm," he chanted, as if every word were a reproach to his colleagues. "Seekers after truth, hear us!" Linus and Teddy between them sent an arc of clashing magics right across the pentarium, and their colleagues' powers-cold and warm, crisp and relaxed-filled in the chinks around it.

The junior demonologists in front of the door kept up the chant without adding much of their own personalities to it. Neil Torecki spoke with the most energy, his red curls bobbing. He cheated every few minutes, reading from crib notes written on his arm. Isaac Graham's face was screwed up as he concentrated on remembering the spell. And Hiram Rho, the natural philosopher standing right in front of the door, odd man out at this, his first conjuration-Rho was a mess.

Rho was in his twenties, a little, wiry, tree-climbing sort of man, with blond hair that stood out horizontally over his ears and pale blue eyes. His hands were small and filthy. His expression was sour. His stance was belligerent. *What would happen,* Warren wondered, *if Rho were so grubby as to not make skin contact with the colleagues holding his hands?* He looked the kind to be wearing a broken chain, mended with old twist ties... Warren shivered, imagining the circle broken and his faculty disemboweled. 'How did this

10

happen?' the dean would ask. 'Did you know the man was incompetent? Did you suspect it?'

He felt himself go cold and then a comforting thought burst on him like sunlight. He was the one furthest from the door. He'd be the one disemboweled, not the one answering questions. Warren gave a sigh of relief and noticed that he was even colder, shivering harder, and the other magicians were all looking to him. They all felt the *cauld grue* that meant a demon stood among them, lured into the pentarium by the summoning charm.

Warren stepped forward another half-pace and raised his voice in the final verse of the incantation, the others chiming in at each word, and he felt his magicians come back from wherever they had been. All their attention was on him and on the words they were speaking, words about themselves and how much they wanted to meet and talk with one of the most powerful arcane creatures. With every word, Warren felt pleasure and anticipation rise warm through his whole body and out into the circle, his magic meeting, clashing and harmonizing with his colleagues' until they formed one thing greater and more complex than any one of them, something any self-respecting demon must investigate. Red smoke began to rise in the inner pentacle, whirling like a distracted tornado, and its cold hit against the circle as if it were feeling for places it could pry apart, and finding none.

***

Rho had no opinion about the words of the invocation. His sour look was based more on seeing

11

that Neil Torecki had written the charm on his arm, instead of wasting time memorizing it. Not that Rho wanted to do anything so unprofessional-it was bad enough working at this second-rate institution, without lowering his standards to meet theirs-but the fact that Neil had a trick and had not shared it confirmed Rho's opinions about the other faculty. About humans in general.

Hiram Rho, natural philosopher and misanthrope, discovered he could understand birds at the age of eight, while watching the neighbor's pigeons. The neighbor came home two days later, and had squab for dinner.

By ten, Rho could hear all the creatures in the barnyard. He ate his own severest critic, picking her out of the crowd around the chicken coop, and after that they watched their tongues around him, but the gift had already gone too far. From sunrise to sunset Rho heard the clamor of wild birds and beasts, from sundown to dawn the arguments of frogs and crickets. When the cries of insects his father poisoned in the fields started drowning out his own family, Rho bolted.

The first bad things that happened to Rho on the streets of Kasidora were his own fault, for listening to the first people he met. The rest were his own fault for not listening to any other people. They were the sort of things animals couldn't warn him about. The tips he picked up on the street did keep him out of some kinds of trouble, though-the kinds of trouble alley cats wanted to avoid, the kinds that involved being shut up and bathed, fed nice food, being flea-combed and having their balls cut off.

The kinds that kept them away from casual sex and violence.

Rho lived eight months on the streets of Kasidora without taking advice from a single human being, until he heard a human speaking cat. By that time he had combined street urchin hygiene with alley cat manners. His mentor was later to say that Rho's true talent lay in making the worst of whatever was offered. Certainly, he had never been able to make understanding animals into any kind of communication. The cats ignored his attempts to sound out their language. So he had listened to the person who could speak with cats. He had followed through alleys, farther and farther from his familiar lairs each time, finally up to an old house by the gates of the university where a plate of scraps sat just inside the open door. The cat-speaker, Baristes, watched in the window, letting strays make their way into the warm rooms in their own time.

In the dark house, Rho learned to speak cat and pigeon. He learned about wine and fabric and the manners of the gentry, but none of it struck home. No more capable of luxury than an alley cat and treated as a curio rather than a servant, Rho learned to endure civilization but not to construct it, and when he transferred from Baristes' mansion to the college barracks he relapsed into squalor as easily as any of the other boys. By then, though, Rho could talk to the animals. He knew his talent was called natural philosophy, and was shared by few. He knew that human rule and human reasoning were arbitrary, designed by people who didn't believe that other creatures truly existed, and that natural philosophers were no more beholden to their own species than to any other.

Small wonder that Warren looked at Rho with carefully concealed dismay and sought his wife's sympathy. Knowledgeable as the mages of Osyth were, as acquainted as they were with interview protocols, with courtly Kasidora and with the oversweet image of natural philosophy, they could not have guessed that the young man who had acquitted himself so respectably in seminars and job interviews would revert to a filthy, hostile scavenger as soon as he was established at the Royal Academy.

The *cauld grue* swept through the pentarium and Rho, who had been half-lost in thoughts of how unsatisfactory his colleagues were, jumped. Those same colleagues were all that stood between him and the demon materializing in the pentacle. Rho hoped he had been wrong about them.

***

Far above the pentarium, sunrise lit the Magic Building, a white castle set on the middle of the ley-line that cut across the northern corner of the Osyth Plateau. It shone on the squat Wizardry Building at the east end of the ley-line, on the Sorcery Complex and hospital between Magic and Wizardry, and on the Alchemy Building sitting in the middle of the isolated triangle of land north of the ley-line.

The sun shone on the city of Osyth, that had spread from the southern edge of the plateau up toward the Academy as far as it dared and then had built a high wall to keep the magic out. That wall and the ley-line bounded a no-man's-land containing Academy administrators, faculty housing, and maintenance workshops. Just behind the wall lay the slums of Osyth. The tall buildings and elegant apartments that Warren had helped build during his wizarding years, before he joined the Magic faculty, rose from the center of the city. Factories and businesses lay to the south, near the cliffs down which pollution could be dumped into the magic-filled canyons below.

At the north edge of the industrial belt, bordering on the classy residential part of the city, stood the large respectable businesses: banks, hotels, and office buildings. On the tallest of these buildings, best warded against malignant strays from north and south, a sign in golden letters glinted back toward the nine o'clock sun. It read 'Salvation Insurance.' Inside this building, Lilian Oldham had just entered her cubicle and opened her e-mail.

Lilian Oldham had grown to resemble her husband over thirty-five years of marriage. Rounded and cheerful, she shared his pink-and-white coloring, though she had hair in bountiful foamy white curls. Like many people who worked in insurance, Lilian maintained a sunny manner. Whatever happened, her smile assured the viewer that Salvation would save its clients. This manner had been ingrained into her years ago when she sold insurance, and her shift into the scrying department had not entirely erased it. This morning, however, the cheerful smile was not in evidence. Lilian looked at her computer screen with a suspicious expression and a feeling that she might be growing tired of bad luck, even though she had made a living from it for over forty years.

Bad luck. Jinxing it. Letting the gods hear how much a person wanted to keep out of the briar patch... the more someone bet on something, the less likely it was to happen. The more likely the misfortune, the higher the premium had to be to fool bad luck into taking it away. In order to set rates, Salvation Insurance hired professional scryers like Lilian to find out just how likely a misfortune was. Her specialty was life insurance.

The computer's screen showed an online application for life insurance, a standard document. Lilian turned on her printer and got herself a cup of coffee while it rattled. Some of the scryers used direct download attachments, specialized soft drives that let the computer copy these data from the forms right onto the tarot cards or bones the scryer preferred. Some were even experimenting with virtual scrying, using computerized images of the cards, but Lilian thought that was going too far. Magic was physical, not just a matter of information in bits and bytes.

She tore the printed application off and ripped it into strips, which she put into the soft green bag that held her scrying bones. The bones were from the only blood sacrifice Lilian had ever made, in her senior year at the Academy; the bag a crooked oblong, its velvet trim sewn on with clumsy stitches. Lilian rubbed her thumb across the velvet and smiled. This had been her daughter Joan's first handwork and she liked to think it added something to the augury, some element of loving care, some understanding of what a family and its well-being

16

meant. She rolled the bag between her hands, losing herself in the feel of it and of the papers and bones rustling inside, and then opened it wide and poured them out in a tangle on the mousepad.

The bones were light and dry, the color of yellowed ivory, covered over with a scrimshaw of scratches. Some lay trapped in the curls of paper, others bounced aside as if they would take wing again and fly. The longest bone, the tibiotarsus, lay wrapped around with paper strips, as usual in Lilian's cases; the life bone of someone who had a good reason to apply for insurance. When she'd begun with Salvation, doing group policies, she'd seen life bones fall free of the paperwork, but it had been a long time since she last dealt with anything so simple. Now all her cases fell out as a snarl of worry and fear, the papers obscuring the markings on the long bone. The paper coils caught up over half the bones, tying them into a tangle.

Lilian teased the mass apart with a delicate stylus, the position of each bone appearing on the computer screen as she marked it, until only a pattern of notations remained to indicate illness, genetic weaknesses, accident and folly ahead. The computer was silent as it did its work, transmitting the scratch of figures to the mainframe for analysis, and Lilian looked at what it couldn't transmit. The strips of paper with the man's wife's name, his children's ages, wrapped around the fragile bones as if to keep them safe.

The next three applications were easier, their results more cheerful. Then came one that needed re-reading, and re-reading again, though it had looked like a standard application; there was no life

17

to the bones or papers, as if she were scrying for someone already dead, and the next two files were no better. Lilian typed in an e-mail.

Another three dead accounts, she wrote to the other scryers, informally. *What's going on?*

No idea, came an answer. *They're all Academy accounts, though. We have two.*

"Damn!" Lilian said, hastily deleting the last message. Some people had no idea of what should and shouldn't be sent over the Salvation network. Still, she rechecked the three dead applications. They were from the Academy, and now Lilian recognized at least one of the names. It was the new man, the one Warren complained about at night. Rho.

***

Warren's first sentence had caught the spirit's attention. It chose a position a little to the right of him in the circle, hovering nearest to Patsy Hoth, who studied incubi, and Linus Ukadnian. It was attracted by their fierceness, but unwilling to approach Susan Teale's more benign aura between them. Warren saw Patsy Hoth's face through the smoke, framed by golden curls and with a look of controlled irritation on her features as she spoke to the cloud and told it a few truths about itself.

"How shall we speak to you?" she challenged the cloud. "As an individual? Hardly, for an individual exists in itself, rather than being defined by those around it."

The cloud hovered, listening, and Linus confirmed Patsy's words with enough arrogance to

18

convince even a demon. "Spirit, penetrated by all around it, is defined only by those points at which its neighbors choose to stop," he chanted. "A being without boundaries is no more than a construction of the stronger beings around it. Matter, alone, exists as itself; matter alone creates its own boundaries."

The cloud retreated a little from this uninvited commentary, but only a little. As fast as the smoke darted, side to side, the magicians were faster. Each line they chanted, each argument, was a new piece of the reasoning that trapped the demon within the pentacle. Each followed from the previous assumptions and the spirit, having paused long enough to admit itself intrigued by those assumptions, was now led by logic into a solid form, a truthful habit, that were alien to it. James Kalin, Russell Cinea, and Teddy Whin wrote these charms of discourse, in consult with a group of theoretical demonologists across three continents, but it was a touchy business. Theoretical magicians got carried away. They were likely to refute one another just for the practice, and a charm would only hold until the demons learned how to refute it. They were always listening.

Warren could hear the magicians by the door reciting the charm of discourse in a steady drone that kept the demon away from them and left it darting between the more experienced magicians. A demon always began by exploring the powers it resembled, fought its way back and forth through the mesh of the magicians' interests and ambitions, and then seized on the neutral powers as a possible escape. It would make its final incorporeal charge toward Warren or Cham Ligalla; this was another reason for placing the senior magicians at the inner end of the room, to draw the near-solid demon away from the door.

The smoke gathered itself together, changing from red to gray. Warren felt its power like the one clear thing in the confusion of the circle. He began the last part of the charm, the words about the meaning of embodiment, and the smoke swarmed toward him as if it rode up a path of his and Cham's attention. Her voice and his, her power and his, met, and where they met, the smoke stood irresolute while the circle of magicians told it about what an individual-a solid individual-was. It curdled in on itself, roiled and solidified, and its pressure against the circle began to fade as it accepted their reasoning and became the solid creature they had invoked. Warren stopped chanting, took a breath, and had the leisure to realize success. Another morning's work was done, and nobody had been disemboweled.

The demon stood solid now, a hulking gray figure with three legs. It balanced on two, waggling the third at the magicians by the door, and then leaned over to suck its own toes while, on the other side, it broke foul wind into Warren's face. The echo filled the room.

"By the logic of your nature I charge you," Warren said. "Make your name known to us."

The demon snarled and spit in frustration, but could find no way to deny the logic of its nature as laid out in the charm. For as long as it remembered to believe the arguments it had just heard, it would speak the truth.

"Nezumia," it finally muttered in a rasping voice as gray as its hide, and Warren saw his magicians' faces light up.

A major demon indeed! A malign power, one of the greatest of the demon lords of Osyth. They almost capered, these magicians who for months in the first semester had been too few to trap any but minor spirits in their pentacle, and Nezumia spun around to look at all of them with loathing. So fast it spun that it lofted itself into the air, and lunged toward the door with a shriek. But the wall of words held, and although the demon frightened those before it, it could do them no harm. Warren cast the last charm, one that set the room as it was against any eddies in the ley-line, and the magicians let go of each other's hands. They had to take themselves and their magic out for the setting-charm to establish itself. The circle dissociated and mages trailed out into the shower room, male and female together. The room was filled with high-fives and bodies capering among the steam, laughter and cries of triumph... but when Warren looked for Rho, the newest magician had disappeared.

"He's probably glad to get out of here," Neil Torecki said, and shook water out of his red hair like a dog. "The big N gave him a scare with that last lunge! I thought he'd break my hand, he held on so tight. Good instinct, that. I like a guy who holds to the circle."

Yes," Warren said. "That's good to hear." He leaned back into the hot water, feeling it beat down on his bare scalp, and laughed. They had done it again, all these magicians he worried and stewed about, sometimes admired and other times hated.

21

All their disagreements had been set aside for one half-hour, and the very force of their desire had called a major demon to speak with them for four hours, five, maybe ten-until it forgot to believe the arguments it had just heard, or stopped wanting to be a creature of reason. All the problems of the day to come seemed far away in another man's future.

***

Rho laughed at himself, stopping on the third-floor landing to pant. Why had he run? Up three flights from the pentarium, now halfway to his tower lab, and already out of breath! More from elation than from exercise, gasping with laughter instead of exhaustion-his heart still racing, shaking his whole chest, his legs full of a trembling that said 'run!' Rho bent double on the stairs and gasped and shook. His blue paper gown rustled like leaves in a windstorm.

The way it had jerked and hit the side of the charm, like a shark in a net, the monster! The way he'd felt it pressing up against his words, the logic he'd been afraid he wouldn't understand or take seriously enough to hold against a demon, and then when it had come at him, that scream! And he'd held so tight, he'd remembered not to break the circle, it had been like steering into a skid or exhaling when he came up from a dive. He'd known it was asinine, if he didn't run he'd be killed, and he'd still held on!

"Yes!" Rho said and slapped the wall, high-fiving the stones. No more being looked down on by magicians who had bound their own demons. No more being just the little man who talked with animals. He, Rho, had trapped a demon! He'd done it! He hadn't fouled it up, and already the feeling was slipping away and out of his mind, he was losing how gray and foul and big and loud it had been-the smell of it, the rot dripping out of those vile teeth, its breath. He shut his eyes, trying to call it back.

We'll do it again tomorrow! he thought, with a thrill. Every morning, as long as they had enough demonologists on campus and a charm that would work, the magicians of Osyth would trap a demon for the day. It was their duty, to pay the International Demonological Association for maintaining the pentarium. Magicians from all over the world would come in today to study Nezumia, and Rho had helped trap it! Every article they wrote would list him in the acknowledgments, because he had done the dangerous work. He ran up the last three flights thinking he'd attend his next conference as a full-fledged demonologist, a master of the trade, and it wasn't until he got to the tower door that he realized his clothing was still down in the pentarium shower room.

***

Theodora Whin used the open showers rather than the private booths, and scrubbed herself more carefully than anyone else in the room. She rubbed shampoo through her brown curls and used herbal-scented soap to chase away the last smells of bittersmoke and demon. Before drying off, she spread a scented oil over her body and let it trap the clean moisture in her skin, and then she put on the most beautiful silk underwear in the entire department. Teddy Whin did not consider it a problem that her colleagues knew what she looked like naked, or that they knew she wore outstanding silk underwear. She was setting a good example in both categories.

"There was another sexist assumption in your third precept," she told Russell Cinea. She had found that Russell was less superior and confident when he was unclothed. "Your imagery was positively phallic. No wonder all our demons manifest as male."

"That's all very well in theory," Russell answered in a peevish tone. "The fact is, if we use your language none of us believe the charm enough to make it work. You have to use the metaphors people were brought up with."

"We could use a different set of the metaphors they were brought up with," James Kalin put in. He sat on the bench near Russell, stretching out his legs and wiggling his toes to dry them. James did not use towels. He believed in taking his time in the morning, and this was another reason that the three theorists had many of their discussions in the shower room. "There's no reason to avoid metaphors of solidarity and unity. Especially solidarity."

"Those are usually as sexist as Russell's discourse," Teddy said.

"But at least they're not classist."

"Who cares what '-ist' they're not, if they're not convincing? If your pet causes were convincing, they wouldn't be pet causes. They'd be part of the dominant culture, and I'd be using them," Russell Cinea said. He had put on his clothes and with them, his assurance. "When you have a major demon in the circle it is not the time to try reforming society. Besides, you can't say my charms are classist! The demons aren't manifesting as effete aristocrats."

"Yes they are," James Kalin said. "They're sure of their inborn superiority. There's no bigger snob than a demon. But do they have to be that way, or have we assumed it into existence?"

"Get dressed," Teddy told him. "Gird up your loins to fight the good fight. We have a conference call from Selanto in ten minutes-my office."

"Fine, I'll meet you there," James said. "No incense this time, please."

Teddy and Russell went out of the shower room together. They were actually good friends, and by the time they reached the second floor their argument had been replaced by a discussion of the coffee shops in town and the latest movies.

***

Warren's computer screen glowed at him and he glowed back at it as he added Nezumia's name to the International Demonological Association's database. When he hit save, computers all over the world changed their displays. Magicians from Kasidora to Selanto, from Sio to Macoma, were looking at what he had entered. They were checking the demon's name against their grants or research proposals, trying to decide whether it merited the cost of an instantaneous visit to Osyth, and typing

25

their answers back in the form of e-mails to the department secretary. There would be a flurry of requests for a demon like this one, more than Osyth could fill, for Nezumia was too powerful a demon for any single magician to bind. It was for things like this that the Royal Academy operated the pentarium-for things like this, and the added pleasure of knowing that none of them were bound to the demon. *To work with the malign powers without becoming malignant ourselves,* Warren thought happily as he stared at the screen. That was the real accomplishment. That was what had turned just another construction job into a life's calling, and it had been Russell's idea, he admitted freely. Russell was the brains behind it all.

If not for Russell, Warren Oldham would never have thought of becoming a magician. He had been successful as a wizard, a specialist in basements and foundations, places from which a person could not fall. Heights made him nervous. Besides, the arcana were found under Osyth, deep in the ley-line, and sometimes wondrous things came up into Warren's basements... maybe he had been interested in magic, even back then. But not in the College of Magic. Not in Demonology, where every faculty member kept a stable of bound demons, full of hate and murder. Definitely not Demonology. Warren would never have set foot in the building if he hadn't been sent there by the Wizardry Department as a matter of professional courtesy, to help fix the pentarium.

Everyone had known why the pentarium had a great hole in it. Everyone had shaken their heads over the latest fatal incident in Demonology, and the way the Academy let those idiots and their demons tear up the facilities. Warren couldn't have agreed more when he saw that beautiful golden room desecrated and felt the remnants of conflict filling it like a bad smell. "What a shame," he had said, shaking his head, and a light voice had answered him from behind in an arrogant Selanto accent.

"It's not a shame, it's a scandal!" That had been Russell Cinea, as tall and slender as he was today, but with butter-yellow hair back then. He had been new to the department, a reformer full of grand talk who never seemed to doubt himself. Demonologists should stop fighting one another, Russell said. They should forget the old ways, the competition over who could bind the most powerful demons, and work together like-like wizards! They should move out of the department and into the city of Osyth. Vampires, ghouls and incubi roamed the city, just on the other side of the ley-line, and where was Demonology? Here, fighting over prestige and ruining their own building in the process. While wizards built the skyscrapers of the new city and sorcerers cured its businessmen of their ailments, magicians sulked in their castle as if the very existence of a mundane world insulted them. "Which it should," Russell said. "Someone may have bound a hundred demons, but if he doesn't do anything worth doing with them, to the mundanes he's just another shabby, useless old man who smells. Whose fault is that?"

Russell was a language magician, with the gift of making other people accept his dreams, but Warren had never minded that. Perhaps he had wanted a dream too badly to worry about its provenance-and he had never regretted it. Except that it only seemed real, any more, when he was actually in the pentarium. When he stepped out into the department, the dream started to wisp away at the edges; when he stopped being busy, he could see it disappearing. The thought made Warren uneasy. He sat up in his chair and looked at the computer screen again, but someone knocked on his door.

"C'mon in!" Warren yelled, and a thin young woman with dark hair and an Academy sweatshirt stuck her head in.

"Nezumia, hey!" she said happily. "Did you get me a spot with it?"

"Oh, hi, Marcie. You've got a choice," said Warren. "I booked from eleven till one for the grad students. Don't let anyone tell you they have those hours." The magicians weren't all above snatching students' time with an important demon, especially magicians from some of the schools where students were still treated as servants.

"All right!" Marcie said, grinning. "D'you want to see what I got from Nograptus last week? I added what it told me into the model and it looks like there's a whole branch of the ley-line we never knew about. So I thought I'd go down to geomancy and see what Linus can tell me about the rock formations in that region."

"That sounds good," Warren said, making his way across the lab to her computer. A three-dimensional model of the ley-line sprawled across it, with the Osyth Plateau an insignificant blip on top. Every time Warren saw this, it thrilled him. The size of it: the depth of power he lived on top of, like a flea on a rhinoceros. "What did Nograptus tell you

28

about the inhabitants?" he asked, and his student looked surprised.

"I didn't ask," she said. "Sorry. I was just working on the map."

"Of course," Warren said. "I ought to have talked to it myself."

"Do you have time with Nezumia?"

"Not today. I have meetings all afternoon."

"Well, write down what you want to know and I'll ask it for you."

"That'd be nice," Warren said. "Only after you get what you need for the thesis, though. And give Tom and Lisa a call, will you? This ought to just about finish off their work." He sat on a lab stool and began to make out a list. He imagined himself sinking into the ley-line, passing through layers inhabited by different spirits. What did a demon see as it came from the netherworld to the ley-line's surface in Osyth? Who did it pass on the way, and what were their lives like, these subterranean arcana? He worked for about ten minutes, trying to pick the best questions to ask the demon, and for that time he was completely happy. He hardly heard the phone ring.

"It's the dean," Marcie said, holding her hand over the receiver.

Warren sighed and pointed toward his office. He went back to his desk.

"Demonology, Warren Oldham here," he said, picking up the phone.

"I know who you are, Warren," the dean said. "I've got your signature all over these papers. Why are we paying to send someone to the Demonological Congress meetings in Selanto? He can't be a Congress member without having bound a demon. You know that's illegal here in Osyth."

"It's a joint meeting," Warren said. "The Society for Veterinary Lechery and the Congress. Rho's giving a paper on incubi in ducks."

"He's registered for both meetings," the dean said.

"He's still a student member at the Congress. This is his last chance to present there. You didn't think I'd hire someone with a demon, did you?"

"I don't know," the dean said. "You bitched enough about how hard it was to find anyone. Well, I'll sign this, but I'm not sure how much I like sending brand-new faculty to scope out the competition. He hasn't been on campus a month, and we're sending him off to talk with head-hunters from Selanto and Kasidora?"

"Oh, I think we'll stand up pretty well against anything Rho sees in Selanto," Warren said, leaning back in his chair with a prosperous feeling. "We called up Nezumia this morning. That's pretty impressive for his first day in the pentarium."

"Is it? That's good," the dean said, in tones of incomprehension.

Warren felt his triumph shrink.

He said the nothings that ended a conversation, looked at his calendar and the list of meetings on it, and sighed. Trying to explain a triumph to an administrator... *Well,* he thought, *I acted the same way when he told me about that educational grant. Nobody cares about anything except their own work.*

***

30

At sunset, the white castle of Magic stood up against the sky. Skylight reflected off cross-shaped arrowslits on the first three floors and larger windows above. Lab lights were on inside some of the lower rooms, but the only well-lighted windows were high in the west tower. A scraping sound came down through the crystal evening as one of these windows swung open; a figure leaned out and a flight of pigeons startled and wheeled around the tower, cutouts against the golden sky.

"You've got a view and a half up here, I'll give you that," said a trifling voice from within the room.

Rho thought Neil Torecki said more obvious things than anyone so young should have thought of. Clichés belonged to grannies, Rho thought, and so he did not answer Neil's remark.

He pulled his head back in, leaving the window open, and a draft followed him. "Where d'you want this box?" Neil went on, shaking his hair out of his eyes.

"In the other room," Rho said. "It's just clothes and such."

"You have clothes? I thought all you owned was that robe." Neil's voice retreated behind the wall that bisected the tower, shutting away Rho's living quarters from his workroom.

While Rho didn't much care for this remark, he had to admit it was justified. He was not a dandy. His major garment was a black magician's robe, worn with disregard for its septic condition. The robe was torn, stained, and buttoned askew over a soiled denim work shirt.

31

Neil came back out, apparently undisturbed at receiving no answer. "I think that's all of it," he said cheerfully, dusting his hands. "This'll be a cozy spot, once you're settled in. Where's your lab going to be?"

"The floor below," Rho said, shutting the window, "as soon as we get the linoleum taken up."

"Stone floors are hard on your feet," Neil said, another remark to which Rho had no reply. He put a chair onto its legs and sat on it, looking around the room with an air of possession.

Rho felt a foreboding that, if encouraged, Neil would make the place one of his haunts.

"I'll work in here until my lab is ready," he said. "I still have a lot to do for my paper at the Demonology Congress, and my plane leaves tomorrow morning."

Neil grinned, ignoring the hint. "Y'got any beer?" he asked. "I'm amazed the dean's letting you go to that. Warren must've pulled big strings for you."

"I'm just a student member," Rho said crossly, pulling two beers out of his tiny refrigerator. "Everybody acts as if just looking at the Congress means I've bound a demon. You can be a student member without having one. Besides, they have a big award for best thesis. I sent in my abstract before I even heard of this job."

"Yeah? Well, we could use someone in with that group," Neil said, following his own line of thought. "I don't think the IDA can afford to be at odds with the Congress."

"Why are they, anyway?"

"Why aren't they! Don't get Warren started on it. First the International Demonological Association set up as competition to the Congress, with all sorts of ethics rules patterned after the Mystic Guild of Alchemists, that kept a lot of the Congress demonologists from joining. Then they outlawed demon-binding here in Osyth-and don't think Warren wasn't a big part of that. That meant no Congress members could work here. Then he led the push to blacklist Congress freelancers from using our pentarium. Warren won't have anything to do with the Congress. He thinks it's mediaeval."

"Why?"

"Well, look at their journal-there's more in there about who gets to command a demon than about what we can do for the field by commanding them. And they don't step in the way the IDA does to regulate disputes. They're working out of the old model, when the strongest magician killed off the others."

Neil seemed more pleased with this than alarmed by it, although Rho guessed he would rank as one of 'the others' in any such battle. But Neil had nothing for another mage to covet, since nobody held title to the demons he worked with. The methods here, he let Rho know, were hygienic and hands-off in the extreme, and therefore probably limited in ways the mediaeval mages of Selanto, who called up demons with spit and blood and sometimes even slept with them, were not. Selanto mages had links with the underworld that Warren Oldham, in his clean lab coat, couldn't even guess at. Or perhaps he could, and that was why he stayed away from them.

33

"So, what do they say about us over in Kasidora?" Neil asked.

"Well," Rho answered slowly, "it depends on who you talk to."

He remembered any number of remarks best not repeated. 'Starter school' had been the kindest epithet his mentor, Baristes, had come up with. "But don't stay too long," he had warned Rho, "or nobody will ever take you seriously again." This was doubtless the sort of thing Neil wanted to hear, as he sat looking at Rho with an eager face, but he wasn't going to get his wish.

"There were a few people who went to school with Russell," Rho said instead. "They thought he was good."

"They ought to!" said Neil. "Did you hear how Russell was the first magician to graduate from Selanto without binding a demon?"

Rho had, but he put on an expression of interest so as to get the Osyth version.

"You know his thesis was all about what binding demons did to the magicians," Neil told him happily, "so he didn't want any part of it. But you had to bind one to get the degree. So instead of binding one, Russell invited all the demons in the department to his defense. I wish I'd been a fly on that wall-imagine a bunch of magicians in there with a hundred demons, and Russell the only person none of those demons wanted to tear apart."

"Yeah, that's why I'm not in a hurry to bind one," Rho said. "I don't want to have to watch my back all the time."

"Then why live here in the building? Nobody lives on campus anymore, except some of the guys

34

over in Alchemy," Neil said, looking around. Rho's workroom wasn't entirely messy, but it was on the way. It still had vacant spaces and unfilled shelves, piles of boxes and empty animal cages stacked in the corner by the sink. The worktable between its two windows was already covered with papers, owl pellets, spiral-shaped grouse droppings, and other detritus.

"I've always lived on campus," Rho said defensively. "I can't see why people bother keeping two places, especially if you work at night."

"We like to pretend we have lives," Neil sighed, and looked at his watch. "Speaking of which... " He got up, groaning. "Next time you move, have Russell invite some demons to help. How're you getting to the airport tomorrow?"

"Warren's driving me."

"Probably wants to give you a last-minute warning," Neil said, grinning. "They've got an agenda here, all right."

"Everybody has an agenda," Rho said with a worldly air. "Everybody human, at least."

"That's right," Neil said. He stood up and stretched before sauntering to the door. "You don't have to take our word for things. You can get advice from pigeons."

Rho bristled, but the door was shutting before he could reply. He sat down and stared out the window, trying to remember Neil's tone and figure out what it had meant. *People!* he thought. People were nothing but trouble.

Rho made no attempt to work on his overheads. He knew he could finish his paper for the Demonology Congress in Selanto in two hours, with time to spare before he caught his flight in the morning. It would take him longer to find clean clothing, to shave and wash and do all the other arbitrary things a conference required and which were really more important to other humans than the content of the paper. He reopened the window instead and slouched in his chair, looking out of it, until a pigeon flew in and sat on his shoulder.

"Warm feet," the pigeon murmured, snuggling and rustling by his ear. "Grain on the ledges. Cat!"

"Wall, hard air," Rho said. "Closed in." The pigeon stretched itself tall and thin, shifting from foot to foot.

"Rap rap, peck, squeeze through," it said. "Airwing. Slip on tiles."

Rho hunched his shoulder and shook it off. With a flurry of wings, it was gone.

"That's the sort of advice you get from pigeons," Rho said, to nobody in particular.

36

Chapter Two

Warren Oldham woke up at three-thirty every morning and worried for half an hour. He let himself be as pessimistic as he liked, wondering what he would do if faculty died, slaughtered one another, seduced students. If demons seduced students. If students seduced demons. If students bound demons, or hacked into the departmental computer files and rewrote faculty resumes. If janitors cast spells at midnight in the faculty offices. If demons used faculty offices at night to run their own academy, with demon students... he never ran out of problems to worry about, but after half an hour he would begin to see them as creations of his own imagination. He would start evaluating them for style and flair, and then he would be able to sleep again.

He usually started by calling up an image of the circle his faculty made during incantation, worrying about each one of them in turn. He went round the circle widdershins, starting with Russell. Russell put less and less magic into the circle each day. Cham Ligalla hardly ever came on campus, and when she did she ignored and was ignored. Nobody liked an exorcist. Linus had been angry for at least fifteen years... in Warren's mental picture, Linus seemed the only one of the magicians aware that he was being thought about. He glared at Warren, and when he did so, the other images began to come to life. The stout dark-haired woman on Linus' right, Susan Merick Teale, pulled away from him and looked the other direction, showing her disgust. That put her closer to Patsy Hoth, the specialist in incubi, who was only a little less fierce than Linus. Warren spent a moment worrying about that, thinking he owed Susan a better place in the circle. Who else could he put between the two firebrands without starting an explosion?

He was limited, by rules of seniority and the number of new faculty in the department. The three new magicians ought to stay near the door until their powers were better developed. Neil Torecki was in his second year and most of the faculty had pegged Neil as a lightweight, not destined for tenure. Linus and Patsy would overpower him. Isaac Graham was prim and got along well enough with Patsy. He couldn't be put next to Linus, though; they were the only two physical demonologists, and tight enough already. Warren feared factions more than he feared demons.

That brought his thoughts to Rho, and Warren heaved himself over in bed with a sigh. *I don't want to mentor anybody!* he thought. *I've mentored a hundred junior faculty and I'm sick of them. I just get them civilized and they move off to some school that doesn't ask that much of them. He'll do the same thing. He already wants to go play with the Congress and have demon slaves and magewars.*

Warren heaved again, raising his head far enough to look at the clock, and huffed into his mustache. *I had to fight with the dean for him, and now I'll have to drive him to the airport, and after all that there's not a chance in hell he'll be worth it,* he thought, but under his griping he felt excitement and knew he would put as much time as it took into mentoring Rho. Because what could be more wonderful than to have a natural philosopher in the department-somebody who could talk to all the creatures on the ley-line and tell Warren what they said?

When I came here, Warren thought, *we were at war with demons. With everything. Now we work with demons, but who thinks about animals? We could all get along.* Didn't everybody want to talk with animals? Didn't everybody love stories, movies about talking animals? About mice in hats, or squirrels wearing breeches... His half-hour of worrying over, Warren drifted into a dream of animals and clothing, where some animal had stolen Linus' bow tie and was wearing it around campus, attending meetings in his place. When his alarm clock went off, he had trouble waking up again.

"Warren!" his wife said, shoving him. "Turn that off."

"Oh? Huh," Warren said. His head was full of his dream. He stumbled in the room, gathering his clothes, and searched a few moments for a bow tie before he quite woke up. But there was no contradicting the clock or the airline schedule, so he took his clothing off to the kitchen to dress while he made coffee.

***

Though he was a flight down and four rooms away, Lilian Oldham could hear every move Warren made in the kitchen. When she was feeling fond of him, the noises were reassuring. Otherwise, they sounded stupid. *Why can't a man do anything*

39

quietly, instead of racketing through life like a June bug on a screen porch? she asked herself. She had seen him work with perfect neatness and order in his cluttered old lab, but get him home and he had to make every movement into a big deal. She got up, scowling, and put on her bathrobe.

"Good morning," Warren said, looking at her with surprise. "You don't need to get up this early. I'm just going to drive Rho to the airport."

"I was up anyway," Lilian said in a long-suffering tone. "Is your mother here yet?"

"I didn't know she was coming over," said Warren. "What for?"

"She needs to stay here for a few days. Her apartment's being exorcised."

"For what? Ghosts?"

"Incubi."

"Since when does Bosie mind incubi?"

"It's a matter of professional courtesy, I think. Apparently they followed her home from the Slap 'n Tickle last night, and the owner wants them back. So Bosie's having the place exorcised and hiding out here until they've given up and gone home."

Warren grinned. "That always happens," he said.

"I would have told you last night, but I was so tired, I just went straight to bed when I got home from work."

"I saw," said Warren. "I was a little worried. Are you feeling all right?"

"I guess." Lilian sipped coffee while Warren looked over the newspaper. She felt like pounding him, but why? It wasn't his fault-not that Rho was trouble, or that she couldn't tell him. "Write

40

something on that," she said finally, pushing the telephone message pad over toward him.

"Eh?" But he wrote something on it about a demon named Nograptus and a new branch of the ley-line, and signed it. Lilian tore the paper into strips and fetched her scrying bag out of her briefcase. When she poured them out the bones and papers were tied into a nasty tangle, ends of bone sticking out in every direction.

"What's it mean?" Warren asked, peering at it sideways.

"I don't know," Lilian said, "but I don't think we should use the program at work to analyze it." The bone tangle sat on the table like a third person in the room, uninvited. Lilian looked at the black windows and saw its reflection. "Do you have to go out?"

"There won't be any traffic this time of the morning," Warren said. "I'll be careful."

"Careful when? When you're driving on icy roads, or when you're calling up a demon?" She poked at the bone tangle, pulling the pad over beside her and making notations. "That paper was about work, wasn't it?" Warren nodded. "Well, it's wrapped right around your life bone." She teased the strip out and unrolled it, revealing Warren's signature.

"That's not about work," he said, leaning over it.

"No," Lilian agreed. The parts of the paper about demons and the ley-line were laced in among the other bones. As she watched, the life bone suddenly slipped out, all on its own. It lay on the

41

table beside Warren's autograph, and the rest of the bone tangle sat unchanged like a sculpture.

"Well... " Warren said uncomfortably, "at least it looks as if work isn't my problem. I'd better go. Rho'll be waiting." He was gone. She didn't have anything solid to hold him with, nothing but megrims and worriments. She listened to the garage door, car door, garage door again, car door... she teased the bones out of their paper nest, noting configurations that meant nothing in particular, and all the time that life bone lay all by itself on the table.

Lilian shook herself, shut her eyes and reached out to the house around her, to the aura of peace she had built up so carefully through years of little rituals. She reminded herself of the fire lighting rites, the holiday spells, the charms she had sung her daughters to sleep with. Whatever overtook the new members of the Demonology Department, Warren would be safe inside the life they'd built together. When she got up for more coffee she moved quietly, self-consciously, like a chatelaine or a domestic goddess-anything but a round and sagging white-curled woman with a broad peasant face and chubby toes. She stood at the French doors, a worried queen surveying her kingdom, and another queenly figure walked into sight.

This one was truly tall and elegant, wearing one of those impractical velvet coats that wrap around with no buttons. The coat swung loose, opening over something black and beaded as the woman bent down to pull a bramble loose from it. She stood up again and lifted her face to the sky, tilting her slender frame back under it, and then turned and walked straight toward the house, carrying her shoes in one hand. Closer and closer she came, with no sign of stopping. Lilian watched, amused and horrified. At the last moment she slid the French door open, before the older woman could run into the glass like a bird.

"Mother Bosie," she said, pulling her arm back.

"Good morning, Lilian dear," Bosie said, marching in without a pause. "I was walking the line out from the city," she went on, "but I'm afraid it doesn't count, not with stockings on. Do you know Warren walked the line in when he switched from wizardry to magic?"

"Yes, of course I know," Lilian said. "We were engaged, remember? I sold him a pack of insurance before I let him pull that stunt."

"Oh my yes, so you were," Bosie said. She shrugged the velvet coat off her shoulders and let it fall in drama to the floor, and there she stood looking ten years younger than her daughter-in-law, her dark curls perfectly sheared into a solid mass around her skull, piquant as a bird's crest. Her darting black eyes and sharp face were the same face and eyes Lilian had seen in Warren on their first night together, so many years ago. Her cocktail dress was simple, black wool with jet beads, but her stockings were shredded away from her feet.

"How far did you walk barefoot? It's too cold outside."

"Oh, never far enough," Bosie said. "I don't know what people see in that ley-line, all these fairytales. Now they said I'd run into demons, or hear the mandrakes chattering to one another or see fairies riding owls, but you know there's nothing at all down there, dear. Except thistles."

"Have you brought any luggage?"

"No, whatever for? I'll just rinse out my tidies in the basin, and they'll be dry by tonight. If I could have a cup of that coffee, dear, and one of Warren's nightshirts to doze in-I always used to steal his father's, did you know?"

"No, I didn't," Lilian said gently, picking up the coat and shoes.

"He was such a beautiful man," Bosie said, still without moving. "He had a wonderfully shaped head. I wished he would go bald, but he never did."

"Warren has," Lilian heard herself saying. "I like it so much. It makes him look benign."

"That could be the white hair," Bosie said. "It can make them look harmless... but maybe you're right, a man with thick white hair can look a positive goat. Especially if he has yellow eyes." She took the cup with a look of surprise, as if she had never thought of coffee, and let Lilian guide her to a chair. "I'm not drunk, dear, I'm just a little sad. Having all those incubi at home made me think of Warren's father. He was such a frisky thing." She stretched her legs out and laid her head back. "I think I'll just sit here for a while and relax. Why don't you go on to work? I'll not let the house burn down, I promise."

"Well-" Lilian tilted her head and felt the climate of the house close around her, undisturbed by Bosie's entry. "That sounds like a good idea," she said. "I'll be back in a few minutes."

By the time she finished finding a spare nightshirt and afghan, Bosie was fast asleep in the

44

easy chair. Lilian covered her and stood looking for a minute at her sharp face. It was hard to believe that face could cover so vague a mind, and getting vaguer every day. *This will be difficult,* Lilian thought, but she didn't dwell on the problem. When it looked serious enough to need something done about it, she would fill out an insurance application and scry to see what lay in Bosie's future, but today, she could not bear one more difficulty. She swept the bones on the kitchen table back into her scrying bag and the papers into the garbage.

***

As Rho waited outside his tower he saw things along the ley-line, always out of the corner of his eyes. He heard things just at the edge of hearing, from inside and outside, moanings and laughter, and pigeons' drowsy noises from where they roosted safe in the high nooks of the building. He was relieved to hear Warren calling from the parking structure. He trotted over, briefcase banging against one leg and an unfamiliar suit coat cramping his movements, ready for a meeting: poised, shaven, artificial. Warren blinked at him, perhaps recognizing the suit.

"Sorry I'm late, he said, and then drove more slowly than seemed possible through the dark.

Rho went over his paper to keep from screaming. Warren didn't seem to notice how quiet he was, and Rho began to feel disapproved of and to resent it. *If they don't want me to attend this conference, they shouldn't be paying for it,* he thought, and the thought hit him amidships.

"Did the dean sign my travel request?" he asked anxiously. "I never got it back."

"Yes," Warren said. "He told me yesterday."

"Oh," Rho said. "I thought there might be trouble about my going to the Congress."

"Not on a student membership. Only if you bind a demon."

Rho sat up straighter, gathering his courage. "Why's that illegal here, anyway? Or why's the Academy here, where the major research tool's outlawed? There's something inconsistent about that."

"We do a different kind of research here," Warren said. "We study more than just demons. Normally a place like this would have two, three demonologists tops, because there are just not that many biddable demons on this ley-line. They used to kill magicians pretty often, even trashed the pentarium. Now we have this collaborative method, and to make it work we need a lot of magicians in the department, so we house people who work on other things. Ghosts or vampires or incubi. Patsy Hoth and Cham Ligalla spend a lot of their time working for the city government." He steered cautiously round a curve. "It gives us a different kind of relationship with the mundanes-and with the demons, for that matter. And with each other. Nobody's in direct competition."

"Oh," Rho said. Warren, once started, couldn't be stopped; he talked on.

"We started working on it thirty years ago," he said roundly, "and look at us now! The IDA's last meeting was as big as the Congress, and we graduated more demonologists last year than

46

Selanto did. All of them undamaged, too. And look at the quality demons we're getting. You just ask around at the Congress and see who's had a chance to work with Nezumia and lived. Every year more of the serious work comes out of Osyth."

This was boosterism at its most bumptious, and made Rho regret ever having come within ten miles of Osyth and its academy. Serious scholars didn't resort to this sort of self-promotion. *When you're reduced to praising yourself,* he thought, *it's a sign that you can't get anybody else to praise you.* He spied out the window for the airport with a desperate feeling, as if this would be his last chance to escape back to the real world.

***

Far below Rho's empty tower window, members of the Demonology Department straggled in to work along the tree-lined walk from the Academy's parking structure. Warren was the first, drinking a cup of gas station coffee he had picked up on the way back from dropping Rho off. Some walked in with an air of switching gears, fresh from family breakfasts and confusions; these were Isaac Graham and James Kalin. Others strolled along in self-conscious satisfaction, these being the faculty who had worked through the night and taken themselves out to breakfast (though not together): Susan Teale and Patsy Hoth. Scattered among them, the single faculty who worked in the daytime-Russell Cinea, Anders Regan, Linus Ukadnian, and Teddy Whin-walked as if going to work was just one more of the significant things they did in a daily program of self-improvement.

Almost last to enter the building were Cham Ligalla, walking with a vague and urgent air as if stopping in between two breakfast meetings (which was the case) and Will Goth-Harding, who trailed along the path, washed-out and listless. In the winter, sunrise came too late for Will, who had to be at the pentarium before the vampires he studied were well abed. The sun came up just as Will stepped out from under the last spruce tree along the walk, and all his amulets and chains flashed as one. Will turned his pale face toward the sun, squinted at it, and sighed. He went into the building through its great double swinging doors, and the path lay quiet in the cold winter light for a few minutes. Then a figure pelted down it, huffing out clouds of steamy breath into the morning. Neil Torecki burst through the doors, clutching his muffler close just in time to keep it out of them as they swung silently closed behind him. The west campus lay quiet and impassive, as if no demonologists had passed at all.

Chapter Three

The University of Selanto was smaller than Rho had expected. He wasn't used to buildings agglomerated into one hive, and when he looked at it from the outside he thought, *It can't be any problem to get around in.* When he got in, however, he found it a maze of narrow corridors ending in fire escapes which had been converted into makeshift connections between wings as new buildings accreted onto the old. He squeezed through passageways and right-angle turns less than a meter wide, and several times ran into ancient barrier spells attached to what looked like prehistoric bits of wall and had to retrace his steps, so he was relieved to finally find something looking like a lobby and containing what looked like other magicians.

"Where do you register?" he asked a stout, good-natured looking man standing beside him.

"I wouldn't know," said the stout man, who Rho now saw wore the gold chain earrings favored by freelance demonologists. "Why don't you ask one of the hosts?" He turned away and resumed private conversation with his colleague, dismissing Rho.

That was unhelpful, but at least he had gestured in a direction, and when Rho looked that way he saw a thicker press which proved to be around a table at which a woman was sitting, wearing a name badge which identified her only as Vivien, head of conference security. She was a very large woman, with lots of magic.

"Which sessions will you be attending?" she asked, without looking up. Rho put his registration form on the table and she began to search through a file box of plastic pouches, each one of which contained an amulet, or two or three amulets, or no amulet at all but a paper-life insurance, Rho presumed, for the really dangerous lectures.

"I don't need one," Rho said. He pulled his own amulet out and showed Vivien. She gave it an expert going-over, washing her hands in bittersmoke before touching it and passing the stone through several small field charms she had set up on her desk. They were the size Rho had seen at the supply companies' demonstration tables but more elaborate, suspended in pentacles of silver wire tied with intricate knots. He couldn't tell what Vivien was learning from them, but it made her view his amulet with respect.

"That will do," she admitted, handing it back. "What kind of magic is it?"

"Natural philosophy," Rho said. "It's a standard broad-field aroynt." Vivien raised an eyebrow at this and he was irritated. He knew what she was thinking. A natural philosopher casting real magic? NPs were supposed to be warm and fuzzy and embrace their study organisms. They used gestalt statistics (if more than five out of a hundred have a bad feeling about a hypothesis...), and their analyses were subjective and had heart-warming morals.

"Well! I must look into that," Vivien said. There's always something more to be learnt, her tone said, even in the most unlikely places. She turned to the next conference-goer, and Rho put his amulet back on.

***

The Demonological Congress did not run a friendly convention, although (to be fair) Rho would have been just as disgusted with a friendly convention, the sort that involved special name tags and breakfast sessions for first-timers. He had never gone to a conference alone before; his mentor had always dragged him, and explained what everything meant. Some of the people here must remember him, but none of them would remember conversing with him. Rho had sat in the corner and watched other students start such conversations, jealous and shy.

Now, when it was too late to do anything about it, he imagined what a reputation he must have-what they probably thought he was brought along for. He imagined he saw speculation on every face when he stood up to give his paper. Shoulders turned and coats rustled, as the demonologists and lechers in his audience looked around-for Baristes, Rho thought, and, not finding him, for whoever else might have brought young Rho this time. That was the sort of gossip that went around the open bars and closed parties at such conferences.

Rho took a deep breath, gathering his resentment, and stated his topic in such a fierce, uncompromising tone that faces all turned round again and raised their eyebrows in mild astonishment. Ducks-even incubus-ridden ducks-

51

were rarely discussed with such an incisive scorn at a meeting of the Society for Veterinary Lechery. Waterfowl, their doings and failings, were rarely presented as if they carried a hidden moral for each member of the audience, as if each bar graph pounded another nail into the sinner's coffin... Rho felt, at the end, that he had done a very good job of presenting his research but that it would not win any prizes at this conference. People looked at him with interest but none of them asked questions, almost as if they were afraid of what he might answer; he took his seat, sullen and insulted, and simmered through the rest of the student papers, ranking them on a scale from pedestrian to stupefying. As soon as he could, he escaped to the refectory.

"To hell with them, anyway," he muttered, and stirred his tea. The room he sat in was made of heavy brown stone, with low arches pushing its inhabitants downward. It had once been a dungeon, according to a worn inscription on the wall, but was now filled with uncomfortable plastic chairs and a booth offering lukewarm drinks. Conference attendees stood around the room, gossiping and checking to see who was there. None of them looked at Rho until a group of four men entered as a unit, a black mass in their dark magicians' robes, and headed straight for his table.

"Rho," the tallest said, sitting down. "How do you find Osyth and the IDA? Wholesome?"

"Very," Rho said, picking up the familiar tone. "Teamwork is all the rage." He remembered them as natural philosophy students from Kasidora, but their names escaped him.

"So how do you like slumming in the colonies?"

Rho bristled at the speaker's tone, but he wasn't about to defend Osyth. That would be impossible, sitting here in a really ancient institution-one that had light fixtures older than Osyth-talking with mages from the only unionized institution of higher magic. Osyth! Rho had a sudden sickening vision of his new Academy, light and young and full of people so naive they should be wearing pajamas with feet.

"I finished another paper," he said. "From the thesis work. Incubi in ducks. They have a nice park system, full of ponds."

"Tell us about the Demonology Department," one of the students said. "Is it true you use charms of discourse?"

"We do," Rho said. "They're IDA charms. They work pretty well."

"Ah, but whose blood do you use for the pentacle?"

"I haven't set the pentacle yet."

"Probably Oldham's," one of the students said, and another laughed.

"That would be why so many people are out for it. Are they your demons or his, Rho? The things you trap in the pentacle."

"He can't have a demon in Osyth," the tall student said, with a fine scorn. "It's illegal. You can't even keep a little incubus for personal use."

"Hah! So much for your love life," the obnoxious student said.

Rho ignored him and answered the original speaker. "They're nobody's, you know that. A charm

53

of discourse only sets up the geas, it doesn't decide who commands it. It's not like flesh magic."

The other leaned back and looked at him with mock sympathy. "You're in the wrong place, then. Stabor, over there, has slept with ten demons, bound them flesh to flesh. The man disputing with him, Ganeel, lost his arm trying a charm of discourse. But he picked up the torn-off arm and used it to bind the demon that had swallowed part of it."

"Ah," Rho said. "Is Baristes here?" The question caused amusement.

"He should have been."

"He has unfortunately canceled his registration."

"He was trying a body charm on a demon," the palest of the four students explained, "and discovered the demon was already bound to Ganeel. Now Baristes finds himself betrayed with unaccountable urges in Ganeel's presence."

"He might have attended the venery session. His condition wouldn't stand out there."

"That session's over," Rho said.

"Or he could have sat by you. He must not have seen your name in the program."

"I sent in my abstract late," Rho said.

"That's it. I wondered why you were in the bunny session. Tough luck," the tall student said, and Rho agreed. Nobody who was anybody had been in his audience, a day before the keynote speakers.

"Just look at them," the pale student said, with disgust, waving at Ganeel and Stabor. "They turn into what they study. Look at the way they make their students into disciples. What use do they have for those poor things, except feeding off them?"

Rho watched the two demonologists, sleek and intent, arguing in the center of an awed and admiring crowd of subservient students as unlike the cynical Kasidorans as anything he could imagine. The combatants came out greasily satisfied: in two words-well fed.

***

The congress demonologists' arrival changed the feel of the whole conference, and not for the better. It was a political specialty, full of big names who competed against each other for big grants and reviewed one another's papers in nasty, high-profile journals, and in the middle of it was a battle waiting to happen between Mages Stabor and Ganeel. They were the two Rho had observed feeding off their students' admiration, perhaps the most benign thing they would do during the entire week.

Stabor and Ganeel, Rho quickly learned, were at odds about the proper form of incantation in advanced demonology. Each held that the other man was sullying the field with private spells that refuted other, major charms. Each wanted the Demonology Congress to rule in favor of his position, outlawing the other's methods before the demons learned enough to break their bonds and commit murder among the lower level mages and graduate students, and both had come to the conference with papers which were mainly excuses to take the podium and rail against each other's methods and results.

Stabor had taken his enmity further this year, and was attending every paper presented by Ganeel's graduate students with heckling questions and cogent criticisms. Most unfair, since these relative innocents had been trained in almost complete ignorance of the merits of his arguments and were unprepared to defend their methods. Each session led to further ill will.

"If Stabor were a fool, it would be one thing," one of the students from Kasidora said, as he pointed out the players to Rho. "But of course he can outargue any student, especially when Ganeel has only taught them one side of the issue. That's why Kasidora should require courses in all the major schools of demonology. You can't make a mark, if your work is swallowed up in one of these feuds."

"Hm," was all Rho said. He was thinking about a newly announced upcoming paper on incubi and pig farming, and that it would be a relief to listen to something Stabor and Ganeel couldn't fight over. He made a note to go in early and get a good seat.

***

Good seats were unobtainable for the pig farming lecture, which drew a large audience. Those magicians who weren't interested in pigs were interested in agriculture or in incubi, or in the other members of the audience-for both the feuding demonologists were present, to Rho's dismay. He sat several rows behind them among a sizable group of cynics who had pegged their battle as the most amusing thing going on at the conference, feeling as if he were trapped in a crowd of sports fans. Bets were on Ganeel to win; he'd begun to court support among the unallied demonologists by restating their findings as verifications of his pet theory and praising their cleverness in discovering it independently. He did this now, flattering the author in terms that made her grin and infuriated his opponent, who had no gift for soft soap.

As soon as the session ended Stabor made a beeline for Ganeel, his followers crowding Rho to the one side of the room, but Rho had seen the author go out a door on the other side, and for once he was not going to defer to the demonologists just because they were loud and ill-mannered. He wouldn't put up with this nonsense any more, he told himself, but as often happens, the only effect of this resolution was to march him right into the line of fire. As he pushed between junior magicians with his bony elbows, ignoring the raised voices ahead of him, the demonologists' battle took its final, lethal turn.

Rho had read about mage duels with lightning and shape-changing, but none of that was possible on the conference grounds. The reality was simpler and more horrible; Stabor leant forward, his face full of venom, and when everyone expected him to spit curses at Ganeel he reached out instead and with one jerk pulled the golden ward loose from the other mage's neck. It was a desperate act, an act against the Congress' and Vivien's power. Even his supporters were appalled. They pulled him back, and Rho was pushed away behind them. But, at the moment the chain broke, he had heard a roar of thick, mucus-laden delight, and while he was still gasping, putting his hands over his mouth, he saw the first gash open on Ganeel's cheek and the magicians of his party leap to form a human chain around him, covering him with their still-shielded bodies.

One of Stabor's magicians grabbed Rho's shoulder. "Fetch Vivien!" he yelled, a welcome command.

Rho wanted nothing more than to run out of the room, away from the blood flowing red and free between the magicians' feet, but he was too late. Vivien was already in the doorway and he was seized as a free set of hands, given one leg of an already smoking brazier and bid set the points of a pentacle around the knot of magicians while she built up its walls, shaping the smoke into glassy surfaces like nothing Rho had ever seen before. It was a beautiful pentacle, a charm of great power; but they were inside it with a demon, still intent on tearing apart the man who had enslaved it, and Ganeel's blood ran toward the lines as if sent to break them and let the monster's friends in. Rho could see their patterns swirling outside, where they rubbed up against the planes of smoke.

"Watch the lines," Vivien told him, holding out a bag of sawdust, and he began to walk gingerly around the perimeter sprinkling it on every runnel and smear of blood. The job brought him too close to the other magicians, too close to being bumped through the pentacle himself, too close to seeing what was in its center. He looked at the floor only. Ganeel was still silent, but there was always more blood, oozing under the dirty cakes, floating crusts of sawdust toward the pentacle lines... He felt a change in power around him and knew the other magicians had taken off their wards to help in exorcism, and then he heard one of Ganeel's students calling names to Vivien. She repeated each name, commanding Ganeel's demons one by one. It was a long list, for his had been one of the major labs.

Rho tried not to listen to any of the assertions Vivien was chanting. He couldn't help hearing familiar phrases about the bond between body and spirit; he would find his own thoughts chanting along and then the charm would take a turn, would mention an argument or reference not used in Osyth, sometimes a name he had never heard. The charms raised a prickle on his back and he stuck to his rounds, wondering how long the sawdust would last. This was taking so much longer than the invocations in Osyth... using discourse to break a demon away from someone bound to it by flesh magic was not the same as entrapping an errant spirit.

He heard frustration in Vivien's voice and a shift in her language, as if she had given up trying to convince the demon with reason. She was using words from hedge magic and witchcraft now, invoking a relationship outside of logic and calling to the demon as a witch calls a familiar. The lure of it dragged at him and froze every magician in earshot. She promised something beyond dreams, an understanding, an attention as close as slipping into the same skin. If Rho hadn't been trapped in himself he would have taken her offer to come into a body so well known, so loved, so cherished... Strange faces leered at him from the floor outside

59

the line, and sweet voices called him in unknown languages. A black piglet appeared from nowhere and trotted past him, its hooves spattering so close to the lines that Rho caught it up and held it, kicking and nipping, out of harm's way against his chest. Its body was warm and hard and full of muscle, comforting. Vivien fell silent. Ganeel was making noises now that Rho didn't like to hear; the other magicians were standing away from him, putting their wards back on with shaky hands, and Vivien had picked him up uncaring of the blood and her robes.

"Where's the demon?" one of the magicians near Rho asked, searching the floor, and Rho felt the little pig kick against him. He held it out with a sudden movement that brought it too close to the walls. It squealed, twisting in his grasp.

"Let down the pentacle," Vivien said, "and let it go. Unless you want it?" The pig hung as a malignant dead weight from Rho's outstretched arms. He had never wanted anything less. He put it gently down and saw it trot away down a long dark space that somehow existed in the three feet between his toes and the wall.

***

"You picked up a demon," they kept saying. First the students from Kasidora, then any number of people Rho hadn't thought he knew. They would wander over, say it, and buy him a drink. Then they'd suggest all sorts of research collaborations, plausible and implausible. He'd become one of the conference events, recognized by enough people to

60

convince those who didn't recognize him that they ought to; when Rho looked dizzily off into corners, he could see the uninitiated whispering questions.

Rho ought to have enjoyed it. He'd disliked being a peripheral nobody, but now that he was a central somebody his earlier sour grapes attitude got in the way of pure enjoyment. It was hard to bask in the approval of people he'd classified just an hour earlier as tasteless snobs and poor judges of character. He wasn't sure he wanted to be part of the Congress, of the grave and hurried meetings that had called all the senior demonologists out of the hall, of the excited factions eyeing one another from different tables. "Smart move," some people told him, and others glared as if he had masterminded it all just to get hold of Ganeel's demon. As the evening wore on he grew drunker and more disgusted-with his admirers or himself, he couldn't have told. He read over the thick Congress Membership application and imagined himself tearing it up in front of them all, leaving a pile of shreds behind as he walked out.

He pulled himself away from the groups inviting him out to barhop in the lower reaches of Selanto and went back to his hotel alone, well before midnight, and once there he ignored all the recommended calming rituals out of sheer spite and instead watched Selanto television in a language he couldn't understand. The thing was still nattering on when he fell asleep in his clothes on top of the coverlet. It had gone blank and static-filled when Rho woke up to find someone dark and silent sitting beside it on the dresser, looking at him with gleaming eyes.

Rho could never say afterwards just when he knew it was the demon. His body knew before his mind was awake, and by the time he looked at the thing, he was full of the *cauld grue*. His skin was drawing itself up into goose pimples so fast it seemed likely to leap off his body entirely and escape. The demon stood up, casually stretching its legs longer until they reached the floor and it could lift its barrel off the dresser. It was vaguely human, distinctly male as it strolled toward him. Rho found himself paralyzed.

It was a pig, he told himself frantically. *A pig, nothing but a pig.* He tried to recapture the pig in his mind, to feel his hands on the warm, flexible, kicking little body, and perhaps the demon shrank a little. Perhaps its fingers were shorter, a little more like trotters, and its barrel more rounded. It was standing over him by then, though, and the fingers that reached toward his throat were still taloned. Was that dried blood in the grooves of its claws?

Rho was ready to run. He thought frantic messages to his muscles, lungs, throat, and they ignored him. The talons were touching his chest now, running upward along his skin, under the amulet that should have held them off. The demon bent low to investigate the amulet, peering, sniffing, licking. It brought its fangs, its hot breath right down to his throat and licked his amulet-and smacked, as if his power were just a snack to it! *It's a pig,* Rho thought over and over, in an unstopping babble, and under it the notion gripped him that he had to keep some kind of control, that the only victory he could hope for was to keep from soiling the bed with anything other than his blood.

The demon sighed luxuriously and licked its lips, and then it hooked one claw in the amulet cord and jerked it off Rho's neck. His bowels did let go then, the sharp release answering the hot line of pain across the back of his neck. The demon laughed low in its throat. It bent over him again, sniffing and snuffling as if it would inhale the very soul out of him, and put its hot mouth over his. Its tongue traced his lips, its saliva bathed them.

Rho lay still, in shock and shame. *Is this what it wants?* He heard the thought changing in his mind to, *Is this all it wants?* As if he were an observer he heard himself wondering, planning, conceding. He saw that this thing that was himself, that had thought itself finished with this sort of thing, would open its lips to the demon. It would do anything, anything to keep those claws from gouging it apart for just one minute more, to buy a few moments or a night before the demon ripped it to shreds. That was what it had done before, what it would always do. If only it had already been ripped apart, torn into pieces, destroyed, that sack of filth, of offal, of vanity and cowardice!

Two hot tears rolled out of Rho's eyes and down into his ears, and just as he relaxed his mouth the demon stood up away from him; it stretched and sighed a sigh of contentment, and it was gone. Rho's lips opened onto nothing more than air, jerking its way into him in three sobs and breaking out again in three more.

He would have lain sobbing, but the filth in his clothes drove him into the bathroom. Once there he threw up again and again. He knelt at the toilet forcing dry heaves, wishing he could vomit up cells,

63

blood, the organs he'd been so frantic to save, all those tripes he would have kissed the demon for. Then he turned the shower on hot enough to parboil and sat under it in a lump. By and by he lay down, curled on his side, and felt the tub's cold strike up through him to meet the water's heat striking down, and in that way he slept a little until the hotel sent someone in to see why the shower was running.

**

Rho was eating a solitary, sour-tasting breakfast when Vivien brought the news of Ganeel's death. She posted it in a big, black-bordered announcement on the refectory bulletin board, and didn't look at Rho; but everyone else was watching him all morning. People came up behind him and said hello abruptly, peering at him with little sharp prying eyes.

Rho didn't jump. He said hello back at them, and kept his own counsel. He looked dignified. He attended all the papers he had circled on his conference schedule, and would not stay in the refectory to talk with other magicians while the sessions were running. "I may not get to any more Congress meetings, and I fly home this evening," he said to the students from Kasidora. "I want to learn all I can while I'm here. I can follow up with people over the computer, if I know what was in their papers."

"I guess you can," the pale student said. "Everyone wants to know you. That must have been a major demon."

64

"Lucky bastard!" the tall one said. "Just starting in the field, and you get to be an owner without any of the ordeals! Most people work for ten years and lose an eye or something before they manage to bind their first demon."

"Yeah, lucky," Rho said.

Chapter Four

Six hours on a plane from Selanto to Osyth translated into an entire night of Rho's life, thanks to time zones. He landed just before dawn in a clear morning full of the scent of a thaw-cold wet dirt and half-frozen greenstuff. Neil Torecki was waiting for him at the passenger pick up, idling his car and staring at passersby.

"You don't look as if you got much sleep at the conference," Neil said, pulling out into rush-hour traffic on the branch road from the airport. Fields covered with mangy snow stretched on either side of the car. "A good one, was it?" Rho slouched deeper in his seat and scowled, and Neil chuckled. "Think you'll be able to do your part in the pentarium this morning? We haven't had anything worth catching for a week."

"Oh, hell," Rho said, caught off-guard. Everything inside him solidified, as if his guts were half-frozen and half-rotted like the world around him. *I can't go into the pentarium,* he thought. *That demon can walk right through my wards...* "Pull over," was all he said, but he said it with urgency and conviction. He had the door open and was leaning out, spewing, before the car stopped.

"Hangover?" Neil asked, reaching across the seat to offer him a tissue.

Rho tried to ignore him. He considered never moving again, staying crouched half out of the car door, but couldn't see how to manage it. Pulling his shoulders back in, he thought fast.

"They had a magewar at the conference," he said. "A demon got through someone's wards and ripped him apart."

"Wow!" Neil said. "That's pretty horrible." But he said it in a tone of envy rather than sympathy, with relish so obvious that he seemed to notice its unsuitability himself and lapsed into a more tactful silence. Rho wiped his mouth and rearranged himself in the seat. "You all right?"

Rho didn't answer.

"That's not going to happen here," Neil said. "We're warded by the Academy, remember? It's not as if you have to look out for yourself. I mean look at me, I work with imps. D'you think I could ward off a major demon right on top of the ley-line? That's why we use the institutional gowns, and put IDA charms on the chains, instead of our own wards." He started up the car again. "Besides, it's a whole different bunch of demons. You know the big ones stay in their own territories."

"Yeah," Rho said, nodding with his eyes shut. He felt better, but he still couldn't imagine himself casting the charm of intent that would begin today's invocation. How could he want-how could he even *say* he wanted to see a demon, that he meant it no harm, that he sought a friendly relationship with it? "What happens if we don't believe in the opening invocation?"

"We don't get a demon," Neil said, in a voice like a shrug. "Big shucks. You give it your best try, if it doesn't work, we all get out early."

"Mm-hm."

Neil kept quiet until they pulled into the Academy's parking garage. He dithered a little over

67

shutting off the engine. "You okay to go straight down?" he asked. "It's nine already. Listen, if this is really bothering you talk to Warren about it. He'll give you the straight dope. Warren may have a bee in his bonnet, but he never jerks people around."

Rho opened his eyes and saw the garage's gray concrete wall in front of him, and stamped into it the golden Academy seal and ward. "Yeah," he said, getting out.

***

Everybody else in the pentarium shower room seemed to be in a hurry. Rho changed his clothes in silence, interrupted by only a few people who told him they were glad he was back in ways that sounded like a criticism of his having left in the first place. Nobody asked about Selanto, but that may have been because they didn't want to irritate Warren, who carried a cloud of gloom around the room with him and banged his locker door.

"Family troubles," Neil whispered. Linus Ukadnian, who had just come out of one of the private showers, snorted.

"A professional leaves his personal life at home," he said. "Well, Rho, I suppose you saw a different side of demonology at the Congress?"

"Yeah, in a way," Rho said. "It doesn't matter. I probably won't see those demons here."

"Why not?"

"It's a different ley-line."

"Nonsense," Linus said. "There are no such things as separate ley-lines. They are all manifestations of a single phenomenon." He

68

smoothed his bow tie and snapped the gold chain over it, and marched into the pentarium to stand at his accustomed place.

Neil and Rho followed, shuffling to one side of the door and backing against the wall so the other magicians could walk past them. Rho pressed his shoulders against the gold wall and tried to think of nothing except its solid warmth.

"We've never gotten demons from Selanto in this pentarium," Neil said. "Look at the records. The major demons have only been found in their own territories, which match the ley-lines. There's even different kinds of imps on the different lines. Sure, the ley-lines may all flow into the netherworld, the same way rivers all flow into the sea, but that doesn't mean their fauna mix."

"Of course they're connected," Linus said shortly. "This poetic stuff about rivers of power is just foolishness. Power is not generated at the surface and funneled down into the netherworld. The netherworld is the source of power and ley-lines rise up from it toward the surface; it is one place, ergo all things deriving from it are connected to one another. This is simple geography. If modern magicians learned even the rudiments of logic and mathematics, we might be able to hold intelligent conversations with one another."

Rho thought it would take more than mathematics for him to hold an intelligent conversation with Linus Ukadnian. He caught Susan Teale's eye as she stepped into her place in the circle. She winked, and for just a moment Rho felt better, as if he and Susan were sharing cozy speculations about what might make for intelligent

69

conversation with Linus. Then Patsy Hoth stepped into place beside Susan, and the twinkle disappeared.

"No shop talk in the pentarium," Patsy said to Linus in a tart voice.

He bristled. "Why not?"

"Read the manual," she said. "It's rule three."

"I suppose you believe everything you read?"

"I suppose you know enough about how this thing works to ignore the operating manual?"

"Oh, be quiet!" Susan Teale said, flaring up. "Both of you!" Linus and Patsy looked at her as if a rabbit had just spat fire, and were quiet.

The senior magicians came in, pacing past as if clothed in long robes instead of knee-length paper gowns, and Rho tried to forget the argument and rehearse the charm they'd be using in a few minutes. He had to stretch to reach between hands, and at a level below the surface he felt relieved. With James Kalin and Isaac Graham missing, they wouldn't call up anything powerful today. He saw Warren step forward and back, testing the power of the circle before they intoned the summoning charm, and then as Rho spoke the words he felt understanding and confidence flow over him like a warm bath. Here in the pentarium, he did want to see a demon. He wanted to see one from where he stood in the circle, strong and in control. He looked at the gold walls and chains that protected him and found himself standing taller, eager for the excitement of a new creature.

The charm they recited was the same, but it felt different. *Perhaps I'm getting used to it,* Rho thought. *After Selanto, it doesn't seem like so much...* The *grue* was barely a shiver down his spine, and even the smoke that spiraled up in the pentacle looked weak. Rho relaxed. *I can handle this!* he thought, but as the smoke thickened, beginning to swirl out in several directions and with more vigor, he began to feel a deadly cold and a heaviness in his chest as if holding his body up were too much work. He held onto Neil's and Patsy Hoth's hands and shut his eyes, breathing hard between lines of the charm. Patsy Hoth's hand closed tight around his and pulled down; Rho bent after it until his head was near his knees but he felt no better, only furious at Patsy for making a display of him. *I can handle this!* he thought, but could say nothing for fear of breaking the charm. He stood up and glared at her. She glared back.

The smoke in the pentacle hadn't solidified; it wrapped and coiled around itself, and looking at it made Rho feel seasick. He began to think someone ought to do something about this, and looked at Warren, who was moving his hands in Russell and Cham's. *Of course they must have some way of signalling one another during the chant,* Rho thought. *Some safeguard they didn't bother telling junior faculty about.* Junior faculty didn't have a voice in these pentarium emergency discussions. Rho scowled. The smoke billowed up between him and Warren, and when it had moved away again the senior magicians had apparently reached a conclusion. Warren looked at Patsy Hoth, who nodded and gave Rho a stern 'follow-my-lead' glance before raising her voice. Rho kept the chant up with her, and as much felt as heard the other side of the circle break into a different charm. Syllables

71

beat against one another like waves at cross purposes or birds fighting in mid-air.

The column of smoke surged up to the ceiling of the pentarium, flattening itself against the pentacle walls, whirled around once or twice before Rho's dazed stare, and subsided. He saw the center of it condense into a brown and red mass, something that seemed to be struggling to form itself, but its edges were ripped away into the cloud still eddying around it. There was movement across the room; Rho saw Warren bending over, just as he had done earlier, and his anger with Patsy Hoth gave one last spurt before dying away. Feeling faint in an incantation wasn't shameful after all. When he looked back into the pentacle the smoke had changed color to a grayish-green and was closing in on the lump in its center, carving what looked like runes into it. Blood, or something like blood, ran across the floor toward him, and Rho's stomach began to climb up his throat, intent on escape. He bent over again. *This has to stop,* he thought, and just as he thought it he heard the voices across the circle fall silent. Patsy Hoth squeezed his hand and stopped chanting. The room echoed for a second, and then Rho heard nothing except somebody across the circle beginning to throw up.

***

Nobody said much in the shower room. Susan Teale broke the silence when she came back in from the pentarium with the mop bucket.

"That was just disgusting," she said.

72

"Sorry," Will said. He hunched on one of the benches, his face paler than his hair.

"That's not what I meant," Susan said. "I just hate Nezumia. It didn't have any reason to come rip up that poor little whatever-it-was. It's just evil." She banged the mop in the bucket for emphasis.

"Nobody does things without a reason," Linus Ukadnian said, putting on his undershirt. "Saying a demon is evil is both a tautology and an excuse for not investigating its behavior."

"Great," Will said. "You go in there and investigate its behavior. Go wild."

"That's not my field," Linus said. "But if it were, I wouldn't resort to facile categorizations as a substitute for causal analysis."

"That's enough!" Warren said. The edge in his voice shut everybody up except Teddy Whin.

"Linus has a point," she said. "Nezumia has to have had a reason for attacking that little demon. It can't have needed to feed off the thing-we were depressed enough in there to keep it fat for a week. And why was it marking the other demon? It only does that at the edge of its territory. For that matter, I'm surprised we got such a minor demon at all. I thought we had something big in the circle."

Russell nodded. "It might have been Nezumia," he said.

"But a minor demon wouldn't come into the circle if Nezumia were already there."

"The *grue* was really weak at first," Rho ventured. "Maybe the little demon was the first one we caught?"

"I think that's a given," Russell agreed. "We got the little one and then Nezumia came after it. It just

73

didn't feel like Nezumia to me. Not until just at the end." He didn't sound very confident.

"Maybe there were three of them," Teddy said. She leaned back against the lockers and started ticking events off on her fingers. "We get the little one first, and a bigger one comes into the circle to feed on it. Then Nezumia hustles up to warn the second demon off its territory. Sound reasonable?"

"The question you should be asking is whether it is testable," Linus said, looking at Warren with a defiant expression. A loud mechanical beeping seemed to second his opinion, and he stood up straight and marched over to his open locker. Patsy Hoth glared at his back.

"If we hadn't been at odds before casting the charm, we might have been able to hold the demons. What we need is another departmental workshop on collegiality and professionalism," she said, but Linus was deep in discussion on his phone, and didn't hear. When the rest of the magicians were showered and ready to leave he was still talking, sitting on the bench and drawing diagrams of the ley-line on a pad he had fished out of his coat pocket.

Rho was happy to leave him there and to follow Neil up five flights of stairs to the second-floor landing, where Neil turned around.

"My stop," he said. "Want some coffee?"

"No," Rho said uneasily. He hesitated on the stairs. "Does that happen a lot?"

"I dunno, I think maybe once or twice a semester. Just what you needed after Selanto, huh?"

"What do you do if somebody passes out?"

74

"You hang onto his hands and chant louder," Neil said firmly, as if trying to convince somebody. "That's what you do. Or you stop the chant and let the demon go. That's why we have the pentacle, and the safety chain. Are you sure you don't want coffee?"

"Yeah, I'm sure," Rho said. "I have to get some sleep." Now that he'd stopped walking, he felt as if he'd never be able to start again. Four more flights to his bedroom. He looked up the stairs, and pulled himself together. "I'll see you later."

At every turn in the staircase he looked at another of the Academy wards, stamped into the stone and touched with gold, and one of them faced him from his own door. When he opened it, the room inside glowed with morning sunlight. It streamed through the tower's southernmost window, turning the dust on every surface into a glowing velvet, a safe and luminous softness that danced inside itself to the same rhythm that motes of dust kept as they drifted through the sunlit air. Rho stopped in the doorway, shocked by the light and by the feeling the room gave him. Sometime when he wasn't paying attention this room had become home, a den and refuge. He shut the door carefully and leaned against it. Surely standing in the warm light, letting it dissolve him into something as lazy and insubstantial as the dust motes themselves, would be as good as sleep.

With his eyes shut Rho could hear nothing except wind curling around the tower, as if he had climbed all the way out of Osyth into some other world where neither demons nor people could intrude. A flurry of wings came from in front of him and a pigeon with a twig in its beak landed on the west windowsill, the one facing away from the Magic Building proper, and strutted along it, head bobbing as it inspected the site. It laid its burden down across the ledge and leaned out into the air, its neck stretched long and its head cocking from side to side.

"Right here," it called to another pigeon out of sight. "Good spot. Safe place." It stepped back, tilting its head to eye the twig critically.

Rho watched as the pigeon made minor, precise adjustments in the twig's position, then walked over it and flew away, the wind from its takeoff blowing the twig off the ledge. He shook his head, grinning, and went to bed.

***

Russell Cinea stood by the cross-shaped arrowslit window in his office, replacing a bulb in his plant lights and wondering if he should go down and bother Warren. Minding one's own business was severely overrated. When he looked down the corridor Warren's office door was shut, though, so Russell turned around. His own office was nicer, anyway.

Russell's library contained as many scrolls as books, all in cylindrical cases with decorative round caps, carved, sequined or enameled and ornamented with tassels. Some scrolls were stored in square cubbyholes, others in a wooden structure like a magnified honeycomb plastered onto Russell's wall, and the most often used in a wine rack standing by the window. This variety of storage, and the tassels, gave his room a festival air. He especially admired a set of scrolls high on the wall, their foot-long tassels complicated with decorative knotwork and carved pendants in an orange stone. While Russell was standing looking at these scrolls, somebody knocked on his open door and Warren came in. He sighed and settled into Russell's ugly old recliner, looking at the scrolls with him.

"Magic is so much prettier than wizardry," he said. "We just had blueprints and computers, and the odd architect's model. You know what I'd like to do? Just go around the building and look at everybody's labs."

"Half of them would think you were planning to reallocate space," Russell said. "Do it some time when you need to distract them from what you're really planning."

"I haven't really planned anything for ten years," Warren said, stretching. "Not since the last of the old guys retired. Everyone on board now is with the program. It looks as if we got Rho back from Selanto in one piece, anyway."

"Yep," Russell said. "Pity he had to come back to one of Nezumia's little jokes."

"Well, it happens," Warren said, sounding defensive. "It's not all hearts and flowers. A natural philosopher ought to be used to things rending each other tooth and claw." He sighed. "I'll talk to him-or do you want to?"

"You take Neil, I'll take Rho," Russell said. "You know, we've got a real promising bunch this year. It'll be fun to see what they turn out to be. I'd say Graham's going to be another cold power, myself. Like Will. He's a nervous Nellie."

77

"That might come from working with Linus," Warren said. The thought made him sad. He was always sorry for people who got their power from fear or anger. "But then, they're probably sorry for people like you and me," he mused, and they had had the conversation so often that Russell was able to follow it.

"No they aren't," he said robustly. "They're sorry for themselves, and perfectly happy about it. So you don't need to bother. Neil, now-Neil's going to be a nice warm power, just like Teddy. One of the complacent ones. We want to keep Neil. How are we going to help him get tenure?"

"I've already talked with James about that," Warren said, brightening. "He's got a lot of imp-related stuff in the field program. Neil could get a good few publications just filling in gaps. Plus, we need a new liaison with Alchemy-they don't take Linus seriously anymore. And what about the Arcane Arts? We've never had anybody with an arts background before. In fact, I saw a grant opportunity for joint arts and magic projects. It's on my hard drive." He looked around Russell's office again. "I wish I could paint," he said. "I'd get all this stuff on record-what the work really looks like."

"I'm more interested in Rho," Russell said. "We need another neutral power. Natural philosophers are usually as neutral as exorcists, but that's not what I'm picking up so far. He looks like another angry one."

"Not this morning," Warren said.

"No. Well, we'll just have to wait and see. Is that what's bothering you?"

"No." Warren frowned at the pile of papers that concealed Russell's desk. "I'm worried about Lilian."

"Is she sick?"

"No, but she's upset about something. She won't tell me. I'm thinking it has to be something at work. Insurance stuff."

"I was going to bring that up myself," Russell said. "I heard something about insurance from Vinca, over in Alchemy. Don't ask me how that man knows these things-but he tells me Salvation's threatening to raise our rates for group insurance. Significantly. Could that be what she's antsy about?"

"Maybe," Warren said, but he looked unconvinced.

"Well," Russell said, "this could be a big one, y'know? What do we do if these rates keep going up? You can't keep a demonologist on staff if you can't provide insurance. The business is just too dangerous, even the way we do it here. By Vinca, they're going to charge us what they charge the other universities. No credit at all for following the IDA guidelines."

"That's unreasonable! We've never had a fatality since we switched to IDA. Not even a serious injury, except the time Teddy fell down the stairs."

"Tell me. At least Jim ought to be happy about it. This is the one that could get his union off the ground." Russell laughed. "I bet administration is busting their humps to get it all cleared up before he comes back next month."

79

"Damn," Warren said, and shut his eyes. "I'll have to look into it. We can't invoke in the pentarium without coverage. Maybe we should shut down the program, just for a while."

"Nobody's going to take a foreboding seriously from you," Russell protested, wishing he had said nothing. "You're not fey. You're just burned out."

"Perhaps." Warren sighed and shut his eyes, leaning back in the cushy chair, which let Russell get a good look at him unobserved. What he saw, though, was only a bit constrained by the man in the chair. Russell had too many memories of Warren as the young wizard worrying over the pentarium, the fellow enthusiast planning reforms over beer and pretzels, the nature and ritual lover who had walked the ley-line into Osyth in high summer, climbing up the cliffs into Westpark with his hair in his face and an expression at once exalted and lost.

Russell had known Warren the minute he saw him for the kind of person language magicians dreamed of, someone who would believe that every word in an argument referred to something real. Unlike the demons, once Warren was convinced of something he would remain so, until new evidence was explained to him, and he would go out and act on what he believed. But Russell couldn't play arguing games with Warren, the way he could with Teddy or James. It would be like hitting a Styrofoam baseball; it would leave a dent. Russell smiled at his friend with condescending affection. "We're doing our best work in years," he said reassuringly. "These new guys have more magic than we've been able to hire for quite a while. It's as close to routine as it's ever going to be. We have a charm the demons can't poke holes in; we have the best circle we've ever had. The pentarium is in perfect condition. Can you really justify shutting us down?"

Warren opened his eyes and sat up. "Probably not," he said, and sighed. "At least I can go talk to Neil. That'll accomplish something."

"Good idea," Russell said. "I'll run up and see Rho." He followed Warren out into the third floor hall and almost ran right into Teddy Whin as she approached his office.

"Look, we've gotta do something about the rank structures we assume in these charms," she said. "Not to mention this predatory, competitive substructure."

"I have to talk to Rho."

"Neil said he's gone to bed. D'you know, one of the magicians at that conference got killed by his own demon? Rho saw it happen. Neil said he was sick on the way back from the airport. And worried about going into the pentarium."

"Damn," Russell said, standing irresolute in the hallway. "I really should talk to him, then. Not if he's asleep, though... "

"Leave him an e-mail. Let's get online and find out who was killed. It has to have freed up a pile of demons," Teddy said. "I was thinking, that's what we might have been getting this morning."

"All the way from Selanto?"

"You ask Linus about ley-line connections," she said sharply. "I've had about as much of him as I can stand. We should get a copy of the list of conference participants from Rho."

"That'll be on the web," Russell said, turning and going back into his office. Talking with Rho would have to wait.

***

A cloud cut off Rho's sunlight at ten minutes to three and immediately he jumped in his sleep and woke up, looking for what had cast the shadow. It took him a few minutes to figure out where he was. The clue was the view from his bedroom window across the Magic Building's roof, towers and gables spread out in front of him like a mountain range with clear skies beyond. A crow flew across his line of vision, cawing softly as it fluttered its body around the sharp edge of a gable.

"Let's try that again," the crow coached itself. "Left wing down, fold a little more, dive-that's it!"

Rho knelt on his bed and pushed his face against the edge of the window, trying to see where it had gone. He could just see past the roof to the unkempt land over the ley-line, brown with bushes and shrubby trees.

Rho pulled his head back and felt himself starting to relax. He stretched experimentally and found everything to be in working order and hungry. He was hungry from head to toes. Even his hair was hungry. With a sense of foreboding, he padded out into his workroom and opened the mini refrigerator under his table, stared inside, and found it was just as bad as he'd remembered it. Two cans of beer, half a jar of peanut butter, and some of those free foil packets of pickle relish. "Damn," he said without much feeling, straightened up, and rubbed his head. He'd have to stand in line at the bank to get money and walk into town for grocery shopping, and another day would be gone without any work on the research. Tenure review one day closer, and his lab no nearer to being set up. "I wish I'd never gone to that conference," Rho said to himself. "What a waste of time. What a pissing match."

He gave himself all kinds of good advice as he unpacked. *Forget about the other schools and fit yourself into this one,* he said and crammed his suit far back in the end of his closet. *Get a few publications and some graduate students. And a grant!* Send emails to all those people from the Society of Veterinary Lechery and find out who's trying to breed better ducks. When he upended his conference bag over the unmade bed, though, the first thing to fall out of it was the application to join the Demonological Congress.

Rho picked the folder up, fully intending to toss it, and the feel of it was all that stopped him-the heavy linen paper, with its embossed letterhead. Baristes had favored this kind of paper. Rho's hands remembered how it felt to write on, how the pen slid over its rich surface. He smelled the application absently, not sure what he was thinking, and slipped it back into the bag. Then he sorted out the cheaper, glossier documents from the veterinary lechers and put them beside his computer. At that moment his body spoke to him again, in unequivocal terms. *Don't even think about turning that thing on until you've eaten,* it said. His stomach clenched up so tight he doubled over, and a wave of hunger so strong it felt like nausea rushed through him.

"Damn!" Rho said in surprise, standing up. His hands trembled. "You don't have to eat every day!" he complained, as if someone were telling him another of Osyth's unwritten rules. His stomach ignored him. "I'm not wasting this whole afternoon in the bank line and walking in town to shop," he told it crossly, pulling on a tee-shirt and jeans and dropping his robe over them. He stomped on every step as he went down to the first floor refectory. His body would just have to settle for coffee and a doughnut, and be glad for that much.

Coffee and a doughnut made a dent in Rho's cash, and to make it worse his stomach clamored for bananas the minute he saw them. He gave in, with an unwanted image of mothers in supermarkets running through his mind. He could see himself wheeling a cart through the market, his stomach sitting in the baby seat and howling 'gimme that!' at every display. *I've gotten soft,* he thought angrily, and jumped when someone tapped his arm.

"We've been waving at you," Teddy Whin said.

She looked full of herself, full of doughnuts. Sleek and complete. Rho didn't feel kindly toward her.

"Come over and join us." Reminding himself that he'd decided to fit in, Rho followed her toward the window and a small group of magicians-Russell, Neil, and Will Harding, who looked half asleep.

"Don't mind Will," Neil said. "He just woke up. Out all night after vampires, y'know."

Rho, his hypothesis confirmed, immediately began to feel better. Maybe he could figure Osyth out, after all! He couldn't help comparing this cheerful room with its wide windows to the dismal coffee bar at Selanto.

"Yeah," Will said, yawning. "No rest for the wicked. I better get changed-and eat something with iron in it." He stood up and made a face at his coffee cup. "I'm so sick of liver. Why did I go into this field?"

"Dried fruits have iron in them," Teddy said.

Will grinned. "I'll tell the vampires that tonight, and let you know what they say about it. Take my chair, Rho. I've gotta go."

Rho sat down between Teddy and Russell and started peeling his banana.

"That guy has more angst per ounce than anyone else on campus," Teddy said as she watched Will leave the room.

"Oh, bull," Neil said. "What about the students?"

Teddy dismissed the students with a wave of her hand and turned her attention to Rho. "Neil says you saw Dolf Ganeel get killed. So, what happened?"

"Someone pulled his ward off," Rho said. "I guess one of his own demons was around, and got him. How'd you find out he was the one who got killed?"

"It's on the net, in the Selanto news service," Russell said. "They just have an obituary, though. Nothing about how he died-just the usual, 'unnatural causes'." He looked at the table, brooding. "I went to school with him over there."

Rho looked at him surreptitiously over his banana, trying to link Russell and Ganeel. It was hard to do. Russell, with his bright white hair and

85

unlined face, seemed to come from a different century.

"We were office mates for a while," he went on. "Dolf was one of the married students, so he and his wife used to host potlucks at their place. They'd host, and then they got to keep the leftovers. That was the rule at Selanto. They had two little kids, so they needed the food. He was always on the fast track, though. Bound a demon before he'd finished his first year there."

"That is so stupid," Teddy said. "What kind of a school lets people bind demons before they know what they're doing?"

"Since what they were teaching was demon binding, the assumption was that if you could bind one, you knew what you were doing."

"Oh yeah? How many of your class got killed before they could graduate?"

Russell looked at the ceiling, counting on his fingers. "Only three."

Teddy made puffing noises, but Neil cut her off. "Were you still in touch with Ganeel?" he asked Russell.

Tact, Rho thought, making a mental note of it. Tact meant cutting off conversations when people got angry. It was preferred, here, to letting them hurl curses at one another.

"No. We kept in touch for a while after we graduated, but I hadn't seen him since his divorce," Russell said. "I wrote to him and his ex a few years later, when the children died, but he never wrote back. I haven't been to Selanto in twenty years or more." He took a drink of his coffee and set it down

86

firmly. "Whenever I go over there, I end up in some argument about the IDA."

"What made you form the IDA?" Rho asked, pretending innocence. Neil grinned at him in a conspiratorial manner. "Neil told me you graduated from Selanto without binding a demon. Why did you want to do that?"

"My father was a demonologist," Russell said. "I saw what it did to him. I went into the field with an agenda to change it-most second-generation demonologists do. There just aren't that many of us."

"Warren's another," Neil said to Rho, but Russell shook his head.

"Warren did wizardry," he said. "He didn't want any part of magic, until we started talking about the IDA."

"The thing is, people who grow up with power devalue it," Teddy said. "They pretend its benefits are insignificant and they've succeeded on their own merits. The new recruits to any power structure based on voluntary total commitment will be the excluded, who can see how big a difference power makes. The privileged move on-they have to, to develop mores that will distinguish them from the newly empowered. As women and minorities move into positions of privilege, the scions of the old guard have to redefine it out from under them."

Russell smiled at her, apparently not offended at all. "What purpose do upstarts like you serve, then?"

"We're decoys," Teddy said. "We situate ourselves in an opposing stance vis-a-vis the actual proletariat, which people like you have forgotten all about. By redefining success to exclude our achievements, you'll eventually find you've empowered our true allies, the people below your radar."

"But after your oppositional stance, they won't see you as allies anymore and you'll go down with the rest of us. What a noble sacrifice! I'm awed. But seriously-" Russell said to Rho.

"I am serious!" Teddy protested.

"Seriously, I couldn't face binding a demon. I didn't want to turn into the sort of person you have to be to keep a demon you've bound from using your power. Hardly anybody manages to stay married after they've bound a demon."

"You're not married, anyway," Teddy pointed out. "Marriage as an institution depends more on restrictive social structures than on the absence of demons. If you take away enough of women's options, they'll put up with demons. That's what they really do at places like Selanto," she said to Rho. "They take away people's options. I bet they did everything they could to make you feel lower than dirt, didn't they? They're all language magicians over there, trying to tell themselves they haven't made a big mistake and ruined their lives. Folks like you and me, we're just meat to them. If they can convince one of us to bind a demon, they'll look at us afterwards and say 'see, it hasn't ruined their lives,' and then they'll feel better about themselves. And they're right, it doesn't ruin your life right away. Not until long after you've graduated and gone somewhere else, and they never have to face it-unless someone like you goes over there with his life not ruined, and shows them what it looks like to still have options."

Russell grinned at Rho. "You haven't seen a magewar until you've seen a bunch of language magicians trying to reconceptualize one another," he said.

"I've seen all the magewar I want to," Rho said, and a moment of silence fell over the table.

"Who killed Ganeel?" Neil asked.

"Someone named Stabor. I suppose you knew him as well?"

"No, I never met him," Russell said. "I try to stay out of these disciplinary spats."

"You know him," Teddy protested. "He's that guy who posts to all the newsgroups. He's written that book about how charms of discourse are going to kill us all, and put it up on his web page. It doesn't make any sense at all," she told Rho. "The guy's a loon."

"What does he think is wrong with charms of discourse?" Neil asked.

"He thinks that because they're not body based, demons can cast them. The problem is, that's been refuted. Demonic power doesn't work with charms of discourse; they don't believe in logic enough. You've seen how hard we have to work to convince them."

"That's the difference between humans and demons," Russell said. "We can believe in things, and they can't."

A silence fell over the table, and Rho wasn't sure why. When the conversation started up again it was about imps and art, topics he knew nothing about. He finished his doughnut and headed back to

89

his lab, not sure whether he had acquitted himself well or ill in Osyth-style social interaction. At least nobody had been torn to pieces-though that seemed an unambitious goal.

When Rho stepped into the stairwell, though, he felt something colder than the *grue* come over him. It was the way Teddy had talked about lives being ruined; that and the noises Ganeel had made. *We're meat to them,* he thought; somebody else had said that, too. They feed on their students-someone at the conference. *The demons take their power, no matter how well they shield themselves, and so they have to take from students... but that's not how it is! They're just people. Baristes wasn't leeching power off me, or was he?* He shut his eyes and wrestled inside his head, trying to wrench loose from the words Teddy and Russell had wrapped around his memories.

"They're the language magicians, the ones who think they've made a mistake," Rho said out loud. "I'm the one who's getting recontextualized. Everything she said about Selanto-it could just as well be true about her and Russell." Absentminded in his struggle, he'd turned around and found himself facing the steps down to the basement. A whisper of sound came up from the live specimens' floor of the museum, a smell of sulfur from the dry specimens' floor, and a sort of ground zero solid feeling from the pentarium.

Rho went down the stairs because he felt afraid to. He waded down through his own reluctance, one flight, two, three, until its cold heaviness had closed over his head and he could see the corridor outside the pentarium locker room, and then he realized he didn't know whether he was allowed to go into the pentarium alone. He stood on the steps for a few minutes, ashamed of feeling relieved, until indignation came to his aid. "Well, dammit!" he said, "I'm not just fresh meat! I'm not just going to believe the last theory I heard." He strode masterfully forward, only to find the locker room sealed with an Academy ward. All the strength went out of him as he fooled with the ward, as if he were casting a gigantic charm. He sat on the steps for a while to recover, and his stomach spoke to him in forceful terms. It spoke about how long the line at the bank was, and how far the walk to the nearest grocery, and how entirely wasted this day would be if he died of hunger with his lab not yet set up, and after a while it was convincing enough to send Rho back up the stairs for his coat and boots, and off in search of fresh meat for himself.

***

Warren loved his wife, but occasionally she went out of control for weeks at a time, and this was one of those spells. There was just no point to repeating the same scrying ritual every morning and evening. Still, a man who had been married as long as Warren had learned when to shut up and cooperate. He wrote a few sentences about whatever was uppermost in his mind, trying to tell himself that writing it out was a useful exercise in itself, and watched her tear the paper up. She didn't even read it. That gave him an uneasy feeling.

It always fell out the same, exactly, in the same tangle of bones and papers, the same life bone leaping free of the rest of them. Lilian sat looking at it every time, the same way Warren himself looked at a problem he could almost feel himself solving. Warren sat with her, the way a loving husband learns to do, but each time he looked at the tangle something grew tighter and heavier within him. It looked more like his life each time he looked at it, like the hours of his day, snarled together with a thousand problems to be solved, each one needing to be teased away from the next with infinite care.

I don't have infinite care, Warren thought. He looked at the snarl of bones as if it were wrapped around him, and drew a breath when the life bone fell free, he picked it up, running his fingers down its smooth shaft, folded the signature wrapped around it into his hand, and turned away from all the rest of it and Lilian frowning at the bones on the table. He wondered whether scrying something could make it come true.

Chapter Five

Pigeons woke Rho long before sunrise. He sat up with a jerk of terror, looking across the room to where there should have been a bureau with something horrible sitting on it, but all he could see was the wall, gray in the light from his bedroom window.

The pigeons' racket echoed across the rooftops. "Cat! Fly away! Cat! Cat!"

The noise came closer and Rho got up in one sudden spasm of movement, still trembling, and stumbled out into his workroom to see what was happening on the west windowsill. Yesterday's pigeon sat there, stretched upright in a litter of sticks that it doubtless thought was a nest. *They're awful builders,* Rho thought.

"My place," the pigeon muttered in a sulky voice, and stretched its neck even higher when another pigeon wheeled in and landed on the ledge.

"Cat!" the second bird said. "Cat on the roof! Fly away!"

"My place! My nest!" Rho's pigeon said, and he sympathized.

He opened the other window and leaned out, cold striking through his nightshirt.

He was looking over the southern end of the Magic Building, with the South Tower standing up against the beginning of light in the sky. The frozen stones hurt his hands and the chill gave him a reason to tremble. Pigeons rustled on the roof of the tower, above him.

"Safe here," they said to one another. "High place. There! Cat cat!"

Looking down, Rho saw a slim black creature prowling along the roof. It turned a white-bibbed face up to him and stared, crouching with one paw in the air; then, as Rho did nothing threatening, it sat down and began to lick the paw.

"Why are you here?" Rho said to the cat, sternly.

"Here? Where?" the cat said, and continued her toilette. She had a beautiful voice, light and husky at the same time.

"Up on this roof."

"Washing," the cat said, without looking up. "I'm here washing. Why are you here?"

"This is my place," Rho said. "My birds. You keep away." He felt sorry to say it. He liked this cat. *I want a cat,* he thought, but amended it. He didn't want some babyish kitten, or a soft domestic idol of a housecat. He wanted this cat, with her smart mouth and bad manners. The cat, meanwhile, had stood up and turned away. She looked over her shoulder at Rho and began to scrape, a calculated insult.

"I have meat," he said in a temporizing tone.

"Good for you," the cat said. "Who caught it for you?"

She suddenly put her ears up and crouched, looking at something Rho couldn't see from his vantage point. He shut his mouth on any retort he could have come up with (who had caught the ground steak in his refrigerator?), for the first rule of cat life was to keep silent during a stalk.

This cat stalked in a business-like manner, no airs and graces. Three steps and a leap, and she was grappling with something behind the roof's edge. Rho couldn't see what it was, but it didn't flutter. It scrabbled at the tiles and howled insults.

"Kill you, idiot! Help! Help, cat!" it screamed. "Cat! Cat murder cat!"

The pigeons above him joined in the chorus. Rho leaned further out the window, to no avail; the shrieks and scrabbles bounced away, further down and out of his hearing.

"Hey! Cat!" he called, but there was no answer except the pigeons'.

"Gone," they said, rustling among themselves. "Cat murder. Bad thing. Sleep safe, high place."

Rho could hear them settling their feathered breasts down on the tiles, their voices becoming muffled as heads were tucked under wings. It was a soft, whispering sound, but he was wide awake in the chill air. He tried to read his watch by the beginning dawn, gave up, and pulled himself back into the room to turn on a light. Six forty. Too late for him to get back to sleep, and far too close to the time when he'd have to go down to the pentarium- Rho didn't want to think about that.

"Oh well," he said, and turned the rest of the lights on. The windows went black, as if he'd stolen all the sunrise and put it into his light fixtures. He started coffee and turned on his computer, but both of them took too long booting up to hold his attention; putting the time to good use, he dug out the Demonological Congress application and read through it. The feel of it reassured him, and as he read the text he started to feel more settled, his nervousness changing to excitement. This was the way he'd felt at every upwards turn in his career. First terror, then excitement and ambition, and finally things began to fit themselves together, as if the happenings in his life had just been waiting for him to decide how to use them. What to make out of them. Rho read through the lists of Demonological Congress members, award winners, grants issued by the Congress to its members, and saw opportunity.

Russell was the first person to get a degree from Selanto without binding a demon, he thought. *Now I'll be the first to join the Congress without binding one!* He spread the application out on his desk, finding it as smooth to write on as he'd imagined it would be. The ink spread into a strong black line as Rho filled in where he had captured his demon-at the Congress meeting-and who had witnessed it-Vivien, he wrote, taking a deep breath. What if they asked him to prove it was bound? He felt a moment's panic. What if Vivien asked him to call it up? *Then I'll stand on my dignity,* he thought. He imagined himself bristling in outrage. *Are you calling me a liar?* he'd say. *I have other options. I do not need membership in an organization that doesn't treat its members with the respect due a professional.* He practiced inside his head as he folded the application and put it into its envelope. When he'd sealed it he sat back, breathing a little faster and feeling as if he'd found some place to stand between the two territories of the Congress and Osyth, something to be that neither group of magicians could define or control.

***

Seven fifteen meant chimes in Russell Cinea's house. Gently, gradually increasing chimes, of the sort meant to draw the sleeper directly from slumber into meditation. The chimes came from a triangular clock beside his bed, and they hadn't been his idea, but he liked them a lot. They had been a gift from Teddy on his last birthday. She tried all these things, picking them up two years before they became fads, and Russell liked that a lot, too. The chimes were supposed to remind him of his business at the beginning of each day, to start him off in the contemplative frame of mind a theoretical magician needed, but as often as not they made him think of Teddy or of their own avant-garde status, instead.

The problem with being a language magician, Russell thought as he looked at the clock, *is that new words, new things, lose their power for you as soon as you recognize and analyze it. The only things you can count on moving you are the ones you were conditioned by before you became a language magician.* So if he had really wanted to be drawn into meditation by his bedside clock, he should have found the kind that sat by his bed in childhood, with the little window on its bottom through which the moon and sun rotated in smiling, fat-faced splendor. Just thinking about clocks like that gave Russell a peaceful feeling, whereas Teddy's clock made him want to go out and debate something. He would have lain in bed considering this, but by seven thirty he was too stiff for comfort.

"You're getting old, Russ," he said to himself, sitting up in bed and pushing his feet into his slippers. And that was a word nobody got

97

conditioned to in youth, a word nobody understood at all until they were too old for words to mean anything unambiguous. By the time people got old, they knew too much about using words for words to help with something as uncompromising as decline. That was why they used 'old' a different way every time, trying meanings onto the word as if they were dressing a doll up for display. It was why the sorcerers had so little they could do about it. There weren't any words of power for getting old.

We'll end up with no magic at all, Russell thought as he made coffee and heated up a muffin in the microwave. *When we've studied all the words, broken all the way out of our conditioning into rational analysis, what will we use to call the magic up in ourselves?* There, he'd thought it. Once, he had started and stopped his little bedside clock with a thought, heated muffins with a touch of his hand, brewed his coffee with a casual word. Now his kitchen was filled with gadgets and he enjoyed having the latest things, the same way Teddy enjoyed giving them to him. Was she, too, playing with the idea of having no magic at all? They never talked about that. They never came any closer than they had come yesterday, talking to Rho about people who had made bad decisions and ruined their lives.

"We'll have to talk about this," Russell said aloud. "When James gets back." He looked out the window with a bleak feeling, as if he had betrayed friends, and that wasn't true. Teddy and James knew everything he knew about demonology. They knew what happened when a person bound a demon. It was just that they were the first language magicians

98

who refused to bind demons, trying to get along with their own power instead of stealing it from their demon slaves. Nobody could tell what would happen to them... *Teddy's not an idiot,* Russell thought. *Neither is James.* They must have thought of this. But they didn't know how much Russell had been able to do with magic, just ten years ago. He hadn't told them how much he had lost.

The microwave buzzed, and Russell took out his muffin and gave himself a brisk talking-to. Nothing terrible had happened to him. Nothing as bad as binding himself to a demon. After all, how often did he need to turn on clocks, or heat up muffins? *I still have enough power to do my job,* Russell told himself. He might not have enough belief in his own words to control the unspeaking world, but that didn't matter. He talked with other magicians now, and with demons, and they heard him through their own conditioning, their own meanings. They made the charms work on themselves. He thought about the demons they would talk with this morning in the pentarium, and about their talk with Neil and Rho yesterday. Teddy was good, he had to admit. It didn't hurt to admit that she was better than he was, when she got off her pet issues. What had she said to Rho yesterday 'We're meat to them.' *I never would have thought of that,* Russell admitted, but it had been so right. 'Meat.' Not a word that meant much to most people, but it had fitted Rho completely. He'd seen it strike in. How had she known?

***

99

Rho almost put some meat out for the cat, but he couldn't. Not and have pigeons nesting on the windowsill. Cats and birds, they were an uneasy combination-and while he liked birds, they always made him jealous. They were so dumb, but they got to fly. Cats were cleverer. Cats didn't care about other animals, though. They tortured other animals for fun. But they enjoyed life so much. The first rays of sunlight shot into his room and he imagined cats curled up in it. He had never been so happy as when among cats, dozing in the sunlight. Birds didn't relax like that.

"Hell, I don't know," Rho said, and sighed as he put the meat back in the refrigerator. Why did he always have to choose between gentle things and charming ones? Why weren't the virtuous ever so pleasant as the wicked? Why did he feel more at home among the things with blood on their lips? He carried the Demonological Congress application down to the outgoing mail on the second floor as if he were making a confession of his true nature, and went the rest of the way down to the pentarium shower room feeling not so much afraid as resigned.

Rho thought about the sick feeling this room had given him the night before and looked around it now with amazement. It was filled with fluorescent lighting, steam and bittersmoke, and the other faculty washing and undressing in it seemed insubstantial, like people without serious concerns. Like pigeons.

When the *grue* came, Rho almost laughed at its insignificance. It sent no more than a passing shiver across him. He heard Russell and Warren raise the familiar arguments about the nature of spirit and

100

flesh, as if they were binding a demon lord; when the *grue* rushed across him again he spoke a mere line of the argument and it retreated. The little cloud of smoke it made whirled around the pentacle twice and then huddled in its center, a pitifully small hump that resolved itself into a one-legged blue demon with fur and long, floppy ears. It sat up, looking at them through watery eyes, and pulled on its ears and cried.

***

"Ctenothrissa? I've never heard of that one."

"I know I've heard the name," Russell Cinea said. "What's it say in the compendium, Warren?"

Warren Oldham was leafing through a large leather-bound book from his locker. "It's not one of the major demons," he said. "Never seen outside the netherworld, it says here, and only seen in the netherworld when you enter from Sio. This is the first time anybody's called it to the surface."

"Well, hooray for us," Teddy Whin said, peering over his shoulder. Warren looked annoyed.

"Don't get bath oil on my book, Teddy."

"Sorry," she said, without moving. "This is pretty good, though. Another first for Osyth. Now, why would an eastern netherdemon manifest here? The charms haven't changed for weeks. Have the demon lords started sending small fry up instead? Or is there some change in the line-some current, that took the summoning charm into a different layer?"

"That metaphor is misleading," Linus Ukadnian said, in his shorts and undershirt and bow tie. "If your charms are as imprecise as your imagery, we might call up anything at all."

Teddy Whin gave him a cool look. "My imagery is more precise than you'd imagine," she said. "There are merely directions in which I choose not to pursue it."

"Insult is the last refuge of a mind that lacks an adequate understanding of mathematics," Linus said. He pulled his pants on and walked away, carrying the rest of his clothing.

"Is he always like that?" Rho asked Neil.

"Oh, yeah. It keeps Warren from assigning him to committees."

Rho thought about Linus while he dried between his toes. "So," he said, "what's the pecking order?"

Neil laughed. "I'll tell you later," he said. "Stop in my office."

"Like you know," Will Harding scoffed, who had been openly eavesdropping.

"Well, he can get both of our theories and triangulate," Neil said.

Rho felt himself on solid ground. Studying pecking orders was something he knew how to do.

***

Pecking order! That wasn't the way Neil would have put it, but it gave him a chuckle. He saw it more as a totem pole, himself. Something with bold, stylized figures. Russell and Warren at the top, looking out over the department like eagles. Then the froglike climbing figures of Teddy and Patsy Hoth, their feet pushing off the heads of the solid

102

rank below them: Susan, bearlike and maternal, with little ratlike Will nestled under her protecting arm; Linus, whom Neil always saw as a snapping turtle with moss on its shell; Anders Regan, who appeared as himself in Neil's totem pole because Neil knew nothing about him. At the very bottom of the pole squatted Neil himself, Rho and Isaac Graham. Who had he left out? Cham Ligalla. Cham the exorcist, who wasn't part of the totem pole at all. Who viewed it from outside, and could unmake it at any time she chose.

Neil imagined the totem pole painted with tribal markings. Almost everyone at the top of the pole except Warren would wear the markings of Selanto, which Neil thought would be jagged lightning bolts in red and black. Russell, Teddy, Patsy Hoth-all had done their graduate work at Selanto. *And it shows,* Neil thought nastily. *Snobs, the Selanto magicians. Full of themselves. But...* He thought about Patsy Hoth and sighed. *Forget it.* He was never going to be in that league.

Imps were such small beer in the Demonology Department. The children's books Neil had published were, well, for children. Painters were like dancing pigs, admired but not envied. What was left for a guy looking to make his mark? (another great turn of phrase)... Neil made his mark, in charcoal, on the edge of a memo. He was probably the only one of them who had a mark of his own, copyrighted too. "That won't get me tenure," he said to it. It was a neat mark, though. Simple. Dramatic. He started to sketch the totem pole he'd imagined.

Research wouldn't make him a place in this department. Putting up with other people might, though. Staying interested in them. Figuring them out. Hitching his wagon to a star-though all the stars in this department seemed to have sharp points-Neil had always been good at dealing with people, because he liked them. Life drawing did that, it taught him how to see something interesting, even beautiful, in anyone. The question was, where could Neil find anyone to look back at him in the same way?

***

Rho slept from eleven o'clock till past noon, when he woke up peacefully for the first time since the conference. He yawned, stretched, surveyed his room with approval, and stretched again. Having slept in his clothes, he only needed to pull on his boots, put a coat over his magician's robe, and check the camera arcana to make sure its crystals were charged before he headed out to photograph birds on the ley-line, searching for individuals possessed by incubi.

Rho spent every afternoon he could spare in this pursuit, which got him out of doors. So far, it had done little else. Most birds attracted incubi in the spring. Woodpeckers, nuthatches, and pigeons were already beginning their mating season, though, as were ducks. Rho's busy season approached, and with it came a feeling of urgency and the need to know the landscape. By spring he must be able to walk the ley-line and the parks of Osyth as an initiate, familiar enough with their normal appearance to catch any changes, and this was a challenge for someone from a different continent. His current walks were still more sightseeing than useful analysis, too filled with inner comparisons to Kasidora and its fauna.

When he opened the tower door the manicured edge of the campus stretched for ten feet before him, replaced abruptly with meadow stubble-teasel, wild carrot, and tickseed tops, all standing up out of depressions melted into the snow by their warmth-hoarding dark stems. The snow glittered around them in dirty grains. Rho followed his regular path out into the meadow, his shadow pacing beside him. By the time the sun had set, in the half-hour of winter twilight that turned the sky and snow alike a powdery, luminous blue, he had walked nearly half the line.

Rho had followed the ley-line between ranks of middle-class faculty houses, all depressingly commonplace. He had reached the place where it spread out flat around a stream, and he saw ducks and drakes glow through the camera arcana with the shifting, rainbow colors of possession. He had followed the tug of magic through bare woods, by dark stands of conifers that stood like sentinels between the ley-line and the city wall, and into the brush that closed in on the line again just before it opened out for the last time in Westpark, the landscape of little hills and large boulders that ended in a tumble down the plateau's edge into the canyons below. Nearly half of the line's length was contained in Westpark, and Rho did not care to follow it. He did not choose to walk the ley-line for six miles to the cliff edge, six miles back in the dark, and another five miles back to the Magic Building.

He turned back, instead, and once more ran the gauntlet of fat, spoiled squirrels in the woods.

"Hey!" one of them yelled from above his head. "Hey, up here! Hey, buddy! Got nuts? Hey! Hey there!"

"It's cheapskate again," another squirrel chittered. "Hey, jerk! Yeah, you! Turdface!"

Rho hunched his head down in his shoulders and walked faster.

By the time the light faded away and he breathed in the black-ice smell of night he was between faculty houses, transformed now by lights in their windows. Rho looked into the windows with affectionate contempt, seeing busy kitchens, walls with framed photographs on them, or the glow of television sets. People who took no risks lived here. He felt himself teetering at the edge of such a life, ready to fall in and be trapped forever in something virtuous, careful, and safe, but when he got close enough to the Magic Building to see a light shining through its arrowslit windows, it was to meet Neil hurrying out along the ley-line toward him.

"Warren's trying to get a quorum together for an exorcism," Neil said happily, stepping on the soggy ends of his muffler. "That Ctenothrissa isn't smart enough to get out of the pentarium by itself. Come on and see the fun!"

***

106

The light Rho saw shining through an arrow slit came from the vampire lab where Will Goth-Harding and Susan Merick Teale worked together. They co-chaired the necromancy licensure program, a dramatic specialty in which neither of them was active-the working necromancer in the program was Roger Klimt, over in the basement of Sorcery's teaching hospital-and they studied vampires, ghosts and revenants, the by-products of dramatic people who took themselves seriously. Even in the magicians' circle, Will and Susan stood by dramatic people who took themselves seriously. Will linked a hand with Teddy Whin, who never noticed him, and Susan stood between Linus Ukadnian and Patsy Hoth and felt herself become smaller, less interesting, more insignificant with each passing minute.

"We're narrators," Will said to her. "We're the people who aren't involved in the drama, but the ones who get to watch it unfold."

"The ones nobody takes seriously," Susan said bitterly.

"The ones who aren't making fools of themselves," Will said, and Susan agreed. It was understood between them that they alone saw the Demonology Department as it was, they alone were clearheaded and not driven by ego issues, and one day they would be the ones to do something important, something that nobody else was able to do. In the meantime, Will and Susan were observers and analysts. They met every evening in one office or another, and there they shared the college gossip.

"Neil Torecki has the hots for Hoth," Susan said, leaning back and looking down into her coffee. "He admires strong women."

"He'd go for a strong man, but there aren't any in the department," Will said. "How did we come to a state where the strongest man in the department is a woman?"

Susan laughed. "You say that as if it were unusual."

"Neil's just the weakest of a weak lot. Pitiful wretches, all of us."

"I wonder... have you read his books?"

"The one on imps."

"I meant the children's books. *Inside the Red Box* and the other one? There's a snarky streak in Neil, and he draws nasty little pictures on the edges of his papers in meetings. It wouldn't hurt for us to check him out a little."

"No point," Will said. "He won't be here for long. You don't get tenure for children's books."

"Still," Susan said. "Let's take him over to *The King's* on Friday."

"Maybe. What about Rho?"

Susan considered Rho. An expert in postmortem manifestations, she had no objections to his hygiene. It called up pictures of many exhumed bodies, and the contrast flattered him. "I'd like to learn about Kasidora," she said. "He seems pretty much of a loner. Living in the building and all that. Has anybody tried to make friends with him yet?"

"I'm sure Russell took him out. He and Teddy take out all the newbies, once. And Jim Kalin's probably latched on to him. If I ever saw a union prospect, that's one."

"Jim always goes after junior faculty. They need more liberating."

"Oh, please," Will said. "The furthest Jim takes liberation is to wear khakis. It's just a pose. Do you know how much he makes?"

"You think everything's a pose. Too many vampires."

Susan knew Will could not deny any part of this statement. He did think everything was a pose, down to his own worldly wisdom. And it did come from vampires. Vampirism was a pose-the pallor, the unnatural beauty, the black clothing and obscenely perverted religious symbols-and the true horror of it, the part of it that gave Will bad dreams and kept him awake days, was that the undead had outlived any interest in this pose. They simply forgot that they had any choice.

"I'd better get on the move," he said, standing up. "While I'm still young and beautiful. As soon as I get crows' feet, that's it for vampire studies." He had the kind of looks a vampire could appreciate, slim and patrician. Deathly pale, with blond hair and dark avid eyes, Will dressed in black from head to toe and wore a tangle of gold and silver chains, wards, charms, and amulets from a dozen cultures.

"So what's Plan B?" Susan asked. "What do you do when you're a raddled old roue?"

"Switch to incubi, I suppose."

"Work with Hoth?"

"Why not? You know, I don't know what it would be like to work with something that didn't scare me," Will said. "Does that blow, or what? Maybe Plan B should be raising cabbages, or

109

something like that." He snorted. "Listen to me whine. Will I attract them tonight, or what?"

"Good hunting."

"I'll see you at sunrise," Will said, then kissed her good-bye.

Susan always kissed Will harder than he did her, to feel the heat under the cool surface of his lips. One day, she thought every time, she'd wait for him at sunup and he wouldn't return. She'd kiss him and not be able to find that spark of warmth. What was Plan B?

She didn't really want to think of one, so she was just as glad when Warren knocked and pushed the door open.

"We're doing an exorcism," he said. "Are you free? Is Will here?"

"Will's gone," Susan said, with relief. Exorcisms scared Will. they scared everybody. She put her cup down. "I wish I hadn't drunk that," she said, getting up. "This makes me nervous enough, without caffeine."

***

"Exorcise it!" Rho said. "Why would we have to exorcise a demon out of the pentarium?" He hung his coat in one of the pentarium shower room's lockers, shoved his boots in after it, and immediately stepped in a puddle of melting snow where the boots had been.

"Because the shielding spells down here don't keep demons out at night," Neil said importantly, unwinding his muffler. "If we leave a little demon like this trapped in the pentacle, something bigger will come hunting along the ley-line and shred it. Then what'll the big demons think of us? They'd stop seeing us as a benign nuisance." He grinned as he leaned down to pry his boots off. "Ever think you'd aspire to be a benign nuisance?"

Rho didn't answer this. The thought of one demon shredding another distracted him. "Who does the exorcism?" he asked.

"Cham Ligalla," Neil said, and stopped grinning. "She's the one who exorcises any of us, too, if we get possessed. Remember the waiver you signed?"

"Yeah," Rho said. He had signed the thing, but that didn't mean he'd thought about it. The whole topic gave him the creeps. Exorcism would drive a demon out of a magician, but it sent all the magic with it. "Did you ever want to be a mundane?" he asked Neil.

"Speaking of benign nuisances?" Neil stopped and thought about it. "Nah," he said. "You?"

"Not really," Rho lied.

**

Cham Ligalla, small and round-headed, walked through the Demonology Department wrapped in a cocoon of distraction that made all who met her feel either spared or insulted by her disinterest. Perhaps because they had so much difficulty catching Cham's attention, all of her acquaintances shared an unspoken conviction that their worth, perhaps their existence, depended on either getting or avoiding it, and this was what made her a talented exorcist.

111

Knowing this, Cham had embraced a lifestyle of overextension. She played to her strengths. In her large, neat office in the capitol building, she never did as few as two things at one time; folders multiplied on her desk and she slotted their offspring into vertical racks as strict as boarding schools, to mature on their own before they would be admitted back into the stack of active files. A few moments of concentrated attention was all a project needed to get it started. Then Cham withdrew and let matters progress on their own, until they merited another glance.

Cham honored the Demonology Department with her attention on only rare occasions. Every morning, she paid more attention than she would have thought possible in the pentarium. That was odd, and she had never figured it out; from the moment she said out loud that she was interested in calling a demon, she was interested. Completely. When it was finished, stepping into the shower room wiped all that concentration away, like mist off a window, and Cham saw through to her own concerns again.

The other times she spent on campus-department meetings, classes-went better, Cham had discovered, without her full attention. Especially the meetings. She didn't have much other business in the Magic Building, except on the rare occasions like these when her beeper went off, at the end of the workday, calling her in for an emergency exorcism. At one time there had been many of these, when a group of demons tried to lay claim to the pentarium, but that had been years ago. Now the exorcisms were of minor, overimpressionable demons.

She could have found her way into the pentarium blindfolded, simply by following the feel of Warren's worrying. It made Cham smile with approval, because Warren was definitely at his best when worrying about something small and helpless. She liked to see a power used appropriately; most magicians, though, were like Warren and never learned how to turn their strengths on and off. She set her briefcase neatly on one of the benches, hung her coat up, and greeted him.

"You remember Neil Torecki and Hiram Rho," Warren said, waving toward two men whose faces she had seen at the other side of the circle.

"Yes," Cham said. "Who else is helping?"

"Susan Teale."

Cham nodded, imagining the circle they could form in her mind. One neutral power, one sympathetic, two undeveloped. "Good," she said. "Nothing to scare it. We can do a friendly exorcism. Tell me about it." She began taking off her clothes. Normally Cham used the private showers, but this time she stayed out in the main room so Warren could tell her about the demon Ctenothrissa.

"It's seen seven students and five visitors," Warren said. "All the students say it's been cooperative and friendly. It doesn't have a very big vocabulary, though, so we haven't gotten much useful information from it. And it's very afraid of the big demons."

"Mm-hmm," Cham said. "Are any of them hanging around?"

"Not right now."

113

"All right." She looked at the new junior faculty, and they became real under her gaze. "You'll be helping to protect me and the demon when I let down the pentacle. None of what I say to the demon means anything about you, so don't pay any attention to it. You'll be using a second level charm of discourse, so it will work even if you can't keep your focus. The only thing you need to do is keep the candles lit and the chant going. I won't be able to tell what's happening outside your circle, so you'll have to tell me if any of you feel a strong *grue*. The signal is three fingers-like this." They both copied her, and both got it right the first time. People always did, when Cham was telling them something. She nodded, and they looked proud of themselves. "Let Warren do any talking to me. You keep the chant going, and don't blow out the candles, whatever you do. If any large demons come around, I'll have to reactivate the pentacle and stay the night to guard Ctenothrissa. Got it?"

***

While Cham Ligalla was telling them what to do, Rho felt important. As soon as she thought he knew his job, though, she looked away as if he were nothing at all. Her brown face shut down, as if she'd gone away to some place full of ancestral traditions beyond his comprehension or appeal, a place in which people like Rho were only minor nuisances. He scowled and turned away. Neil grinned, and Rho felt like punching him.

"You can't do anything about it," Neil said as they went into the pentarium together.

114

Ctenothrissa was sitting in a lump in the exact middle of the pentacle; it looked up and brightened, and Rho felt better. He squatted just behind the chain and wiggled his fingers at it, and it hopped over toward him. "Hey there, cutie," Neil said to it, and went on about Cham. "Wouldn't you love to see her do that to the dean, though?"

"To Linus," Rho said.

"Somehow he's never available for these occasions."

"What happen?" Ctenothrissa asked.

"It's night," Rho said. "Time to rest." He pantomimed sleep, holding his hands up against the side of his face. "Where do you sleep?"

Ctenothrissa imitated the gesture and sighed. "Never tell," it said. "Somewhere safe. Somewhere deep."

"Is it far?"

The demon nodded its head and looked smug. It pulled its long ears down, wrapping them around its face, and rocked gently. Rho felt the door open behind him and Susan squeezed past; when the demon saw her it uncoiled and stretched its long arms out, like a child asking to be picked up. Susan didn't say anything to it, or look at either of the other magicians as she walked to the far side of the circle. Rho wondered if she was mad about something, but then Warren and Cham Ligalla came in and he had no more time to wonder.

"Here," Cham said, handing him a candle, and he felt himself flicker into existence and out again. He stood up and shuffled to his place in the circle, examining the candle to keep his mind off Cham. The only special thing about it was the gold cap

115

covering the wick end; this cap was perforated by five holes, spaced equally around its upper end and connected by an engraved pentacle. A gold mesh bag hung from the cap by a chain, and opening this Rho found several herbal plugs, an instrument like a tiny cork-borer, and a gold card with a charm engraved on it. Looking to the right and left, he saw Susan using the little cork-borer to drill into her candle through the holes in its cap. Not wanting to have Cham give him directions, he copied her and inserted the herbal plugs, and as he did so the whole apparatus made sense. It was a portable smudging set. *Cool,* thought Rho. He read over the charm on the gold card, impressed with himself for even using such a professional, organized kit.

When he looked up from the candle, Cham Ligalla had gone into the circle and was sitting cross-legged between two points of the pentacle. Ctenothrissa was squatting uneasily in the middle, looking at her with distrust, but she was busy taking items out of her bag. The only one Rho could recognize was a mirror mounted in an oval frame. Cham set this up on a stand that held it at eye level and flicked it with her finger. It swung around freely.

"What happen?" Ctenothrissa asked again, in a small voice, and Cham nodded up at Warren.

"Don't worry," he said, pulling a cigarette lighter out of the gold bag attached to his candle. "We're just shutting down for the night. Time to go home." He lit his candle and passed the lighter to Rho. After a few minutes the herbal smoke began to swirl up and Warren nodded at each of the other magicians. He held up his card and they all began to

116

read the charm, and for a while Rho forgot to watch what Cham was doing. When he knew the charm well enough to look away from it, she had already let the pentacle down and was sitting quite close to the demon, looking into its eyes through the oval frame; the mirror spun so quickly that he could see it only as a flicker between them.

"Tell me about yourself," Cham said, in a voice that promised she would take whatever was told her and find its significance. "Tell me what the magicians say you are." Whatever Cham heard would turn out to be important, to fit into the scheme of the world, and the teller would never have to wonder again whether he belonged, whether he mattered or was just a mistake of nature...

The demon was answering her, but Rho couldn't tell what it was saying. He saw its face, eager and excited, and heard it stumble over its words. Cham began to answer it, in a language Rho could not understand but that he knew contained the explanations everybody longed for. He had to look away then, back to the card, or he would have strayed from the charm and begun to tell Cham his own secrets, just to hear those answers. He chanted more carefully, concentrating on every syllable, and the air felt solid around him.

When the solid feeling disappeared Rho almost dropped the candle to clutch at something, anything; at first he thought he was feeling the *cauld grue*, but there was nothing so real as cold in this sensation. Yet nothing had changed-no, Cham had stopped the twirling mirror. She held it edgewise, so she could look at the demon past it, and her voice was withdrawing like a clam closing its shell.

"Do you really think that's true?" she asked the demon, and Rho saw it pull in on itself. "Does any of that matter?" It doesn't, said her tone.

Rho felt himself break out in a cold sweat. None of it mattered. Everything he had ever thought about himself was meaningless, childish nonsense. He'd been found out... Warren's voice came toward him, clear and strong in the chant, and somehow Rho was able to keep speaking as he watched Cham Ligalla turn away and Ctenothrissa dwindle into a lump, a vapor, and nothing at all.

***

Cham Ligalla seemed to be gone even before she had left the pentarium. Rho couldn't tell when she was there and when she was not. He began to feel real again gradually as he showered and dressed. He bumped into things-the benches, the locker, and Susan Teale, who jerked away as if his touch had burned her. "Sorry," he muttered.

"No problem," Susan said, an obvious lie. She shut her mouth tight and tears began to pour out of her eyes.

Rho was half terrified and half as relieved as if he were crying himself.

"Uh-" he said, backing away and looking around for Warren, who came over and put his hands on Susan's shoulders as if it weren't at all dangerous. He held them there, standing behind her and blinking hard, and Susan kept still for a minute. Then she punched the locker door in front of her, a tremendous bang that made Rho jump away and hastily start buttoning his shirt.

118

"Bitch!" she said, and punched the locker again. "I hate her. Sadistic bitch!"

"Uh-huh," Warren said, somehow turned Susan around, and put his arms round her shoulders.

He made 'get out' gestures with his head at Rho and Neil; Rho was glad to obey, and even gladder that, for once, Neil had nothing to say about it.

***

Warren Oldham had been home for an hour before he managed to catch his wife's attention. Since he had tiptoed in late, it took him a while to realize he was being ignored. He waited, first in his office until it began to seem that Lilian would never call him out. Then he went into the kitchen until all his offers of help had been rejected and he realized the fluster over preparing supper would last as long as he stood there. Then he sat in the living room, folding laundry, while Lilian flustered between her computer and the telephone. When he found himself getting irritated, Warren shut his eyes and did breathing exercises. He imagined a shell of calm radiating from his chest, pulsing in and out with each breath. When he had done this for twenty minutes, Lilian came and stood over him.

"I wish you wouldn't do that," she said. "I'm entitled to a crisis if I want one."

Warren looked past her out the French doors that gave onto the snowy garden and the ley-line. He heard bare bushes rattle above the line, though there had been no breeze when he came home.

"I wasn't trying to calm you down," he said. "Just me."

"You said everything was fine, when you called."

"So what are you having a crisis about?" Warren asked. He knew the tone was wrong the moment he used it.

"Maybe about having my husband stay late to do an exorcism, when he knows something's about to go wrong."

"It has," Warren said. "Salvation's raising the insurance rates. That is what you were really worried about, isn't it? Something you found out at the office. All the bones told you about me was that I have a life outside of work."

"What do you expect me to do about it? I don't decide what the policies cost."

"Nothing," Warren said.

"Then why did you bring it up?"

"You know something about why they raised the rates." He glared at the windows for a minute, and something familiar came into his stomach. Something he had felt in the pentarium, one morning, when he had looked across the circle. He had felt it and then thought about being the one the demon killed... He looked at his wife with the expression he used on plagiarizing students. "Was it when the new guys applied for insurance? Isaac Graham and Rho? If something's going to happen to them, didn't you think it might happen in the pentarium? Didn't you think it might involve a demon getting loose and killing all of us?"

"Dammit yes, of course, yes I thought that!"

"But you didn't do anything about it."

"I can't tell you about other people's records!" Lilian said. "You knew that when I took this job."

"Lili, if Rho or Graham goes during an invocation-they're new. They're my responsibility. I have to be able to tell them if something like this is happening! And if one of them goes, the circle's broken. We could all be killed. Damn! And I had Rho help with the exorcism tonight!"

"The circle's just as broken if you go," Lilian said. "And you haven't done anything about that, have you? I've told you every risk factor you've had for twenty years, and you haven't done a thing. What about exercise? What about your blood pressure? You go down there every day, as if you think you're invulnerable. You risk everybody's life."

Warren fell silent for a moment. "I don't think I'm invulnerable," he said quietly. "I never think that."

"Then what do you think?" Lilian asked. "What do you think?"

Chapter Six

"I'm shutting it down," Warren said to the first magician he saw coming down to the pentarium, a dark lump in the poorly-lit stairwell. "We're not insured. No demons until the insurance is straightened out."

"What?" The magician stepped into the light and opened her eyes wide.

Warren cursed internally.

"Why aren't we insured?" Teddy asked. "Were we insured yesterday? Has everybody's insurance lapsed, or just some of ours? How did you find out about this, and when was anybody planning to tell us?"

"I found out yesterday," Warren said. "And I was going to tell you as soon as I confirmed it with the dean, which is now."

"Hey," Neil Torecki said, crowding Teddy.

"We're not invoking," she told him. "Our insurance is out. Bureaucracy!"

"Where's Warren?" Patsy Hoth's crisp voice cut through. "Warren, is this true? I would have appreciated knowing before I came back onto campus."

Warren heard her heading back up the stairs.

"Don't bother," she was telling people she met on the way. "Some administrative snafu."

He heard Cham Ligalla muttering something vague in return, and a bang as the door closed behind Patsy.

"This is a hell of a note," Teddy Whin said. Her eyes shone and she showed no signs of leaving. "Just when the new boys come under coverage, huh?"

"They've been here all semester," Neil protested.

"Yeah, but they don't go on insurance till their second month. And Salvation can't just change rates any old time," Teddy said, who had been on faculty senate. "They review them once a year. I remember when we hired Will and the insurance threw a fit about vampirology."

"Why?" Neil asked, and Warren was grateful.

"Well, think about it! The undead-that's never-ending coverage. If Will turns into a vampire, they'll be paying his dental bills for all eternity. And the liability... " Distracted, Teddy chattered her way back up the stairs with Neil.

Warren let out a whoof of relief and sat down on the bottom of the staircase.

***

Rho dawdled in his room, enjoying the morning sunlight and unwilling to go downstairs and see Cham Ligalla again, so he had to rush to the pentarium at the last minute; consequently, he ran straight into Neil Torecki and Teddy Whin as they came up the basement steps.

"Hah," Teddy said. "Here comes trouble."

"We're not running the pentarium," Neil told Rho. "Warren says there's some problem with the insurance."

"Insurance?" Rho gaped. The conference room in Selanto came to mind, and the noises Ganeel had made. Had the man merely been complaining about what the incident would do to his insurance premiums? Rho shook his head. Teddy Whin looked at him with a questioning, summing-up expression.

"You work on what-ducks?" she said. "Nothing dangerous about that. Maybe it's Graham."

"Elementals are pretty unpredictable," Neil said.

"What? What about ducks?"

"We're trying to figure out why Salvation's giving the Academy insurance problems," Neil explained to Rho. "Their scryers must have picked something up. It doesn't have to be someone new, though," he told Teddy. "They have everybody's application forms, don't they?"

"They can't just go over all those applications on spec," Teddy said, opening the door onto the second floor. "I don't have a clue what they actually do down there. Warren's the one with family at Salvation, and he's taking this seriously enough to shut down the pentarium. That's why I think it must be one of us."

"But Isaac isn't even here." The two of them turned down the corridor, and Neil looked back at Rho. "Want to come for coffee?"

"No." Rho turned the other way, brooding, and walked back up the tower stairs. He hadn't gone three steps before he heard light footsteps patter up behind him.

124

"So, one less brush with death," a casual voice said. "Is there anything nicer than an unscheduled hour?"

Rho turned around and found himself almost nose-to-nose with Will Goth-Harding, a man with a different sense of personal space. He took a step back.

Will was the same height as Rho, the same build, and also dressed in black, but there the resemblance ended. One magician was dusty, unkempt and pale-eyed, in a ratty voluminous robe; the other perfectly coifed and clad in black clothing a hint too form-fitting for good taste. Will wore knee-high leather boots over black jeans, and a turtleneck under a black leather jacket. At first glance he looked like a bad boy, but Rho was used to bad boys and knew better. Will Harding was something different, but what?

"We look like a before-and-after ad," Will said, returning Rho's stare. "But before-and-after what?"

"Insurance, perhaps," Rho said.

Will laughed, and clapped a hand on his shoulder.

"Don't worry about it!" he said. "It's just corporate posturing. Come in and have a coffee." Determined to refuse, Rho nevertheless found himself turning from the stairs into the third-floor corridor, walking through double doors, and stopping inside the spotless vampirology lab, with its clean white benches and glass-fronted cabinets. He stood in the middle of the room, looking around, while Will poured two mugs of coffee.

Rho knew Will Harding worked late. Some nights, as he sat at his own table looking through the

125

day's notes and listening to cries from the live specimens' floor of the museum, he was acutely aware of it, glad to know there was another person in the building. But he had never come down to Will's lab, because Rho distrusted theatrical people. The prejudice had some empirical basis, for he had met many theatrical magicians in Kasidora, but his attitude had predated actual experience and survived it.

Females, he felt, were entitled to be theatrical, their lives being performance art of a sort, designed to have a predetermined effect on the observers. Gay men had an even better excuse, having to sort out a small, covert subset of the observers on which to have the desired effect. Will Goth-Harding fell into neither of these categories, however, and Rho could not figure out how to take him. Who was the man trying to impress with his looks, his dress, his manner, and why did he waste them on Rho? Surely, it was not for Rho's benefit that Will now leaned back and propped his black-booted feet on the corner of his desk, a position which tilted his blond head back into a dazzling cross-shaped ray of sunlight.

"Salvation's just jerking the Academy around again," said Will. "They do it every four or five years-pick someone as an excuse to raise the rates. They did it the year I came on, and then again five years ago when Social Magic started to work with witches. Can you imagine? Witches! As if it costs more to insure against fake magic than real. Then there was the time they decided it was too dangerous to have mundane janitors."

"They are mundanes," Rho said. "Aren't they?"

126

"Not a one of 'em. Hard to believe, isn't it? Nope, they're all minor talents. Tell me that doesn't blow. What kind of a magician sweeps floors for a living? If it was me," Will said, "I'd be more worried about what those folks might get up to than about funded research. I see the day coming, when the insurance companies run their own countries, or fiefdoms. It'll become so hard to get insurance that the government will make it a right. Next thing you know, we'll all be born into one insurance tribe or another. They'll arrange marriages, decide what career you can have and where you can live. Everything we do will be dictated by the laws of our tribe. Multiculturalism." He stood up in a smooth, urgent motion that made Rho step back to leave room for the leap or twirl that it must flow into, but the movement led into nothing. It stopped, suspended.

"Still, it's nice to know there's a job for us if the old talent goes, isn't it?" Will Goth-Harding said.

***

From nine o'clock until ten, the Demonology Department buzzed with gossip. Magicians at loose ends tried to fill the hour with productive work, but their schedules overcame them. Appointments could not be moved up. Of all the magicians present in the department, only Patsy Hoth put the hour to good use. She could hear the bustling outside her door, as she typed email messages to other professional lechers across the world.

Patsy Hoth had taken years to come to terms with Osyth and its sloppy informality. Thank

127

goodness for Warren, and for his wife in the insurance industry who made him at least aware of the risks around him. Not that he did enough about them. Linus Ukadnian was one of the things Warren did not do enough about. Hiram Rho was another. The rest of the department were inoffensive enough, and seemed to know their jobs. Patsy Hoth did not ask for more. Modest as her demands were, she rarely got them, she reflected as an unwelcome knock sounded on her door.

"Come," Patsy said, not wasting time on unnecessary words. The door opened and a musty black figure stepped in. Rho seemed to move in a cloud of dust, and Patsy Hoth wished she could get up and cover her glassware before he contaminated it.

"Do you have a few minutes?"

"Just," Patsy Hoth said.

"I've been recording incubus possessions in the ducks along the ley-line," Rho said. "I'd like to compare the camera arcana images with your archives, to see if we're tracking the same incubi."

"That makes sense," Patsy admitted. "My archives aren't all here, though. Most of them are housed downtown in the Department of Public Health."

"Can I look through them?"

"Sure. I'm going down there this afternoon, if you want to come along." Patsy Hoth gave Rho's robe a doubtful look. "I'd appreciate it if you don't wear that robe, though," she said. "The government people here in Osyth don't take lechery seriously. I've put a lot of work into developing a professional image for the lab."

"What? This is professional garb, for a magician."

"It's not professional garb for someone in the Office of Public Health," Patsy Hoth said. "Just dig up a suit and tie-something clean and conservative. It'll significantly increase the amount you accomplish in that office."

"Oh," Rho said. "Well, when should I be here?"

"Two sharp," Patsy Hoth said, and looked back at her computer. She didn't watch Rho leave, nor did she waste more than a few seconds congratulating herself on how well she had handled him. If Warren would only make a minimal effort, he could have this department acting like professionals. It was not that much work.

***

Warren sat on the stairs until he had warned all the magicians, and a while after. Stairs had a special meaning for him.

In Warren's youth, when he was in the middle of his wizardry program and exhausted, one of his favorite professors had died. The man had come out of class, sat down on the stairs, and perished in an instant, and the event had caught Warren's imagination. Every day for months, and ever since when he was exhausted, he had taken the first step up every flight of stairs with the thought that he might collapse right there and then. He might not have to climb that flight to the top; he might not have to take one more step; to write that paper waiting in his office; to interview that job candidate; to make that phone call. Pleasant and unpleasant

129

tasks alike featured in Warren's list of things he would not have to do if he only collapsed, right on those stairs, with his head on the third step above him and his feet sliding out below and nothing his responsibility any longer.

Warren had heard of people who didn't face stairs this way. He had read stories about people who leapt out of bed, glad to start the day, and bounded up the stairs to their offices with enthusiasm, but he didn't believe those stories. The closest Warren came to that attitude was when he had so much on his mind that he didn't even notice the stairs he was climbing. He stood up now with a feeling that to turn around and look at the pentarium stairs would be a bad idea. He walked forward instead, through the pentarium shower room and into the golden chamber itself, and sat down in there with his back to the wall. He was still sitting there when Russell Cinea found him.

"Warren?" Russell said, squinting down.

"Yeah? What's up?"

Russell seemed relieved as he sat down. "You all right?"

"I'm fine," Warren said. "I figured this was one place nobody would look for me, for at least an hour." He leaned back against the pentarium's smooth wall. "We shouldn't be talking in here."

"It isn't on," Russell said. "You're worrying too much, again. Take a vacation. Take Lilian somewhere and leave Bosie to watch the house."

"Good idea," Warren said, with resignation. When Russell decided to watch over somebody, nothing would stop him. Two days in a row. What was the man worried about? The insurance, of course, but there must be more. "If only I could be two people," he said. "Or stay home and send my body in to work for me."

Russell sighed. "If only," he said longingly.

Could a body do that? Warren wondered. Of course spirits could exist apart from bodies; demons did that all the time, and only had bodies for as long as they believed they had them. He had heard that argument chanted in this room for fifteen years, and seen it work every time. He'd seen demons materialize and then dematerialize, later, as they forgot to believe what they had been convinced of in the morning. *Perhaps I only stay in my body because I forget to believe I have a choice,* he thought, and he almost said it aloud. It seemed so striking and exciting an idea, though Warren knew he had thought of it a hundred times before. It struck him anew every time he had it, because he couldn't remember to believe it in between times, and Warren began to wonder about that as well.

He looked at Russell without really seeing him. It felt as if Russell and the room behind him were being passed before Warren's eyes, as if Warren's only obligation was to be physically present. He sat and watched the other magician, feeling as if something inside him had become unnecessary over the years and he was just now realizing it.

Sitting here made less sense the longer he did it, and Warren thought about stiffening his muscles to stand up, uncurling his legs, pushing his hands against the golden floor. But none of this happened. Nothing happened, and as Warren tried to think this through something clutched at him all at once, closing its grip over every muscle and organ at the same time. He tried to howl and double over, but his body did nothing. His thoughts raced in circles, around and around in something that felt like a combination of guilt and nausea, and his body sat unmoved.

Russell stirred beside him, said something, and rubbed at his eyes. Warren tried to look at him, tried to move his eyes or refocus them, to scream or to pull himself away from the stiff body that was ignoring him, and with a jerk he did; he pulled himself apart from the body, at least far enough to feel only half in it, only partly aware of its lungs and heart and senses, and the swirling around him began to pull him even further away into confusion and failure.

That terrified him, and he scrambled to get back in, to align his spirit exactly with the parts of the body, but some attachment had been broken and now he was like a person mimicking another's stance. He could put his mental legs and arms exactly where the body's were, he could pretend he felt the floor's pressure on his ankles and butt, but the pretense lacked conviction. He was making it up. As Warren realized this, feeling it sink into him like the conviction of sin, his body got up without him and all pretense of sensation disappeared. He had a faint sense that his legs were still there, poking right through his seated spirit's torso, but he could see, hear, touch nothing.

I have to stay calm, Warren told himself, and automatically tried to concentrate on his breathing. But he had no breathing to concentrate on. Only failure, misery, guilt and despair-and mixed with them all, growing stronger with each second, impatience, as if Warren were not measuring up to some unknown standard. He was letting everybody down. *Perhaps the body'll do better without me,* he thought. A familiar depression filled him, and he had the feeling of something throwing him aside in disgust. The failure and misery disappeared in an instant.

I'm not afraid! Warren thought, shocked out of his depression. He automatically tried again to concentrate on his breathing and found none. But neither, he realized, did he have any stress to reduce-no sour stomach, no tension in his neck, no pressure headache. Perhaps he could manufacture them, but he wasn't going to. *Something entirely new has happened to me,* he thought. It felt like springtime-cold indifferent air with a new year's scent in it. And just after that came a hint of something like looking into a wood fire, then a second of something like smelling roses. He couldn't interpret the feelings any other way, as he had no language for them.

He spread himself out into the unknown surrounding him and felt his moods shift fast as light. A spot of determination here, a trace of guilt running across him and away again, and Warren felt exhilaration grow and spread inside him. He remembered hot showers, jumping into the snow, the first time a woman had touched him; things he'd been afraid of, that might have hurt but had been wonderful instead, things he had never classed together. They had been so different to the body-to the spirit, they were the same, a thing without a name, for Warren had never even thought of learning the names of things of the spirit. The body had always distracted him. He spread himself out further, then drew back in and felt the safe, cozy feeling of watching a cat curl into a ball, sinking down in something soft, or filling his belly with warm food.

It's like being a baby again, he thought. *I think everything I feel is happening inside me, the same way a baby thinks the whole world is part of itself. I'll have to learn the names of what I feel, and what they mean, and by-and-by there'll be a world made up of these things for me to explore and live in. It won't be so bad.* But meanwhile, what would his body be getting up to? He could no longer detect even the ghosts of his legs. *The body could be anywhere, doing anything,* Warren thought. The body could be going upstairs, holding his office hours, chairing a department meeting. The thought amused him, and he wondered if any of his colleagues would notice. The body would finish up Warren's day- *this is as good as having a vacation,* he thought-and then go home for him in the evening.

Home to Lilian, Warren thought, and although he couldn't muster up a cold sweat or pounding heart something else came over him, something like having a spike driven through his hand or discovering he'd eaten something deadly or hanging up the phone with things unsaid. He had to find the body that had walked away, out of his sensing. He had to get it back, to stop it, before it did whatever it might do to Lilian, and Warren didn't know whether he was more afraid of its doing nice things or nasty ones.

***

Russell Cinea always enjoyed looking across the pentarium, but this morning the view was overlaid by irritation. If Warren had finally given in to his worrying, to making mountains out of molehills, could he close the pentarium for good? Of course not! Russell's better sense scoffed at the rest of him, and he agreed with it. But he had already moved on from the question. It wasn't having the pentarium closed that gave him that gray feeling. It was the thought of not talking with the demons. Not doing magic on the only things he could do magic on-no, that wasn't true. *Be honest,* Russell told himself. It was not persuading others to do the magic he couldn't do himself. That was what he didn't want to lose.

He felt a moment's hatred for Warren. How could this simpleminded friend keep his magic, grow stronger every year, when he, Russell, lost power with every bit of wisdom he gained? Russell blinked fiercely and refocused his gaze on the other side of the pentarium, and as he did so he noticed something askew about himself. It was a minor vision problem, almost as if his internal eyes weren't tracking with the eyeballs as they moved across the room. His eyes still focused on the wall in front of him, but his attention seemed to be on something they weren't aimed at.

"That's very odd," Russell said, and rubbed his eyes. This was a bad idea; it made him feel as if he had pushed whatever lived behind his eyes back into his head, and it looked out his pupils from a distance that left dark rims around the view. "Very odd indeed." Russell wondered if he could turn whatever it was around and look into his own head, and he did so, and found that the inside of his own head looked just as he had always suspected it would. *No surprises there,* thought Russell, unnaturally calm, as if he were a child again and magic happened to him every day. He choked off that thought before it could dissolve the wonder and floated out of his body into the middle of the pentarium. From that vantage point, he watched Warren get up and touch his own body on the shoulder. He watched it stand up and walk out of the pentarium with Warren. Warren hadn't noticed a thing. Russell was there on his own, hovering in the middle of the pentarium, and all he could think was what he had thought when he first floated out of his white-sheeted crib as a boy. *It's magic, it's magic,* he thought, and if he was still in his body he would have wept. *It's the magic; it's come back to me. It's been here, waiting for us, all along. I just never sat quietly enough to notice it.*

He looked around the pentarium and saw it with new eyes. *How bright it is!* The gold shone like magic itself, as if it had treasured up all the charms cast in it over the years and was offering them back to Russell now, when his need was greater than its own. Russell felt outward, giving up his human form to spread out like a cloud of sheer vigor, brushing aside everything in his path. Bits of worry and fear struck at him and he knocked them away without even a thought. He was his old self again, he hadn't led anyone astray; they were all going to be fine, here in the magical world he had gone to at night, as a child, where anything could happen and nothing could go wrong.

**

Hiram Rho did not realize how much he hated Patsy Hoth until one thirty, when he finished his lunch and discovered that he owned no clean suit jacket. The one he had worn to Selanto had blood on it. He considered sponging it off, considered sponging off his magician's gown, but when he looked at them in that light, through Hoth's eyes, both were hopeless. The answer was obviously to stop looking at them in that light.

"I went through hell to earn this robe," Rho said, putting it on. "It's more professional than anything they wear in the government." As he said this, his feelings about Patsy Hoth crystallized. He would not have to worry about her again; she had been categorized, and Rho could use stock responses from now on in his dealings with her, which saved a lot of time and effort. He was almost grateful to her, because without her, he might have forgotten this coping mechanism that had seen him through so many years of life. He buttoned up his robe and marched down the stairs toward her office, so pleased with his own emotional efficiency that he expected Hoth to approve of him as well.

She didn't.

"I told you we had different standards of dress here," she said, looking at his robe with disgust. "If you need to borrow a jacket, I can find you one."

"And I told you this was professional dress," Rho said. "You may be ashamed of being a magician, but I'm not. You don't have any right to tell me what to wear."

"Fine," Hoth said. "You don't have any right to come down to the DPH in my car. Have a nice afternoon."

"It's a public office! I can go there whenever I want to."

"Not as part of my team, you can't. I have professional credibility to maintain."

"I wasn't hired to be on your team," Rho said. He felt himself turning beet-red, an infuriating weakness. She would see it and gloat. "In case you hadn't noticed, I'm not one of your lab techs." Patsy Hoth looked at him with apparent concern and said none of a million things, but Rho heard all of them. She shook her head slowly.

"It's not just that it's a robe," she said. "It's filthy! Look at yourself. If you were going downtown to a government office on your own, instead of with me, would you go like that?"

"Forget it," Rho said. "If this is the kind of support I can expect from my colleagues, I'll work independently. I don't need you to vouch for me."

"No, I guess you don't," Hoth said, and left.

Rho stood in the corridor outside her office for a minute, wondering if he should follow her downtown and make her acknowledge him, but that was a poor idea. When he went downtown, it would be to make an impression. All of Hoth's friends would ask her why she hadn't introduced them to this wonderful new magician at the Academy. They would work with him instead of her. They'd make her feel like a boring prude, when she saw him talking with them the way men really talk with each other, when they don't have to watch their tongues because a prissy woman is in the room. He would be the power downtown, and Hoth would be frozen out... standing in the hall outside her office didn't fit this plan, though, so Rho got his camera and headed out onto the ley-line.

He didn't pay attention to the trees and grasses this time. Several birds flew by him unnoticed, because he was going over what he should have said to Hoth, what she probably would have replied, what that would have led to. He walked twice as fast as usual, muttering to himself and casting scornful glances at the faculty houses he walked between. By four he was in the middle of Westpark, where the stream he'd been following for a mile spread out into a pond right over the ley-line. Here he set up his tripod and camera and focused on a flock of ducks dabbling in the shallow water. The camera picked up the glow around two drakes beautifully.

Out of twenty ducks and drakes, only two had an aura. They were also the two most interested in mating this afternoon. The ducks, especially, wanted to feed; they found these two drakes a nuisance, and scudded away from them when they approached making virile displays and loud noises. Nothing would discourage the two, however. They paddled between a duck and the bank and attacked her, biting at her nape and holding her head down until she pulled loose and swam underwater, rowing with her wings, toward the opposite shore. When she popped up, shaking her head, the rest of the flock joined her and all of them got out, apparently preferring to stand in the snow on safe land. The two glowing drakes stayed in the water for a few minutes, rearing up and flapping their wings with quacks of excitement or triumph; then they got out and waddled round the flock, trying to drive ducks back into the water. Rho recorded all of this on tape and in his notebook. Too soon, though, a group of children ran screaming toward the pond and the ducks flew away. The afternoon turned from interesting to dreary, he was miles from home, and the sun was almost down.

Rho thought of catching a bus back to the Academy, but the crowd at the bus stop deterred him. Not that they would look askance at his magician's robe, but because he didn't feel like associating with the motley crowd of grannies, nannies, and teenagers, all modern middle-class ranch house types; he looked at them for only a moment before turning to walk back along the ley-line. There he found his rage at Patsy Hoth, which had been set aside while he filmed the ducks, waiting for him unaltered as if it had been in refrigeration.

It was a bundle, wrapped up in words like a spider's dinner, and he could only look at the outside of it at first. *Leave it that way,* he thought. *Don't start with that.* But even those words were part of the bundle; he'd used those words before to think about this anger, and using them again started the wrapping unraveling. Every word he thought of was part of another strand of blame, argument, rhetoric.

Strings of words spooled away from the black bundle and wrapped around Rho. He was tethered to it, and all he knew to do about it was think harder,

140

and thoughts were words, and every thought tied him to it a little more. He gave up, with a voluptuous feeling. He wallowed in his anger, made up scenarios about it, called it to him as he would an invisible friend. As dark came down he became bolder, less ashamed to stride along talking to himself, gesticulating, rehearsing what he would say to Hoth if she ever dared treat him so again. He spoke it aloud as he walked along the ley-line until he was hot with it and the cold mattered not at all, and he was not alone any more, but had called on all the spirits around to witness his righteousness.

He was hardly surprised when one of the silent witnesses put its arm around him, which burned hot and cold at once against his side, and familiar claws scratched along his neck. He even turned toward the demon and spoke to it, yelled at it, hissed things he meant for Hoth at it, and it laughed in his face. The stench of rotten meat and sulfur shocked him out of his anger. The demon spoke in a language Rho couldn't understand, its voice deep and inviting, and it leaned toward him. Rho pulled back, suddenly full of the *cauld grue*. His voice dried up in his throat as he fought the strong arm around his shoulders, tried to pry up the talons digging into his arm; he sank to his knees in the struggle and the demon sank with him, pulling him against its chest, into the shelter of its great black wings.

"Let go," Rho said, in a croak, and the demon laughed again, and none of the other invisible witnesses to Rho's righteous wrath said a word.

141

Chapter Seven

A man who worried too much should be better off without a heart to pound, shoulders to knot, or blood pressure to soar into the danger zone. With nothing physical to tell him how apprehensive he was, however, Warren worried even more than usual. In the moments when he wasn't anxious about Lilian and his errant body he was concerned about whether he was worried or not, how he could learn to tell, and what invisible, unknown health hazards awaited a Type A disembodied soul.

Probably it becomes a ghost, he thought sourly. He imagined himself wafting through the halls of the Magic Building as a turmoil of cold air, an unnoticed shriek of frustration, but that was drama. The Magic Building was one place where a ghost would not go unnoticed. If Warren were in the Magic Building he would soon be discovered and dealt with, and what would that mean? More than anything, he wished for a set of stairs where he could sit down and hold his nonexistent head.

Literature on ghosts-and Warren wished he had read more of it-had them as place bound as cats. Unhappy in unfamiliar spaces, tending to roam back to their old haunts no matter how many times removed. Using that model, Warren decided, he was most likely to be either in the pentarium or in his office. Those were the places where he had always worried the most. He tried to convince himself that a plausible scenario had him and his body both haunting the same office, and miracle of miracles!

the office faded into his sight, with his body sitting at the desk. Warren seemed to be hovering just where a ghost would expect to hover, below the ceiling in the far corner of the room. From the pale blue light at his office windows, it was either early morning or late afternoon.

Warren's body was doing just what he expected, as well. It was reading the day's mail, sorting it into piles. After a few minutes of this it scratched its bald head and sighed loudly, got up, and poured itself a cup of coffee. Next, Warren thought, it would look out the window; and it did. At this, Warren became suspicious.

Now it will bark three times, he thought, and the body obediently barked three times. It had a hoarse, baritone bark, rather like a bloodhound. *Scratch behind your ear,* Warren thought, and the body scratched. This displeased the hovering spirit mightily. *Either I control that body, or I'm making all of this up,* Warren thought. He turned his spirit eyes toward the door. *Three ballerinas in pink tutus will come in right now,* he thought, and the door burst open onto a froth of rosy gauze.

***

"This is really a nuisance," Lilian said into the phone. "We called you three days ago about this. How long are we supposed to put up with it?"

"Look, lady," the voice on the other end said, "we've got infestations all over the city. If you think your mother-in-law's incubi are more important than the ones in the Wilmer Boys' School, you can talk to my supervisor."

143

Lilian had to admit his point. "It's just awfully inconvenient," she said, and caught Warren out of the corner of her eye. He had his coat on. "Just a minute, please. Warren! Are you going to work?"

"Yes," Warren said.

"Did you forget you have to take Bosie to the dentist this morning? We talked about it yesterday."

"But I have to work," Warren said plaintively.

"Lady, I don't have all day," the man on the phone said.

"I'll call you back. Do you have any idea when you'll get around to us?"

"Not until they stop popping up," the voice said. "We've already got more than this ley-line ever let out before. Your guess is as good as mine."

"Well, thank you," Lilian said, and hung up. Warren was trying to sneak out the kitchen door. "Warren! You promised. It's written down on the calendar, see? You told me the pentarium would be down this morning, and I said in that case, would you take Bosie over to the dentist so I don't have to be late for work. It's right here in black and white."

"So it is," Warren said, in a tone of relief. "What else do I have to do?"

"Check your appointment book," Lilian said, exasperated. "I don't know what else you have scheduled. Why are you so vague this morning?"

"I don't know," Warren said, looking in the appointment book. "It doesn't say."

Bosie came into the kitchen, still wearing the cocktail dress she'd put on the night before. "I'm ready whenever you are, dear," she said. "Such a lovely night, wasn't it? I actually saw a ghost or something of the sort, out on the ley-line. Of course, who can really tell what it was? But I hardly ever see anything like that, so it was a treat, whatever."

"I wish you wouldn't walk along the ley-line at night," Lilian said.

"But it's the shortest way here," Bosie said. "At least after the buses stop."

Lilian sighed. "You know I wish you wouldn't stay at nightclubs until the buses have stopped," she said.

"Oh, if I hadn't done that, you'd have no husband," Bosie said, ruffling Warren's fringe of hair. "Not that you would have been an old maid, I'm sure, but you wouldn't have this husband. Now, do you think I really have to go to the dentist?" She bared her teeth and hissed air in through them, testing. "Oh, dear, I'm afraid so."

Warren looked up from his appointment book. "When do I have to be home?" he asked, and wrote it down.

"And bring Bosie back here before lunch, if you can," Lilian said. "I'm expecting the plumber."

***

The sun rose at two minutes to nine, struck through the arrow-slit windows of the vampirology lab, and made a red spot on Susan Teale's notebook. She swiveled her chair around to look out. Susan had to crane her neck and lean on the desk to see the path from the parking garage, but she only had to hold that position for a few minutes before she saw Will coming toward the Magic Building. She sat back with a sigh of relief, letting the cross-shaped sunbeam warm her face. The beam had turned from red to golden, and moved down a bit toward Susan's neck, when Will came into the lab.

"Hey," he said, then kissed her.

"Hey yourself," Susan said. "Still alive?"

"Just," Will said. "What a crazy night! They were feeding all over the south quarter."

"No way!"

"Way. Big time. Did you check the news?" Will stretched over his desk and turned on an old black-and-white television set. The set had no picture, but its sound came through fine.

"I haven't lost an ounce," a self-satisfied female voice said, "and you won't have to, either! Make yourself lovely for only twelve low payments of twenty-nine ninety-nine. Beautiful Dreamer-Osyth's source for books, supplies, and instruction in basic enchantment for over fifty years."

"It's on the hour," Susan said. "Nothing but commercials for another ten minutes." Will turned the set off. "The pentarium's still down. Let's go out to breakfast," she suggested. "We could run up and ask Rho to come along."

"Better not," Will said. "I saw him creeping in last night when I was creeping out. He looked wrecked."

Susan got up and put on her coat. "Word has it he had a run-in with Patsy Hoth yesterday," she said. "Something about professional image."

"If Hoth was on my case, I'd go get pissed. I probably wouldn't even wait till after hours. Maybe I better rethink incubi," Will said, looking down at himself. His black outfit was clean, but it smelt of face powder and cigarette smoke, and it was still a little too tight. "I don't suppose she'd think this was a proper professional image, would she?"

"For a lecher? I think it's entirely suitable," Susan said, grinning. "When's your first class?"

***

The same sun shot a big square of red through the door from Rho's workroom onto the wall beside his bed. He woke up, looked at it, and buried his face in the pillow, sinking into a dream of smothering in the dark. In a few seconds he jerked awake again, just as he had been doing all night. Awake, he curled up in a ball and held on to his knees.

A demon alone was trouble enough. An affectionate demon was worse. *And it could get worse yet,* he warned himself, but it felt inauthentic, as if he were counterfeiting prudery. In Rho's adult experience, kissing and embraces were part of a series which led to only one ending. It would be dishonest to pretend the prospect surprised him.

Nobody who spent his adolescence with alley cats, and the people they watched, could be naive or idealistic about sex. Sex was something people wanted. They would do things far out of the ordinary in the hope of earning sex-kind things or cruel-and Rho could usually steer them in the direction of kindness. Money, food, shelter, jewelry-people would give the most amazing things for sex, and even then, they never thought they deserved it. Their faces afterwards were ashamed or defiant.

147

Sex with a demon might be something different entirely. Or then again it might not. *Either way, I'll make the decision,* Rho thought. *That's what really matters.* The frightening thing about this demon was that it could reach him through his wards. So could any street vagrant, though, and while Rho might have slept around in Kasidora, he had never been raped. "And I never will," he said, looking into the mirror, standing up straighter and more confidently than, he feared, the situation warranted. He put on his robe and shook it into position on his shoulders.

Rho spent the morning before his class on the computer. He emailed Vivien and some of the magicians he had met at Selanto, but he stopped short of asking the demon's name. The moment he clicked that 'send' button, he would turn from a respected professional into a bad joke. Picked up a demon without knowing its name! they would laugh. That's the sort of person they hire in Osyth. No wonder they can't get insurance... Rho stared at the screen without seeing it. This was what Salvation had predicted. He was a danger to all of them when he stood in that circle. Sure, Neil had said the Academy wards would protect them, but Neil had also said demons stuck to their own territories. Neil had been wrong and Linus had been right, an unpleasant thought in itself. Rho was not about to seek help from Linus, and be told it was all his own fault for not knowing enough mathematics.

As he thought it over, his panic ebbed. He'd have to tell someone, but the person to tell was one he trusted-Warren-and not right now. *With any luck, I can bring him a solution as well as a problem, before the pentarium starts running again,* thought Rho. His computer came back into focus.

Rho searched the online literature in every demonological database the Academy subscribed to. His teachers at Kasidora had been highly skeptical of the Internet, a self-fulfilling prophesy which, Rho discovered, was shared by all too many. Few Demonology Departments had even begun transcribing their records onto the web. By ten he was ready to give it up and prep for class, and after noon he switched over to the Magic Library, a modern white concrete building named after some Osyth nonentity. He looked up charms in an unfamiliar system that used numbers instead of letters, and arranged the numbers in an odd fashion, so that eight-hundred twenty-five came before eighty-three. Osyth seemed less respectable the longer he lived there. They couldn't even count properly, and they split their books of charms into ten or fifteen different areas, interspersing them with anthropology books, the autobiographies of witches-errant, and tomes on philosophy.

He rectified this painstakingly, moving all the dispersed volumes into one carroll, before being told he had not signed it out and it belonged to another patron. That needed a trip downstairs and negotiations, and when he came up again to move the books to the carroll he had obtained at the other end of the building, some officious flunky had put half of them away again. One day was not long enough to do this library justice.

He felt better when he had established his territory and hung his coat over the front corner of the carroll as a mark that the owner was in residence, and he picked up the first book, *Elementary Charms of Essence*, with real anticipation. But its title was too accurate, and nothing inside it enlightened Rho at all. Certainly it contained no clues as to how he might discover new aspects of his own essence and shape them into charms with enough power to ward away a demon. He turned to the next, which proved no more than a treatise on the virtues of self-knowledge, such as belonged in the self-help section of an amateur magic shop.

Charms of essence were not well understood in Osyth, Rho concluded regretfully as he leafed through the pile. A pity, for nothing else could be relied on to protect him while he slept. He turned to the next heap and the charms of intent, pushing aside the question of how he might stay awake and intent on protecting himself through the night hours.

Two students came scouting through the stacks as Rho riffled through the index of the next book.

"Nothing!" one of them said, in a querulous, paper due sort of tone.

"What did you expect? Nobody'd leave a book of good charms in a library," the other voice said. "No one even writes the good charms down. Who'd want to share them?"

"I don't see how you're supposed to learn something if nobody will write it down," the querulous student said.

Rho agreed. The magicians of Osyth pretended to be innocent and team-spirited, but they kept secrets and jockeyed for power just like anybody else.

What I need, he thought, *is someone's private grimoire.* A lawless and desperate notion. Stealing another magician's grimoire would be a bad way to start at a new job. Still, Rho pushed the book of charms away from him and contemplated the other magicians. Who among them might teach him new charms? Not as a gift, but as a trade-which of his new colleagues was green enough behind the ears to accept an offer of trade, without wondering what Rho stood to make out of it? With half his mind on this problem, Rho turned to the pile of books on flesh magic, its risks and benefits.

***

Neil Torecki listened to folk songs in his office after five o'clock. He locked the door, turned a tape on high, and pulled his sketch pad out from the bottom drawer. Perched over the table where he spread out the relics of imps by day, Neil made watercolor cartoons of his colleagues. Tonight the pad on his drawing board showed a long dim room, lit with one candle; any Osyth magician would have recognized the dry specimens' floor of the museum, with the brownie perched on its tall stool, cataloguing.

Neil had spent many hours lurking in that cavernous space, breathing in the odor of study skins and mothballs, before he caught a single glimpse of the brownie. He had not begrudged a minute of the time. Brownies were imps, after all. They were his business, and the natural stuff of children's books. A brownie that stuffed cockatrices instead of milking cows, that slept in the rolls of

151

taxidermists' cotton instead of in sweet hay, and that listened to the banshee scream from the floor below instead of the sleepy grunting of pigs-this intrigued Neil. It cried out for a book. *The city brownie and the country brownie,* he thought, as he made the edges of his painting darker and more sinister. Just as he got it as spooky as he wanted, a knock at the door made him jump.

"Just a minute," Neil called, turning off the drafting lamp. Anybody might be in the building at this time of night, but few of the magicians would bother one another during prime conjuring hours. Casual visits took place during the daytime, between their morning congregation in the pentarium and lunch. "Hey!" Neil said, opening the door. "Rho!"

***

Rho stood in the hallway, thinking. Once again, Neil had made a remark that seemed to admit of no reply. "Hello," he finally answered, sounding lame even to his own ears.

"What can I do you for?"

"May I come in?"

"Oh, sure," Neil said. He let Rho into a dim room with an oval rug, couch and chair, and framed pictures creating a homey nook to the right of the door. This put Rho off-balance, and not even the sight of a work table and standard lab cabinets, off to the left behind Neil's desk, could entirely restore his perspective. What sort of magician put an end table in his lab, with a little bowl of mints on it?

152

"Have a seat," Neil said, and sat down in the armchair, leaving Rho with the couch. He sat on it gingerly and stared at the bowl of mints. "Would you like a mint?"

"What? Oh, no. I was wondering if you'd like to trade charms," Rho said.

"What kind?"

"Whatever. I know a lot of charms from Kasidora. They aren't in the books in the library."

"Oho," Neil said. "Trying to build up the old grimoire, are you? Well! I can't say I wouldn't like some plums from Kasidora, but I don't think I've got much to trade you. All my upper-level charms are drafting stuff."

"Oh," Rho said, without comprehension. Neil grinned.

"No offense, but I've seen you doodle. Unless you're hiding something, you can't draw a stick. So I don't think you'd want to trade me much for a charm that starts out, 'Draw a portrait of the administrator in question'."

"No, I guess not." They sat a minute longer.

"Well-"

"I guess I should go," Rho said.

"It's just that I was working on something."

"Yes, of course." Rho stepped back out into the corridor, with a flat and foolish feeling. *What a dolt! They're charms of essence, remember?* He'd have to find someone with an essence like his own to learn charms he could actually do. Neil Torecki, with his sunny manner and sketchpad and sofa, was probably Rho's worst match in the whole department.

***

Neil Torecki swaggered a little as he went back to his painting. It was flattering to have the new guy want to learn his charms. Even more flattering to have the new guy find himself too unskilled to use them. Neil pulled out another watercolor block and made a quick color sketch of Rho's face, pinched and dirty. He couldn't use it for the country brownie-not unless the country were having a famine or the plague. Neil shook his head. *Nah, not in a children's book.*

***

Rho's course from Neil's lab to the tower stairs took him past Warren Oldham's office just as the man himself was coming out and locking the door behind him.

"Good night," Warren said cheerfully.

Rho muttered and hunched a shoulder in response. Before he had taken another step, he had identified the opportunity he'd been hoping for. He turned around.

"Who would you suggest I talk with about learning some of the common charms here in Osyth?" he asked Warren.

"What kinds of charms?" Warren answered. "You're already getting the cutting edge charms of discourse."

"I meant charms of essence and intent," Rho said. "Charms one person can cast. I'm trying to build up my grimoire."

"Hm," Warren said. "I have to get home. You could come along and look through my stuff, if you like. Borrow the books for a few days."

Rho was flabbergasted. "You're sure?" he asked. "I'll trade you charms from Kasidora."

"Sure," Warren said. "I'd like some new charms from Kasidora. All I have are what my father picked up when he taught there. But I can't stand around here. You don't need your coat-it's nice out, and I'll give you a ride back."

Rho turned away from the tower door and followed Warren along the hallway, and to the parking structure. The walk took them between rows of blue spruce, their needles tipped with gold from the setting sun's horizontal rays and their shadows lying out powder blue behind them. Little birds, titmice and chickadees, foraged in the treetops and flew one by one across from one line of spruces to the next.

"Here," they called softly to one another. "Over here, children. This way, dear. Over here."

Warren Oldham's home was the most modern house Rho had ever been close to. It couldn't have been more than a hundred years old.

"Pretty, isn't it?" Warren said, with a smug smile. "It's on the Osyth Heritage List. What I really like is the way the stones are cut up under the rafters, there-and there, isn't that precise? They don't do work like that nowadays."

"Oh," said Rho, who had seen better stonework in Kasidoran privies. Warren opened the front door into a little vestibule.

"Lilian!" he yelled as they took their coats off. "I've brought someone to dinner."

155

"She's not home," a voice from somewhere in the back of the house said. "She went for a walk."

"Oh, all right," Warren said, as if his approval mattered. "We'll sit in the living room and have a drink with my mother. What's your poison?"

"Whatever you're having," Rho said.

"Beer?"

Warren led his guest, who felt more unexpected by the minute, into a plastic kitchen and showed him out the other end of it into a big room with windows overlooking a snowy garden and the ley-line. It all looked like something off a television show about urban professionals, the sort of thing students at Kasidora had marveled at when they happened to see it-as if everything in the house had been built new for Warren by somebody with no imagination. *Pale,* Rho thought, trying to put a word to it. *Insubstantial? No-insignificant.* This was an insignificant house. It gave nothing to the people in it except comfort.

"You look like someone who doesn't see a square meal every day," a voice from his right said. "Probably cook for yourself, right? Another of Warren's bachelor magicians." The speaker was an old woman sitting in a recliner, but an old woman of a type Rho knew. Her hair was perfectly dyed and trimmed, her makeup flawless, her manner imperious. She belonged in Kasidora, not in Osyth where new was good and old was apologetic. "I'm his mother," she said, just as Warren came into the room with beer.

"This is my mother, Bosie Lane," he told Rho. "Bosie, this is Hiram Rho. He's new at the Academy this year."

156

"Well," Bosie said. "Get me a sherry, would you, sweetie? You ought to like Osyth, Magister Rho. We have a long tradition of bachelor magicians in this town. I married one myself."

"Oh," Rho said again.

"Yes indeed," Bosie said. "He was a regular stage-door Johnny. Of course, he could send better flowers than any of the others. He made 'em grow in the Academy greenhouses, amazing things. At first I thought he was just an enchanter, you know, making carnations look like orchids. Then for a while I thought he was an alchemist and was really making them out of thin air, as if an alchemist could get away with something like that. You know their guild has to approve it every time they-well, you know. Anyway, he turned out to be just a magician, with a greenhouse. But by then I was intrigued, wasn't I, dear? And he knew how to keep a girl intrigued. Make a note of it, young man, a girl likes a man of mystery. As long as he isn't too mysterious to let her know how happy she makes him."

"Oh," Rho said.

"Mysterious and happy," Bosie said. "That's the winning combination. It works every time."

"Rho's from Kasidora," Warren said.

"Now my goodness, there's an exciting town. Why I haven't been to Kasidora in a dear's age, indeed, but I'll wager nothing's changed. Tell me, dear, is the old Black Magic Pub still open?"

"Yes," Rho said.

"You know I used to dance there, when Warren's father was on sabbatical leave at the university. It wasn't legal of course, you know it's impossible to get a work permit in Kasidora if you're nothing but a wife, at least back then, but the kind of dancing I did wasn't strictly legal anyway, not in a regular student bar, so it was a horse a piece, wasn't it? But I'll always remember the university and how those three great big mansions were built right into the wall and the gatekeepers lived in them to keep the demons in. My goodness, I itched to get inside one of those, but everybody told me they were old and cold and dusty and people only really lived in the kitchens. Like old ladies who inherit houses too big for them, you know. That's why I sold my house right after Warren's father died. I have a horror of turning into one of those old ladies with sixteen cats and papering the walls with newspapers every fall to keep warm and a million dollars under the bed. Every time I think of it, I give something away or move into a smaller apartment."

"Oh," Rho said.

Bosie looked past him toward the French doors. "Here's Lilian now."

Looking where the old lady pointed, Rho saw a figure walking up from the ley-line in the dusk. Inside, in the light, she was just another middle-class, middle-aged Osyth suburbanite. She was dumpy and white-haired, wore a pink sweater and jeans under her coat, and her first order of business was to kiss Warren.

"This is Rho, from the Academy," Warren said to her. "Rho, this is Lilian. My wife."

"Pleased to meet you," Lilian said, not looking pleased at all. "I see Warren got you a drink."

"I asked him for dinner," Warren said, a little guilty.

"That's fine, there's plenty. Let's just set the ward and relax a little while, then I'll get into the kitchen."

"I want to help," Bosie said.

"We'll all help," Lilian said. "If you don't mind?"

"No," Rho said. "I'd like to learn how it works."

"Well now, you must know a lot of wards already if you're from Kasidora, dear, don't you?" Bosie asked.

"Yes," Rho said truthfully. He had known an awful lot of wards, enough to impress Vivien. An awful lot, to let a demon through in one moment... "I always like to learn more," he said.

"That's wise, dear," Bosie agreed. "Life's always exciting if you're ready to learn more, isn't it? I've often wished I knew less, so I could learn more."

"Here we are," Warren said, digging in a drawer in the highboy. "You need to take your shoes and socks off."

"Why?"

"So your flesh touches the floor," Warren said. "It's okay if you're on the carpet, though." He bustled about, pulling a coffee table and chairs into position so they could all sit in arm's reach of one another.

Rho saw that Lilian had taken her own shoes off and gone out into the garden with a blue ceramic bowl.

"Does it matter what bowl you use?"

"It has to be a special bowl, dear," Bosie said. "Something with real value. Now I gave them that

159

one, it was a wedding present. Warren's father bought it for me when I was pregnant. He used to bring it in every morning just full of white violets."

"It's all associations," Warren said. "The bowl isn't made of anything in particular."

Rho was watching Lilian, who had come back in. She wiped her feet five times, and cleaned the snow off the bowl with downward strokes-seven of them. The bowl was full of snow to a little above the brim, with a wedge sticking up almost an inch at one side. Lilian held it with that side facing away from her, toward the north when she put the bowl on the table. Warren had spread a placemat there. "It's just a mat," he said, before Rho could ask. Then he set a short purple candle in the snow. "Any candle will do, as well. This is the charm." The booklet he handed Rho was old and ragged, its corners worn soft.

Rho paged through it carefully. A book of spells he'd never seen was a treasure. The home ward charm was a simple one, a rune and mantra with specific syllables after specific breaths. He tried it a few times and nodded.

"The trick is to do it with the pattern," Lilian told him.

"You and Bosie sit on the sofa," Warren said. "That way you can have the book on the table, in case you need to cheat."

The four of them sat around the coffee table, watching while Warren lit the candle and he and Lilian traced a rune in the dew on the bowl's surface. Rho watched Lilian's hands carefully. Where her fingers touched the bowl it became clear, as if they had wiped the color off it with the condensation. That was more skilled than it looked, for two people to make the rune and have it match perfectly. Even for one person, it would be a challenge. Warren and Lilian leaned back and Rho took Lilian's hand on one side, Bosie's on the other. He looked at the pattern of light shining through the rune onto the table and tried to breathe.

At first the light got in the way, its flickering cutting across the mantra and his breathing. Rho struggled with it, feeling as if his heart beat too fast and his mind worked too hard. He shut his eyes and worked on the mantra alone, then the mantra with breathing, and then opened his eyes to find himself in rhythm with the flickering candlelight. It pulsed and pulled back, grew and ebbed with every breath. Parts of it flickered bright and then paled again, until it made a blanket of light across the floor right up to the dark outside. It lay over Rho's own knees in a scribble of lace, and he felt vessels under his skin open and close with it. He saw Warren and Lilian frosted over with light, the mother and father of all the world, and as the light reached his own face he laid down all the horror of last night, set it aside and opened his mouth and breathed in the light and safety, down into the very center of his being.

***

Lilian watched the pattern of light and fought with her temper. It was really too bad of Warren, when she was worried sick over him to start with, to bring home another of his lost puppies. Especially this one, the one all the trouble seemed to be about-though Warren couldn't act as if he knew that, she admitted. Still, if this Rho was possessed, what would that do to the house aura? He was like a mass of darkness, spreading out into the light and stirring it up; they might sit there all night, and just get crosser and crosser with one another. The pattern stuttered and balked, as if she were trying to push it outward all by herself. But after about ten minutes she could feel a change as if something began working with her instead of against her, and her black mood lifted. In ten minutes more the room even began to feel clean.

This has been a long time to keep Bosie concentrating, Lilian thought, and gave her mother-in-law a smile as soon as the peace and comfort had come back into the room. Warren stretched a little and Bosie leant back. Lilian looked at Rho and what she saw in his face made her cringe. Another one who wanted a mother. Why did they keep hiring these babies?

"Isn't that lovely?" Bosie said, stretching. "The perfect end to a perfect day, isn't it?"

"It is indeed," Warren said. "I promised Rho he could have a look in my grimoire. Does he have time before dinner?"

Lilian gasped. "Can I have a word with you in the kitchen?" she asked her husband. When she stepped out of the living room, she had the odd feeling he wasn't following, but he was right behind her in the kitchen doorway. She motioned for him to shut the door. "You always said it was dangerous to try spells from someone else's grimoire without supervision," she whispered. "What's this all about?"

162

"Oh, he'll be all right," Warren said placidly.

"He is not all right! It doesn't take a scryer to notice that. He's wound as tight as-" *As tight as you usually are,* Lilian thought, and looked at Warren anew. He was smiling at her, holding his mug of beer like a man without a care. *This is not the man I married,* she thought. "How much beer have you had?"

"This is my first. Why, would you like it?"

"No." Lilian turned her back. "Do what you like."

"All right," Warren said cheerfully. "How long until dinner?"

"Forty minutes." She heard Warren going out of the room, and his voice came muffled through the door.

"Is it charms of essence you want, or charms of intent?" he was asking. "I don't think you have time to look through both books before dinner."

***

In Warren's study, a small room off the side of the living room, windows looked onto the ley-line. The room didn't even have four walls; a sliding door was pulled open on its inner surface, giving a view of the washing machine across the hall. Here, in this niche filled with books and a computer, Rho watched Warren pulling his grimoires out of hiding. They were in a cardboard box with several different labels written on it in different colored inks and scribbled out with yet other colors, and they were not warded at all. This wasn't the picture he'd been given of grimoires, but when Warren pulled out the

163

three big books they met all expectations. Magic shimmered through their green leather covers.

"Wow," Rho said. He reached out to touch the top one, and Warren stood back with a complacent smile. The book's binding was soft as butter, its pages thick and fleshy-and the charms! Charms written in blood, some of it hot to the touch. *That's dragons' blood,* thought Rho. Charms in different hands and scripts, some that rearranged themselves under Rho's gaze and others which seemed to turn their backs on him and shut him out. Different ones to be drawn and to be sung and to be thought or not thought about. Charms written inside ornate borders, some held in by the border until it would be erased; others mere decoys, for the border was itself the charm. Blank pages to be looked at under a special lamp or the moon, or in particular company or a certain mood... Rho's fingers shook when he touched some pages and slid over others. What he needed must be in here, and relief took all the strength out of him. He leaned against the desk until Warren, still placid, pushed a chair up against the back of his knees; Rho sat down with a bump, looked up at the older magician, and knew this was a true friend.

"Don't you want to know why I need this?" he asked.

"Only if you want to tell me," Warren said, unperturbed.

"A demon followed me back from the Congress," Rho said. "It belonged to one of the magicians there, but it got loose and killed him. I don't know its name or how to command it. What would you do?"

164

"Has it threatened you?" Warren asked, and took a drink of beer.

"No, it seems to like me," Rho said. "The Congress thinks I've bound it, and I don't want to tell them I didn't. But it can get through my wards."

"There are plenty of wards in here, but they're all advanced meditative charms," Warren said. "Oh, I'm sure you can handle them. It doesn't sound like you want to use anything strong enough to hurt it. Seems like a friendly demon?"

Rho laughed, wondering how just naive people were in Osyth. "Oh, yeah," he said. "Real friendly. At least it hasn't come into the building. But is it safe for me to be invoking in the pentarium? How much trouble is this going to cause?"

"You don't wear your own wards in the pentarium, anyway. If you haven't bound it, you've done nothing illegal."

Rho felt a mixture of relief and embarrassment, a little like what he had felt in the exorcism. He'd been dramatizing his situation, looking for troubles. Why had he thought Warren would be angry?

"I used to know quite a few demons, to talk to," Warren mused. "Still get the odd visitation now and then when I'm walking the ley-line. They always have something interesting to say."

"You wouldn't worry about it, then."

"No, not at all. There's dinner," Warren said. "Why not just leave these here. You can take them home with you afterwards."

"Just the charms of essence," Rho said, feeling that someone had to exercise a little prudence. "I'd rather not have your books all at once. There's no safe in my rooms."

Warren shrugged. "Whatever," he said cheerfully, and sniffed. "Smells like chicken."

Rho, following him, found the commonplace house transformed into something completely different, a place where everything was as pleasant as it seemed and there were no dark mysteries. Dinner was simply chicken, grimoires were just books, and demons-demons were acquaintances. That was all.

Chapter Eight

Teddy Whin liked to know what was going on in every area that affected her life. For example, she preferred to know whether she had health insurance or not, but for once, Teddy met her match in the Academy's business office. Though she spent an hour inquiring the first thing on Monday morning, she could not find out anything about the Demonology Department's insurance or the Academy's.

"Tell me about my own, then," Teddy said. "I have a right to know whether I'm personally insured, don't I?"

"Certainly," the receptionist said. "I can't tell you that, though. You need to contact your personal insurance agent."

"I don't have a personal insurance agent!" Teddy explained, in a tone that would have made the other demonologists back away. "I have group insurance, through the Academy."

"Then it's not personal insurance," the receptionist said, "and I can't tell you anything about it. You could contact Salvation and request your individual records, if you want to."

"Would that tell me whether my group insurance through the Academy is currently active or not?"

"I wouldn't think so."

"Look," Teddy said, leaning on the desk. "If I call up a demon today as part of my contractual obligation to the Academy. And that demon rips my leg off. Will Salvation pay for the hospital?"

"I couldn't say. I don't know if that specific event is covered in your insurance."

"If it were."

"I'm sorry," the receptionist said. "You'd have to ask an insurance agent that kind of question."

"I have a better idea," Teddy said. "Why don't I call up a demon right now, and let's see what happens?"

"I'm calling security."

"Or we could do that," Teddy agreed, and left. Anybody who didn't know her would have said her short figure was stumping back to the Magic Building in high dudgeon, but that would have been an error. Teddy Whin admired a worthy adversary. She whistled a happy tune as she went into her office, hung up her muffler, and called the Demonology Department secretary.

"What was the name of that lawyer who came over here and left a card for us year before last?" she asked. "When the Wizardry students levitated the courthouse." She was scribbling the name on her desktop when Russell Cinea came and hovered inside her door. "'Lo, Russell," Teddy said. "What's up now?"

"It's nine o'clock," Russell said. "Heading down?"

"What?" Teddy said. "No, I got it. Thanks." She hung up. "Are we invoking?"

"Of course we are," Russell said. "It's in my calendar, isn't it in yours?"

"Warren said we were shut down."

"That was last week," Russell said. "He's already gone down. I think we're the last."

"Oh," Teddy said. "Well, how'd this come about? How were they able to fix anything up over the weekend? Has the Academy made peace with Salvation? Or did we get a new policy? What's this going to do to my paycheck, and will I be able to keep my primary care sorcerer? And who makes these decisions, anyway? Who's our rep on faculty senate?" She left a trail of questions in the corridor, even after the door to the basement stairwell had closed behind her and Russell.

***

Rho's head hurt from trying Warren's charms. He'd spent most of the weekend hunched over the grimoire. He'd slept over it, falling into the crabbed script in his dreams, but none of the charms had done what the book said they would. There had been no peaceful lacy lights, no sounds or smells. He began to suspect that his and Warren's essences were entirely too different-Rho, after all, would never have let anybody else take his grimoire, even for an hour. *Maybe I can't work any of them,* he thought. *Maybe Osyth magic and Kasidoran magic are completely different things. Maybe I don't have any power at all, over here.* In this mood he answered his phone, and found the pentarium was operating again.

"Hell and damnation," Rho said. But he went down the stairs, showered, put on his blue smock, and took his place in the circle. The chant rose around him, red smoke welled up inside the

169

pentacle, and Rho began to relax. The demon hovered, listening as the words of the charm persuaded it into physical form. A foot put out here, a hand there, unknown organs and appendages grew out of the mass of flesh, and last of all the thing created itself a head with eyes-five of them-the better to see the magicians, and ears-three-to hear them with. It stalked, lumbered, ambled around the inner walls of the pentacle until it came to the side facing Warren and Russell, and there it stopped. Its back eye blinked at Rho.

This demon made no dramatic shrieks and no lunges to escape. It simply walked toward the two senior magicians, and the pentacle went down before it like smoke.

"Crap!" Neil Torecki said, next to Rho. "What the hell!"

Rho gave Neil a glare of equal parts fury and terror, and chanted louder. The charm rose in volume and pitch, magicians' voices shifting into a high tone of desperation. Rho thought he heard Vivien's voice among them, and Ganeel making the wet, abject noises he still heard in dreams. He felt cold sweat slicking the hands that gripped his.

Warren and Russell neither moved nor blinked; they spoke on, calm among their horrified colleagues, as if their seniority alone were enough to keep any demon at bay. The demon swiveled its head around until all five eyes had had a look at each of the magicians. It was choosing the weak spot, Rho knew, and that was him. But when the demon moved, it went straight toward Warren.

Up to the gold safety chain it walked, and bent down to look at the links. Then it hooked a three-pronged appendage under the chain, raised it up, and bit through the gold. Almost before they could realize it, the magicians were face-to-face with the demon, unprotected except by their own chains and wards. The chant broke then, faltered into gasps and exclamations. Only the senior magicians spoke on, undisturbed. Were they brave or insane?

Rho's heart was racing so fast he couldn't think. He looked from Warren to the other magicians, and saw them looking from Warren to one another, each one trying to decide whether to break the circle or to trust the senior magicians' apparent belief that this link of frail bodies could hold back a lord of the netherworld.

The demon swiveled its head again. It made a thick low stalking noise and began to walk sideways around the circle, pausing in front of some of the magicians, but because of its structure, Rho couldn't tell where its attention was. It had two mouths, set crooked in the sides of its neck. A long, misshapen purple tongue lolled out of one side of the mouth facing him. Magicians shifted when it drew near; Rho smelled sweat and urine as the thing came closer. It was in front of Linus Ukadnian now, halfway to Rho, pausing beside Susan Teale, two-thirds of the way, looking at Rho with its leftmost eye, that tongue licking where it had no lips...

The demon stopped, laughing a deep laugh like bubbles bursting in some thick, rotten liquid, and Rho knew it was thinking of him. But it had stopped in front of Patsy Hoth the lecher, whose gold-curled head only came up to its chest. Nobody laughed at Patsy Hoth. She looked the demon straight in the nipples, opened her mouth, and began the chant

171

again in her fierce, precise voice. When they heard her, all the magicians joined in. And the demon took a step away from Patsy Hoth, trampling the chain lying on the ground, and began to sidle back toward Warren and Russell. They were the ones it walked up to, the ones it reached out to with that three-pronged arm, and it touched them as if their wards were so much air.

The two magicians did nothing. They stood still and undisturbed, keeping up the chant as the demon handled their arms and heads, and that was when Rho realized they were insane. The whole group of them had stayed in this room with an unbound demon, because they put their trust in these two. *We're all going to die,* he thought.

The demon was shaking Warren's and Russell's arms now, trying to make them let go of each other's hands, and they were still ignoring it and chanting. As if it had simply lost patience, it pulled Russell's left hand off at the wrist and walked through the broken circle. Blood shot into the room in fountains. Rho felt Neil Torecki pull his hand loose, just as Isaac Graham grabbed tighter. Every voice shouted something different, and below them all was the sound of Warren and Russell, still chanting the charm of discourse. Frantic, Rho looked for Neil, to grab him before he could run out the door or perhaps to follow him, but Neil wasn't there. Rho had clutched Will's cold hand before he finally caught sight of Neil running toward the demon.

Neil ran straight to the emergency switch behind the senior magicians, the switch that wasn't magic at all but Alchemy, that would shut the pentarium off from the ley-line with spells that might be irreversible. Rho saw Neil's hand over it, half-hidden by the demon's tentacles as the thing began to reach for him; saw Russell Cinea, standing as if nothing had happened with blood spurting from his arm, and Warren standing next to him holding the severed hand in his own, still chanting; saw Neil pitch forward, his face caught in a shout or a scream, and felt himself go flat as the magic left him. The demon went out with a pop. There was only a basement room and a broken chain and twelve people, and the blood.

Silence. Then a puff of breath from ten throats at once.

"Neil," said Isaac Graham said, as if he were calling on a god, and that started the babble.

Rho could make out Patsy Hoth's voice cutting through it all.

"That was good work, Neil," she kept saying, over and over. "Good work. Good work, Neil."

The magicians let go of each other's hands and swarmed through the pentarium, gripping arms, patting backs and straightening one another's chains as if they needed to touch each other, to be reassured they were all alive. Isaac ran into the shower room to call security and someone whose name Rho couldn't remember was trying to bandage Russell Cinea's arm, but Neil Torecki just stood beside the emergency switch with tears running down his face. *He's only been here one year longer than me,* thought Rho.

"Warren," the person bandaging Russell's arm said, "are you all right?"

Everything seemed to stop as Rho realized the chanting had gone on through all the hubbub. Warren stood in his accustomed place, as calm as he had been last night, repeating the charm of discourse over and over as he looked happily into the blood-spattered pentacle.

The person who had bound up Russell Cinea's arm, and whom Rho had since identified as Anders Regan the herbalist, ran the department in Warren's absence. He called a meeting that afternoon. Ten of them sat around a table meant for thirteen trying not to stare at Neil Torecki, who still looked fragile. He shuffled his papers and kept his eyes on the table.

"Our first order of business is to thank Neil," Regan said. "I think we all agree that most of us would be dead if not for his quick work and courage."

"Hear, hear!" someone down the table said. A spatter of applause started, but Patsy Hoth silenced it by standing up. She walked around the table and shook hands with Neil.

"Thank you, Neil," she said formally, and walked back, and as she did the rest of the department rose.

Isaac Graham was the first, as formal as Hoth, and one by one they all walked or leaned or reached across the table to shake Neil's hand. Anders Regan gave Neil a big warm hug that made him sniffle and have to blow his nose.

Then Regan, who seemed fond of celebration, led a round of applause, and then he said "Speech! Speech!" which Rho thought was a little too much.

"Don't get used to it," was the speech Neil made, mopping his eyes. "I'll probably screw up tomorrow." But when he sat down, he didn't look at the table any more. All of them seemed refreshed and ready to tackle business, so Rho had to admit all this fuss had been a good idea.

"The first order of business is to call in Alchemy and see if we can salvage the pentarium," Regan said. "I've already informed the IDA. We can expect an investigation starting tomorrow morning, and all of you need to let me know when you're available for interviews." He passed a calendar to Isaac, on his left.

"How's Russell?" Teddy Whin asked.

Everyone looked at Cham Ligalla, who had gone over to the College of Sorcery's Teaching Hospital with the injured demonologists.

"They reattached the hand and he's in stable condition, physically. You did good work on his arm, Andy."

"I didn't have any of the right herbs," Regan said, flipping a hand. "How is he otherwise-and Warren?"

"Fine, says the sorcerer," Cham said. Her tone left no doubt about her view of sorcerers. "All they know about is the body."

An uncomfortable silence filled the room. Rho imagined they were all, like him, thinking about the scene in the pentarium when Warren and Russell had done nothing while a demon touched and savaged them. *How do these magicians feel about it?* he wondered, to avoid thinking about how he felt about it. He looked from face to face, but they were so uninformative-tight, closed-in human faces. If they had been cats, ears and tails would have given

175

him a clue, but humans hid everything. Humans lied.

"Perhaps the demon enspelled them," Susan Teale said in a tentative voice, as if it were a hopeful comment.

"Anything like that should have gone away as soon as the pentarium went down," Will said.

All the magicians began to perk up, Rho among them. Trying to figure things out was more cheering than just worrying about them.

"Did the demon get out because there was something wrong with the pentarium, or because there was something wrong with Warren and Russell?" Teddy Whin asked, rhetorically. "Or was there something wrong with the pentarium that affected them? And if so, was it something inherent in the pentarium design or something that developed with use? Was it from the fleshly world or the spiritual?" She leaned back in her chair, ticking the points off on her fingers as she made them, and with each point her round face became more remote and peaceable. The list was having the opposite effect on her colleagues. Rho counted six unused fingers.

"That's what the IDA will try to find out," Regan said.

Two or three people tried to speak, but Teddy Whin talked through them.

"As members of the IDA, are we entitled to be part of the investigation? Or are we recused, having likely been affected by whatever damaged the pentarium? Since the pentarium was operating according to IDA standards, is it likely that an IDA investigation would discover any flaw in its basic assumptions? And should we insist that the

176

investigating team contain representatives of other ideological schools than classical demonology? Do we know whether this is a problem with the pentarium alone, or another change in the ley-line?"

The last was a fatal error, a question someone could answer. Linus Ukadnian jumped in, too loud and determined for even Teddy Whin to interrupt. Eyebrows bristling, he raised his voice in passionate rebuttal.

"Rubbish!" he said. "Total rubbish! The recent changes in the ley-line have been entirely compensated for. The pentarium monitors report no changes in power since I adjusted them two days ago. Maintenance reports no unusualness of any kind. I have spent all morning investigating these inane ideas. They are rubbish. Are they not, Magister Graham?"

Isaac Graham, who was as new as Rho, answered more tactfully. "The elementals don't mention anything out of the ordinary," he said. "There were only one or two of them around all week, and they were just passing through. All the records say there won't be much action on that front till March."

"The IDA's first order of business will be to find out what kind of power is affecting the pentarium," Anders Regan said, a little desperately. "We don't really need to argue about that ourselves. They'll send in experts."

"They'll never find out," Teddy Whin said. "Of course it's Alchemy now. The safety wiped everything else out, didn't it? So we'll never know whether it was magic, sorcery, enchantment, wizardry, necromancy-whatever. Or it could have been a kind of power nobody knows about. In the long run, though, what does it matter? All these classifications of power are less important than what the power's used for. That's why the details of their procedure are worth investigating. The assumptions behind normal IDA processes could be causing or reinforcing the problem."

"The first step in any analysis is to identify what you're working with," Patsy Hoth said. "You can't counteract a charm from its consequences alone. All you end up doing is treating the symptoms, instead of curing the disease."

"The symptoms are the disease," Teddy said. "If it didn't have symptoms, you wouldn't call it a disease. We only think this charm-or whatever it is-is a problem because it let the demon out."

"Where did the demon go?" Rho asked. There was a moment's silence.

"I don't know," Regan admitted. "Warren and Russell are the ones who know most about the pentarium. I've never looked at what's in that safety switch-anybody here know how to read Alchemy?"

"They don't use words," Patsy Hoth said, giving Regan a look Rho was familiar with.

"I've already called Magister Vinca," Regan said. "He consulted when the pentarium was built. I think he even made the emergency switch. But he's out of town for the rest of the week. In the meantime, we should all just go about whatever business we have. Does anybody know how to get hold of James Kalin?"

"The secretary should," Patsy Hoth said, as if stating a moral principle.

"She will not," Linus said. "He is working in the Keral Range for another two weeks. You can reach him by radio from the Geomancy reading room, if you must."

"All right. Why don't you help me do that?" Anders Regan said. "Unless anybody has other business, this meeting is adjourned."

***

Most probably, Russell Cinea was making up everything he saw, felt, heard and tasted. He was pleasantly astonished at the idea, and at the variety and wonder of his imaginings-so much better than they had been when he visited these wondrous worlds in his bed, at night, as a child. The glassy waters, great swells rising below him and then tilting and sliding him into their hollows; the long shifting spears of sunlight that shot downwards around him, sometimes blocked off by his body and other times passing through as if he were not there at all-when he thought of it, Russell could feel every mote of sunlight strike against his skin, or he could choose to feel the waters flow through him, around muscle and bone, or he could spread out entirely in the light and motion, feeling little shocks as sea creatures swam into him and pushed their way across.

Then he could regather himself, into a body undefined but as powerful as the water itself, and leap into the air or plunge down to where the rays of sunlight stopped and left him to go on by himself. Fish burst past him, shaking their rigid tails from side to side, with their great eyes staring and their

179

mouths open to the water. Smaller fishes, just as rigid but narrower and silver, dashed upward, leapt into the air to escape on stiff outstretched wings. Russell dashed, leapt, and glided with them, and from high in the air he saw the islands, palm-fringed, floating where air and water met at the horizon.

I'll never go back, Russell thought in the time it took him to fall down into the water, into the splash and swirl of bubbles.

***

Rho woke at sunset with his face pressed against Warren's grimoire, making a wet spot. "Crap!" he said, jumping up and looking around for a towel. He finally mopped the book off with the corner of his bedsheet, noting with relief that the ink hadn't run. "Damn and blast," Rho said, sitting down heavily in front of his desk. A sleepy pigeon cooed at him from beyond the glass before tucking its head under its wing. His tower room seemed musty, the air solid and meaty-tasting in his mouth. Rho sat up, thinking, glaring at his own blurred reflection in the window, and thought about hurling the useless book through it.

"Idiot!" he told the reflection, and it looked back at him with disgust. What must he have looked like Friday, when he thought Warren was going to save him from everything? A simpering fool, a lost puppy, believing the first and loudest lies-just like always. Rho snarled. Would he never learn? There was no doubt about it, Warren was insane and this starter school was likely to be Rho's end.

He put Warren's grimoire aside and went back out into his workroom, where he had stacked the real books of magic-everything he could find in the library, and Russell Cinea's thesis on flesh magic from thirty years ago when Russell wasn't crazy, or was crazy in a way Rho liked... He thought of the young magician inviting a hundred demons to his defense, and shivered with pleasure. That was showing them! But what had it led to?

Rho recognized every page of the thesis. He had read it too often in the past three days, this compendium of ways to bind a demon and what that binding did to the person who performed it. The injuries sustained as one clung to the demon, keeping in physical contact as one spoke the spell. Hands, arms ripped off, demon blood or semen turned to flame, burning its way out of the magician. The more subtle damages that came after, through years of intimacy with the bound monster, and the final death at its talons, when the aged magician's powers began to fail. *What for?* Rho shuddered as he closed the book. *So those snobs at the Congress won't think I'm a fool? I am a fool, if I do any such thing.*

Before he could lose his courage, he sat down at the computer and composed an email to Vivien:

The demon you enchanted into a pig has followed me to Osyth.

I do not know its name. Can you send me its name or call it back?

But at the last moment, he couldn't send it. He saw her face when she had picked up his ward. *Natural philosophy?* he imagined her saying. *That little man who talks to ducks...* Any answer he might

181

find in the Congress' archives would be out of reach once they discovered he wasn't one of them, just another of those incompetents from Osyth.

"Hell and damnation," Rho groaned, putting his head down in his hands. The picture of Vivien slid in his mind until it was a different face, Cham Ligalla's, turning away, closing off, finding him of no worth or significance. He felt the same lurching in his stomach, the same cold sweat he had felt during the exorcism; it was the last straw. "I'll take care of it myself," Rho said to both of them, sitting up. "I can't do worse than the rest of you."

He hit 'delete' with a steady hand, and the email disappeared to wherever unsent messages go. The cold sweat came again, though another shiver followed it, and another, and then his body was gripped by the *cauld grue* and the familiar scent of rotten meat was all around him.

Rho sat still, first in shock at the idea of his demon's appearing inside, by its getting through the Academy wards. But hadn't he just been analyzing the Academy's weaknesses? Here was object proof. And this time, he was taking charge. A real magician had to learn to cope with demons. "I've seen demons before," he said to the demon, looking at its black shape reflected in the window. "You're nothing new. The question is, what's in it for me?"

The demon laughed, a more glutinous sound than before (if possible, Rho thought), and licked his hand. Rho pulled it away.

"I know what you want," he said sharply. "But do you know what I want? Do you have anything I want? And I don't believe we really have a language problem."

At this he turned and looked the demon full in the face, something he had never done in the light, and found it was not bad-looking. If one ignored the smell and the shivers of revulsion, and in the few moments when it was not grinning and showing its jagged teeth, this demon had much to recommend it. Its face was human, chiseled, with a cleft chin, but covered in matte ebony skin of a color and texture never seen on a human body. Rho thought of Will Harding in his black leather. Black leather looked classier on its original owner. The demon grinned and spread out its wings behind it, and Rho was glad to shift his eyes from that grin to the great black feathers. An oversized louse crawled out from under one feather and in behind another. "I thought demons had bat wings," he said.

"Not when we're visiting a bird person," the demon said. "Manners. Courtesy. Does this form please you?" It leaned toward him, letting the tip of its tongue show. The tongue, also, was black.

"It's not bad," Rho allowed. "Can you do anything about the smell?"

"It pleases me. If I learn to enjoy what pleases you, you must learn to enjoy what pleases me," the demon said.

Rho heard the student from Kasidora saying, "They turn into what they study," and something colder than the *grue* settled into his bones.

"What can you give me?"

"What do you want?"

Damn, Rho thought, *that is the question*. "If I knew what I wanted, I'd have it by now," he said, in as haughty a tone as he could muster. "What use are

183

your powers, if you can't teach me what I most need to know?"

"That was a brave answer," the demon said, and touched his cheek with one finger. "Few have the courage to answer that question truthfully. But for all who dare to give that answer, it is true. When such a man discovers what he wants, he will have it."

Rho felt as if he had been hit in the stomach, struck by kindness. He looked away, blinking.

"What are you here for?" he asked in a less haughty voice.

"Kindness," the demon said, caressingly. "A friendly touch. Support and respect. Does anyone need more?" Its voice was soft, deep, hypnotic. "You took pity on me when I was trapped in a body not my own. I will protect you from your enemies in this world. We will encourage one another."

Rho was quiet for a minute. "I didn't know demons were like this."

"I am no more like other demons than you are like other magicians," the demon replied. "We need each other. We have no equals. Inferior minds are all around us; they would be glad to see us fail; how will we grow, how improve, if not by championing each other against them?"

Rho remembered Patsy Hoth and the look on Warren's wife's face. He thought of Neil Torecki, whose charms he couldn't use, and all the glory Neil was enjoying for doing nothing more than throwing a switch, and of the way the red demon had walked through all the powers of Osyth as if they were nothing. He looked again at the black demon beside him. His skin and guts and bones all disapproved of it, threatened to resign if they were asked to work under these conditions, but they were not in charge. Courage was all a magician truly needed.

"Go on," he said.

***

Teddy Whin was watching late-night television when Anders Regan called her, long after normal people should be abed. She was lounging in a hammock-chair swung from the beam in her bedroom, propped up with pillows, and had to struggle to reach the phone. When she had it, the chair began to twirl and wrapped the cord around her.

"Yeah, what? Oh, Regan."

"It's about Russell," he said.

Teddy didn't like that. She didn't like Regan, or his tentative tone of voice. "I just got back from visiting him a few hours ago," she said, in a 'don't tell me about Russell' tone, and untwirled herself.

"How was he?"

"Just like last week," Teddy said, curiosity overcoming irritation. "He didn't seem upset about any of this. He's been preoccupied lately. Did they find something else wrong with him?"

"Here's what they just told me," Regan said. "Apparently the arm wasn't healing the way it should have, when the sorcerer came in this afternoon. They thought there was some necrosis, so they called in Roger Klimt from Necromancy to clean up the dead tissue."

"Yeah? Was that before or after I visited?"

"Before," Regan said. "They just got through talking with Roger now, that's what held this up. Roger said he fixed the arm, and cleared out some blocked arteries and a valvular problem, rectal polyps, cataracts and a little liver disease. I guess he got confused and thought he was cleaning Russell up for an organ donor."

"How was Roger able to do all that? I thought necromancers could only handle dead things."

"Well, that's the point."

"But Russell isn't dead! He was talking to me an hour ago. Didn't Roger notice that he was working on a live body? Do the organ donors usually talk to him?"

"Yeah, Roger thought that was odd."

"He's not dead," Teddy Whin said. She turned the sound off on her television.

"If Roger Klimt can heal him and the sorcerers can't, he must be dead," Regan said.

"Crap. If someone's walking and talking, they're not dead."

"Unless the demon went into him. They've moved him into a secure wing of the building, and they want some of us to come over and check it out. I thought you're the one who's closest to him, in the department."

"Andy, I was in his room an hour ago. There wasn't any demon."

"Can you meet me over there?"

"Yeah, in twenty minutes." Teddy hung up the phone and stared at voiceless figures on her television screen for a few seconds. Then she threw the remote across the room, into a large painted gourd. "What kind of friend dies without telling anybody?" she asked. "Dammit to hell, that's not collegial."

187

Chapter Nine

Rho sat at his desk in the morning sunlight and answered his email. One of the first items in it was his password to the Demonological Congress' listserv and website, and Rho grinned. How close he had come to giving this up, in his panic yesterday! He felt like a new man, no longer looking for leaders but forging ahead in his own path. He leaned back in the sun and sighed happily.

The room smelled faintly of rotten meat, but Rho didn't mind that. The faintness of the smell was mute witness to his ability to stave off an affectionate demon, even though the institutional wards of Osyth had been unable to keep it out of the building. His first independent parley with a demon had gone well. It had been like a discussion with a new friend-a challenging friend, who switched at a moment's notice from invective to flirtation to analysis. Rho was tired, but he felt lively in a way he had not felt since he'd come to Osyth, as if he had been using his brain to think with after too long a time of simply storing up new rules and wondering whether any of his previous learning would ever apply.

And how much he had learned about the local demons and what they looked like from the other side. Nezumia and its taste for anxiety and Warren, its hostility to visitors. The minor demons that flocked along the ley-line like so many sheep, and what it felt like to absorb one of them and use its power as one's own... He hummed as he opened the word processor and began entering his notes.

As he typed, Rho's confidence began to ebb. Talking with the demon had been a triumph, but believing what it had said might be a catastrophe. Was it as ignorant as it claimed of whatever had happened to the pentarium, to Warren and Russell? It had found Rho by searching through the ley-line, that was all it said. The way had opened. It had shrugged its wings as if a non-demon could never understand, and insisted it could tell him nothing more without knowing the charms of discourse used in the pentarium-and those, Rho knew better than to give it. He was sure he hadn't told it anything useful. Positive.

Rho felt yesterday's confusion and guilt creeping up around him again, and he was not about to stand for it. "So the ley-line led it here," he said fiercely, getting up. "So what? We have people who know about that sort of thing." Before he could talk himself out of it, he pulled on his robe and ran down the steps to Linus Ukadnian's second-floor lab.

The lab looked like a prison, with its contents locked up in stark gray cabinets. Even Linus' books stood behind metal-edged glass doors. In this strict atmosphere Linus pottered and smoldered, and glared at Rho as if about to erupt.

"I wanted to ask you something about the pentarium," Rho said.

"Damned foolishness," Linus said, as if he meant to be encouraging.

"The morning I came back from Selanto, something changed in the ley-line, didn't it?"

"An abnormally large fluctuation," Linus proclaimed loudly, standing up straight and apparently speaking to someone other than Rho. "It indicates the utter inadequacy of our predictive algorithms. We have underestimated the lines' sensitivity to initial conditions. I speak of chaos in the mathematical sense, not of the facile metaphors into which it has been distorted by antirationalist poseurs."

"Um-all right," Rho said. "I'm more interested in why it changed."

"I have just told you the problem is beyond our current understanding."

"Could I have had anything to do with it? Because I'd just come back from Selanto, and I touched a demon there. Neil told me they don't let anybody with a bound demon use the pentarium."

Linus glared at him. "Have you bound a demon?"

"No!" Rho said, getting angry himself.

"If you had, the question would still be irrelevant. The magicians who built the pentarium had all bound demons. Most of the current users have touched demons. I suggest you do your background research before offering to take responsibility for geological events. Someone less concerned with accuracy than myself might take you seriously."

"Fine," Rho said, damned if he would thank Linus for this advice. He was snarling when he pushed open the door to the stairwell, almost banging it into Will Harding and Susan Teale.

"Hello, Rho. Come along to breakfast," Susan said. "We're certainly not invoking today."

Rho's first instinct was to snap at her, but curiosity stopped him. Susan Teale had a lot more going on than her appearance would indicate. Rho had admired Susan's broad pale face, ample frame and the hair that flowed over her wide back like a brown river even before she told Linus and Patsy to shut up and called Cham a bitch. She seemed an asexual being, solid and reliable. Next to her Will looked tawdry in his black leather jacket, with circles under his eyes. "I could use some coffee," Rho said.

"Then come along," Susan repeated. "You've hardly had any chance to see the city, have you? It's a beautiful morning. This thaw can't last much longer. Get out and enjoy it."

"I do," Rho said. "I walk the ley-line every day."

"That's right, it's part of your research, isn't it? So tell me, how's it going?"

Before Rho knew it he was walking along beside Susan, telling her about Osyth's ducks and their doings. Then the three of them were in the ground floor lobby, out the big double doors, and the time for deciding whether to come along or not had completely passed.

"Let's walk," Susan suggested, but Will complained.

"I've been walking around all night. You drive, my eyes are sore."

"Oh, all right," Susan said. "Quite a day yesterday, wasn't it?" she asked Rho, who blinked at her a minute before switching gears.

"Oh? Yes," he said, trying to sort out the parts of yesterday Susan might know about from the parts he wanted to keep secret.

"I'd be jumpy too, if I were you," Will said, who apparently missed nothing. "Just signed on, and we lose two of our best magicians in one morning. I bet you're wondering where we get off, calling ourselves an academy."

"What nonsense," Susan said. "Nobody asked that when three of the wizards dropped a girder on their own heads. Nobody asks that when patients die over in sorcery. He's like this before he has coffee," she explained to Rho. "It's from spending all night with vampires. Vampires put everybody down, just for being alive."

"That's true," Will said. "They call it buying into the system. Why play a game you can't win? That's what vampires want to know."

"I'd like to ask them what they think they've won," Susan said. "It sounds like an eternity of high school, if you ask me. Cliques and factions. The red sedan over there."

She pointed it out to Rho. Conversation was suspended as she got them out of the parking garage and onto the road that ran along below the city wall. The snow along the roadside was littered with cans, beer bottles and other less savory garbage.

"What I'd like to know is why people don't feel safe enough to come over here in the daytime and learn something, but they do feel safe enough to trash the place at night," Susan said.

"Millions for offense, but not one cent for tuition," Will said from the backseat.

"And all the same," Susan said. "They're as much bought into it as any of the rest of us. Vampires. They do a lot more to stay alive than I would. In fact if you think of it, vampires have less to lose than I have and they still do more to avoid losing it. It's not as if they'll die if they don't feed."

"Vampires have no socially redeeming features," Will said.

"So what do you study?" Rho asked Susan.

"Ghosts and revenants, poor things," she answered. "Neither soul nor body. Reminiscences, I guess you'd call them. Echoes. Durrell's?"

"Fine," Will's sepulchral voice said from the back seat.

"D'you like Durrell's?"

"I've never been there," Rho said. "I usually eat in my rooms."

"Oh, where's the fun in that?"

"There's a nice view."

"I guess there would be," Susan said. "But any time you want company, come down to the lab. I usually go for breakfast around seven, when we're going to be invoking at nine. It's only days like this, when the pentarium's down, that I wait for Will. Speaking of which, have either of you heard any news about that?"

"No," and "Nothing," were the responses from Will and Rho.

"I ought to go over and visit Warren and Russell," Susan said. "Remind me when we park, and I'll call up and see what the visiting hours are."

"Here's the gossip I do know," Will said. "The vampires say some of the Academy's wards are down, and they might come feeding over here-but

193

they won't. They're scared of the demons along the ley-line. Not that demons can kill vampires," he explained to Rho, leaning on the seat back, "but they make fun of them. Treat them like fierce bad rabbits. Vampires have their dignity to maintain."

"I'm scared of the demons along the ley-line myself," Susan said, "especially after yesterday. Maybe I won't work nights anymore until this is cleared up. You shouldn't be staying in the building at night, either."

"Oh, I'll be fine," Rho said. "Don't worry about me."

Susan had turned in through the city's north gate, and the car rattled through a narrow street lined with shops. Durrell's, which stood out with its big neon sign, already had a full parking lot.

"Pest," Susan said. "Find me a spot, guys." As if the demonologists commanded traffic, three cars pulled out and made way for them. "Good work!"

Durrell's bustled. Bright, crowded, and full of food smells and jabber, it engulfed the three demonologists and reduced them to regular people indistinguishable from truckers, bankers, and the other mundanes filling the booths. They were all just folks, said Durrell's clean windows and gum-chewing waitresses, and the reward for being just folks was sausage.

"The best sausage in town," Will said. "Don't pass it up."

A squadron of lawyerly types in gray suits marched across the parking lot, turning into just folks as they stepped through the door. Rho watched with amazement.

"Who are these people?" he asked.

"That's Grant and Ellis, and a few of their friends," Susan said, pointing out the lawyers. "You'll have seen their commercials? Ambulance-chasers. The old guy at the end there, he's Lord Failek. Those green uniforms are capitol city messengers, they hang out in here until they get work. Their office is next door."

"That's Warren's mother," Rho said, as Bosie Lane came in the door. Not even Durrell's could change Bosie, in her high heels and cocktail dress, into just folks. Susan and Will gawked.

"His mother?" Will said, shocked. "She was in a club on the south side last night. Closing it down, in more ways than one. Warren's mother!" He grinned and elbowed Rho off the seat. "Ask her over, you know her."

Rho had to stand up or fall to the floor, and in standing up, he caught Bosie's notice. She made her way over to the booth.

"Magister Rho," she said graciously. "And these would be your friends from the Demonology Department?" They introduced themselves, Will with a knowing grin that Bosie seemed not to notice. "You're the vampire people, now aren't you?" she said, sitting down beside Susan. "So sad, I've always thought. To see them sitting at the bars, pretending they'd be too sophisticated to dance with us even if we did ask them. Sour grapes. There was this lovely young man, I might even have married him instead of Warren's father, but he was so afraid of dying. His mother had, you know. And he said it wouldn't make any difference, but of course it did, because nobody seems worth spending all of eternity with. Well, they wouldn't, would they?"

"Oh, I don't know," Will said, looking at her with appreciation.

"How's Warren?" Susan asked, just as their breakfasts arrived. They leaned back from enormous plates of sausage and eggs, and Bosie spoke to the waitress about her own order.

"Warren?" she said, after the waitress left. "Why, that's the most peculiar thing, dear. I've just come from visiting him. You know he's always been one for getting up early and not fond of hospitals at all. He was quite upset about missing the invoking this morning, poor dear, but that chart on his bed was very clear that he has to be there for all sorts of tests and dosages and checkings and so on."

"What's peculiar about that?" Susan asked.

"Nothing," Bosie admitted. "It's what the hospital did last night that was peculiar. Why, do you know, they called up poor Lilian at home and told her he was dead? Can you imagine? How careless of them. Poor girl, she was there all night as if she could do something if it were to happen, you can't and there's no use trying."

"Dead!" Susan dropped her fork.

"What?"

"But he's alive," Rho said. "You said you were just talking to him."

"That's right," Bosie said. "Not twenty minutes ago. He's as merry as a grig, whatever a grig is."

"I believe it's a type of cart, or maybe a salamander," Will said. "But the hospital shouldn't be making mistakes like that. I wonder-ow!" He glared at Susan, who glared back.

196

"Oh, go ahead," Bosie said. "I know you're all dying to talk about it. I was married to a magician myself, you know. I can tell you one thing, he's not turned into a vampire. There was a big ray of sunlight right across the bed, and it didn't bother him a bit. He's always been that way, Warren has, as fair as he looks now, he never burns. So convenient, when he was a little boy. But then he was dark, of course, like me."

"Maybe he's possessed," Will said. "Maybe the demon got him."

Wow! Rho thought. *Possession!* This was the most exciting thing he'd ever been around. Then his eyes fell on Susan, who was looking sick, and the picture of Warren hugging her flashed into his mind. Warren setting the home ward in his house; Warren, giving Rho a ride to the airport, loaning Rho his grimoire, shutting down the pentarium when the insurance lapsed. Warren had nothing but good deeds to his credit, and Rho had only thought Wow! when the worst thing in the world might have happened to him... Rho glared at his plate. The most exciting thing that might ever happen in his life, and he'd always remember it like this. *I hate this place,* he thought. *They can't keep crap from happening, but they can keep you from enjoying it.*

"Will!" Susan said, jerking her head at Bosie.

"It happens," Will said defiantly.

"Well," Bosie said, "I wouldn't know myself, I've never been able to tell a demon from everybody else. Warren gets it all from his father. The hospital had someone check out his aura last night, though, according to the chart." She waved to someone behind Rho's head. "It's shift change at the hospital," she explained to him. "Things will get frantic in here in the next five minutes, just watch."

Rho turned around to watch the people coming in and keep his gaze away from Susan.

"Good thing we have a booth," Will said. "Hey! Keep an eye out for Roger. He'll tell us all about this. Roger Klimt's the necromancer over in the hospital."

"I know, dear. Warren's father was the one who wanted to hire him at first, but the Magic Division voted against having necromancers on staff. Such an unfortunate prejudice, I always thought, but they said bodies and demons didn't mix in the same building. Worried about possession. People used to worry about that all the time. They go in and out of style, these worries. Now everybody's worried about child abuse and handguns. When I was a girl," Bosie mused, "it was white slavery and the yellow peril."

"At least that was colorful," Will said.

"There's Roger." Bosie stood up. "Hoo hoo! Roger!"

"Squeeze over," Will told Rho, who made room for the necromancer with mixed feelings. In Kasidora, necromancers had looked on the other magicians as no more than potential cadavers.

Roger Klimt stood a head taller than either of the younger men. He had a narrow, intelligent face, glasses, dark hair going to salt-and-pepper on the sides, and long, delicate fingers. He smelt slightly of decay and formaldehyde.

"So is Warren dead, or what?" Will asked.

"By my criteria, he's dead," Roger said, giving Bosie an uneasy glance.

"But he's not a vampire," she said with a bright smile. "Don't worry, Roger, you know I'm not easily upset. Better you should tell me than poor Lilian."

"Well, that's true, he's not undead," Roger said, still looking uncomfortable. "He had a regular dinner."

"Could he have lost his soul?" Susan asked, pushing her plate away. The smell of sausage rose up around Rho, and guilt rose with it. He stared at the plate.

"That's the diagnosis we're working with," Roger said. "The Demonology Department sent somebody over last night with a camera arcana, and he didn't have any aura."

"Mundanes don't always have an aura, either," Will said. "Does that mean they haven't got souls?"

"Oh, I wouldn't think so," Bosie said. "There was a young man once... no, I've known some terribly soulful mundanes."

"But, Roger... " Susan looked at Bosie helplessly. "This is serious," she complained.

"Some mundane scientists say souls don't even exist," Will said helpfully. "They claim that people just think we have souls because the same random brain activity that generates actions also generates thoughts about actions, so it feels like we've planned the actions."

Roger took a clinical interest in this. "Where are they getting these soulless bodies to investigate?" he asked. "We could obtain one, and compare it to Warren. D'you mind?" Susan shook her head, and he reached across Rho to take one of her sausages.

"Have mine too," Rho said, just to be saying something, and Susan looked at him as if they both understood something the others were missing. She pushed at Bosie. Rho stood up as well, not entirely sure why except that if he let Susan go and stayed behind, he'd keep feeling guilty. "I need to get out," he said. When he got out he didn't know where to go, except with Susan.

"I'm going to call the hospital," she said to him. "Come along." He followed her out into the parking lot, where instead of calling anybody she wrapped her arms around her coat and stood on the sidewalk. Quiet sunlight filled the space around them and their breath hung in clouds. "I don't think I can go back in there without hitting someone," Susan said. "How can they just talk about it! It's Warren's soul, and he's out there with demons after him. What could be happening to him right now, and his own mother eats sausage."

"She doesn't seem too worried," Rho ventured.

"I know! And I can't say a word about how serious it is in front of her."

"The necromancer isn't worried either."

"He never deals with anyone who still has their soul," Susan snapped. "What does he know?"

"Warren wasn't afraid of demons," Rho said firmly. It needed to be said, and said often. "He had friends who were demons. He thought we ought to be relaxed about them. That's what he told me-not to worry."

"If you'll excuse me, I'll worry!" Susan said. "There's a reason losing your soul is supposed to be worse than death. Demons can do anything they

200

want to in the arcane world, and it's not as if a soul can die again and get away from them."

"You don't know what happens to souls."

"I know what happens to ghosts. They lose everything that made them persons, bit by bit, until all they are is little blobs of emotion. Walking obsessions."

This wasn't what Rho wanted to hear. He had wanted her to calm down and tell him it wasn't so bad, he now realized, but Susan was obviously a person who couldn't be counted on to do that. She was one of the people he'd never be sensitive or kind enough for. "We can stand out here scaring ourselves, or we can go back and see what to do about it," he said, and wished he had eaten his sausages. They'd be gone by now, and they were. Will and Roger were still deep in conversation over the empty plate, Bosie watching them with tolerant amusement.

"The thing is, if his soul is loose, we might be able to call it back," Will said. "There are a lot of charms for contacting the departed. We could use a seance, or a ouija board."

"Have you done that?"

"Sue does it all the time. She's a pro." Roger looked at her as if he had never thought of that, and Will smiled as if he were showing off a prized possession. "We can get right on it, can't we? Better to do something than sit around worrying."

"Maybe tonight," Susan said.

"Don't do that. We'll never get a handle on this if every faculty member with an interest puts their oar in," Roger said sternly. "He's a real person, not a case study."

"Sorry," Susan said.

"That's all right. Just don't go trying things on your own; we have to put together a treatment plan."

"And we have to get back for classes," Will said. "Don't you have an eleven o'clock, Rho? Eat up."

"There's nothing left," Rho said. "I didn't want it, anyway."

***

From the fact that Warren was now a disembodied spirit, a few things followed. It followed that there existed a spiritual realm and a material one. A demonologist, Warren had always accepted this. Now, however, it was practical knowledge rather than a working assumption.

If the spiritual realm existed, it existed in tandem with the material realm. It somehow mirrored that realm-for he was a spirit of Warren, not part of some amalgam. He thought as himself, which meant the spiritual world was divided into entities along some of the same lines as the material world. If he could learn to perceive them apart from his own vain imaginings, he could find places, things, and persons he knew. He could navigate through the spiritual world. What that would accomplish, Warren tried not to ask himself. But it was a moot point. Anything which depended on turning his mind outwards, on silencing the inner voices, would have to wait until Warren had finished worrying.

His whole life long, nobody had ever let Warren worry as much as he wanted to. Someone had always come and tried to cheer him up. The only time he got close to worrying as much as he wanted to, his mother had put him in hospital where the sorcerers filled him up with confusing spells until he could hardly think at all, let alone look at things in their true horror.

Now he was free to stew and carry on. Without any apparent effort, his mind conjured up the situations he anticipated. Like the audience at a horror-movie festival, he could see all the things his body might be doing; from the fantasies of benign neglect, in which it just went along about its business while the department dissolved into factions, to the scenarios of homicidal mania in which it murdered Lilian and Bosie, or threw their souls out of their bodies to create peers for itself, to the most horrid scenario of all in which his body did everything better than he had and ended up receiving academic honors Warren had long dreamed of.

Like the horror-movie audience, Warren was becoming desensitized. Each scene had to be worse than the previous one to have the same effect, and they were beginning to tax his imagination. And none of them were getting him any closer to getting his body back. Warren finally decided he had to stop worrying and look outward, find out what was around him in reality.

It took a mighty heave and pull for him to jerk himself out of the storm of worries he conjured up, almost as great an effort as it had taken to loose himself from the body in the first place. He could

203

only maintain it for a few seconds, at first. To stay out of his worries felt like determining to do something wrong, admitting to himself that he was the sort of person who ignored responsibilities and that he intended to live with being that sort. It left an empty space like a lost tooth; the only way he could stop poking at it was to remind himself that the most moral act of all was to perceive the world as it was, so far as he could. That thought gave Warren a stern righteous feeling that let him put his worries aside for a few moments as childish toys and keep putting them aside again and again, a hundred times in a minute. It was his duty. A new world awaited his attention.

***

Teaching made Rho too nervous to think about anything else. The students seemed to change before his eyes; at one moment attentive and respectful, then sardonic or sullen, closed off, refusing to believe a word of what he told them. Animals talk! Ha! They couldn't hear it, and how could it be real if they couldn't hear it? Rho wiped the sweat of frustration off his forehead with one of his sleeves and wondered again why the Academy let people with so little talent into their classes. Not one of this group was going to pass, and it was no fault of theirs. They read the book and did the assignments, but nothing could put talent into a head it wasn't born in.

"In Kasidora, you had to discover your own talent and then go begging for a teacher," he told Neil, who stood next to him in the hallway watching their classes file out. "What are these students going to get for their money?"

Neil shrugged. "If they do the work, they get a passing grade," he said. "They'll at least know what magic's about, and not start pogroms or witch-burnings. It's good PR to have people with Academy degrees running the local businesses."

Neil took everything lightly, Rho thought.

"Don't you have any opinion?" he asked. "Are you content to be doing PR work instead of teaching real magicians?"

"Hell, yes," Neil said. "You know what goes along with PR work? Air conditioning. My own house. A car. I have more stuff than senior magicians have over in Selanto. My salary is twice theirs, plus we have real sorcery coverage and a pension plan. There aren't enough students with talent to support me in the style to which I'm accustomed."

For a sunny, open-faced kind of guy, Neil worried Rho a lot. He seemed to represent a malignant force, one which dressed itself up in modern clothes and masqueraded as just folks until you were in its toils. Then it called in your debts, and you would find your soul sold for air conditioning. Rho hugged his filthy robe around him as if he were cold, and rustled up the stairs to his tower room. He had almost washed it, that robe. Almost hung it outside in the sun until it smelled fresh and innocent and modern, like the robe of someone with a washing machine and a car. Shaking his head, he packed his field gear and headed out onto the ley-line.

The midday sun made the children in Westpark into dolls in bright colors, clean and plastic as the toys they played with. Young mothers ran out bundled in ski parkas and swung the children up over their heads, whirled them around, carried them off to station wagons. Rho sat on the bench in a black lump, watching them and dozing.

He'd come out to film ducks and found himself too tired to do the work. He felt himself dissolving in exhaustion, as though he'd been doing heavy manual labor all the day before. Or all night. *Ridiculous!* Rho thought, pushing his head upright again and forcing his eyes open, but in his heart he excused himself. It wasn't every week that he barely escaped one demon and sat up all night with another.

A cat walked around from Rho's left and sniffed at him. A large ginger tom, he stood four-square and raised his scarred head in Rho's direction.

"You have meat," he said. "Give me some."

"I don't," Rho said, and the cat jumped a little and flattened his ears.

"You have meat," he repeated. "I smell it. Give it here!"

"I ate it all," Rho answered, a single casual sound often heard among cats. In some areas, it served as a greeting between equals; this tom seemed to accept it as such. He looked Rho over carefully, from one end to the other.

"I fuck here," he warned Rho. "Where do you fuck?"

"Over there," Rho said, nodding in the direction of the Academy. Territories established, the tom relaxed and sat down, knuckling his front paws under his breast. He half-closed his eyes.

"Nice sun," he said.

"Nice sun," Rho agreed, and shut his own eyes. The park sounds surrounded him, children squealing and mothers rebuking them. High above, he heard the clamor of geese.

"Hurry hurry, what sun, move over," the geese sang. "Look at that, well I never, lovely day. It doesn't, it doesn't get better, better than this, better than this."

Chapter Ten

Teddy Whin made an effort to get something done, even though most of what she had to do needed to be done with Russell. Working out charms of discourse on her own, with no prospect of bouncing them off either him or James, made her uneasy. Single-magician arguments were trouble; they gave the demons too much insight into how the magician's mind worked. Nothing she did would be of any use, either, if demons got hold of Russell's soul while it was sojourning away from his body and made it explain how to refute her work... but that wasn't to be thought of. Not if one wanted to get any work done. Teddy put in a solid morning reading through Russell's notes and devising her own modifications of them. She was working through lunch when Anders Regan came in and sat down in her office.

"Do you know anything about Russell's financial situation?"

"Not really," Teddy said. "He must be pretty well off to keep going on those cheesy vacations. Why?"

"Salvation called the Academy. They won't pay for keeping him in the hospital any longer," Regan said.

"But they say he's dead!"

"You don't usually keep people in hospital for that, do you?" he snapped. "Sorry. This is starting to get to me."

"Andy, don't apologize. That's the first remark you've made that I understood."

"Picking on one another never solves anything. We have to support each other."

"Go back to why they're kicking Russell out of the hospital," Teddy advised.

"He isn't sick, so Salvation wants them to release him. Where will he go then? I visited this morning, and he seems to be assuming he'll come back to work."

"He can't work. There's not a breath of magic in him. Though if there were, I'm sure the Academy would expect him to work long after death," Teddy admitted. "We thought it was a victory for us when they abolished mandatory retirement, Hah!"

"He could still teach."

"Send someone dead into the room to teach students? There's a lawsuit in there somewhere."

"You're not helping." Regan put a hand over his eyes. "Oh, I wish Warren were here. What happens to lost souls, anyway?"

Teddy didn't like this question. She had been up all night surfing the web for answers, and found none that pleased her. They sat in silence for a few moments until Teddy got that feeling again as if her head were a bubble of water, with her thoughts just a thin skin over it. The bubble kept growing as she sat there, wobbling and shivering atop her neck, and no matter how hard and fast she layered thoughts over it, it was going to break, her whole head was going to turn into a fountain of tears... *And leave one more headless faculty member,* she thought sarcastically. *Maybe we should just kill off the whole department, and save on benefits.* She shook her head and sniffed.

"Warren is here," she said. "He's in the same wing of the hospital as Russell. I saw him yesterday afternoon. So let's go ask him what to do. He'll still be functional; you don't need a soul to be an administrator."

"Dammit, Warren's a good man," said Regan, "and I'm sick of your nasty comments about him. Some demon could be tearing his soul apart, and you mouth off."

"All right," Teddy said. "I'll try not to be a smart-ass around you, okay? But you have to try and not get me into this sitting around contemplating the situation, because that's not how I cope with things. Let's just deal with the problem at hand, and find other people to sympathize with us, on our own time." She knew the look she was seeing on Regan's face. It meant the other person was saying, *You bitch,* inside his head. It meant she was right and he knew it.

***

"Salvation won't cover these bills," the person at the hospital desk said. "These bills are for treatment dated after the person's deceased. Your policy doesn't cover postmortem treatments."

"He's not dead," Lilian said. "Do you want me to bring him down here and show you?"

"I'm sorry, but all our records show he is dead. We have a death certificate and a donor preparation voucher from necromancy."

210

"You are not taking one organ out of my husband." Lilian jabbed her finger in the man's face. "Is that clear?"

"He signed an organ donor card."

"Not now, he didn't," Lilian said, tearing up the proffered paper.

"That was a copy," the man said. "We also have a living will on file. The loss of a loved one is a terrible event, I know. Many family members find some comfort in knowing he made his last wishes clear, and in carrying them out. Do you think maybe you should speak with one of our grief counselors?"

"Does this look like grief?" Lilian bared her teeth at him. "I'm checking him out. Right now. What do I have to sign?"

"I'm sorry, but you can't check him out directly," the man said. "Osyth law mandates that you need to do it through a licensed funeral director. We have a list."

Lilian felt herself swelling up like an overfilled balloon. She thought of all the things she might say to this officious twit, but she took the list.

"Where's a phone I can use?" was all she said. If they wanted to play games, she'd play along. This early in the morning, it should have been easy to get hold of a funeral director, but she had to wait on hold for almost ten minutes before someone came on the line. "I'm trying to get my dead husband out of this hospital," she said, and the voice on the other end took on a tone of professional sympathy.

"Of course," it said. It was a deep, somber, reassuring voice. "Allow me to express my deepest sympathy for your loss."

211

"All the sympathy I want is to get him out of here before they cut him up for parts," Lilian said. "I want to take the body home."

"We will certainly do all we can to help you in this stressful time," the voice said, with a temporizing sound that made Lilian's heart sink. "Why don't you let us make the arrangements for postmortem preparation and cremation directly with the hospital. I presume you want a viewing."

"I do not want a viewing. I want to void his organ donor status, and I want to take the body home unprepared."

"Both of those are difficult," the voice replied. "An organ donor card represents the deceased's last wishes. Going against last wishes is a very bad idea, for you as well as for the hospital. And the disposal of dead bodies is restricted by several laws. I'm sure you realize that a dead human body is raw material for most of the nastiest forms of black magic. I'm sure you wouldn't want that happening to your husband's remains."

"Oh, hell and damnation!" Lilian cried, and slammed the phone down. She went back up to Warren's room, where at least the nurses seemed to care about her, and they brought her a lukewarm hospital lunch. Warren was reading his chart.

"It looks as if I could leave after four," he said to her. "I'm scheduled for some kind of a scan at three twenty. There's nothing after that."

"It's not going to be all that simple," Lilian said. People who really needed organs would not have left their donor sitting all day. She stayed by Warren's side, reading everything she could find about hospital policies, until the sorcerers finally

212

came in at three o'clock. *About time!* A gaggle of students filed into the room, following a severe-looking woman with spiky gray hair who looked at Warren as if this were all entirely his fault.

"Sorcerer Pim," Warren said cheerfully. "This is my wife, Lilian."

Sorcerer Pim's face cracked into a smile as if she had never smiled before. She shook Lilian's hand, which didn't seem right, but then, Lilian reflected, they also shook hands before duels to the death.

"I've been going over Warren's papers," she said to Pim, "and I see that he is an organ donor, and I don't have any legal rights to stop you from taking his organs. However ridiculous it seems to declare someone dead and keep feeding him meals and carrying his bedpans, but set that aside. You don't need family permission to harvest organs. But you do need my permission to use anesthesia, and I'm not giving it." She folded her arms and stood back, nodding toward the bed. "Go ahead. Knock yourself out."

Warren smiled cheerfully at Sorcerer Pim from the bed. All the sorcery students looked nervous. Pim raised her eyebrows.

"What's that again?" she said.

"The hospital won't let me check him out, because he's been declared dead and he's an organ donor. Don't they tell you what's going on, either?"

"Apparently not." Sorcerer Pim picked up Warren's chart. "It says here he was declared dead yesterday evening at ten twenty-four." She flipped the chart and handed it to a student. "Tell us about preparation for organ donation, Mr. Tomko."

213

The student looked at the chart and cleared his throat nervously.

"After declaration of death, the body must be treated by the necromancer to repair any damage to the organs," he said. "That was done in this case before the declaration of death, which is irregular but not unheard of, especially in cases of accident. Organs must be removed within half an hour of death under the supervision of a licensed sorcerer or necromancer, or the body must be maintained on life support or by a necromancer until they can be harvested."

"And?" Sorcerer Pim prompted.

"Well, the only part of that which was done in this case was the initial necromancer's screening," the student said. "That was... almost nineteen hours ago."

"No life support."

"No."

"There you have it," Pim said to Lilian. "Nobody would use his organs. They've been sitting around dead entirely too long."

"Oh." Lilian sat down. Tears filled her eyes. "But how can I get him home?" she asked plaintively, looking up at the sorcerer. "The funeral director says I can't take a dead body home, for fear I'll do black magic with it."

"There's some sense to that," Pim said. "Something very unusual has happened to your husband. It might even be black magic. I don't think you should take him home."

"We can't afford to keep him here. Since he was declared dead, the insurance won't pay any more." Lilian had a sudden vision of herself as a piteous supplicant at the sorcerer's feet, wrapped in a ragged shawl. She straightened up and blinked fiercely. "Never mind, it's not your problem," she said. "We'll think of something." Students in the door rustled and dithered away from it, and something short and solid bulled its way into the room.

"Excuse me," it said. "Is Sorcerer Pim in here? Hello, Warren. Lilian."

"Hello, Teddy," Warren said. "How did the invocation go this morning?"

"Didn't bother," Teddy Whin said. "Not with you and Russell out and the pentarium still down. Vinca hasn't had at it yet, he's at a conference. Sorcerer Pim?" She stuck out her hand. "I'm Theodora Whin. The Academy sent me over to clear things up about Russell Cinea, but I just missed you in his room. Could I talk with you when you're done in here?"

"Are they taking Russell off the insurance too?" Lilian asked.

"They are," Teddy said, "and nobody can get into his bank account to pay the hospital. So I guess you're working for free, eh?" She grinned at the sorcerer.

"I'll be glad to talk with both of you after rounds," Pim said, "but I really don't set insurance policies."

"Yeah, but you're the one who's supposed to care what happens to these patients," Teddy said. "Can I stay in here and hear what they say Warren's got?" she asked Lilian. "I'm betting it's the same as Russell." Lilian nodded and the sorcerer held up the chart, which Mr. Tomko had given back to her.

215

"Whose case is this? Ms. Dilnijki?"

"The patient is a sixty-two-year-old Caucasian male, brought in with no apparent injuries yesterday at nine thirty-two in the morning, in company with another patient who had suffered injury due to demonic attack. This patient initially presented with normal vital signs but showed confusion and disorientation to surroundings. He persisted in chanting a charm until ten o'clock, when he suddenly stopped and appeared to be normally oriented to his surroundings. Neurological examination showed no gross abnormalities. Drug tests negative. No meds, no history of neurological or psychological problems except a brief episode of stress-related depression thirty-one years ago. Discharge was delayed until a cerebral scan could be performed. In the early afternoon the other patient was discovered to be clinically dead and necromantic investigation of this patient discovered that he also responded to necromancy. An aura scan with camera lucida last night showed no aura. The provisional diagnosis is loss of soul, cause unknown but presumed demonic, prognosis unknown."

Demonic! Lilian thought, and shuddered. She hated demons, always had. They were so-evil. Horrible, evil, hate-filled beings!

***

Clearing his mind with no breathing to focus on, no beads to run through his fingers with a mantra, no body to inventory from toes to crown, felt like balancing on a pinpoint. Warren could do it for only a split second before he toppled over into

216

something made up, either sensation or speculation. *There is no difference between the two, now,* he thought bitterly. The stutter in his concentration launched a familiar vision, the one where he hovered in his office, the door opened, and his body came in and turned on the lights. Warren snarled at the body, howled at it in silent rage. He made its head explode, and the satisfaction gave him the strength to concentrate for another few seconds, searching for something-anything real, anything from outside his own mind.

In the moments between illusions, he felt like something insubstantial-perhaps a wisp of air sliding across other layers of the atmosphere, whipping into one eddy and out of another faster than thought. Other times, it seemed he must be like a blind man, a deaf man, creeping through a new world with no way to tell what he had come upon but to touch it and see if it stung or burnt. Warren crept or slid or sailed through a world of emotion instead of sensation, trying to create a map of it as he had once mapped the netherworld.

In it there was a place, or a thing, or a person he liked best, and that was like looking at a woods in springtime, a kind of soft wonder. All around it there lay something like trumpets and knights in armor, an adventuring feeling that might come from just stepping away from the gentle. Then there were the feelings of looking at a sleeping cat, watching it turn over and stretch and longing to curl around it and become as soft and boneless; the solid, trusting feeling that was like drinking out of a spring that never stopped; the feeling of having built something sturdy... Warren catalogued them, but he could not tell if they were places or people or things; if they came to him or he to them. He pulled his attention inward again, but this time to devise experiments rather than look into his own imaginings.

Warren had spent years building maps of the netherworld, translating demons' own accounts of their realm into models. This was much the same. The arcane elements of his old world would appear in this new one. The ley-line, the pentarium, the magicians, and other things with arcane power. These would be his landmarks, and he had surely already met with them. He had only to identify which was which.

***

At the westernmost end of the ley-line, Rho fell out of a tree. He didn't fall far; he woke up in midair with a moment's feeling of flight, then a thud that jarred every bone in his back. The flock of ducks he'd been watching waddled down to the water in a flurry of quacking and splashing.

"What, what!" they said. "Watch out, get out of the way. Into the water right now, girls. Move along."

Rho lay still a minute, furious, and then sat up smeared with mud and dark green duckshit. He'd gotten it all on tape.

"This can't go on," Rho said aloud. And it didn't; when he went over to rewind it, the camera arcana was on the blink. He shook the thing, swore at it, and kicked the ground to emphasize his words, but none of these lower-level charms had any effect. "I will disassemble you with a blunt screwdriver,"

218

Rho said to the camera, glaring at it, but the red warning light continued to blink at him. He finally packed it up and took it to a shop just inside the city walls where a small bald man poked at its innards, clucked his tongue, and sold Rho six overpriced crystals.

"You need a higher power crystal for this kind of work," he told Rho. "We can recharge them for you here, if you don't charge your own." Having laid this groundwork, he then sold Rho a necklace in which to recharge the crystals by wearing them next to his skin, and six uncharged crystals to wear in it.

"I have to get a grant," Rho said to himself, fingering his empty wallet as he stepped out into the winter twilight. "This can't go on." He walked back to the Magic Building half asleep, and encountered Teddy Whin coming out the big double doors as he went in. She looked away from him.

"Regan wants to see you," was all she said, before brushing past in a hurry.

What have I done now? Rho thought. He'd had about enough of this week. Regan wouldn't criticise him with impunity. When he looked into the man's office, therefore, it was with an unfriendly glare.

"Whin said you wanted to see me."

"Oh, yes, I did," Anders Regan said, looking up with a worried expression. "I wanted to ask you to pick up Russell's section of Fundamentals of Magic. You're working off the same syllabus, so it won't mean an extra prep."

"It'll mean extra grading," Rho said. "I have to get my research program going. They don't give tenure for picking up extra courses."

Regan looked shocked. He obviously hadn't expected a junior faculty member to stand up for his rights.

"We'll hire you an assistant to cover the grading," he said. "But there's no way we can find a part-timer to lecture, not this late in the semester."

"Why not one of the maintenance staff?" Rho said. "They're all magicians, aren't they? Not that it matters, if Russell's class is anything like mine. Anybody can teach students with no talent."

"Look, I don't need an argument," Regan said. "I'm picking up Warren's job on top of my own. All I need is someone to teach Russell's class for two weeks till Jim gets back from the field. Is it yes or no?"

"Yes," Rho muttered, ashamed of himself but not sure why. "When does it meet?"

"Same days as yours, eight o'clock."

***

"I can't believe I let him talk me into that," Rho groaned. "Eight o'clock!" It meant getting up before dawn. No more breakfasts with Susan and Will, unless they waited for him... He didn't mention that to the demon. He had secrets from the faculty, from the administration, from the Congress, and now from the demon. Was this a triple or quadruple life? *But I'm only getting enough sleep for one.* Rho put his head down on his arms. He moaned again.

"How did he persuade you?" the demon asked. "Threats?"

"Not exactly. They never really come out and threaten you. They just let you see that you're being

220

difficult, and then you start wondering how much better than anybody else's your work has to be to make it worthwhile for them to have someone difficult on staff." Rho lay still, fuming. "I wouldn't be difficult if they'd just get off my back! Everybody has something to complain about. I'm not clean enough for Hoth, I don't know enough math for Ukadnian, I can't draw as well as Neil, I don't pick up double loads with a smile like Regan. And Whin probably thinks I'm sexist or something. She thinks everybody's sexist."

"Kalin approved of you."

"Only so long as he thought he could get me involved in his stupid union. He dropped me fast enough after I told him what I thought of that." This was quite unfair, since James Kalin had been in the field, but filling out the list was more satisfying than fairness. "The only one who was really decent to me was Oldham." Rho stopped at the name. "And he's lost his soul. I don't care what you say, you know something about that. You're not getting the time of day from me until you tell me what happened to him and how you're involved."

"Oldham?" the demon said, knitting its brow. "I'm afraid I never met the man. I took no notice of this little Academy, until you. What is a talent like yours doing buried in this obscure country? Tell me about the attractions of the department. I hear Magister Hoth is quite busy. The little incubi absolutely tremble at her name."

"I don't want to talk about her. I want to talk about Warren. It's been awfully convenient for you demons. You appear here, and all of a sudden

221

everything's shut down. What happens to someone who loses his soul, anyway?"

"There are a million ways to lose one's soul," the demon said, in tones of relish. "It is really of little interest to us. Human souls are much the same in and out of the body. Like shrimps with or without the shell." It ran a claw over the back of Rho's hand and he shivered. The *cauld grue* was leaving him, but it came back at inconvenient moments.

"You eat souls?"

"We taste them," the demon corrected him. "We savor them. We enjoy their company. We seek out those few with outstanding souls and protect them, lest the world destroy what is too noble for it. That is where the old stories about binding demons arose."

"But you hurt Ganeel."

The demon hissed. "He dared to command me!" it burst out, in a hot stinking puff of air. "Ten years he abused and toyed with me. For ten years I strove to please one whose only desire was to be acknowledged my superior, to see me grovel before him. That is what humans truly desire, when they meet one greater than themselves. They will not rest until they have broken it to their will. The magicians here are the same. They see your worth, and will not rest until they have made you into a tool for their use. Is that not what Hoth tried to do? To turn you into one of her assistants?"

"I said, I don't want to talk about her," Rho lied.

"Oh, are you grateful for her advice? Will you be happy to work in her laboratory, under her direction, and have her introduce you as part of her team? Hoth dreams of making every magician stronger than herself a slave to one of her organizations and alliances. But perhaps that is what you need, someone to direct and control you."

"I can take care of Hoth," Rho said, a little desperately, "But I can't do it tonight!" He yawned so hard that his eyes watered. "I have to sleep." The demon said nothing, but he could feel its disapproval. "I'm sorry," he said.

"Never mind," the demon said. "It seems I have overestimated you. I hardly relish your company, tonight."

"You said you wanted to be friends," Rho defended himself. "If you make friends with a mortal, you have to put up with his being mortal. We have to sleep."

"Not when you need something from me."

"You're right," Rho said, after a bit. "We spend all our time talking about my problems. How are things going for you?"

"I would hate to intrude on your self-pity." The demon sneered.

Rho felt a white, sharp shock of fury race through him, as if he'd been struck by lightning. The demon grinned and began a chuckle, leaning forward, but then the lightning feeling flashed across Rho's chest and stopped, exhaustion replaced it, and the demon's chuckle died away.

"I see you cannot deny it," it said, in a biting tone.

"I'm too tired," Rho said desperately. "Come back tomorrow and I'll get mad at you then. I just can't do this right now."

The demon stood up and gathered its wings around itself. "Perhaps Magister Hoth was right about you," it said. "Strange, you seemed like so much more of a magician, over in Selanto." It faded away into a shimmer of dust, and Rho fell forward onto his desk. He stayed awake just long enough to tell himself that he'd resent that remark, too, tomorrow.

Chapter Eleven

A language magician, Russell Cinea gained his power from words and ideas. That, Russell had always thought, was the best kind of magician to be-focused on one's work, rather than on the flighty and changeable outside world. How strange and surprising, then, that his mind now conjured up the outside world with ease but could remember so little of his work. He floated face-up and looked into an endless blue expanse sparkling with silver spray and dust motes. Insects, spiders, and even snails had traveled across the oceans on winds like this breeze that rocked him. *How marvelous the world is!* Closing his eyes, he basked.

Though he could have been at the islands with a thought, Russell had instead found a current that would take him slowly there. He felt the water warm around him as he moved from the deep blue channels into shallower, saltier slopes and lagoon waters. The wide sweep of the open ocean's lives changed around him as well, into more focused, detailed, intense little dartings and pokings; through some sixth sense Russell felt a hum of busyness, judgments and negotiations happening below him. He rolled over and opened his eyes onto a cityscape in miniature. The fleshy pastel apartment buildings of soft corals, filled with little worker creatures all reaching limber fingers out of their windows waved beneath him between sterner, more solid hard coral constructions of greenish-gray and yellow. All around them little fish went about their business, poking and prodding and hovering in display positions.

Russell felt ambivalent about all this. Part of him, charmed, wanted to sink down and watch the colorful world at its work. Another part of him felt it was too much like home to be a true vacation. Why, there was doubtless a fish academy somewhere down there, with fish wizards and magicians and sorcerers... Even as he thought this, a larger fish stopped beneath him, gaping, and four little ones began to go over its head and gills with a professional air. Russell watched this, and for the first time he began to put words around what he was seeing as he catalogued their clinical motions. He would tell Teddy about this. It was too funny to just look at, it had to be made into a story.

***

Hospital coffee stank, but Teddy Whin drank it, nonetheless. Life was hard enough without eschewing coffee. Visiting Russell was hard enough. It made her feel slow and sluggish visiting Russell, and that hurt worse afterward, when she had time to think about it and about how being with him used to perk her up. They used to play off each other, bouncing ideas higher and brighter with every word. There were things Russell used to say just to get her going, and things she used to say just to find out if he'd thought up a new way to disagree with her; it had all been fun, because they both knew how much they liked each other. Teddy had depended on the energy that came from being liked,

226

showing off and being admired for every trick she knew.

All that was gone now. He'd only been in the hospital two days; he looked the same, his voice was the same, he was nice and polite, but the spark had gone. Talking to Russell now was like performing for an audience that had gone to sleep or teaching a class of dullards. She tried to believe that the thing in the bed was still Russell, but it was more obvious every minute that she was talking to a corpse. That it wouldn't notice if she never came again. That Russell was, really and truly, dead.

Of course it was imagination, pitiful perhaps, but when she wasn't actually facing this corpse, Teddy made up stories about Russell coming back. Russell stepping out of his office as if nothing had happened, and while in a standard story she would be the only one to see him or everyone would suddenly realize nothing had happened after all, it had all been some kind of illusion. Teddy had no use for such hackneyed cliches. In her stories they all saw him and remembered that he had been dead a minute before. Russell would be brisk, in Teddy's stories. Matter-of-fact.

"Oh yes," he'd say, "but it was boring being dead. Not at all what it's cracked up to be."

That was where the story fell apart, because not even Teddy Whin could imagine that somebody would give up being dead to spend the rest of eternity at the Academy, just to make her happy. To be honest, honesty being one virtue Teddy bought into, she wasn't prepared to take on that responsibility. Some day she'd want to leave the Academy herself, and what would become of the

227

resurrected Russell then? It would be worse than having a dog, Teddy told herself, and then she cried again because it was so true that Russell was lost and she was more concerned about how it made her feel than about what might be happening to him. Was his lost soul hoping she'd do something to help him, or did he know her better than that? Was he floating beside her reading her mind, knowing after just a little while she'd stop missing him, stop wanting him, and he would simply be gone? These thoughts hit her at inconvenient times, making her clamp her jaw shut and look fiercely into the distance, and then everyone else looked away with odious sympathy.

It was better, on the whole, to come over to the hospital and deal with the real Russell, with the insurance hassles and the necromancer hassles and the funeral director and inheritance law hassles and the general confusion around disposing of a dead body that still sat up and talked and fussed about everything written in its appointment calendar. Nobody at the hospital had any sense, Teddy soon realized. Nobody had thought of just getting him a new appointment calendar, and taking away the one with classes and meetings written into it. Now Russell's calendar had his medications and tests in it, and he was a good patient. Teddy knew how to manage him, but that was not why she had been friends with Russell for fifteen years. She had never, ever, wanted to manage Russell. She glared into her coffee and stirred in another packet of sweetener.

"That won't help," a tired voice said, and Teddy saw Lilian Oldham standing by the table. She sat down, looking as if she hadn't slept in a week. "Nothing helps, everything makes it taste worse," she said. "I'm having Bosie bring me in a thermos from home."

"Are you staying here?"

"I feel as if I have to," Lilian said. "Warren signed one of those wretched organ donor cards, and though they say someone who's been dead three days isn't a donor unless he's been on life support, they've kept on feeding him, which I think counts. I don't want to be at home when they decide they need an emergency donor and some bright bean counter figures that out."

"Wow," Teddy said. "So you don't think he's dead?"

"Of course not," Lilian said. "That's just a technical definition. An insurance definition. Neither of them is dead."

"Russell is." It was the first time she'd said it aloud, and it felt like the ultimate in betrayal. *You don't even care whether he's dead or not. You just want to give up on him and go find someone new to admire you, and it's only been two days!* Stirring too hard, Teddy poked her coffee-stirrer through the side of the cup. "Crap," she said, and put her finger over the hole.

"No, they're just missing," Lilian said. "They'll come back."

She didn't try to pat hands or say anything kind, and Teddy appreciated that.

"Our job is to take care of their bodies so they have something to come back to."

"How are you managing the money?"

"I'm not. We'll be in debt forever. How are you?"

"We can't. He didn't have a will. It'll take months to figure out who gets his estate, and he certainly won't be one of them, so we can't spend the money on his postmortem treatment."

"No relatives?"

"No."

"Did he have funeral coverage?"

"Hey now!" Teddy said. "What does that cover? The Academy provides that, at least to demonologists, so Warren ought to have it too."

"You know, I never thought about it until just now," Lilian said, awed. "It's amazing how stupid you get when you don't have the person you're used to bouncing ideas off, isn't it?"

"Absolutely," Teddy Whin agreed.

***

Once Russell began putting what he saw into words-a familiar pleasure, one that ought to have increased his enjoyment of the wonders below him-he began to lose concentration. Parts of the reef became vague generalities, only coming into focus as he described them, and Russell began to feel displeased with himself. If his mind could conjure up all this, it ought to be able to look at what it had conjured up without missing the details, he should not have to choose between living and observing. Having identified this problem, he set himself to think it out of existence, but nothing happened.

Perhaps, Russell thought, *something in me has changed. Perhaps I no longer have the level of control I had before.* He made his body small and dense, sinking down toward the bottom, and followed a single fish as an invisible waver in the water, and while he concentrated on doing this the reef came back as bright and sharp as ever, but as soon as he began to describe the test to himself, taking mental notes, the fish in front of him began to fade out of reality.

Well damn, Russell thought, brooding on a sandy patch of the sea bottom. *This is irritating, to say the least.* But, if he was in a mood to describe things, he might as well enjoy it. The only problem was that things have to be described to someone, and Russell swam these seas alone; he thought a few minutes more before rising to the surface, where he stared at a nearby wave and concentrated. The wave thickened, solidified, and Teddy Whin appeared in it, doing a competent breast stroke. Having seen Teddy both naked and in her underwear, Russell could create an accurate picture of what she would look like in a bathing suit. He looked at the simulacrum as it paddled toward him, and sighed.

"But you're not real," he said dolefully.

"You can always find something to complain about, if you look hard enough," the faux Teddy said, treading water beside him. She looked down. "I see you've done some editorial revision elsewhere," she added. "Did you ever consider that my appearance is my own intellectual property? I don't appreciate being reconfigured into a swimsuit fantasy."

"That's what you look like," Russell protested. "You've marched around me in your underwear enough times!"

"Which I have a perfect right to do," Teddy retorted. "However, my breasts are at least two cup sizes smaller than this, and my waist three inches larger. I am not built like a supermodel, nor is any normal woman."

"Well, this is how I see you. You might as well keep it; none of this is real anyway."

"And you probably think it's a compliment," she sighed. "I can't even begin to list all the arbitrary value judgements implied, and that's if I leave out your epistemology. Since when do 'real' and 'unreal' exist in the spiritual realm? If they did exist, would that justify valuing the real over the unreal? On what grounds? Aren't you tacitly assuming that virtue inheres in conforming to whatever exists in the solid world, hence any deviation from constraints of the solid world in the spiritual world represents an unavoidable loss of 'reality' which releases you from moral and ideological obligations?"

"You're the one who's complaining about inaccuracy," Russell responded. "If nothing's real, nothing can be either false or true."

"I'm complaining about ideologically pernicious standards of physical perfection, as displayed in your representation of my appearance."

"Physical perfection has nothing to do with the case," Russell shot back. He flapped his feet in the warm water, and was content.

***

232

Rho stood outside the classroom and thought about coffee. He should, he supposed, have been thinking about the new students he had just lectured at for an hour. A dedicated teacher would have been trying to learn their names, or making note of the things about them he would have to ask Russell. This morning Rho was not a dedicated anything, except perhaps sluggard. He wavered, swaying forward into the packed hall and backward again until he banged into the lockers behind him, and wondered if he could possibly survive his eleven o'clock class, why Fundamentals of Magic had to meet four days a week instead of three, and whether he could just cancel it for the rest of the semester. Then he caught sight of Anders Regan at the other end of the hall and took to wondering how he could back out of teaching this early morning class or, failing that, kill Regan and destroy all records of the agreement.

Rho's eyes blinked half-shut and his whole world turned the mustard-yellow of the corridor, a loathsome color. The mass of students raced and chattered past him like a permanent structure, part of the architecture. Leaning his head against the cold metal, he began to lose himself in the flow and noise. It reached out to him, drew him forward, then hands reached out of the hurley burley to grasp his arms, his shirt front. They pressed against his chest and held him upright. He jumped and shook his head.

"You were falling into the freeway," Susan said. "Don't get trampled. It's so traumatic for them when they kill a professor."

233

Looking to his left, Rho found Will Harding's face once again too close for comfort.

Will smiled sweetly. "Coffee," he said, an incantation. "Cooofffeeee."

Rho straightened up. "Oh yes," he said, and Will laughed.

He and Susan broke a trail through the students, and Rho followed close on their heels. Susan looked back at him. "Tell me if it's none of my business," she said, "but what are you wearing around your neck?"

"Huh? Oh, I'm just charging crystals," Rho said. He fumbled with his robe and pulled the necklace out. The crystals were partly charged, each with an iridescent center and dull gray edges.

"Whoa, Nellie!" Susan exclaimed, and stopped dead. "What are you planning to run, the pentarium?"

Will forged a few steps ahead and then turned around.

"What?" he said crossly, and caught sight of the crystals. He whistled. "Bigger than mine," he said, and grinned. "If you're carrying around that much hardware, you'll need more than coffee. Durrell's?"

"Not unless you can buy," Rho said. "I spent all my cash on this hardware." He tucked the necklace back down his shirt, pleased to be invited two mornings in a row. They pushed through the double doors that separated Magic's classroom wing from the research labs, and quiet fell onto him like a blanket. All three stood up straighter, using more space.

"Just let me pick my keys up in the lab," Susan said. "I'll take you by the bank if you want to get some cash. But first tell me what you're using those crystals for. They're industrial size!"

"The camera arcana," Rho said. "The video one."

"No way! That thing uses itty bitty chips."

"They burned out when I was filming incubi in ducks."

"This I doubt," Susan said. "Can I have a look at it? I'm good with cameras."

"If you get her started fixing something, we'll never eat," Will protested. "Make an appointment, and don't bring the thing to breakfast. She'll try to take it apart while she's driving."

***

The sunny air hit Rho. It felt thick, full of damp smells. "It's spring!" Susan said. "What's that bird saying? Or do people ask you that all the time?"

"No," Rho said.

"I can't believe it," she said. "What a commentary on human self-absorbtion. So what's the bird singing?"

"The same thing you hear in any bar at about ten p.m.," Will said. "Right?"

"Pretty much," Rho said. "It's saying... " He cocked his head and listened. "C'mon, baby, here I am, you know you want it bad, my branch is highest, my song's loudest. Oh, baby, c'mon, you know you want it bad."

Will hooted, and even Susan burst out laughing.

"I don't know why I think that's cute," she said. "I'd pulverize any human who said any of those things to me."

"We have pretensions," Will said, leading them onto the tree-lined path. "Supposed to be able to think of something else. Like publication, or tenure. Maybe we'd be better off as birds."

"It'll only be saying that for about a month," Rho said. "Then all they talk about is their homes and kids. Then they do it all over for a second brood-they do in Kasidora. The season might be shorter here. Then they get travel happy, and then they go. It's like they have no real personalities at all, migrating birds."

"What is a personality, anyway? It comes from the soul, right?"

"Well-" Rho said, ready to be interrupted, but both of his companions looked at him with attention. "I think it's the things you do because they're natural to you, rather than to the circumstances you're in."

"The stuff you do whether it makes sense or not," Will said.

"Yeah, sort of."

"That would explain why people do so much stupid crap," Will said, nodding. "But vampires don't have souls, and they're as stupid as anybody. They all have these poses."

"Maybe they need poses because they don't have souls. People with souls generate our own stupidities, without having to memorize a set of them or depend on hormones-right? Isn't that what you meant? So if you never did anything stupid, would you have a personality?" Susan asked, opening the car doors.

"I bet you wouldn't!" Will said. "Don't you think that's what happened to Warren and Russell?

236

They always did the right thing, and one day they just woke up and found they weren't there anymore. I bet it happens to a hell of a lot more people than we know about."

"What happens to a soul once it's out of the body?" Rho asked.

"They say it has to interact with the demons on their terms," Will replied. "On their turf. What exactly that means... " He shrugged. "For that matter, they say Russell's the best magician on the continent. He ought to be able to take care of himself. And Warren's supposed to be friendly with them, for what that's worth. It'd be a different story if Linus or Patsy were out, hey?"

"It's not a joke," Susan said to the ignition.

***

Grayson, of Grayson & Sons Funerary Directors, stood six feet four in his socks. He was not a man who stood around hospitals in his socks, but Teddy Whin had checked his shoes and made an estimate. Grayson stood before Lilian, immaculate in charcoal gray and a dazzling white shirtfront, and bowed his sympathetic head. He had the thickest, blackest hair Teddy had ever seen, and she wondered if he dyed it.

"Allow me to express my sympathy for your loss," Grayson said. He cut his eyes at Teddy for a fraction of a second, wondering no doubt how she fit into this, but she said nothing to enlighten him. Lilian at least had the right to dispose of the dead man in her care; they would start this experiment with the simplest case.

"Don't bother," Lilian said. "Let me introduce you to the deceased."

"Ah, of course," Grayson said, straightening up.

Lilian led him into Warren's room, where Warren was sitting up in bed doing a crossword puzzle.

"Good morning," Warren said cheerfully. Grayson looked at Teddy again, but she said nothing.

"Good morning," Grayson said. He looked down at Lilian and from his vantage point must have seen nothing except white curls, which couldn't have helped.

"This is my husband, Warren Oldham," Lilian said. "That is the name you have on the insurance, right?"

"Yes! Yes, but-"

"And you have the official certificate of death, from the hospital, and the Release of Human Remains form."

"Is he-" Grayson stopped, looking at the ray of sunlight that lay across Warren's hospital bed. It made little white hairs sparkle on Warren's knuckles as he moved the pencil. "He's not undead," Grayson went on. "We have funerary protocols for the undead and the possessed, but the certificate didn't specify which of these conditions applied."

"They don't," Lilian said. "Neither of 'em. He's as alive as you or me, as you can see."

"Ah," Grayson said again. "Then I should not be here."

"The hospital won't release him to me," Lilian said. "Because he's dead, you see."

"If I remove him from hospital on the grounds that he is dead, I won't be legally able to release him to you either," Grayson said. "I'll be responsible for cremating him."

"Or storing the body under appropriate security until conditions allow its cremation. It says right here on page three of your flyer."

"We don't have appropriate security for a body of this type. You can't expect me to keep him in the freezer!"

"It says here that when you don't have appropriate facilities, the Royal Academy Hospital will provide them."

Grayson seemed to catch his balance. His look brightened. "Just what are you people trying to do?" he asked, with amusement in his voice.

"Make his insurance cover his treatment," Lilian said, relaxing. "The sorcerer says he has to stay here, but Salvation won't put it on his health insurance because he's been declared dead. What I need is for you to agree with the sorcerer that this is appropriate storage for a body in this condition. Unless you could say that staying at home is appropriate storage?"

"I don't think I could go that far," Grayson said, looking back at Warren. Warren scratched his head and yawned.

***

Fortified with sausage, a man could survive another encounter with the Royal Academy's student body. Rho taught his eleven o'clock well, enlivened by the boa constrictor one student had

239

brought in for a lark. The snake, like any bored pet, told Rho things about its owner which earned him points when he repeated them to the class and enhanced the prestige of natural philosophy. When he had seen the disgruntled snake owner and his classmates off, Rho brought the video camera down from his own rooms to the vampire lab, where Susan was working on delicate shreds of ectoplasm in a glove box.

"No, I'm glad to be interrupted," she said. "My hands are about frozen. If I keep on, I'll make some stupid mistakes. So how are you fitting the new crystals into this? See, the instructions call for the little chips. Let's have a look at the crystals that burned out, I bet they were much smaller."

Rho fished them out of the case, blackened. They were indeed smaller. "That's what you should have been using in a camera this size," Susan told him. "See, he had to readjust the crystal pack to take the large ones. What did he think you were using it for?"

"What would it need bigger crystals for?"

"Dealing with larger spirits," she said. "You use little crystals for incubi and ghosts. The major demons give off too much power for small crystals. When Teddy took the division's camera over to the hospital, to see if a demon had possessed Russell, she used the adapter for larger crystals than this. I saw it on the sign-out sheet."

"Crap." Rho looked at the burned crystals. "I thought demons didn't manifest during the day."

"They don't, usually. They aren't supposed to like sunlight. Are you saying these burned out in daylight?"

240

"Yeah. It happened about two thirty. I was filming ducks."

"Some ducks! Show me." Susan got up.

"Now?"

"I mean show me the tape. I have a player right here."

The familiar pond appeared, with the ducks. Three of the drakes shone, the camera arcana picking up shifting iridescent auras. "How lovely," Susan said. "I never get over how pretty incubi are." She leaned her elbow on a knee and watched as the glowing drakes chased the others around the pond, onto dry land and back into the water.

"Those two are the ones that always have incubi," Rho said, pointing out the thinner drakes. "I'm going to band them and take blood samples for hormone levels. But we don't know whether the high hormone levels attract incubi or are caused by incubi."

"Mm," Susan said. Suddenly something flashed through the picture, top to bottom, and the screen went a poisonous green and turned to static. "What was that?" she exclaimed, and rewound.

Rho saw himself falling out of the tree, asleep, in slow motion. He saw his body jerk awake and twist a little, land flat on its back with a bump, and then the screen went green again.

"It wasn't the ducks that burnt out the camera," Susan said. "It was you. What were you doing?"

"You saw," Rho muttered. "I fell out of the tree."

"Does that happen every time you fall?"

"I've no idea."

241

"Well, let's find out. We can use one of my ghost monitors." Crossing the room, Susan pulled a case out of the cabinets below the arrow-slit windows. "Rewind the tape, and we'll use it to calibrate the meter," she said, and came back with a handful of equipment.

Rho saw a small black object like a wristwatch and a meter the size of a transistor radio in a leather carrying case.

Susan plugged the meter into the video player's audio jack. "Look at that," she said as the tape ran again. "It goes off scale when you hit the ground." Replaying the scene again and again, she adjusted the meter until the needle just stayed on scale.

"What would cause that?" Rho wondered, looking at himself on screen. "Maybe contact with the ley-line, or adrenaline. It could have been the incubi and not me. I almost fell on that drake."

"I think it's you. You have to have some kind of extra power, to be charging up those crystals. If I wore that many, they'd drain me." Susan grunted in satisfaction, and brought the wristwatch over to the meter. She pushed minuscule buttons on its side and grunted again. "Here's how it works," she told Rho. "You wear the remote, and the receiver will keep a timed record of your power flux for up to two days. Then we feed it into the computer. You have to keep an activity diary as well. Instead of marking down what time it is when you do things, use the time marker that's showing on the remote. Or you can press the record button here, and speak into the receiver."

"Do I have to wear the receiver as well?"

"No. Traces this strong should go through the wards; it ought to work even if they're not in the same room."

Rho wasn't sure he liked this plan. He pictured himself pulling a pad out and checking his wrist. Demon appears, t=900, he would write. Or push a button and speak into the device on his belt. 'Discussing colleagues with demon, ten p.m.' "Can you teach me how to run the computer program?" he asked. The only way he'd do this was if he could edit the record before Susan saw it. He played with Susan's computer and borrowed a copy of the program to install on his own. It wasn't precisely legal, and that made him feel better about perhaps lying to her. He considered putting the monitor in a bottom drawer and forgetting all about it; in fact, he did put it in a bottom drawer, but as dusk came on, he found himself digging it out and strapping the remote onto his wrist. It was just curiosity, he told himself.

***

The most solid thing in Warren's world was the sleeping cat feeling. A combination of longing, envy, and total relaxation, it overcame him whenever he stumbled upon it. Warren gave his imagination full rein to interpret this feeling, and found himself in a wasteland of tumbled rock and brush, climbing upwards at an uncomfortable incline. His feet were bare, he realized as a sharp rock turned under one heel, and then he knew where he was and what that longing for simple, unjustified existence led him to. This was the ley-line.

Of all the experts in Osyth, only magicians walked the ley-line. The traditional walk began at the river, thirty miles west and half a mile below the Osyth Plateau. A soft grassy path had been worn into the meadows by other creatures' feet that walked during the night. The river's shallow riffles concealed creatures more sullen than crayfish, shyer than darters. None of them needed a reason to exist. They were enough in themselves.

Warren had spent his early life among people who thought they were enough in themselves, or pretended to think so. He had seen them staggering out of nightclubs in the early morning. They had welcomed him into cheap hotel rooms. He had spent summer afternoons with them, sitting on old car parts in greasy backyards as semiprofessionals bilked each other at poker.

The little boy had sat, impassive, watching nothing in particular under the trees. He's a deep one, they had said, he's planning something, and he had been. He had been planning a more worthwhile life, one justified by something more than body temperature and rationalization. A life like his father's, mysterious but publicized, validated by scout badges, honor rolls, dean's lists, certificates of participation, awards, degrees, credentials, buildings erected-and, maybe, the love of a good woman with high standards.

Not until Warren had all these things to his credit had he been able to relax and look at himself. In his early thirties Warren had found himself unable to ignore, any longer, the person he had been before that little boy laid those plans. He had looked at the creatures around him, the ones for whom sitting in the sun was its own reward, with an envy and longing that could no longer be denied; he had given up his appointment in wizardry, left buildings unfinished and contracts unwritten, and walked the ley-line, making peace with the arcana who set their own worth. When he climbed up the last fifty feet of jumbled rock onto the plateau, dirty and bruised, he had not been able to tell which of the people who faced him were mere humans and which were magical. He had felt the ley-line itself stepping forward to wrap its arms around him, to accept him and welcome him into the list of the worthwhile. His mother, vivid as an army with trumpets. Lilian, gentle and wonderful like the dawn through new leaves. Russell, like a spring bubbling up in sunlight.

They were all here, Warren realized with a start. Here, now, in this void where he had been trapped, or trapped himself, and which must be a completely different place to every person in it. They were here, and he had already met them.

Chapter Twelve

Thursday morning after his eight o'clock class Rho had time to work, to get outside and study the late-morning birds, but instead he was inside plugging the ghost monitor into his computer and grumbling to himself. Rho told himself about a mythical earlier time when he hadn't had to worry so much about what he was or did. A time when he simply did whatever it took to get through the night alive, and forgot about it when morning came instead of graphing and reviewing it. The computer whirred and clicked, and a set of graph coordinates appeared on its screen, with the time across the bottom, and the power along the left side. The monitor's trace, a green line, scrolled across it.

Nothing but a straight, flat, dull line. For a half-hour of the graph's time, nothing. Then the time marker and peaks began to appear on the graph. Rho's life, a featureless plateau, gained variety when the demon appeared. Up and down the line darted, but it always dropped back to the plateau. Rho looked at it with confusion and reeled it back. Up, down. Plateau. Up and down again. Up, wavering high for a long time, down. What had happened with this rhythm so early in the evening? Up and down, over and over again for half an hour, then the line sloped up and up to a higher plateau, one with lumps and bumps and jiggles in it, and Rho suddenly knew what that looked like. He scrolled back, looking at that disgusting trace, and it seemed to him that anybody who got a glimpse of it would read it instantly. *I don't have any power of my own,* he thought. *I just steal the demon's. Everybody thinks I have enough talent for this job, but it's a fraud.* He erased the file, all of it. "Nothing yet," was all he said to Susan, when he saw her in the halls, and he was too busy to go to breakfast.

Rho kept himself too busy to talk with any of his colleagues. He got his jacket cleaned and went down to the Department of Public Health, copying their files of incubi into a database of his own for future reference. He trapped ducks and drew blood, took it over to sorcery and had their lab analyze it for seventeen different components; he collected feathers, as well, and banded their irate owners, and learned six new swear words in duck, and he recharged the large crystals completely, stored them in a lab cabinet and laid aside the necklace he had worn them in.

This isn't so bad, Rho told himself. *I could never have done all this on my own.* But he didn't feel glad in the evening, when time came near for the demon to appear in his lab. He sat in the last glow of sunset, looking out the window, and his mind turned to the things a man with a demon could never do. He thought about bars and nightclubs, or just walking along the ley-line in the dark. He thought about having someone human in his rooms at night. He thought about getting a cat, and about a peaceful full night's sleep.

"I see you are in better spirits," the demon said.

Rho only snarled, which seemed to amuse it. Before it could say so, though, someone knocked at the door.

"Yeah?" Rho yelled, in unfriendly tones.

247

"It's Susan," a voice answered. "I need to borrow my ghostmeter back."

"All right," Rho said. He opened the door just a slit, passing the little square case back to her with a mixture of disgust and relief. He didn't invite her in.

"Who was that?" the demon asked, as soon as the door closed on Susan's retreating back. "A new romance?" It had dematerialized when Susan knocked, and Rho had hoped himself rid of it.

"Someone from the department," he said. "Borrowing equipment. Nobody important."

"Oh," the demon said. "They are polite enough when they want something from you, are they not?"

"She's not like that," Rho said fiercely. "She's always nice."

"Nobody is always nice. If she sees profit in it, she will turn against you in a moment." The demon's voice was low and its movements gentle as it settled itself in a crouching position beside Rho's fireplace. "You can never let your guard down," it said. "Any person who says you can has plans for you."

"And you don't."

"I thought I had made my plans very clear," the demon said.

***

"Of course I can, dear," Bosie said. Her voice chirped, and Lilian suppressed a groan of dismay. Staying home at nights bored Bosie, and she spent the time drinking whatever Lilian had left in the house. By now, she might well have progressed to vanilla extract and floor polish.

248

"I'll see you at eleven, then," she said into the phone, rubbing her eyes. "Goodbye, now." She hung up in the middle of whatever Bosie said in return.

Lilian leaned forward over the flimsy hospital table and put her head in her hands. Finances, housework, children, her job, the department, Bosie, all chased each other through her mind in an unstopping circus of worry. She sat up like an old drugged woman and glared at Warren, who was doing his endless crosswords. "You don't even care," she said bitterly to him. He looked up and gave her that inane childish smile.

"I'm sorry," he said, "Was I supposed to be caring about something?" He looked to his left-he actually looked for that damned hospital chart, with the time of his next medication on it!

"About me!" Lilian said, through gritted teeth. "You're supposed to be caring about me!" She knew what Teddy Whin would do. She'd snatch that clipboard away from Warren and write 'Care about Lilian!' on it in big red letters. That's what Teddy had told her to do. Don't put yourself through this, Teddy had said. Tell him what you want-but Teddy hadn't written anything like that on Russell's chart, Lilian noticed. For all that she visited him twice a day, and sat in there making innocuous small talk, which Warren had never described as a characteristic of Teddy Whin. Now Lilian's mind was whirling around Teddy and from Teddy to all the other members of the Demonology Department, persons she did not ordinarily give a rat's ass about, even that dirty little man Warren had brought home just before he...

249

Lilian sat up straight, thinking. She looked at Warren again and he smiled at her. "Whatever happened to your grimoire?" she said. "The charms of essence?"

"Oh, I think Rho must still have those," Warren said carelessly and went back to his puzzle.

"What could happen to a magician if somebody-did something-to his grimoire?"

"It's just a book," Warren said.

"But it had your essence in it."

"No, it just had the kind of spells my essence can cast."

"Warren! You used to tell me grimoires were dangerous! And then you just handed it over to Rho as if it didn't matter! What the hell was going on?"

"Goodness, I've no idea," Warren said, looking up at his wife with bland approval.

"I'm getting a coffee," Lilian said. "If the sorcerer comes in, I want you to call me on the cell phone. Got that?" She reached across his bed and wrote it on the chart, across an order for some kind of scan or other.

"Yes, dear," Warren said.

Lilian headed out into the hall as if she were running on steam, charged up with enough energy to take off and fly herself over to the Demonology Department right then and there, in one great leap.

***

Susan Teale leaned back against the lab wall and sighed. A single calm star looked in through the arrowslit, criticising her. *If I had a life of my own,* she thought, *I wouldn't waste time worrying about*

250

my colleagues. Who really weren't hers to worry over. They had passed the age when Mom could tell them to stand up straight or brush their teeth, wash their robes or not lose their souls or stop listening to vampires... *But he was coming along so well,* she said to herself in excuse. *He was starting to come out of his shell, and go to breakfast and talk with people, and now it's all back to the way he was a week ago. Ever since I loaned him that ghostmeter.*

She looked at the meter in its case and the blank computer screen next to it and thought that a real mystery-solving academic, the kind in those murder mysteries, would hack into the file Rho had erased and find out what was bothering him.

I'm not one of those academics, though, Susan thought, and then stood up with a start. The meter's needle was moving. It was reading something, something strong enough to pass through the warded walls of the building. *Nonsense,* Susan told herself. *It's just picking up traces here in the lab.* But the little remote monitor was nowhere in the black case. Susan looked at the meter for a minute, and set the computer to record.

The trace jumped up and down like nothing she had ever seen before. Sometimes it went up for five or six minutes, then down again even faster than it had risen; sometimes up and across the screen in a flat line, but always down again to levels lower than she had expected from someone with Rho's credentials. Susan pushed a button and the computer screen divided into three ranges, blocks of color showing the mundane, arcane and demonic ranges. She normally used the monitor for ghosts, weak arcana, so that range filled most of the screen; even with this distorted view, Rho's trace was definitely falling down into the mundane range and then rising back up through the full arcane range, offscreen into the demonic. She scrolled upwards and whistled to herself as she followed the trace up and up to the levels of power possessed by only a major demon.

"This isn't good," Susan said, sitting back and drumming her fingers on the keyboard. She reached for the telephone.

"Campus security, please," she said to the operator. "I think we have a demon loose in the Magic Building."

***

"You are losing your edge," the demon said. It was smoking. Not a cigar or cigarette, just smoking, curls of blue smoke with the smell of burning plastic seeped out of its slit-shaped nostrils. Every few minutes the demon closed its nostrils tight and inflated its barrel, with what looked like a sigh of contentment, and then let out larger, paler puffs of smoke. "All this talk about ducks! You do not really care about birds."

"Birds are what I do really care about," Rho said. "What I've always cared about."

"No, there is nothing in you when you talk about birds. No fire. No passion. What you really care about is professionalism," the demon said. "You are meant to show this Academy what a real magician is like. To stop them from peddling their cheap imitation to the few students with real talent."

252

"I'm doing my own work," Rho said. "The way they run the Academy isn't my problem, as long as they let me do my own work."

"When they needed someone to pick up another course, who did they choose? The natural philosopher, of course. The little man who talks to ducks."

It puffed for a while while Rho mulled this over.

"They are laying up complaints against you. Wait and see; every time you stand up for what you believe in, it will be one more nail in your coffin. But what they truly hate you for is your power, your standing head and shoulders above them. Everybody is jealous," the demon whispered, leaning against Rho's shoulder. Its smoky breath tickled his ear. "The less real work they do themselves, the more they resent a person who is working. The less power they have themselves, the more they resent a person who has power. They will try to stop your work, lest it serve as a reproach to them."

It is true, Rho thought with resignation. *It all fits into place.* That was how people always treated each other, and it was a damned shame. But if he accepted it, he could file all these puzzling, confusing interactions into a working model, stop looking for anything better, and just get on with his life. People tried to fool and confuse him, and when he mentally listed his acquaintances he preferred the malignant ones to the friendly. Patsy Hoth and Ukadnian had made their positions clear. The others-if the others couldn't state their intentions in

253

plain language, they couldn't expect him to take a chance on them.

If he once decided on what people were up to, he could set it aside as finished business. He wouldn't be able to ignore them entirely, no more than he could ignore an enemy in the next alley, but he wouldn't have to care about them or wonder whether they were right and he was wrong. He would never have to look at his life through their eyes. The enemy's spitting and snarling didn't mean anything; of course the enemy criticized him, simply because they were enemies. Rho sighed. It would be so much easier... still. He sighed.

"I had this idea things would be different, once I was faculty," he said.

"No, the world is the same everywhere," the demon said. "You have one or two friends who take pains to please you, and you have many enemies who take pains to hurt you. That is all there is; what else did you think there could be? The only answer is to fight them off. Accept no abuse. Show them you are nobody to be trifled with."

At this inspiring moment, someone knocked at the door to Rho's lab. He sat up with a jerk.

"Another colleague, borrowing equipment?" the demon asked.

"Hshh!" Rho said. The knock came again, an imperious rapping. "I'd better get that. Coming!" He stood up, bundling his magician's robe around himself. When he got to the door and looked back, the demon was still sitting beside the fireplace. "Hsst!" he said to it, gesturing vaguely. "Get out of sight!"

"Oh?" the demon said, raising its eyebrows. "In here?" It pointed toward the door to his bedroom, and Rho rolled his eyes. Grinning, the demon sauntered through the door.

Another rap came on the wood near Rho's ear, a decidedly ill-tempered banging, and he opened the door.

He couldn't identify the person in the shadowed tower stairwell. "Hello?"

"Hello, Magister Rho? I'm Lilian Oldham."

"Oh, yes," Rho said. "Of course. What can I do for you?"

"I'm sorry to bother you," Lilian said. "Did I wake you up?"

"No, no. I-I was still up." A pause, and Rho realized she expected him to let her in. "I, uh, can't invite you in right now," he said. "I was in the middle of something touchy."

At this the demon gave an amused whoosh, and smoke began to spread into the lab through the bedroom door. Lilian looked at it with a concerned face.

"I think it may be boiling over," she said. "Or on fire."

"No, it does that," Rho said, not looking at the smoke, "but I can't leave it for very long."

"I just wanted to get Warren's grimoire back, to see if anything in it can help us."

"Oh," Rho said. The smoke stopped and silence replaced the whooshing from his bedroom. "All right, just wait here." His bed was empty. He felt a moment's relief, until he reached for the grimoire on the bedside table and his hand touched something hot and solid. The demon was crouched before the table, holding the book. "Give it here!" he said, under his breath. "It's not mine."

"Oldham's!" the demon said, just as softly. "Oldham's grimoire! Do you know how many would sell their souls for a look into this book? This is your greatest asset, and you would give it away to a housewife!"

Rho laid his hands on the book where it stuck out from beneath the demon's arm. "It's not mine, and nothing in it works anyway."

"It will after you trap his soul in it," the demon said.

Rho stopped pulling.

"What?" a voice echoed from behind him. "What's going on? Is there a problem?"

The demon folded both arms over the grimoire and grinned at Rho, showing all its fangs, and he turned away. Lilian was wavering in the doorway. He leapt over to it and stretched an arm across her path.

"You can't come in here, it's not safe. And I don't have the book, anyway. I just remembered, I gave it back to him on Monday morning. He wanted to use one of his charms to check the pentarium."

"Well, why didn't you remember that when I asked you?"

"Because I've been up for four days, and I'm in the middle of a delicate procedure," Rho said. "Are you calling me a liar?"

"N-no," Lilian said, in a very doubtful tone. "I'm sorry. It's just that this has been a dreadful week. I shouldn't have troubled you this late at night."

256

"Don't mention it," Rho said, ushering her back out. "Walking around this building at night isn't really safe, though. Would you like me to see you out? You could get into Warren's office in the morning and look for the grimoire. I'm sure it's in there someplace."

"Oh, no," Lilian said, looking back at the bedroom door. "I think your potion is boiling over again. You'd better get back to it."

***

Warren had been relaxing in the springtime forest feeling. As long as this lasted, beautiful and untouched, Lilian was safe, he told himself, but the gentle feeling he enjoyed changed even as he thought about it, as if his springtime forest now contained a dragon. It felt more solid, more like something outside Warren himself.

As he wondered about this change, something like a storm came over Warren. A feeling he did not like, as if he had given his reputation into someone else's keeping or bought something he could not afford-a feeling of retribution around the corner-went around and around in him, like a whirlwind, blowing hot and cold at once, passing weather and edging into disaster, sirocco, ghost wind, the screaming air that rips flesh from bones, and as suddenly as it had started, it paused, as if it had seen him, as if great golden eyes pressed their gaze down on him until it saw through all his pitiful ambitions and burned his worth away. Warren had nothing to scream or run with, but he would have jerked himself out of his resting place, he would have

257

spread himself out into nothing at all to escape-as quickly as it had come, the feeling ebbed away and he was left in what might have been the quiet place of moments ago, but it felt burned and tired to him now. It felt helpless.

She needs me, Warren thought, and pure guilt overwhelmed him. Here he had lain, luxuriating in being able to recognize his wife, while in the mundane world she had to cope with his loss. She had to be dealing with whatever his body was up to, whatever problems he had left behind. *Knowing where I am isn't enough,* thought Warren. *It's nothing! I have to know how to get back!*

***

Rho shut the door and leaned his back against it. A stream of perfect smoke rings was drifting out of his bedroom into the lab. When he went back in the demon was sitting on the bed, reading Oldham's grimoire by the light of its own eyes.

"Do you have the other ones? The charms of intent and charms of discourse?"

"No," Rho said. "I was looking at this one first."

"First! He gave you a chance at them all, and you took only one?"

"I was only interested in charms of essence."

"Why?"

"I thought his essence might be enough like mine that I could make some of them work."

"You had this and were too ignorant to use it," the demon said. "Did you never learn that to steal a man's grimoire is the first step to stealing his soul?"

258

It laughed at Rho's face. "So there is something that even the clever students in Kasidora have not ferreted out of their masters' libraries. You could have owned Oldham for your slave, if you had known how to call on the grimoire. Now his soul has gone flitting, and you will have to catch it."

"What are you talking about?"

"Trap the man's soul in his own book, and he will cast the charms for you as often as you command." The demon leaned forward, its eyes gleaming at Rho over the book. "Now will you believe I mean you well? I am telling you the secret my master sacrificed his own children to perfect. All you need do is find Oldham's soul, and nothing can stand against you."

"I wouldn't do anything like that," Rho said. "He's the one who was halfway decent to me."

The demon looked at him as if it could not imagine such a foolish statement. "Are you not aware those are the dangerous ones?" it asked. "The ones who seem so sensible, so reasonable. Oldham has probably half-convinced you to become a good little suburbanite." Its tone dripped sarcasm. "How many magicians do you think he has destroyed with his decency? Nobody worth noticing has survived Oldham's rule in this Academy. But if that is what you prefer," it shrugged, "there is nothing forcing you to become a magician. You have the perfect appointment, if your true desire is to abandon magic and become a good citizen. If you bought a decent suit, Hoth would take you on and teach you how to behave."

"I'll be a magician on my own," Rho said. "Not by using someone else's power."

"Of course," the demon said, and went back to reading the grimoire.

Rho felt himself flush. He had just opened his mouth to answer when another knock came at his door.

"Rho!" Susan's voice called. "I know you're in there. Campus security is clearing the building, there's a demon around."

"Let her in," the demon chuckled, looking up from the charm for trapping souls. "We'll need blood."

"All right, just a minute," Rho called, glaring at it. The demon sighed and stretched out one of its taloned hands, spreading the claws wide.

"Whether you let her in or not, we'll need blood," it said casually.

Susan knocked again.

"Campus security," a deeper voice. said "The Magic Building is being evacuated. I'd appreciate it if you open the door, sir."

"I'm in the middle of something!" Rho shouted. He made flapping motions at the demon. "Get out," he whispered. "Do you want all Osyth trying to exorcise you?"

"All Osyth means nothing to me," the demon said, grinning. "But your being in jail would be inconvenient, I suppose." It began to fade out of sight and Rho grabbed at the grimoire, too late. His hands went through the book's covers; the demon grinned at him again, and it was gone.

260

Chapter Thirteen

Gossip! Neil Torecki loved gossip, all the more because, as a new guy, he caught only the few bits of it people let fall before they realized he was listening. Overheard snatches of conversation between two security guards walking away from him, snatches he hadn't even dreamed were about his building until it was too late to ask for more detail. One or two words between Will and Susan, both of them looking washed-out and betrayed as they went into their lab, words about Rho and last night. Neil jumped with excitement inside, for he was the only one, he felt sure, who knew Susan and Will were lovers. He had watched long hours before drawing that conclusion, and had shared it with nobody. But Susan working alone in the building all night; Rho, living alone in the building all night; oh, he'd seen it coming. He pretended to feel sorry for Will, but only for a second.

Then Lilian Oldham, looking like death warmed over. Was it true she'd handed Warren over to an undertaker while he was still alive? Just a few words between her and Teddy Whin, about someone named Grayson-and going by Neil's phone book, Grayson meant either funerals or agricultural machinery. Or, if it were spelled with an 'e,' office supplies. And when he popped out after consulting the phone book, Lilian again, coming out of Regan's office, and the word 'grimoire' floating down the hall. Hadn't Rho been trying to build up his grimoire? Oh, Rho was at the center of this somehow. Rho and the grimoire, Rho and Lilian, Rho and Susan in the building at midnight with a demon.

"Damn," Neil Torecki said, admiringly. He'd underestimated Rho, just because the man couldn't draw. He shut himself in his office and lit some incense, doodling with his eyes closed, because that was how he got the best scryings, but when he saw what he had doodled, Neil blushed. *You have a dirty mind,* he said to himself, tore the paper off his pad, and burned it.

***

"You don't accuse someone of black magic unless you're ready to prove it," Teddy Whin said. She leaned forward over her desk toward Lilian.

The top of Teddy's desk was covered with runes, spirals, geometric shapes, some of them deeply scored into the wood. Every paper on the desk had its border of delicate scrolls. Lilian looked at Teddy Whin's hands and saw bitten nails, ragged knuckles, and a pen dented with toothmarks. The edges of all these indentations glinted under Teddy's desk lamp, but the rest of the room lay in semidarkness in the dim February morning.

"He had something in his bedroom that blew smoke rings," Lilian said.

Teddy grinned. "Who hasn't?"

"He told me it was an experiment."

"To repeat, who hasn't?"

"He wouldn't give me back Warren's grimoire! He said he gave it back to Warren on Monday, but it isn't anywhere in Warren's office."

Teddy stopped smiling. "What was Warren doing, lending someone his grimoire?" she asked sharply. "Would this be before or after he lost his soul?"

"Who knows? He loaned it out on Friday evening, and his soul was gone Monday morning."

"What was he like in between?"

Lilian frowned, thinking. "He was relaxed," she said. "He sat around talking to Bosie. We played bridge on Saturday night-otherwise, he didn't do anything I can remember."

"Was that normal?"

"No, he usually has paperwork. I remember asking him if he had anything... and he showed me his day planner, with nothing in it."

"Mm-hm," Teddy Whin said. "It doesn't mean anything."

"It means his soul was gone, just after he loaned the grimoire to Rho!"

"It could have been gone before he loaned the grimoire to Rho," Teddy pointed out. "That would explain why he did such a damn fool thing in the first place. Or he could just have been fed up that weekend, taking a break." She picked at a hangnail, looking across the room.

Lilian looked at the shelves behind Teddy, trying to categorize what stood there. Books, of course, but they were almost hidden behind statuettes, pictures in frames, shells, and lumpy objects she couldn't identify.

"Still, it's odd," Teddy admitted. "Have they found the grimoire yet?"

"No."

"The thing is, you can't accuse Rho without proof. It's too serious. It's like saying somebody committed murder to say he stole Warren's soul using black magic. Though if you accept the existence of the soul, stealing one should really be equivalent to kidnapping. There's some kind of double standard here, isn't there? An assumption that the soul's real importance is to keep the body alive. You could question that, on several different levels."

"What?"

"Sorry. What I mean to say is, if you really think he might have done it, you ought to go to the police."

Lilian looked at the scored desktop. "I didn't think about it being like that," she said. "Warren's not dead-nobody's been acting as if this was as important as a murder case." Confusion began to blend into rage, as if something gray were being stirred around in her brain, turning red as it moved. "Nobody's been acting as if this matters at all!" she said. "They've been treating it like a disease, as if Warren caught it all on his own hook. Where have the police been?"

"They haven't thought it was a crime," Teddy said. "If somebody did it on purpose, it would be serious. Hell, if I thought someone did this to Russell, I'd have him hung. But if Rho did it with Warren's grimoire, why would it have happened to Russell at the same time?" She swirled her mug around, slopping coffee. "Nobody's taking this seriously except you and me," she said. "It's been five days, maybe longer if they lost their souls last week, and nobody has any idea what might happen to a disembodied soul in that time. We don't even talk about it, because it's so frightening. Isn't it time we stopped being good little girls and took matters into our own hands?"

***

Cham Ligalla listened to her voice mail while booting up the computer, sorting her paper mail, and pouring a cup of coffee. Throughout, she thought about the day's itinerary, the paper she was delivering in Selanto in a month, and whether the *Journal of Magic in Public Policy*, which she edited, should run a special issue on legal rights of the possessed. The phone rang, and Cham looked at the row of red lights along its base. Seeing her private line lit up, she picked up the receiver and skimmed her email.

"Cham Ligalla, Public Health," she answered, switching to the news window on her computer and scrolling through bulletin boards.

"Hi, Cham, this is Teddy," the voice from the other end said. "What else are you doing?"

"Email, coffee."

"Well, stop."

"What?" Cham continued to scroll.

"We need a reverse exorcism, for Russell and Warren."

"I know that," Cham said. When dealing with Theodora Whin, it was best to establish a few things straightaway. "I've already had a half-dozen messages about that."

"Oh! From who?"

265

Whom, Cham thought. She closed her newsreader and opened her daily planner. "The hospital, the insurance company, Grayson's funeral home, Anders Regan, Sorcerer Pim, Sorcerer Klimt."

"Then why haven't you done it?"

"There's no such thing as a reverse exorcism," Cham explained patiently. "What you're all talking about is an invocation. You know how to perform an invocation better than I do. You design them."

"Well, give us some information then. What happens to a soul you banish with exorcism?"

Cham looked back at the computer. Paying attention to a question like this could only make the answer worse. More real. "All the data we have are suspect," she said. "Supposed sightings by people having out-of-body experiences."

"And what do they supposedly sight?"

"Demons, or other forces of some kind, attacking the souls. You know all that's just symbolism. The witnesses are making up images to express what they feel. It's more your field than mine."

Teddy Whin was quiet for a minute. "I've read this eyewitness crap on the Internet," she said. "What I want to know is your professional evaluation."

"My professional evaluation is that you reap what you sow," Cham said. "Demons don't go after the out-of-body witnesses. Demons are creatures like the rest of us. They have motives. They attack people who've attacked them."

266

"Oh, I see," Teddy said. "What happens to someone's soul is their own fault. Not an issue for government intervention."

"Of course not." Cham closed the day planner and opened the paper she was writing on Possession and Place, for an upcoming Urban Planning Conference. "Losing one's soul is a private matter. Public Health has no say in what people do with their souls. The state can only intervene in what you do with other people's souls, which falls under black magic."

"But somebody stole Warren's and Russell's souls."

"Nobody has filed a complaint to that effect," Cham said. "It would be a police matter, if they had."

Teddy was silent for a moment. "You don't care at all, do you?" she said at last, and her tone was so downcast that Cham actually stopped editing the document.

"I do care," she said gently. "I just can't do anything about it. I've gone through all the similar cases I could find, but this just isn't a matter for exorcism. If you design an invocation, I'll drop everything else to help cast it. But I can't unilaterally involve the government. You know the Academy wouldn't let me, if I tried. They would never give Osyth City Government a say in regulating what you do in the department. You wouldn't support that yourself."

***

267

Teddy Whin put the telephone down with a snarl. "Is there anything more irritating than being told to figure something out for yourself?" she asked rhetorically. "If I wanted to figure things out for myself, I would hardly own this many books."

"Who was that?"

"Cham Ligalla," Teddy said, in tones that left no doubt of her opinion.

"I don't think I've ever met her."

"Don't lose sleep over it," Teddy said, and picked the phone up again. "I shouldn't have called her in the first place. When you get an exorcist involved, everyone gets hurt."

Warren said that, Lilian thought, *or something like that. He said exorcists hurt everyone they touched.* Just thinking about it gave her a lost feeling, as if the world were less real and more strange than she had ever imagined. *What would it be like to live knowing that your presence only brought pain?* Teddy hadn't dialed the phone; she was looking at Lilian with a concerned expression.

"Are you all right?"

Lilian felt herself filling up with tears. "I have to get Warren back," she said hotly. "He was always glad to see me." She looked at Teddy and felt that for just this moment they had cut through all the talk, that she was seeing a real person who was just as sad and afraid as herself.

"Yeah," was all Teddy said. She shook her head and punched phone buttons.

***

268

A tiny crab, jewel-colored in red and amber, squatted at Russell's fingertip. He moved the fingertip, adding another stripe of gold to its delicate leg. *This must be what it's like to be an alchemist,* he thought. "What do you think?"

"You've gone from experience to theory to experiment, as if this were a real world," the faux Teddy said. "Who are you trying to fool? What will building a crab tell you about a world you've already built?"

"If you want to get analytical, nothing in this world is going to tell me about anything except myself," Russell said. "I'd rather not think about that and just enjoy it."

"There are a lot of assumptions embedded in that statement," Teddy said. "Is the world within you intrinsically less enjoyable or worthwhile than the world outside? You could argue that we only privilege the outside world because failing to adapt to it can kill us, and that freedom from the need to make it first priority is every human's dream. If you chose to naturalize values to that extent, you could infer from the universality of that desire that the proper subject of human analysis is the world within oneself. As the patriarchy has always implicitly accepted, with its unceasing attempts to delegate life maintenance and other dealings with the outside world to lesser genders and races."

"What part of me do you represent?" Russell asked.

"The part that didn't ask to be on vacation. The part with things to do."

Russell lay still and thought about this answer. Shifting blades of light glanced through the pandanus leaves above him, making the little crab's colors sparkle and deepen as it moved in and out of shadow. The soft sounds of the ocean and the breeze filled his ears. Was there any part of him that didn't want exactly this?

***

"I guess that thaw's over," Will said. He stretched, groaning. "Shit on a brick, I froze last night! What's this about a demon chasing you home in the wee hours?"

"I knew I should have stopped working nights." Susan hung up her coat. "I almost got myself killed for nothing but a stupid habit." The flat morning light made their lab look even neater and more antiseptic than usual, with its bare countertops and white walls. Susan and Will posted no mementos and kept any cartoons or clever sayings that amused them in scrapbooks. *It's funny what little things a relationship can start with,* Susan thought. As little as having the only two naked doors in the department.

"Sounds as if you might have saved Rho," Will said now.

"He didn't seem to think so," Susan said. "I'm sure those readings were coming from his lab, Will. The demon was in there with him. He said he returned the remote to me, but it wasn't in the ghostmeter case when I came back. It was in the stairwell."

"Could you have dropped it?"

"It was all the way down on the second-floor landing. When I got it back from Rho, I went up

270

from this floor to his lab, and then came back down here. Do you see me dropping a piece of equipment a whole flight further down and not noticing?"

"No," Will agreed, "but anyone who doesn't work with you might. That remote is tiny."

Susan drummed her pencil on the table. "He was up there with a demon, but he wouldn't tell me about it. What does that say to you?"

"It says he has one of his very own, doesn't it?" Will sat down and propped his feet on the desk, stretching back in his chair with a lazy grin. "A demon lover, how romantic. He's not going to tell you, is he? It's against the law over here. Life's so tough. He probably got an A in demon binding over in Kasidora, and now when he gets a job he can't even put it on his web page."

"What should I do?"

"Well, shit, what can he do about it? It's the same sort of crap Salvation put me through, when they got their tails in a knot about the undead. Only worse," Will said thoughtfully. "I could give up vampires if I had to, but you can't get rid of a demon you've enthralled. If he lets it go free, it'll come back some night and tear his balls off. Give the poor fucker a break, Sue. It's not like you're in charge of enforcing the rules." He sat up and shrugged. "You don't have any real evidence, anyway. The good thing is, if it's Rho's demon it won't be able to hurt anybody without his say so. We could have a lot worse things roaming around, after what happened Monday."

Susan looked at the desk. "If Warren finds out... " she said doubtfully.

271

"If Warren finds out, he'll fire the kid's ass out of here. Except Warren isn't exactly the demon lord, these days. Warren isn't high on my list." The telephone rang. "Demonology, vampire lab," Will answered. "Oh, hey! Teddy! How's the big guy?"

***

Though Warren lacked a body, he had a memory and the knowledge stored in it. Ignoring this had been a tremendous oversight, he realized now. How could he have been so intent on discovering where he was, and so forgetful of what he was? *Nobody knows more charms than I do,* he told himself. *Nobody is better able to link body and spirit. There must be a dozen such charms in my grimoire, even leaving aside charms of discourse.*

He reviewed them methodically. Charms for creating a familiar, either by blood sacrifice or enticement. Golem building. Invocations to nature spirits. Traps for nature spirits. Charms to make ghosts manifest themselves as ectoplasm. Old-fashioned venereal charms to invite possession by an incubus. Necromantic charms to recall the spirit into a dead body. Translations to switch spirits between bodies. Bindings to trap a spirit in an inanimate object. Everything from witchcraft to black magic was in the Oldham grimoires, those compilations of a family's knowledge. There was no dearth of charms, but as Warren went through them, he began to perceive a major obstacle. They all needed props. Quite reasonably, the Oldhams had only collected charms that could be cast by material beings, using material objects.

Reluctantly Warren laid aside the charms. Each of them required something more impossible for him to get, from blood to rats to mud to the grimoire itself. He brooded. *How does something spiritual perform magic, anyway?* The demons did it, endlessly, but only in their own realm. Alchemists cast charms without props or words, simply by the desires of their own hearts, but Warren knew he was no alchemist. He had tried hard enough in his youth. Alchemy was nothing that could be learned, it was working out of one's nature.

Relaxing from thought, Warren noticed he had the sleeping cat feeling and the springtime forest feeling at the same time. *Lilian must be near the ley-line,* he thought. He hoped she was safe at home, getting some rest.

***

"I'm forming an ad hoc committee to reincarnate Warren and Russell," Teddy Whin said, sitting on the white benchtop.

There were plenty of chairs in the vampire lab, Susan thought, but Teddy always had to be different.

"Nobody's doing anything about this," she went on. "I think it's up to us."

"Roger Klimt told me to keep my nose out of it," Susan said.

"He hasn't done anything himself," Teddy said.

Lilian Oldham nodded. "He really hasn't," she said. "He got someone from the public prosecutor's office to come in and try the charms they use to

273

revivify bodies, but that didn't work. Ever since, all they've done is run tests."

"So I figured, anyway, we could try some of the other incarnation charms," Teddy said. "That's where you come in."

"It's backwards," Susan said thoughtfully. "Usually you have the haunting and try to identify the ghost. You don't assume there must be a specific ghost and search for where it might be-no, it makes more sense to invoke them the way you would demons, in the pentarium. After all, we know their names."

"The pentarium might not be up for weeks."

"We could try the invocation anyplace, I suppose. Start with someplace special to them. Warren's office, perhaps."

"We can't bring the body over here," Lilian said. "The hospital won't release it."

"Then that's where we have to invoke," Susan said. "Can you design a charm?"

Teddy lost her assurance. She avoided Susan's eyes and pleated the loose fabric of her trousers over one knee. "I write charms of discourse," she reminded them. "The whole point of those is to convince creatures of free agency to embody themselves. But are human spirits creatures of free agency? Can they affect anything in the material world?"

"Poltergeists can," Lilian said, but Susan shook her head.

"They're using the power from a living source. Regular ghosts can only produce ectoplasm. I see the problem, Teddy. But we don't need Warren and Russell to make bodies, just to reinhabit them."

"It's the spirit-material barrier," Teddy said. "After all, if souls could get into their bodies, something would have by now."

Susan wished Teddy had not said that in front of Lilian. "What if we used ectoplasm?" she asked, hurriedly. "We could try a seance instead of an invocation, and get them to leave some ectoplasmic relicts we could take over to the hospital. That should lead their souls to their bodies."

Teddy bounced on the benchtop. "That's it!" she crowed. "It sounds like a plan!"

"When can we start?" Lilian asked.

"Not until next week, at the soonest. It takes a lot of preparation to set up a seance. And ectoplasm only lasts about a day. We should do the seance the day before whatever we plan to do with it."

"That's all right," Teddy said. "We still need to figure out how to get the spirits back in the bodies, once we've got 'em in the same room. It's not all jam yet."

"I hate to be a blight," Will said, "but have you thought the safety switch might have done it? We don't know that they went into the pentarium on Monday without their souls. We just know that after the switch went off, their souls were gone. I mean, if their souls were loose or something, they might have gone out. Like the demon."

"You're saying their souls could have been destroyed?" Lilian's voice was stern. Susan didn't dare even look at her.

"I don't know. What happened to the demon?"

"We don't even know what demon it was," Teddy said angrily. "If they're gone, we won't find them in the seance, will we?"

275

"Okay," Will said.

"Well? Will we?"

***

Rho sat in his tower room, watching the colorless sky darken and waiting for the demon. He ran over the plan again, the plan in which he asked to look at the grimoire, to con over the charm he meant to cast, and then seized the book and ran to the only safe place in the building, the pentarium. It wasn't a nice plan, but the pay off! He imagined himself a hero, using the grimoire to lure Warren's soul back into his body, though that would require explaining how he came to have the thing. Rho didn't like thinking about Lilian Oldham. *I'll make something up after I have the book back,* he told himself. At least he had the pentarium up his sleeve. He reviewed every step, every motion, so lost in thought that the demon appeared beside him unnoticed.

"You are preoccupied," it said.

"I've never stolen a soul before. Are you sure it will work?" Rho asked. "I'm not sure I trust those charms. They didn't work for me before."

"Oh yes, I am sure. I have seen such charms used before, and the grimoires they produced. I have seen mages kill one another over them. You will be the greatest magician in the world, with his power and mine," the demon said. "With Oldham's power, you will command all the demons of the Academy. Nothing will be able to stand against you."

276

"I don't know," Rho said, considering. "Let me have another look at the charm."

"That is not necessary," the demon said. Its voice was full of confidence. "Reading something like this to yourself is dangerous. Touching the book, letting it know you-you have done too much of that already. You might cast your own spirit into it, and then where would you be? Simply focus your mind on Oldham for five minutes, and then cast the charm." It held up a hand to forestall Rho's reply. "Five minutes only."

"I don't think it's that dangerous," Rho said. "I like to read something through before casting it, to get the pronunciation."

But the demon merely shook its head with an indulgent smile, and held up five fingers again. He sat down and stared into the dead fireplace. The demon amused itself by lighting the tips of its fingers on fire, one at a time.

"Open the window, if you're going to do that," Rho said.

"Oh, very well." The demon opened the window beside Rho's chair and leaned out.

The cold draft hit Rho's neck.

"It's been five minutes," Rho said. "But I won't do it unless you let me read the charm over first."

"Do you not trust my judgment?" the demon said. It stood back and leaned against the wall, beside the open window. "Have I ever misled you?"

"I don't know yet," Rho said. "But you said you wanted to be friends. Friends humor one another."

"Oh, friends," the demon said.

It seemed to lean forward, closer to Rho, and the draft from the window made him shiver.

Goosebumps rose on his forearms under his robe's loose sleeves. The demon's muzzle was longer, its face less human and its barrel rounder, more like the form it had taken in the hotel in Selanto, and Rho found himself pressing back in his chair, shaking with the *grue*.

"With enough power, you can make anybody act like a friend. Which you have not done, so far. I have been disappointed in you, Rho."

When it spoke his name, Rho felt a tugging inside.

"I have not asked you for that much," the demon said. "Not that much at all. You have tried to play games with me, Rho. Do you think I do not know what you were searching for in the grimoire? Or what you were trying to do with the crystals around your neck? You seek to steal my power and deny me yours. But that is natural, I bear you no malice for it. Only follow my directions, now, and we will have enough power to share."

"I-didn't," Rho said. It came out as a squeak.

"Here is the book," the demon said, ignoring his protest. "Here, the charm. Cast it."

It put its hand on Rho's shoulder, and he felt the pulling inside grow stronger. He found himself taking the book and laying it on his lap. His mouth shaped itself around the words he looked at so he dragged his eyes away. "These don't work for me."

"I have enough power to cast any charm, through you," the demon said. "But I forgot. We need blood." It took half a step sideways and shot its hand behind it, and out the window at an impossible angle. When it pulled the hand back in, it held a squawking, surprised pigeon.

278

"Help!" the pigeon screamed. "Teeth! Eyes! Killer! Help me! Fire! Help!"

The demon held the pigeon by one wing. "Blood, I think," it cooed, and dangled the flapping bird in front of Rho. "Show me what you know of black magic."

Rho felt his hands reach forward, the demon's grip on his shoulder hot and firm.

"No," he said, as he took hold of the pigeon. It looked up at him with recognition and stopped flapping.

"Safe," it gasped. "Monster, fly away. Fly far-" Then it screamed again.

Rho tried to cry out himself; he turned his eyes away from what his hands were doing, and they fell on the book. Syllables in a language that sounded like Cham's exorcism began to force their way out of his mouth. They mixed with the pigeon's screams, forming something like the web of light he had felt at Warren's house, but this web burned.

"Stop," cried the pigeon. "Friend, please-"

Rho fought to let go, to stop his voice or turn his gaze away from the book. Tears of helpless rage filled his eyes and his hands kept moving, but his voice faltered, fell silent.

"Go on," the demon said.

Rho felt his hands still moving, felt blood flowing free down his wrists and heard the pigeon moaning, but he said nothing. He could not see the words to read them. He burst into a cold sweat when the demon put a finger under his chin, tilting his face upwards.

"Oh, poor thing," it said. "This is sad. You are just not ready to be a magician, are you? Perhaps we

279

will have to try another night, with another sacrifice. We have all the time in the world." It patted Rho's shoulder and picked up the blood-spattered grimoire. "Not to worry," it said. "I will not give up on you so easily. Come along. We can try this again tomorrow."

He saw it gesture toward the dark door of his bedroom and felt the weight of its hand shift on his shoulder as it straightened, pulling him to his feet.

"Oh, you can leave that here," it said.

He felt his hands put down the pigeon, still moaning. He tried to pick it up again, at least to break its neck, but the demon laughed.

"You must learn to enjoy what I enjoy," it said. "Come along."

"I-I'm going to throw up," Rho said, jerking his head toward the sink.

"Do what you must," the demon said, "but do not take long." It let go of his shoulder and walked into the bedroom.

Rho stood still, shaking. He turned away from the demon as it disappeared into the darkness and took three big silent steps, and then he was fumbling his door unlocked and running down the dark tower stairs. His whole body cheered him on. *At last!* his legs cried, and *I told you so!* his skin said, and his heart yammered *Go go go,* as he ran and slipped down the steps, hearing the taloned feet and thick chuckle behind him. Its laugh followed as it let him run, flight after flight down in the dark to the levels where not even red 'Exit' signs lit his steps, until he ran into the pentarium shower room and into an entirely different kind of darkness and

280

silence, as if he had gone blind and deaf in the night.

"Oh," Rho gasped, stopping to listen. He heard nothing but his own heaving breaths. His arms prickled with gooseflesh and tremors, not from the *grue* but the subbasement's chill. He could hear nothing on the stairs. Was the demon out there? Could it tell where he had gone? He turned in the darkness, and nothing seemed more horrible than to be standing here waiting to find out whether it could reach him. The temptation to put his head out into the stairwell was almost irresistible, but Rho pushed against it. One step at a time, he backed up until he ran into cold metal lockers. He pressed himself against them as if they could make him invisible, choking in tears and snot but too frightened to cry aloud. He put his hands over his face, rubbing until he saw black lights inside his eyes, and tried not to think.

Nothing disturbed the silent darkness, and Rho began to believe he was safe. He breathed more easily; he took his hands down from his face and began to feel cramps and scrapes along his body, and a stiffening cold. *The emergency switch must have turned off the heating as well,* he thought, with a little pleasure. *Freezing to death in the subbasement in February would be so much better than living as the tool of a demon...* Perversely, as soon as Rho thought that, he began to turn his mind to ways of survival. *After all,* he thought, *I can always kill myself in the morning. If I'm going to live through the night, I need blankets.*

He began to fumble at the lockers, stubbing his thumb against locks, until he came to a full-length

281

closet with nothing except a dead ward hanging from the handle. His hands plunged into folds of velvet, fur, plush and brocade; magicians' court gowns, lined with silk and satin. Rho leaned into the closet. The fur along his arms and shoulders felt like a great cat curled around him, ready to purr. He embraced the gowns, he lifted and heaved and tugged them out with a clatter of hangers falling away to the invisible floor, and made himself a nest half under the benches.

Just as he began to feel warm, a horror of the shower room seized him-maybe it was not as cut off from magic as the pentarium, maybe the demon was toying with him and would appear as soon as he had relaxed-and he crept out from the bench again, scooping up an armful of robes and running through the dark to where he thought the pentarium door would be. Like a blinded bird he ran full tilt into benches, falling over them in the black, and crawling through the door when he found it with a sob of relief. He sat on the cold floor hissing through his teeth, rocking as he nursed his barked shins and stubbed toes. He shut his eyes and built up in his mind a picture of the pentarium and its strength, its warm golden walls and the alchemical safety switch. "I'm safe in here," he whispered in a voice softer than his motions. "It can't get in here. I'll be fine. It's all right." By and by he bundled himself up in the robes again, tucking them around his shoulders and feet, and slept.

***

Warren kept as still and small as he could imagine. He had been in the springtime woods feeling, with the trumpets and banners feeling of Bosie beside it, and that wind had come again; it had torn at him, threatening to drag pieces of him away; it had felt like seeing somebody tortured, or reading about inquisitions, or dreaming of hell. It had almost pulled him away from Lilian and now he was worrying again, conjuring up on her dear body all the horrors he had ever read of, like someone forced to watch the worst he can imagine. But it was all his own imaginings, Warren knew. The threat had been to him, not to Lilian; whatever horrors his mind created now, beneath it all was the woodland, still standing, still green.

She's not safe, though, he thought. *Not while I'm hiding here.* For the first time since the beginning, Warren made up a dream on purpose. He made up the forest, sunlight between new leaves. He made up bird song and the feel of the air and his wife standing in front of him, the way she felt in his arms and how her hair smelled. He held her and kissed her, and did not let himself make up what she would have said about what he was going to do. "Goodbye, Lili," he whispered into her hair. "Goodbye, my darling."

283

Chapter Fourteen

A yellow light woke Rho. It wavered along the far wall of the pentarium and over the floor, coming toward him and then moving away again. Rho froze, pressing himself flat against the wall next to the door.

"I will need better lighting," a courteous voice said very near to him.

"I'll go check the breaker," a more familiar voice said. Rho couldn't place it.

The light withdrew, however, and he heard the voices retreat to the shower room. He jumped up and scrambled to gather up the robes. The voices came no closer; they went back and forth, apparently at the other end of the shower room, and then disappeared. After a few seconds, Rho poked a wary head through the door and saw wavering lights-flashlights-going up and down by the exit at the room's other end. Regan's voice came, muffled by the shower stalls sticking out from the wall between him and Rho. It was a plaintive, aggrieved voice. Rho could hardly believe how much it grated on him.

"The dead zone seems to extend out into the corridor here," he was saying, and the other voice-a light, urbane, amused voice-answered him.

"My goodness, so it does indeed," this voice said. "How very intriguing."

Rho darted into the dim shower room, over to the locker he had left open, and shoved the robes in any old way. He held his breath while he shut the locker door and crept along the shower room's wall; Regan's voice was retreating as if he were walking along the corridor for the room's entire length, trying to map how far the dead zone extended. He would be near to the second stairwell, Rho estimated, and when he peeked into the hall, this was indeed the case. He stepped out, and had just time to catch his balance when the urbane voice spoke again.

"We have company," it said. "Somebody to see you, no doubt."

The lights went on, catching Rho in their yellow glare.

"Eh? Who's in here this early on a Saturday? Oh," Regan said. "It's Rho. Magister Rho, Magister Vinca. From Alchemy. Did you need something? I hope you didn't spend the night in the building."

Rho snarled inwardly, and swore to himself that he would never give Regan the satisfaction of knowing what was going on. Being helped by someone like this-it would be worse than having a demon. The alchemist, though, might be useful.

Rho had never seen an alchemist, but he possessed firm ideas of what one ought to look like. Alchemists, after all, were the most powerful of all things, human or arcane. They changed the world whether it agreed or not, forcing all realms to do their bidding, and should by rights be dark, mysterious, and sinister. Bound by blood oath to their governing body, the Mystic Guild of Alchemy, all alchemists bore the guild's brand as a reminder of how they would burn if the guild ever voted to censure them. Power and bondage, it horrified Rho and at the same time fascinated him, and he would not have been an alchemist for anything. Unless he had the talent.

Magister Vinca betrayed all such notions to the point of insult. He gave the impression of having chosen to be little, round and white-haired, dapper and beautifully dressed in the style of a bygone era, and of having chosen it specifically to annoy other people and to contradict their notions of alchemy. He extended a tiny, immaculate hand, seeming too polite to notice the dried blood on Rho's.

"What brought you down here?" Regan asked, and Rho shrugged. "Security will raise hell if they find any of us in here at night," Regan fussed. "Didn't you get my memo? I thought you took a room in one of the warded hotels. The department will reimburse you."

Rho nodded, muttering an insincere agreement.

Vinca smiled at him, reassuringly. "Let us have a look at this pentarium, shall we?" He led the way back through the shower room, and Regan followed him. Rho tagged along, putting off the moment of his return to the tower. Vinca stood in the door of the pentarium with his hands behind his back, teetering forward and back on sparkling shoes as he looked around the room. "Well, my goodness," he said. "This brings back the old days. I remember when we dedicated this room, back when it was used by one magician at a time and they never even told one another what they did in here. My, my, times have changed."

"It's been a good facility," Anders Regan said. "The question is, can we fix it?"

"Oh well, that is a fine question," Vinca said. He walked around the room, tapped and prodded its

286

walls and even poked his nose up against them, sniffing. Then he looked at the floor, bending at the waist and half-squatting with his hands on his knees. He pulled a snow-white handkerchief from his pocket, dusted a place on the floor, and folded the kerchief back up before putting it away. He hitched up his trousers and knelt on the spot he had dusted, looking at the floor in front of his nose. The pentarium floor did look odd. It shimmered, along the line where the pentacle had been and over toward the far wall, where Russell Cinea's blood had been cleaned away, and in the spot where Rho had slept.

Rho saw a hundred golden reflections of Regan's flashlight down in the floor when he bent over it, but when he touched the spot there was no trace of magic. This was just the way the floor looked-as if the gold had become transparent as well as reflective, very pretty. He stroked the spot again, thinking it felt like the magic mirror from a story. Where would he go if he fell through this mirror? Rho leaned over so close that his breath should have made a fuzzy spot, but the mirror showed no flaw and the hundred reflections stayed as bright as they had been when he first saw them.

Vinca had been carrying out a similar series of tests; he stood up, cleaning his hands with the handkerchief. "This is very interesting," he said, looking down into the shiny place under the pentacle.

"Did the demons cast it?" Rho asked.

"They might have," Vinca said. "Although I believe if you were to clean this room, you would find it extends throughout. How often do you clean in here?"

"I don't know," Regan said.

"Ah, well," Vinca said. He took his kerchief out again and unfolded it, scrubbing at another part of the floor beside him, outside the pentacle. "Yes, see. Here it is."

Rho crouched and saw the same vertiginous depths in the newly cleaned area.

"But what is it? Can you tell what kind of magic it is?"

"Not at first sight," Vinca said. "I'll need to perform some tests. I may want to bring some of the other alchemists over. Bill Navanax is our metals man."

"Can we help?"

"Not at all," Vinca said. "Alchemy is a matter of belief, not argument. In fact, the further away you stay, the more easily it will go."

"The IDA wants us to get it up as fast as possible," Regan said.

Vinca stood up straight and looked at him with theatrical surprise. "Do I hear you correctly? You wish to shortcut the reactivation of a contaminated pentarium? Even if you had the authority for such a reckless action, I would be bound in duty to report your intentions before the folly could be accomplished."

"I'm not in charge," Regan said defensively. "The IDA's coming in to investigate, unless they have some deal with the guild so you can do it. Either way, I don't decide when the pentarium's safe."

"Usurp the authority," Vinca said, bending back down to look into the pentarium floor. "Perform a coup. You'll find it the most useful of academic skills." He stood up and stretched himself. "I think the IDA will be satisfied with any conclusions I reach on behalf of the guild. We will work on this through the weekend," he said cheerfully, "and let you know its prognosis on Monday."

He led the way out of the pentarium and into the stairwell, and Rho climbed in company as far as the first floor. There, both Regan and Vinca turned to leave the building. They looked questions at Rho. He knew he should tell somebody, but not Regan. Not prissy, pusillanimous, butt-covering Regan. And not Vinca, with his soul sworn to whatever the Mystic Guild dictated. These were not people a man could trust; they would sacrifice him in a minute to advance their own careers.

"I-I have to get some things from my lab," he stuttered.

"Don't stay in here after dark," Regan warned. "Are you sure you're all right?"

"Yes, sure," Rho said, and the door closed. He cursed the luck that had sent him only people he couldn't trust, that had landed him in this horrible place with its laws and politics. He pounded his hand on the stone wall, new blood slicking over the dried, but none of that changed the stairwell. None of it changed the darkness at the top, or the fact that Rho stood alone at the bottom.

He would have to go up, because he could not go away wondering if the pigeon was still alive, lying mutilated on that table. *If I can't do anything else, I can at least kill it,* he told himself, and moved his foot to the first step. Like a stiff old man he crept up the stairs, and he imagined he could already smell a charnel scent from his rooms. He stopped and squeezed his eyes shut, listening. No sound came down the dim stairwell. The arrow slit window above him showed only a gray sky.

When he reached the top, Rho found his door locked. He had to fumble with his key. *Anything inside knows I'm here by now,* he thought as it clicked and slid in the lock, and swallowed bile. Was it the *grue*, or pure cowardice, that made his body sweat and shake? He pushed the door open just a crack, far enough to see the table, and drew in a deep breath. The pigeon could not be alive; its body was torn from crop to vent and its head wrenched loose, set on the table where it seemed to fix him with a reproachful, glassy stare. He pushed the door a little further.

The demon had amused itself after Rho's departure. His rooms were decorated with shreds of pigeon, and the stench of meat and brimstone filled them. Sickened, he wavered at the threshold, but then a hot, familiar feeling began to flood into him. "I won't put up with this!" he said, weakly at first but with more conviction as he stepped into the room. "Nobody treats me like this! These are my rooms, nobody does this sort of thing in here. Nobody." All lies, but buoyed by the sound of them he walked across the room and cast the window open. "Nobody," he said firmly to the world outside, and turned around, rolling up his robe sleeves as he turned. If it took the rest of his life, this room would be clean!

290

He had scrubbed for two hours and emptied his fourth bucket of bloody water out the window by the time the impulse wore itself out. As if coming back to himself from an illness, he sat on the table and looked around his wet rooms. Cold, raw air blew around him into the corners and Rho had to admit the rooms did not look much better. Removing pigeon parts had made only a superficial, cosmetic change in their appearance. The smell had thinned into a hint of blood that caught at the edges of Rho's nostrils when he turned his head.

It'll probably just mess the place up again, tonight, Rho thought. He didn't care. He wasn't going to be there to see it. Picking his way between wet patches, he opened the warded cabinet door and took out his treasures-a computer disk containing his thesis, the external drive on which all his current work was backed up, and his grimoire. He stuffed them into a worn black backpack. In the bedroom, he considered the bedding and judged against it. *I'll buy a sleeping bag,* he decided, and the notion gave him an absurd feeling of adventure and luxury. *Maybe even a pillow.* Locking the tower door behind him, Rho set his steps for Osyth and camping supplies.

***

In the early afternoon, Rho stood in the road that ran along Osyth's walls. To his left it stretched west, curving slightly as it reached Westpark. To his right, it made a sharp turn in through the city's north gate. A little red car pulled out of the gate, turning too fast, and honked at Rho. He jumped back, into slush, and the car roared past.

Rho shook his fist after the car. "Road hog!" he yelled, wishing he knew some really potent curses. Making a car burst into flame might relieve his feelings.

He'd searched for new ways to deal with the demon for hours. He had asked indirect questions in sober offices, and over the phone. He'd approached the topic obliquely in libraries and shops, asking about supplies and books, hoping to find something relevant without telling the bored attendants his business, but no luck. When he paged through the books in his carrel and in downtown bookstores he saw nothing but the most elementary charms, even though he looked five or six times to make sure.

Frowning, he walked along the sloppy margin of the road. *I could jump in front of a car,* he thought, but without much conviction. He would hide in the pentarium tonight, after all. It was not yet the time for extreme measures. But soon the sun would be down.

Rho sighed as he shouldered his backpack and sleeping bag. He crossed the road into the park, joining another vagrant on one of the benches. The man popped his whiskery head up out of stiff, soiled layers, gave Rho a distrustful glance, and pulled it back down. He muttered to himself. Rho set the backpack on the ground in front of him and pulled out his grimoire. He opened it to the middle, the last full pages, and scanned the few charms he had been able to pick out of the library. He had copied them in haste, frantic to get the job done before the demon might appear in that dark, empty corner. All

292

day he had panicked in dark, empty places. He wondered for a minute how the pentarium would look when he reached it, and put the thought aside. Instead, he read the defensive charms over. To make a person blind. To stop a person's speech. To paralyze for hours. Rho shivered, and the vagrant at the end of the bench reached across and nudged him.

"Hey, buddy, have a slug," he said, holding out a bottle in a paper bag. "You look like you need it more than I do."

***

The ley-line spread around Warren like mist, dense at its center and fading into near imperceptibility as he spread himself away from the core, yet, like a mist, coloring his perception of things outside it as well as within it. But mist was a poor analogy. The word brought up images of damp and cold, mystery, and senses closed off. In the ley-line, Warren's feelings were the opposite. He could not claim to see the world more clearly, having no eyes; nor did he touch it, having no hands, or nerve endings, nor hear it without ears; what he felt, rather, was the satisfaction of his desire to see and touch and hear the world.

How often in his life Warren had stood, spellbound, before something too beautiful to be real. He had known the beauty would change as he walked into it-that misty distance, that ray of sunlight, that field white with dew-it would all back away from him as if it stopped being real when he came too close. It would never let him in; look as he might, reach as far as he could, he could never quite get to it.

He had lain flat on carpets of moss, marveling at the millions of perfect plants below him, and wanted nothing more than to dissolve and lose himself forever in such beauty. He had seen shafts of sunlight through the trees, or slanting between gilt-edged clouds, and wanted only to flow up them into glory. When the sea beat against rocks below him, he had wanted to blow away in those rough winds...

He had pretended, for a while, to be content to lose himself in the joys of sex, of work, of holding his baby daughters, and those had certainly been the closest he had ever come to what he wanted until this moment. But now, in the ley-line, Warren felt himself dissolved, swept up, lost in the beauty of the world. Without knowing clearly that anything surrounded him at all, he knew whatever did contained every one of those transcendent moments and that he was one of them, at last. For the first time, he began to wonder if he wanted to return to his body. How long had he been drifting away from it? Surely by now, it had done its worst.

**

The pentarium shower room was lighted from within by something hot and white, an industrial sort of lighting. Rho saw it more clearly under the door as the tower stairs darkened. At first he wondered about the light. *What could it be? Something as magical as a tamed star, or as mundane as a garage lamp?* Rho distracted himself with speculations. What he really feared was that they would come out dusting their hands, with the look of mechanics who had repaired a motor, and say the pentarium was fixed.

The alchemists finally did come out at eleven o'clock, when Rho had found a place to wait in the corridor, pushed into what he hoped was the dead space Regan had mentioned. The dark emptiness was making him unhappy, and he was stupidly delighted when they emerged. Vinca stood in the block of light from the shower room door, dusting his cuffs with a fastidious but, Rho thought hopefully, unfinished air. A second man stepped out beside him, reached a long arm back in to douse the light, and plunged the corridor back into darkness.

"That was premature, William," Vinca said mildly.

"Crap," the tall man said. He stepped toward Rho, feeling for the corridor light switch. When the lights went on, dim in comparison to the dazzle the alchemists had produced earlier, Rho blinked up at him and he blinked down at Rho.

This new man looked the alchemist through and through. He might have been any age between thirty and fifty, and everything about him was long, from his tall frame to his lantern jaw and long nose. On a Saturday, he nevertheless wore a white shirt, brown dress pants and a tie. He leaned back stiffly from the waist to look down at Rho, crumpling his long chin down into his neck until it lay in folds of skin like a bloodhound's, but his voice, when it came, was sharp and quick. Voices like that snapped out of windows and then their owners threw boots.

"What's this?" the man said to Vinca.

295

"Magister Rho, Magister Navanax," Vinca said, waving a hand in introduction. "You are an amazingly conscientious young man, to wait this long."

"I live in the building," Rho said.

"Hence the bedroll?"

"They belong down here in the storeroom."

"Ah. Well, if you are not planning to take your ease in the pentarium, perhaps you will join us for dinner. I believe the faculty club is still open?"

"Till two," Navanax said, as if Vinca knew the answer and was pretending ignorance, to be cute.

Rho hesitated. "It's not safe walking around the building at night," he said, but Vinca pooh-poohed his fears.

"One of us will walk back with you, if you have business here," he said. "No demon will attack an alchemist."

Persuaded, Rho shouldered his backpack, left the sleeping bag inside the shower room door, and started up the stairs. "Did you find out what was wrong with the pentarium?" he asked.

"It was demonic," Vinca said, dusting his hands with his handkerchief. "Of a sort."

"What do you mean, of a sort?"

Navanax laughed, a short sarcastic noise. He pulled on the brown leather jacket he had been carrying. "It's a short circuit, that's what it is," he said. "It's one of your own charms."

He came toward Rho up the stairs. Rho backed up in front of him a few steps, and then scooched himself flat against the wall so Navanax could pass. The man smelled like hot metal.

296

"What kind? There are all kinds of magical charms."

"It left very interesting traces in the metal, almost like an alchemical spell. Our first hypothesis was that your pentarium was not originally gold, and someone had enspelled it to make it into gold," Vinca said, waving Rho ahead of him. "Go on, go on. However, that is not the case. Some very powerful magician has used a charm of definition on gold to turn it into gold."

"At least it's legal," Navanax said. "Making anything else into gold outside the bursar's office would get you into deep shit. This is just stupid enough to get away with."

"I doubt whether it is a foolish a spell as you suggest, William," Vinca said. "I do not believe the intent was to make gold."

"Well why don't you tell us, then?" Navanax said, with half a sneer. He treated Vinca in an offhand way that Rho admired.

"Nobody would try to make gold with a magical charm. An alchemical spell is the only kind which will force the world to comply with it," Vinca said. "Yet here we have a charm which tells gold to be gold. By logic, it ought to do nothing. Yet, from the very appearance of the room, it has done something. I believe this spell has been used to create a superimposed replica of the pentarium; a demons' pentarium, in which demons cast their own charms. Rather more than a mere ornament."

"What would demons want a pentarium for?" Rho frowned, walking sideways to look back at Vinca. "And they can't cast magic charms, anyway."

297

"Two very good points," Vinca said. "What would demons think they might do with a pentarium? Where would they gain the power to use one?" He smiled, too sweetly. Navanax stopped and looked back at him for a few seconds, thinking, and then smiled himself.

"What?" Rho said.

"Ah, there is where we cease to be of use to you," Vinca said evasively. "You know more than I about the nature of the spells cast in this pentarium, and the assumptions underlying them. I am sure your department will spend many hours discussing the issue."

Rho was silent as he followed Navanax to the first floor exit. He didn't know more than Vinca, Rho was sure. Vinca appeared to know something he didn't.

***

"This club has the strongest protective spells in twelve countries," Vinca declaimed, raising his glass. "The only facility to match it is the harem of the Emperor of Selanto, blessed be he."

"He has more to take care of," Navanax said. He didn't exactly look around at the other faculty members, comparing them with a harem to their disfavor. He just held his head as if he might.

"Have some more, Magister Rho."

"Just Rho," Rho said. They were drinking brandy from a bottle reserved for Vinca and handed to him by an awed student bartender, and Rho knew he was meant to be impressed. Osyth brandy.

"A pale imitation of Kasidoran luxuries," Vinca said. "You will doubtless have tasted much better."

"Not that much better," Rho said, and Navanax gave a sudden bark of laughter.

"Ha!" he said. "You've met your match, old man."

"Oh, Kasidora," Vinca said, shrugging. "They cut their teeth young."

"Too young. How old are you, anyway?"

Rho bristled. "Twenty-six," he said, and Navanax laughed again.

"Now, William! He's old enough to sleep in pentariums, and that is as old as anybody needs to get," Vinca said. "Are you trying to avoid the demon that injured Magister Cinea?"

"Huh," Rho said, sipping the brandy. He wondered if this was his third glass or his seventh, then decided he didn't care. Vinca refilled them before they were empty. "That demon's nothin'."

"Compared to... "

Rho put down the glass, trying to keep his head balanced on his neck. He looked across the table and Navanax, stretched out long in his chair, looked back.

The alchemist swirled his glass and cut his eyes toward Vinca. "This is statutory," he said.

"Do not judge everyone by yourself," Vinca answered. "So, Rho. Tell us about the other demon. Or are there several?"

Rho opened his mouth, almost ready to tell them everything. He thought just in time of the oath mark somewhere on each of them, the brand that made them unable to break rules or help rule breakers, and nothing came out except a gurgle.

"He's sloshed," Navanax said.

Vinca sighed. "There, I fear, you have the right of it. It's past time you were in bed, young man. Let us walk you back to the pentarium. Unless you have another destination? A hotel, perhaps, as Magister Regan so wisely suggested?" Rho shook his head miserably. "Ah, are you a purist, then? One who needs to be on the ley-line?"

Rho could not answer; he hung his head, watching the table sway in and out of his view, and Vinca took one of his arms and gently guided him out into the night.

"This is as far as I go," Navanax said, turning into the club's parking lot, and Rho saw the tall alchemist climb into a brown convertible with its top down before Vinca steered him the other way.

Chapter Fifteen

By Sunday night, Rho had the necessities of life squirreled away in his locker. Sleeping bag, even a pillow, an alarm clock that ticked loudly through the night, a flashlight, with spare batteries, and an assortment of junk food. He had added five more protective spells to his grimoire, and could send mortal attackers into a torpor, make them unable to speak any known language, turn their vision upside-down or right to left (these meant to be used by unsporting swordsmen in the course of a duel), and paralyze the hands of a gesturing opponent. The work on ducks, however, was suffering.

Rho spent most of Sunday away from the pentarium, so he was unaware of how the alchemists' repairs were progressing. It was not until Monday morning, when he returned after his eight o'clock class, that he ran into them again. An almost comic line of respectable-looking men was ascending from the subbasement. Rho balked, nearly stumbling into the first of them, and backed away to the landing, waiting until he saw Navanax come up, rolling down his shirt sleeves.

"What's going on?" he asked, darting forward to the alchemist's side.

"We've reset the pentarium," Navanax said, doing up his cuffs. "You'll have to find somewhere else to sleep."

"You mean demons can get back into it?"

301

"That's right. It might work pretty much as always, once you get your magicians back on line. Tell Regan it's in his court."

Rho stood on the stairs, watching the line of alchemists march upward, and felt himself left behind in the dark. In the pit.

***

The ad hoc committee for reconstituting the senior magicians met at nine o'clock Monday morning in the vampire lab. Susan had invited them, being unable to think in Teddy Whin's cluttered, incense-reeking office. They pulled chairs away from the benches and sat in a loose cluster; Will, a member only because it was his lab, propped his feet on the desk. Teddy Whin sat on the desktop and grandly ignored them.

"Lost spirits is the closest we can come to it," Susan said. "There's actually quite a bit of literature from the early days of ghost studies. Mediums who lost their spirits when contacting the dead; sometimes the ghost took over the body, and other times it just remained in a trance."

"Warren isn't in a trance," Lilian said.

"Warren and Russell have a lot more power than your average medium," Teddy said. "And they're on the ley-line. How did they deal with these lost souls?"

"They didn't," Susan admitted. "The cases all end up in the death of the left-behind body. There's only one report of the spirit ever being contacted again; that was a pair of mediums who were lovers and co-workers. After she lost her spirit, he was

302

able to contact it. But they never did get it back into the body."

"Lay out what they tried, and you at least know what doesn't work," Will suggested. "Your sample size sucks, though."

"Perhaps ghost studies isn't the answer," Susan agreed. "What did you find?"

"There's a lot about incarnate arcane spirits in witchcraft," Teddy said. "I went over and talked to the leader of a local coven about creating familiars." She pulled a pile of xeroxed articles out of her briefcase. "There are two ways to make a familiar, and both of them require a witch who has a loving relationship with the body." Will grinned at this, but Teddy kept her eyes firmly on the papers. "In one, the witch performs the invocation to draw a specified spirit to her and when the spirit manifests, she sacrifices the creature that will serve as the host body. The spirit is drawn into the body as its soul departs. In the other, the witch cajoles the spirit into creating the desired body, with invocations describing what it's like to be in the body. That's not too far removed from charms of discourse, except it works through affective persuasion instead of logic."

"We're not going to sacrifice Warren," Lilian said. "And I don't want a duplicate of him, either."

"You're passing up the most obvious examples," Will said. "What spirits possess bodies at the drop of a hat? What spirits make a public nuisance of themselves?" He put his booted feet down with a bang. "What spirits do we have two bonafide experts on in the department? Incubi, ladies, think incubi."

303

"He's right," Susan said. "We need Patsy in on this."

"Fine," Teddy said, but she glared at Will. "Don't tell Rho a word about it, though."

***

Rho lived through his eleven o'clock. No more could be said for his performance. He kept his head down at the end of it, bulling his way through the students into the office wing and climbing down the nearest staircase. Coming upon the pentarium from a new angle he startled Vinca, who stood in the hallway admiring something quite invisible to Rho.

"Ah, Magister Rho," Vinca said. "I hope our work meets with your approval-oh, I see it does not."

Rho opened his mouth to say a hundred things, but what came out was a minor question. "Where would you put something you wanted to keep safe? From arcana as well as the material world."

"In the safe in the Alchemy Building," Vinca answered promptly. "Nothing can get through alchemical wards. For those of you without access to that office, the Bank of Mammon maintains a similar facility. May I ask what it is that you wish to protect from such a variety of dangers?"

"My grimoire," Rho said.

"Ah yes. The Bank of Mammon, I believe, is chosen by many who do not wish to keep their precious documents ever on hand."

"Mm," Rho said. He stood looking at the pentarium doors. "Will the pentarium work the way it always did?"

304

"Ah well, an excellent question," Vinca said. He returned his attention to the walls and teetered back and forth on brightly polished shoes. "We had to make some changes. The guild has imposed new restrictions since this facility was built, and approved new materials. Still, William has really done an excellent job," he said happily. "One could hardly tell the facility had ever been damaged."

"What exactly did he do?" Rho asked. "What makes the difference between a working pentarium and a nonworking one?"

"I am not fully cognizant of William's methods," Vinca said mildly. "Have you asked him?"

"He doesn't want to talk to me," Rho muttered.

"Not true at all! William is a most congenial person, once you get through his outer crust. He's shy."

"You think I should ask him?"

"Oh, I think you should," Vinca said. "His number is in the book."

But Rho could not bring himself to call Navanax. If he heard that sharp voice snap at him over the phone, he would hang up. Instead, he outlined a route for himself. Into the city, to the Bank of Mammon, then back, through the Academy quadrangle and across the ley-line between sorcery and wizardry, into the wooded triangle of land around alchemy.

Rho took three false trails before he was able to find the Alchemy Building. The footpaths led him off the campus proper, through leafless woods and along the slushy bank of a thin stream, into the territory of large black squirrels with poor attitudes.

305

"Look'ee here!" they yelled above Rho. "Another little lost lamb. Walk in circles, ya will, till ya starve or freeze. Ha! We'll chew yer bones, baby. Think ya can figure out east from west? Only if ya can tell the sun when ya see it, greenhorn."

Rho bore these remarks with dignity as he retraced his steps.

"Try this'n," called the squirrels, from down the first false trail. "Na, it's one ya haven't tried. You're turned around. This here's north."

Ignoring them, he tried each path methodically until he saw treetops sticking up above a wall of red stone. Set in the stone wall he found an iron gate, but beyond it... beyond it lay nothing but a lodge of the same red stone, something like a Kasidoran noble's country home. No Alchemy Department at all, no spells, no magic. None of the mystic powers that controlled the world. Disappointed, Rho retraced his steps along the outside of the wall until he found a parking lot full of cars, Navanax's brown convertible parked at one end of it with the top down. He stood beside the car, baffled and unable to focus. Whether from the demon or the alchemists' protective wards, his head wasn't working right; sun and trees looped around him, and he shut his eyes to escape from their acrobatics.

***

Something had come down the ley-line. Something like a cloud of sparkles poked at Warren, pushed into him and withdrew... his memory cast up a cloud of damselflies, their bright wings in the sun, and his rational mind sternly brushed them away.

But the sparkles remained, little prickings of a feeling more intense than anything he had met here but that never stayed long enough for him to recognize it. The little bits of excitement gave him a dancing feeling, like watching waves in sunlight.

The sparkles that bumped into Warren were not all alike. Some were stronger than others, or strong in different ways; a number of them were filled with a bright energy and others with something more like a need. He spread his perceptions out, imagining himself a cloud all around the sparkles, and tried to find one and watch it. He finally picked one of the needy ones out of the crowd and followed it as it darted through him, around the others. Although the sparkles bounced into one another as often as they bumped into Warren, this needy one never seemed to meet up with its fellows. *Is that what it needs?* he wondered, feeling a little sorry for it, and then suddenly it disappeared almost entirely. He felt the ghost of its motion, something a little like the *grue* without the cold-a feeling of almost but never quite touching another realm, of the worthlessness of a life that could not reach beyond itself-and then the sparkle was back, brighter and merrier than any of its fellows.

Warren felt himself come to attention. Where had it gone? What other realm would he, in the spirit world, only dimly perceive, if not the material world? In all his wanderings he had found no sign of his old world's existence, yet this sparkle had leapt into it and come back refreshed.

***

Bill Navanax loved his convertible, even when it was too cold to love a convertible. He would have skinned anybody who climbed into it for a nap, yet he was no better impressed to find Rho leaning against its side, asleep. The kid hadn't even dared get in-it was abject. *I always knew there was something sick about Kasidora.* He went to poke Rho with his foot, but instead he found himself squatting and shaking the kid's shoulder, more gently than he intended. It felt like shaking a bird.

"Hey, wake up," he said. "You're on my car." The kid blinked up at him, dazzled. *That's flattering,* Bill thought. "What are you doing here?"

"Waiting for you," Rho said. "What did you think?"

"I don't think on my own time," Bill said. His knees griped at him, so he stood up, four times as tall as the huddled lump before him. "Don't you sleep at night?"

"Not on my own time," Rho said.

"You don't look like you eat, either. Oh, hell," Bill said. "Get in. It's too cold to stand around here trading cracks." He drove home with this strange kid in the car beside him, and all the way he made a story up about it in his head. *Sitting there like a street rat,* Bill thought. *It was too weird to pass up.* But who would he tell the story to? Who would listen, laugh, add a new twist-he drove too fast, and stopped too fast at the traffic lights. "Don't they have seat belts in Kasidora?" he asked when Rho fell into the dashboard.

***

308

The house smelled bad.

"Your fish are hungry," Rho said as soon as he got into the living room.

"So feed them." Navanax disappeared into another room, and Rho opened the cupboard under the fish tank. A babel of voices arose.

"Light! light! Big-run! hide!"

"You have roaches," he said.

"And I care."

Rho scouted through the jumble under the tank until he found a half-empty box of fish flakes. He fed the fish, and they called him a god.

The room had two of everything. Two chairs with two little tables by them, two lamps, two dents in the sofa. But it felt cold and smelled dead. "Do you live here alone?"

"Why?" Navanax reappeared with two glasses of something golden. "What is it you want, anyway? What do you do in Kasidora, once you've gotten a strange man to take you home with him?"

"Slit his throat and rob the house," Rho said, glaring. "So, is there anyone else I should be watching out for?"

"No," Navanax said. "The knives are in the drawer under the sink. Unless as a professional, you have your own." He handed Rho one of the glasses and sat down with his own. "I like you," he said abruptly. "You took Vinca down a peg. But I'm not going to put up with much more of this mystery act. Any fool can tell that some demon's got your tail; now what do you expect me to do about it?"

"Nothing," Rho said. "I don't need you to do anything. That safety spell made what I want. It made a place the demons can't get into. Right? So

309

now it's part of the real world that places like that can be created. I don't need you to remake it, any mundane could do it if they knew how. I can do it, if you tell me how."

Navanax scratched inside the back of his collar, stretching his head down. With his eyebrows raised, his face became a pile of folds: neck folds below and forehead folds above. "You think I can tell you?"

"Why not? It's possible now, isn't it?"

"Well, sure, it is," Navanax said. "But I don't know how. I make the world, I don't study it. Figuring out how to make that happen again without alchemy would be a hell of a big job. It might even be impossible. We tried to make it so specific that it wouldn't happen by accident. You'd never get all the factors together again."

"I can try."

"Look-" Navanax sighed. He got up. "Come on," he said, leading Rho through an unvacuumed hall, past closed doors. They went into a small room claustrophobic with books-piled on shelves, stacked high on the floor, teetering off the corners of every flat surface. Navanax swept one pile off a chair and started picking new books off the shelves to replace it.

"These are the ones about gold and how it works," he said. "Here's one on the geology of the ley-line. It's not the best one for what you need, it's an old textbook from when I was in school. This one is on the hydrology under the plateau. And you'll need to go over to the plant and grounds office and get a blueprint of the pentarium and the Magic Building. They've put up two wings of the

310

teaching hospital since then, so you'll have to find out how much those siphon off the ley-line. I don't have any of the books on soil chemistry or astrology or the atmospheric stuff, and the guys who worked on them are at other schools of alchemy."

Rho looked at the chair, which was almost full. Navanax went across the room, to a warded cabinet. He opened it with a gesture.

"All I really know about is the metals part." He pulled the door wide to reveal stacks of paper. "These here are the texts they thought would become true when the safety spell went off. These... " he grunted, heaving great reams of computer printouts, all clipped into heavy gray binders, "these are the new facts about gold, with predictions of how they'll change the old facts. Here's the new truth about how the metals in the wiring work, and the geological composition of the Osyth Plateau. I don't have a clue about the rest of the new order. The others have it locked away in their own offices in all the other schools that work with the IDA. Now that they're true, all these papers can be submitted to the Mystic Guild of Alchemists for review. They'll read 'em, in five or six years, and decide how much of it ought to be published. Then they'll issue it. You ought to be able to buy a bound set in oh, ten years." When he added the binders to his chair, it creaked. "Go ahead." Navanax waved at the heap. "Knock yourself out."

"Get real," Rho said. "We're talking about the mundane world."

"This is the mundane world." Navanax kicked the chair. "The mundane world is a hell of a lot of hard work. No charms of intent in the mundane world. Wishing doesn't make it so, for them. Mundanes have to fight for every scrap they get, and they're a damn nuisance. I spend ten percent of my time working out an idea and ninety percent making sure it doesn't ruin their sweet little lives.

"And magicians are worse. Magicians are people who could change the world, but they won't step up to it. They don't want the work of figuring out what it would do to the mundanes, so they sit back and comment and pretend that's a contribution. If you want your safe spot, you're going to have to sweat blood for it." Navanax turned away. "Take whatever you want. I'll give you a lift back to campus when you're done."

Rho stayed in the little room for about half an hour, but he didn't waste his time with the books Navanax had piled up. He looked through every other drawer, instead, and the only interesting thing he found was a heavy gold ring in a desk tray, right in front as if it wanted to be stolen. The alchemist knew metals, though, so Rho only looked at the ring, for fear it would cry out to its master if he touched it. He went back out into the hall, wishing he dared open the closed doors, and down into the living room. Navanax's empty glass sat on the table; its owner was lying on the sofa, lumped across the two dents in it. He looked uncomfortable, but he had closed his eyes.

"Your drink's in the kitchen," he said. That gave Rho an excuse to look around the kitchen. Dusty chrome-plated machinery stood on all the counters, and pots of long-dead herbs blocked the small window. The walls were hung with pans and spoons, and on the stove stood a filthy frying pan, with the grease in it pushed to one side.

"You don't cook very much, do you?" Rho asked, taking his drink back into the living room.

"No," Navanax said. "Never trust a man who cooks. All that chopping and mixing. It's nothing but an excuse to think about things. If we were meant to think, there wouldn't be hockey."

Rho had never thought about hockey, so he didn't reply to this. He just listened.

"Alchemy isn't like magic," Navanax said. "Magicians think it's the same sort of thing, but it's not. None of these meditative disciplines, for one thing. No molding your mind to the world in alchemy. It's the other way around. That's why hardly anyone can do it."

"All I know about alchemy is those old stories about three wishes," Rho replied.

"Those are crap. Nobody's a big enough whore for that. You don't set your heart on something just because some fisherman asks for it. Can you really see some alchemist making his life hang on whether an old woman has a pudding stuck to her nose? Not for a minute. Do you know how much work it is to care about something? I mean really care. The kind of caring the world has to notice, not the kind that whines in a corner.

"And once you care that much, you have to submit it to the guild," Navanax said, then let out with a short bitter laugh. "Please, sirs, is it all right for me to have this? It's only the most important thing in the world to me. Take a few years, however much time you need, just let me know... at least I

313

work with metals. My projects don't die while I'm waiting for an answer.

"Nine times out of ten, the answer's no. Oh dear no, that would interfere with a tribe of sixteen mundanes living in a hole in Lower Tombolian. It would mess up the exchange rate between the great cities of Graft and Corruption, or make the land the peons live on worth more than the land the nobles live on, or cut some CEO's bonus this quarter down from six million to five and a half. So that's how my day went, how was yours?"

Rho didn't even try to give an informative answer.

"Is it true that nothing can get through an alchemy ward?" he asked instead. "I was down at the Bank of Mammon, and they were advertising it."

"Don't use Mammon," Navanax said. "Their interest rates are the biggest swindle in town. Never give your money to anyone named Mammon. Look, do you want dinner here or down to the corner?"

"If you don't cook-"

"Right." Navanax heaved himself upright. "The corner it is."

The corner was a bar, one of the featureless buildings with the front corner lopped off that Rho had wondered about since he came to Osyth. He looked around him as they went in, checking out the tiny vestibule.

"You've never been to a bar?"

"All the time, in Kasidora," Rho said. "They were different." Different indeed. Pubs in Kasidora had been homey, well-lighted, with comfortable chairs and quiet conversation. The den Navanax led

314

him into was almost pitch-dark. Its only windows were two narrow strips running below the ceiling, too high for anyone to look out of, and its interior lighting was obscured beneath thick glass shades advertising unfamiliar beers. When Rho's vision adjusted, he saw a plywood bar with red leather stools before it and a flyspecked mirror behind. Half of the room was paneled and the other half walled with particleboard; half was floored with linoleum and the rest with concrete. The finished half, to the left of the bar, was dominated by a large pool table. On the unfinished side sat three tiny tables, each with four chairs around it.

"It's easier to eat at the bar," Navanax said when he saw Rho eyeing these tables. The bartender came over as soon as they sat down and put a double whiskey in front of Navanax.

"What's for you?"

"We need food." Navanax took a large sip of the drink.

"We got the usual. Beans, brats, burgers, slaw, fries, rings," the bartender said, and braced both fists on the bar.

"How's the slaw?"

"Same as yestiddy."

"Beans and rice." Navanax took another drink. The bartender looked at him without moving.

"No rice," he said.

"Fries, then."

"What'll you have?"

"Uh, beans and slaw," Rho said, "and a beer. Whatever dark beer you have."

Navanax shook his head, but said nothing. He was nearing the bottom of his drink. The bartender brought a new one with Rho's beer.

"So, what's this research?" Navanax asked. "Ducks?"

On a safe topic, Rho was able to talk. He did, eagerly, but by the time they had eaten Navanax was on his fourth drink and Rho began to worry. The windows were rapidly fading into night; he could not go back to the pentarium, or to his lab. He paid up silently and followed Navanax back down the block in a brown study.

"You're quiet," Navanax said. He swayed just a little. "Look at that! The Northern lights."

Flashes of white and green moved silently above the housetops, so faint and quiet they seemed unreal. Rho stood in the dark looking at them, acutely conscious of the lighted windows around him. People were inside these houses eating decent suppers and talking with family. They were tucking children into bed and turning on the evening news, and he was always watching them from outside in the dark.

Navanax shook himself and walked up his own driveway to the dark house. He stopped beside the convertible.

"Guess you want a ride back," he said. "Or what? You don' like having the pentarium up, do you? No place to hide."

"My stuff's in your living room."

"Oh. Yeah."

Rho followed Navanax into the dark house. As if it was an afterthought the alchemist turned on a wall sconce and stood beside it, looking at Rho. The light cast his eyes into black shadows.

"Let me stay here," Rho said.

"Stay the night? What for?"

"Whatever you want," Rho said. The man stood looking at him for long minutes, while Rho felt again the house's dead emptiness behind them.

"I can't do this," Navanax said, swaying a little. "Maybe you can do this, just for a lark. Maybe magicians are like that."

"If you don't like the way people are, change it. You bitch about the world, but who makes it? Not me."

"You show me an alchemist old enough to work who can still b'lieve people are decent, and I'll vote for every change in the world he suggests," Navanax said, with effort. "On the other hand, he'd be an idiot."

"I'm not asking you to fall in love with me," Rho said, laboring to explain the obvious. "I'm offering you a deal. You fancy me, and I need somewhere to sleep until the Magic Building's safe again. Vinca said nothing can get through your wards."

Navanax looked at Rho with disgust. "Is this how you got your degree?"

"Now who's naive?"

"I don't fuck people I don't love. Alchemists can't afford to do that sort of thing. We have to keep clear 'bout what we... really want, or the worl' stops taking us seriously. The minute you settle for second best, that's all you are."

317

Rho felt himself flushing angrily. He shrugged his shoulders in a pretense of indifference. "I still need a place to stay. Can I rent a room?"

"Damn! Brazen li'l thing," Navanax said, but he said it with admiration. "Stay the night if you like. Just keep out of my bed."

Chapter Sixteen

Rho shut his eyes and stood in the middle of Navanax's spare room, breathing it in and ignoring the dead, unused feel of the place. *That didn't work out quite as I expected,* he told himself. *Still, beggars can't be choosers...* He swung between awe at his good luck in having a safe place for the night and an unexplored chagrin at Navanax's rejection. Words like 'second best' and 'brazen' lay in his mind like stones, but he was too tired to concentrate on them. He undressed as if he were moving inside a soap bubble, trying not to burst it, and fell asleep with the same precarious feeling.

It must have been the middle of the night when he woke in a sullen mood, feeling as empty and disregarded as the room he was lying in. With nothing to distract him he went over the evening in detail, replaying every remark until he had decided what it should have meant and what he was going to claim it had meant when he faced Navanax in the morning. On the whole, Rho judged, he came out better than the alchemist. He had at least been sober, and if anything complimentary; the other had made some statements he would regret, if he could remember them.

Rho would have to be magnanimous about some of those statements. 'Second best!' 'Is this how you got your degree?' There was enough truth in that to make it worth resenting. Rho began to wax hot. It was too bad that he had to put up with this sort of thing, after all. If only the Academy took proper care of its building, or of its new faculty, he would not have to expose himself to such abuse. "They didn't call me second best when they hired me," he said aloud to the empty room. "They save that for after you're committed. How much crap do they think I have to take?" Indignation felt comfortable, warm and solid. It built on the rest of his experience of Osyth and Osythites and their hypocritical moral codes; with indignation, he was accomplishing something that mere confusion never would. He was closer to developing a game plan.

"These people aren't that hard to deal with," Rho said. "Pretty predictable."

"Not very intelligent," a voice agreed from beside him in the dark.

Rho went cold all over. *Navanax!* Turning his head, Rho could just make out a dark figure beside him, standing at the bedside. His indignation withered at the thought of the alchemist sitting in the dark, hearing his own hospitality abused, and rebloomed at the idea of being spied upon in his sleep.

"I thought you didn't go for second best," he said nastily.

The dark form turned half toward him and opened its glowing eyes.

"I have missed you," it said gently. "Did you forget we had business to finish?"

The *grue* hit Rho all at once. He retched.

"And I am pleased to see you," the demon said, catching his wrist in its hot strong grip. "Cast the charm, and we may put an end to this unpleasantness." It held something out before Rho's face. "Ah. Lights." With an appendage he couldn't

320

see, it turned the lights on and Rho saw again Navanax's nondescript spare room, with old magazines piled neatly on a shelf next to guest towels and spare bedding. He blinked watery eyes against the light and tried to look anywhere but at Warren's grimoire under his nose.

"We will need blood," the demon said, tilting its head as if listening to the house. "Warm blood." It turned its face back toward Rho and grinned. "You will have to help me with that, as well," it said, and twisted his wrist upwards. It licked his palm and pulled its head back a little, baring its teeth.

Rho jerked his hand back and gabbled the charm for paralyzing an enemy.

The demon stopped for a second. "For that, I will hurt you," it said in a strange, remote voice, and bit into his palm like a thousand knives.

Rho heard himself start a gasping scream and clamped his teeth together. His mind's eye saw the door opening, Navanax looking in with a suspicious air, and then... he stifled another cry as the demon chewed deeper. It pulled away, ripping through skin. Rho gasped and swore under his breath. The demon laughed at him and spat a mouthful of blood into his face.

"The book," it said, poking his chin with the grimoire. "Do your part."

Rho took a deep breath and tried to turn his eyes away. Unable to do that, he crossed them, and this took the demon a moment to figure out. While it was trying (making his eyes shift from side to side wildly, so the room-two rooms-dipped and swayed), Rho did the only thing he could think of. He licked his lips, and with his own blood in his mouth spoke the silencing charm. He swallowed just as his vision cleared.

"Now," the demon said calmly. "We will discuss your disobedience later. Read the charm."

Rho saw the words, knew how they sounded, and moved his mouth to the right places, but no sound came out. The demon put the grimoire down on the bed and grabbed him by the hair. It shook his head roughly, and pushed it down to the book.

"Read," it said, its tone harsher.

Again Rho read, silently. The demon made a noise of frustration, and Rho jerked his head out of its grip. He'd beaten it! Rage and triumph filled him, and with his free hand he punched the demon square in the face.

"Hhh!" gasped the demon, rearing back. It looked less angry than it had a minute ago.

Rho hit it again, catching its upper arm and doing no damage. He tried to pull his mangled hand away from its grip, and the pain made him howl with fury-silent fury, but the demon saw it and smiled.

"I had forgotten why you interested me," it said, complimentary. "You are stronger than anyone at this cozy Academy can guess." With these kind words it slapped at Rho, claws out, and he felt his shoulder rip open. He fought back with all the strength he had.

***

A hint of wind came up around Warren. Just a touch of doubt, a passing wonder if maybe the

322

things he had hated were as much here in the next world as the things he had loved. *Plausible,* he thought, focusing on it. *More than likely.* But the sensation was small, weak, dying away ... The notion might come back, but Warren would not invite it. He turned his attention back to the other small things around him.

The longer he adventured alone, the more Warren was perceiving. The part of the ley-line he had now reached swarmed with spirits in constant motion, interpenetrating one another, creating a collage of moods and ideas. The smallest and least complex were the avid sparkles he had encountered earlier. Between them lay long, slow stretches where he felt himself concentrate on nothing more than time and existence; into these, then, would come an upwards feeling, or an urge toward hiding and darkness, or a leaping, breathless excitement. At times Warren felt busy and precise, a collector of details, and during those moments he swept those niggling thoughts aside impatiently. He imagined himself floating through an overlapping, constantly changing swirl of colors, taking on whatever momentary hue it gave him.

The world he floated through had a floor, as well. The hints of something else he had felt the sparkles dive into were stronger, though still unclear and unsettling. They cast a feeling around them like a cloud of denial. When Warren strayed too close to one, he began to slip into a mood in which the wonders around him were not truly real. He began to think it was all made up, must be made up, that there was no possibility of its being anything other...

323

He pulled himself away from that place as fast as he could, back into the vivid reality of the ley-line.

***

Even when he had a hangover to distract him, Bill Navanax hated mornings. He especially disliked his own stubborn habits in the morning, the way he rolled over onto the other half of the bed before he was even awake so he always woke up reaching out to nothing, telling himself he preferred the smooth cool sheets after all. That was a bad way to start, for someone who didn't like lying, and it usually got worse. Bill's brain was so used to hearing something from the kitchen in the mornings, or smelling coffee and bacon, that he spent the whole time of shaving and dressing either hearing ghosts, smelling ghostly smells, or noticing their absence.

His solution to these doleful mornings was the simple traditional one: he drank enough the night before, to make just standing up and shaving a full-time job. The same strategy took care of the dreams, at least the ones where Gordon came back and wouldn't explain himself. It didn't do much for the dreams where the guild inquisitors asked Navanax questions all night, but those didn't bother him so much. He'd never cared much for the guild, and now they couldn't do anything to him that would matter. Not even in his sleep. No, the dreams that left a nasty feeling in the morning were the ones about how Gordon had kept him out of it all along, hadn't used a penny of the money on the house,

324

hadn't even set foot in Bill's lab from the minute he started the scam.

Gordon's boss had known. The conglomerate that paid for it had known. Even the mundane scientists who planned the experiments had known, because they had to write the whole thing out beforehand so Gordon could create realities just before they 'discovered' them. But not Bill. Not Bill, and not the lab tech who found one of those notebooks, with the results the next week's experiment was supposed to generate. If they'd brought the lab tech in on it, Bill would have been the only one who didn't know.

That was what galled. Bill thought about it every morning while he was shaving, if he could think while he was shaving. He looked in the mirror at his own face, which really didn't look that foolish. Actually it was a nice-looking face, an intelligent one; it didn't look like a face that could go happily about its business, congratulating itself on a good relationship, while its lover committed capital crimes. It did look like a face that had witnessed a guild execution, especially on the mornings when a hangover was turning it green, and that was the down side of drinking too much. Bill hadn't quite figured out how to compensate for that.

This morning something was a little different, though. The house felt different. Bill felt different-off-balance, as if he might have heard something in the night, but what? So he was listening for something, trying to remember, from the moment he rolled over and stretched into Gordon's half of the bed. That was interesting. When he went into the bathroom he kept on listening. Something smelled different, a little like sulfur and blood-iron, Bill could tell iron anywhere, but he had never had an ironworker in the house. Not even any iron cookware, it was all the new stuff Gordon's company made. None of the illegal compounds, of course. Gordon had been careful about that. As if on cue, Bill's headache kicked in and he stopped listening for anything in the house, but some subterranean memory nagged at him under the throbbing. He shaved without criticizing his face in the mirror, too busy juggling hangover and mysteries, and started a bath. When he headed back to the bedroom to get his clothes, he found himself facing the closed door to the spare room.

Bill stopped and stood looking at the door, feeling more foolish than he liked. Something of what was bothering him, he decided, lay behind that door. He opened it, quietly, and peered into the darkness within. The smell of blood was in here, and what looked like blood, too-smears on the wallpaper and the tumbled bedding, and a sort of jangle of magic against Bill's house wards. It was a combination that made a man's innards congeal, as if the air caked in his lungs. Bill switched on the light and saw his spare room trashed, wallpaper hanging off in strips, stuffing and shreds of bedding scattered across the floor. Some little guy-Rho, his brain volunteered-was sitting on the side of the bed, holding his right hand in his lap and glaring into it as if he were casting some sort of charm or scrying in a palmful of his own blood.

Rho looked up, scowling, as if he were going to order the light turned off, but Bill saw his assurance disappear as he followed the alchemist's gaze around the ruined room. His back hunched and he stopped whatever magic he had been working at, and the more he diminished, the more expansive Bill felt, because this kid so obviously expected him to howl over a messed-up guestroom. *Kid, you don't know what trouble is,* Bill thought. He felt himself growing taller, bluff and in control and good-natured.

"Crap," he said cheerfully. "I was going to redecorate, but this wasn't what I had in mind."

Rho hunched a little lower on the bedside, something easily accomplished because the mattress beneath him was gashed and shredded, partly disemboweled in the spot he was sitting on.

"Is that all your blood?" Bill asked, and the kid looked around as if he had to check-which meant he had fought back-and brightened a little.

"Yeah," was all he said.

"I hope you got in a few good licks," Bill said.

"Oh, yeah," Rho said. "I guess I threw the first punch, anyway."

Bill sat down on the bed beside him and felt the mattress cave in like a dead thing. "Let's see that hand," he said.

Rho held the hand as if he didn't want it poked at. "It's not that bad," he said. "I can fix it if you'll take the wards down."

"I thought that horse was out of the barn. How did whatever it was get in here, if the wards were up?" Bill could feel the difference when he spoke the words that let the wards down, though, and he looked at Rho with even more interest. Rho was glaring at his hand, as if the sight enraged him, and mumbling under his breath. The blood obscured any

327

changes, but after a few minutes Rho stopped scolding the hand and began stretching it, closed it into a fist, and wriggled the fingers one at a time. "That's pretty good!" Bill said.

Rho shrugged. "It's just first-aid," he said.

"Can you fix my headache? Just joking," Bill said. "Hell, my bath'll run over! You use it. You're dirtier than I am."

Rho jumped up. "What time is it? I have to teach at eight!"

"Call in sick. It's already a quarter till."

"I can't call in sick," Rho said. "I don't have tenure!"

"What, you're not going to get sick for seven years? Good luck," Bill said.

Rho had turned an ugly shade of brindle; he sat down again and put his head between his knees.

"You can stay here and explain all this to me," Bill said, "or you can go wherever and I'll call Magic and complain about my spare room, and find out what you're up to in the newspaper."

Rho glared up at him. "It's my problem," he said.

"But it's my spare room," Bill pointed out, "and my bathroom floor. Why don't you get in there before it's a swamp?" He had to hold Rho up to get him across the hall. "Use this stuff on those scratches," he said, rummaging in the medicine cabinet. "Towels are under the sink. And take two of these-no, make that one. I'll call Magic for you."

"Don't... " Rho said, and stopped.

"You have a better idea?" Bill peered at him. "You have any ideas at all? No? Then get in that tub."

328

He didn't half like going downstairs to the kitchen, leaving Rho in the bathroom. *At least I don't have any razor blades up there,* he thought, *or any sharp instruments.* Still, he left the door open and kept half his attention on the sounds from upstairs while he dialed Anders Regan's home number.

"Navanax," he said when Regan answered. "Is this Regan? Yeah, listen, do you guys have the wards back up in your building?"

"Not yet," Regan said, his voice heavy.

"That's what I thought. Because I've got your new guy over here, trying to get away from demons. He's taking a sick day, right?"

"Oh, dear," Regan said. "Is he all right? I thought he was staying at a hotel."

"He's a little messed up," Bill said. "I don't think he's slept much the last few days."

"I said all along, these tower-room living quarters were a poor idea. It's classical enough, but if something goes wrong, where are you? All alone over there, with the ley-line and the live specimens."

"So what's your problem with the wards?"

"Warren and Russell set them," Regan said. His voice was shifty. "They're indisposed."

"Indisposed, crap," Bill said. "You're not making me believe you had a whole building warded with charms of intent. Those guys didn't sit around twenty-four hours a day willing the demons to keep out of their labs. And what kind of 'indisposed' voids a charm of essence?"

"Will you keep quiet about this? Please."

329

"I don't make promises like that," Bill said. "If you want to keep secrets, make sure your new faculty have someone from their own department to run to at midnight." He heard too much splashing from the second floor. "Gotta go." But it had only been Rho getting out of the tub. He was kneeling beside it, scrubbing its sides with Bill's nail brush.

"You don't have to do that," Bill said, taking the brush away.

Rho sat on the john, kilted around with a green towel.

"What's the 'G' for?" he asked.

"What?"

"In the monogram." Rho's head was nodding as he spoke, and Bill wondered if even one of the sleeping pills had been too much. Stripped, the kid was smaller than he'd thought.

"It's not my towel," he said. "Take it with you when you go, or pitch it. I don't want it. Now let me see that hand."

***

Bill Navanax went into the Alchemy Building with none of the difficulty Rho had encountered. He walked purposefully, as if it were a normal building, and once inside he turned to the left and strode down corridors inlaid with fanciful birds and beasts, past arched doorways. At the third arch on the right, he banged on the door once with his fist before pushing it open and stepping into a small laboratory. Dark wood cabinets lined the room, their glass fronts half obscuring their contents-books, glassware, dried and fresh specimens. More

330

specimens sat on the benchtops, tagged and arrayed in neat rows. A soft breeze came in the windows and riffled the papers on Vinca's desk, an expanse that dwarfed its immaculate owner.

"What are you trying to do to me?"

Vinca looked up with his usual air of benign interest. "I have never quite decided that," he said. "I consider you a work in progress."

"You sent that damn little magician after me."

"Magister Rho? I merely suggested that he ask you the questions he was asking me about you."

"Oh, yeah? That must have been quite a conversation. If he was asking you what he asked me, he thought you were my procurer."

"Oh, my goodness."

"He shows up at my car last night, looking like the thin end of nothing. So I take him home to give him a good feed, and the next thing you know he's offering to do anything I want if I let him stay the night. I put him in the spare room, like the damn fool I am, and when I get up he's let a demon in through my wards, and it's ripped the hell out of him and the room. You'll pay for that wallpaper, or Magic will."

"Is Rho hurt?"

"Of course he's hurt," Bill snapped. "But he did mid-level sorcery on his own hand-what he calls first aid. What's going on with that boy?"

Vinca's expression changed. "That's a very good question," he said seriously.

"What's your point? D'you think he's one of us? Or that he cast that spell in the pentarium?"

"No. One of the demons cast it," Vinca said. "But it needed cooperation from a magician. Rho

331

was right-demons can't cast charms themselves. They have to steal a magician's power to do that." He sighed and twirled his chair, looking out the window. "The fields are blurring more and more. With charms of discourse, magicians are defining the arcane realm by persuading demons to reconceptualize it. Now demons seem to be trying the same trick on magicians, from the other side of the barrier."

"If you're saying they changed the pentarium, that's not the arcane world."

"No, but the pentarium is in the ley-line. When I removed a fragment of the gold from the ley-line, the charm on it disappeared. That is the only bright spot in this picture," Vinca said. "We apparently do not have to worry about either demons or magicians reshaping the mundane world. Still, it is interesting that none of this happened until Rho appeared, and that the demon was able to get at him through your house wards. What have you done with him?"

"I patched him up and put him to sleep in my bed, and fuck all if I know what I'm going to do with him when I get home. If he isn't gone, and all the silver with him. Don't fix me up, Vinca. I mean it. Especially not with a little tramp like that. He probably has diseases from three continents."

"Is it not possible that the boy was desperate-"

"Thanks so much."

"-and could not conceive of himself as having anything of value to offer, except sex?"

Bill glared at the older alchemist and Vinca looked back at him big-eyed over the top of his reading glasses. "Well damn," Bill said at last, "why didn't you just get me a puppy?"

332

At noon the sun reached its nearest to vertical. It shone in the south windows of Osyth, which meant it lit up Patsy Hoth's lab. When the sun covered her desktop, it was time for lunch. Patsy Hoth took out her sandwich, kicked her shoes off, and picked up a journal.

The venery lab was old, with much-scarred black benchtops. Under Patsy Hoth's administration it was spotless. Beakers stood in regimented lines in her cupboards, graduated cylinders marched in file along her shelves, each of them topped with a little hat of sterilized aluminum foil. Before every experiment, the benches were covered with white acid-resistant paper. Every sink held its lining of plastic webbing. The iridescent mists of incubi swirled in glass boxes along the north wall, the one nearest the ley-line, and neat red labels marked those boxes which had contained an incubus for three days and whose contents must be released into the rabbit colony down the hall before the day's end.

All this stood in great contrast to the general run of venery labs, which were traditionally happy-go-lucky places filled with pin-ups and the chatter of small animals. Venery, as Patsy Hoth had told Rho, had a poor reputation; persons who entered the field, who became professional lechers, were thought to have unseemly interests. The general public still viewed incubi as either sex toys or lame excuses for misbehavior, which Patsy Hoth thought was most unfair. Incubi, she had told the members of her department, were the most oppressed of

333

creatures. Everybody could be whipped up to some sort of concern, however hypocritical, about prostitutes or child pornography, but who cared for their spiritual equivalents? The other women in the department should not have viewed her askance for this opinion, which she had not belabored. She had not wasted her time repeating it more than once. But, as Patsy Hoth had noted on more than one occasion (inefficient repetition in itself), life was not fair.

Someone knocked on the door, and Patsy Hoth gave it a look. She had posted her schedule on the outside of that door, with details of where she could be found at each hour of the day and *Lunch* written clearly across noon to twelve thirty of each day. It did not seem, to her, that difficult to understand. The knock came again, and she put down her sandwich.

"Yes?"

The door opened onto a pale yellow hallway containing Teddy Whin and someone Patsy Hoth did not immediately recognize. As they came into the lab, she identified this person as Lilian Oldham.

"Teddy," she acknowledged. "Mrs. Oldham. How is Warren?"

"Just the same," Lilian said.

"We're trying to figure out ways to get his soul back," Teddy said. "Thought there might be something in venery to help us. After all, incubi jump in and out of bodies all the time."

"They do," Patsy Hoth agreed. "Do the sorcerers know about your efforts?"

"Since we haven't done anything yet, no," Teddy said. "Time enough to worry about who's in charge when we have an idea."

"All right," Patsy Hoth said, and Teddy looked at her in surprise.

"You're in?" she said, a little defiantly.

"In what? You say you haven't done anything. But it's an interesting problem. There's a large body of literature on the mechanism of incubus possession. I've been considering a few projects on the topic."

"What do you know that might help Warren?"

"I'm not sure," Patsy Hoth said. "Let me pull some notes together. Can I get back to you tomorrow?" When the two women had left she picked up her sandwich again, but this time she ate it swiveled away from the desk, looking out across the Academy quadrangle toward the administration building. The thought of doing something about Warren and Russell, instead of waiting for sorcerers to twiddle their thumbs, was extremely satisfying. At twelve thirty exactly, Patsy Hoth folded up her lunch bag and opened her filing cabinet.

***

Rho woke up to dazzling light, heat, and a smell of burning metal. On second breath, he liked it. With his eyes shut, he moved gingerly in the warmth, feeling the scratches on his back pull as he stretched, and it was with a feeling of regret that he sat up, admitting he was awake, and looked around the room.

He might have been transported back into his old life in Kasidora. Everything in Navanax's bedroom looked older than Osyth. Rho looked at furniture so old its wood had turned black: the four-poster he was sitting in, a cane-bottomed chair, a tall dresser with one of those mirrors that swivelled mounted across its top. The mirror, tilted upwards, reflected part of the ceiling and a sunlit patch of dusty yellow wallpaper with brown diamonds on it. Rho turned toward the flood of light pouring over him, trying without success to look out the dust-covered window. The light, impenetrable, pushed all attempts to see through it back into his face. When he looked away again, the rest of the room had disappeared into a shimmering black and purple void.

Rho blinked, feeling less contented, and stood up. He tottered and shivered, standing in the cold shadows, reopened his dazzled eyes, and went out into the hall. In the bathroom mirror he saw himself, a wizened thing with bruises round his eyes, and turned away with disgust. *Better just to go,* he thought. He'd caused enough trouble here. But his clothes-either shredded, or in the spare room. Rho looked at that door and sidled past it, his back against the opposite wall. He went down the stairs, instead.

"Hey," a voice said. Navanax was sitting in a room Rho had never noticed, a sunroom opening off the living room. The same aggressive light blasted from behind him, whittling his edges away, and bleached the papers on his table.

"Hey," Rho said.

"Have some coffee." Navanax went back to his work. He had piles of books and papers, some binders, and an open laptop.

Rho couldn't tell whether the alchemist was angry or just busy. He filled a mug with stewed coffee and took it out into the sunroom as quietly as he could.

"How's your hand?" Navanax asked him, without looking up.

"Fine."

"It ever scratch you like that before?"

"No."

"Hmf."

Rho hunkered on a sofa and drank his coffee, watching the steam curl upwards in the sunlight. At first he snuck sideways looks at Navanax, but when these were ignored he became bolder and stared. It was the first chance he'd had to look at Navanax in a good light. *Some people,* Rho mused, *might say it was forward to offer a man sex before you'd had a good look at him, but those people didn't know how the world wagged.* Anyway, nothing he was seeing now made him regret the offer. Perhaps it was because of the man's long farmer's face, with the skin hung carelessly over its bones, or because he recognized a fellow spirit in the invariant uniform of brown slacks, white shirt and tie-Rho spared a thought to mourn his own magician's robe, no doubt destroyed upstairs-or perhaps it was the way Navanax was working, calm and concentrated, with his clipboard and slide rule, but Rho thought that if anybody had to know his problems, this would be a good person. He was looking at the slide rule when Navanax put his pen down and looked up.

337

"What kind of slide rule is that?"

"Alchemical." Navanax passed it over and Rho saw one scale of numbers, one of alchemical symbols, and one he couldn't read; it shifted and squiggled under his gaze. He gave it back, feeling queasy. "You haven't had anything to eat yet, have you?" Navanax jerked his head toward the kitchen. "Get yourself something and then come back and tell me just what went on last night. I'm big on knowing about things."

Rho didn't like making himself a sandwich in somebody else's kitchen, unsure of whether he was allowed to use the new jar of mustard or the good china, but he still dawdled over it. *If only things could stop now,* he wished, *right where they were, before anything has to be thought about or talked over or planned out.* But there was a patch of sunlight on the kitchen wall, and Rho could almost see it marching upwards in front of him. No amount of wishing would stop the approaching night. When he went back to the sunroom the light seemed paler, its aggression more like bluster. He sat down and looked at Navanax, who had his hands folded in an expectant manner, and it was just not possible to think up a good lie.

"It's a demon I picked up in Selanto," he said. That sounded entirely too flippant, so he had to hastily explain how he had really picked it up, really, and watch Navanax look amused. There was simply no getting away from it. He was little and talked to ducks, and he had picked up a demon without catching its name, and nobody would ever take him seriously! He bit into the sandwich and pretended it was the mustard that prickled his eyes.

338

"That's quite a story," was all Navanax said, in a too-polite voice.

Rho stared out the window, chewing hard, and thought about how they all were jerks. After a while he felt better.

"Still, that doesn't explain why it's here," Navanax went on. "They're supposed to stick to their own ley-lines, or so I'm told."

"That's what Neil Torecki said, but Linus Ukadnian told him it was crap. He said all the ley-lines were connected and demons could range through them all."

"Linus!" Navanax said, with a nasty grin. "How is dear old Linus?"

Rho was thinking of something else.

"He said it in the pentarium!" he said excitedly. "He was talking about it and Patsy Hoth came in and tore a strip off him for talking shop in the pentarium. Could the demons have heard him?"

"I'm sure they did, but what of it? If the ley-lines are connected, the demons probably know about it without asking Linus. He didn't make you pick up this demon. He didn't get it in here through my house wards, either-or use mid-level sorcery on his hand and call it first aid. What kind of magician do you call yourself?"

Rho bristled in reflex, but the question flattered him. "Natural philosophy," he said. "We're not really magicians. Not according to most people. We just hear animals."

"Uh huh." Navanax raised his eyebrows and push his chin down.

Rho hoped he would say more, but he didn't.

"Anyway, I have this demon. Warren gave me a lot of happy talk about being its friend, but I'm not sure how much of that I should take seriously," he went on. Not mentioning the grimoire gave him a heavy feeling that talking about Warren relieved, a little. "I don't know how seriously I should take Warren at all," he said fiercely. "Everyone at Kasidora thought this program was a joke, and maybe they were right. Here we are two months into the semester, and the senior magicians have lost their souls-and I don't even know what that means over here. In Kasidora, if someone lost his soul you assumed he was a goner. But it's never happened there."

"Ha! That you know of," Navanax said. "I could give you some good history books on Kasidora. How long has it been since they had someone torn apart in his sleep-two years? Folks around here take Warren and Russell pretty seriously. They run the only demonology program the guild pays any attention to." He shrugged. "What do you expect, though? All the other universities will say, 'That's Osyth.' Wizardry and sorcery will say, 'Those fools in magic don't know what they're doing.' The folks in social magic will say, 'Natural magicians act so superior, now look at what they've done,' and all of you will say, 'What did Warren do wrong; has he been doing that all along?' There's always a moral for somebody else. It's always somebody else's fault."

"My problem isn't," Rho said, feeling solid and righteous. "I'm the one who picked up a demon without knowing its name. Now what am I going to do about it?"

"Good question. Got an answer?"

"If I can pick up some new wards and protect myself, I might be able to do what Warren said and strike up some kind of an equal relationship. Or I suppose I could offer it to Vivien. She already knows its name. Or I can just give it what it wants. People already think I sleep my way up."

Navanax had the grace to look embarrassed. "Sorry," he said. "I wouldn't have said that if I was sober."

"No, you'd just have thought it. Who cares? It's the truth. If I didn't do whatever it took, I'd still be getting buggered in the back alleys of Kasidora. It's no big deal."

"Well, that's a valid point," Navanax said. He opened his pen and doodled on the corner of his paper, probably to avoid Rho's gaze. "I don't think sex means all that much to a demon, though. What d'you think it really wants?"

"I never thought of asking that," Rho said slowly. "Damn." He thought for a minute. Of course he had assumed it was sex, as if it were another of those pitiful prowlers in the alleys. "Damn," he said again. "It has to be power. That's what it always is with demons." Feeling stupid made him cross. "I might as well ask what you're after," he said. "You want to know everything about me, but you aren't giving anything away yourself."

"What d'you want to know?"

Rho had no idea. He looked around the room, and tried to think of a question. What did people ask one another about? "Who used to live here with you, and what happened to him?" As soon as he'd asked it, Rho was sorry.

341

Navanax looked at his papers and drew tiny, precise squares down their edges. "Gordon Weyerhauser lived here, and the guild executed him two years ago," he said, in a colorless voice.

"Oh," Rho said.

"If you find that anything useful can be done with that information, be sure to let me know," Navanax said, still without looking at him, and abruptly got up and went into the kitchen.

Rho heard the refrigerator door and the pop of some can, and hoped it wasn't beer. *Does he get drunk every night?* he wondered, not sure whether he liked Navanax better or worse. If the guy didn't want to answer questions, he shouldn't invite them! Oddly enough, though Rho had liked the idea of having found a strong, rational friend, it was almost as nice to have a friend whose life was as messed up as his own. He felt more like an equal. He went out into the kitchen himself, and found Navanax looking at a set of dark green pots hanging on the wall. The can was a soda.

"Look, I'm sorry," Rho said.

Navanax continued to look at the pots. "Do you know anybody who cooks?" he asked, and his voice was normal again. "I'll never use these things. They're top of the line. You want 'em?"

"No, I don't cook," Rho said. "Maybe some grad students?"

"Yeah, I'll put an ad up. So it's what, three hours till dark? What's your plan?"

"I don't know." Rho sat on the kitchen counter. "I thought your wards would keep it away."

"Why?"

342

"Vinca said nothing could get through alchemical wards."

"I don't use those at home," Navanax said. "Sleep in the lab. It'll probably give you a headache, but I don't suppose you give a crap about that." He led the way back into the sunroom and dipped into his briefcase, pulling out a wooden amulet on a cord. A flock of tiny birds were carved on it, some feeding at the base of the charm and some flying up it toward the sky. When Rho put it on it weighed him down; he felt all of his body limber and weak. "You'd better wear that all afternoon, to get used to it," Navanax said. "It's changing your nervous system."

"Will I change back?"

"If you don't wear it too long," Navanax said. "What do you need to get from your own place?"

***

Rho could hardly stand up in the driveway leading to the Alchemy Building. He wished he could look at it the way he had before, see a country house, and turn away. Every step toward the low red-stone building ground against his nerves.

"Headache?"

"Hell," Rho groaned.

Navanax took his arm and hustled him forward. "Soonest begun, soonest done," he said. "The charms are strongest outside. Shut your eyes." Every step a pounding, grating wrench, Rho felt himself scraping through gravel, stubbing his toes on stairs, slipping on polished floor. A heavy door sucked air from in front of him and slammed behind

343

his back. A sudden silence fell, the sounds of night and the textures of the spell fading together, and Rho opened his eyes.

He stood in a dark lobby with a black staircase curving up from his left. Behind it, to the left and right, arched corridors yawned.

"I'll leave the lights off," Navanax said. "It's easier on your eyes."

The spells inside the building made Rho feel stupid. He seemed to be missing almost everything; he couldn't have said whether they took the right or left corridor, how many doors they passed, whether they turned right or left into Navanax's lab. Whenever he tried to think about it, his sinuses buzzed. When Navanax turned on the light in his office, revealing many more things Rho couldn't think about, the buzzing got worse.

"You see," Navanax said, "a demon would have a hard time in here."

"I wouldn't know if it killed me, in here," Rho said.

"Same thing. I've got a cot here, for when I work through."

Rho just barely recognized the cot and blankets. Touching them worked better; he shut his eyes and felt for the pillows.

"You all right?"

"Yeah," Rho said. "Good night." He could hear the alchemist hesitating by the door.

"The john's down the hall-oh hell, here's a beaker. Use that. Look, are you sure you want to stay here alone? I can bring over Vinca's cot."

Rho gritted his teeth, trying to think. His own worries were easy to visualize, compared to the

344

things of alchemy. "If it gets in here, you won't be able to stop it," he said. "Go home."

"Crap," Navanax said, in an admiring tone. "You have guts. I'll be in at seven o'clock, and pick up the pieces."

Rho heard him walking away down the hall. He'd left the lights on, and Rho didn't want to try looking for the switch. He climbed into the cot with his coat still on and pulled the covers over his head, and there he lay in an uncomfortable untidy lump, waiting for the demon.

Nothing happened. Rho lay still until he warmed up and began to sweat inside his overcoat, which he unbuttoned by feel and eased out from under the covers. That disarranged them enough to uncover one side, which then felt chilly, and it reminded him that his boots were still on. "I'm hard on bedding," he said to himself, sitting up with his eyes still closed. A clank told him he'd kicked over Navanax's beaker. "Hell." Rho opened his eyes.

His head filled with pictures, shapes, colors, and a buzzing, foggy feeling around all of them that made it impossible to tell how they fit into the world he knew. Rho shut his eyes again and made up an office out of his own imaginings. Any office would have to have a desk in it, with drawers. A computer. A chair. Lab cabinets, and a sink. When he looked again, he searched for bits of these and was able to assign some of what he saw to the categories he'd decided to find. Only the novel and unique parts of Navanax's lab remained mysterious. A pity, because when would he ever have such a chance to go through an alchemist's stuff? He stared hard at the desk, but could not tell what any of the things on it were until he had already decided what he wanted to see there. Long things turned into pencils, pens, chalk, scalpels, as Rho thought about them. He was even able to convince himself they were licorice whips, and when he picked one up it felt like rubbery candy. Still holding the thing, Rho looked away from it. He thought it was more likely to be a pen, and felt it harden in his hand.

Rho put the long thing back on the desk, wondering how he should feel about all this. If he wasn't in a real place, how could it really protect him from the demon? He choked off the thought. *I might conjure the thing up just by thinking about it, in here,* he told himself. *Think about something else. Will this room turn into whatever I want it to?*

When he opened his eyes the next time, the desk looked like an antique and the rest of the room had arranged itself to be his old lab at Kasidora. Mysterious objects still lay along the benches, but they lay along the scarred, stone-topped benches Rho had known by heart. The beaker at his feet had grown short and squat, with flowers on its porcelain surface-the chamber pot Rho had used for three years. *Not that it mattered much.* Rho swiveled on the hard cot. He shut his eyes again, concentrating, and the cot grew thicker under his butt. Its pillows puffed up to nudge his thigh, and his inquiring hand felt thick blankets. Rho laughed. He tried to think his borrowed clothing into silk pajamas, but that had no effect; still, he was pleased with himself as he stood up and shucked most of it. He thought the light into a glow of candles, used the chamber pot, and crawled into the best bed he'd ever slept in.

Perhaps I have more magic than I thought, he said to himself. *Magic and guts.* With this, he fell asleep.

Chapter Seventeen

"Wake up!" said a voice, then laughed.

Rho jumped so hard the cot rattled. He felt a moment's sheer panic, looking at something standing over him and unable to decide what it was. Black or brown, or something else? Wings or overcoat? Glowing yellow eyes, smell of rotten meat, or brown eyes and toothpaste?

"It's me," the thing said, and kicked the cot leg. "Navanax."

"Oh." Rho sat up. He felt the cot turning thin under him again, and shivered as his warm blankets dissolved into old army woolens.

"You turned my pens into licorice," Navanax said, and Rho thought he was amused. "I hope you didn't eat any of them, did you?"

"No. What would happen if I did?"

"Good question. Maybe if you stayed in here till they were digested... let's not try. So it worked."

"It did!" Rho felt himself grinning. "If the demon did get in here, could I just think it into being something else?"

"Who knows? What would you turn it into?"

"A pig," Rho said promptly.

"Oh yeah, sure, of course."

"Why, what would you turn a demon into?"

"I tend toward inanimate objects," Navanax said. He seemed to be sitting on the desk, which seemed to be gradually turning back into modern furniture under him. "A paperweight, or a spittoon."

Rho got up and pulled his pants back on.

"The sink's over there, if you want to wash up," Navanax said. "There's soap." He didn't say what kind of soap, and when Rho found the sink he had to stare a while before a white cake with an embossed gold monogram came into focus-the soap he had never been invited to use in Kasidora. The monogrammed towels matched it. "Pretty nice for lab use," Navanax said. "You must have had some life over in the old world."

"I never got to use these," Rho said, muffled. "I just saw them."

"Hm." Navanax dropped the towel. "What were you, some kind of servant? No, forget I asked."

"Make up an answer you like," Rho said, bristling.

"If I do that, it'll be true," Navanax said. "At least in here. Let's get breakfast."

"I can't," said Rho. "I teach in half an hour." He wanted to get out of the Alchemy Building, to a place where he could actually see the person he was talking to. Where he could feel proud of himself for surviving the night, without the fear that the mere feeling would turn into something unexpected and obvious. "Can I sleep here again tonight?"

"Sure, as long as you don't eat the equipment. Come over after work and I'll let you in."

"About six?"

"Fine," Navanax said. "Did you get anywhere with figuring out what the demon wants?"

"Power," Rho said. "I figured that out yesterday."

"I meant what it wants with you. As opposed to shopping itself around to some other magician."

349

"I'm working on it," Rho said. He hated being nagged.

"Whatever," Navanax said, in a voice that was like a shrug.

Rho thought he had turned his back and was bending over the things on the desk. Everything in the room had turned back into whatever it was the day before, and Rho couldn't look at any of it without his head hurting. But the spells helped him, now that he was on the way out; he walked down the corridor with ease, knowing where to turn, and the steps and gravel drive welcomed him as if they led downhill, to a place of rest. When he looked back from outside the gate, the lodge lay as unofficial as ever, and Rho could have sworn he saw some leisured noble ride a horse around its eastern edge.

***

"The traditional theory is that incubi bypass the mind and soul," Patsy Hoth said.

Lilian admired her ability to ignore Will Harding's feet on the desk in front of her.

"The theory is that incubi, rather than displacing the soul already in residence, possess the body directly. This suffices because the functions of interest to them are, essentially, mindless."

"But we don't want to lure incubi into them, we want their own souls back," Lilian said.

"If their bodies are uninhabited, there shouldn't be any barrier to the soul just stepping back in—except the wards around the hospital."

"But those wards are keeping demons out," Teddy said. "It's interesting that we don't have any wards which distinguish between malignant spirits and human souls. In every other field of endeavor, we distinguish rigorously between humans and the rest of creation. What does this say about the world views of the initial magicians?" Nobody seemed to care.

The group of five sat silent in the long room, considering, while the cross-shaped patch of light through the arrow slit worked its way from red to white and across ten books in a glass-fronted bookshelf. Will leaned back and looked at the ceiling, twiddling the toes of his boots. Lilian leant forward, propping an elbow on her denim-covered knee and listening to snow-melt drip off her sneakers onto the floor; if they had not all been so quiet, she would have gotten a paper towel to mop it up. Instead she looked around the room, marveling at how light and airy Susan had made a lab with only those little arrow slits, and wondering where they kept the vampires. Susan's eyes were shut and she was leaning on the bench beside her in a slovenly manner, her long loose garments puddled around her.

Teddy Whin and Patsy Hoth sat exactly opposite one another in the group, and both sat in silence with all the trappings of extreme concentration: Teddy cross-legged on the desk, hands folded into a meditation posture as if they just fell into it through habit, and Patsy Hoth straight upright, legs crossed in immaculate nylons, writing ideas down in her leather binder. Patsy Hoth was the one Lilian would go to for legal advice. Susan

351

was the one she'd want for a friend, to have tea and discuss decorating problems with, and to bully into believing she was lovely, taking off those mud-colored draperies and wearing something that would knock Will's smug smile right off his face. *Just as well we're not friends,* Lilian thought as she looked at his wagging boot tips with their silver caps. *He wouldn't have any use for a woman he couldn't outshine.* Teddy Whin-here in the Magic Building, Lilian could not imagine herself doing anything with Teddy Whin. The woman had seemed so different over in the hospital, so much more human. She sighed, and Teddy opened her eyes.

"There has to be some way to induce the souls to reenter the bodies."

"You know where that's leading," Will said. "You go inducing a human soul to enter something-that's black magic. Right there is where you cross the line." He pulled his feet off the desk and put them down with a thump. Patsy Hoth nodded.

"Perhaps we can find something in the venereal literature about facilitation. Any number of aphrodisiacs facilitate incubus possession, and that's not viewed as binding or summoning. I can review the principles involved in that. And what is there in the meditative disciplines about opening the mind to spirits?"

Teddy nodded. "I know the disciplines Russell used," she said. "I had him doing them in the hospital. But over there, he's warded against any kind of spirit. The problem is, what if we let a demon into one of them? They're the best magicians in Osyth. If one of them were possessed by a demon, we'd have serious trouble. It would

352

compromise charms of discourse throughout the discipline-not just the current charms, if it was Russell they got. The underlying principles and all their possible refutations... "

"You'd have to exorcise them, and that would take away their magic," Lilian said. "Then we'd be as badly off as we are now."

"No, we'd be much worse off," Patsy Hoth said. "Without magic, they might never be able to get their souls back. We'll have to proceed very cautiously, with careful planning, and involve sorcerers at every step."

Lilian looked over at her. The woman seemed entirely unmoved, unlike Susan, who was swiveling unhappily around in her chair, or Teddy, who was gnawing at one of her fingernails. Lilian felt safer just seeing Patsy Hoth sit there neat and businesslike, as if no situation had ever been bad enough to distress her.

***

The grayness below him nagged at Warren. He could not believe his previous life had been that gloomy, that saturated with meaninglessness and dismal tedium. *I was there, dammit!* he thought, as he floated among the airy spirits, and he began to drift closer and closer to the enervating material world. The sparkles dipped and dived into it, and came out renewed and dancing. If he did so, would he be able to get back out again? Or would he find himself trapped inside whatever he had recklessly entered-a tree or a tapeworm?

Warren could not be afraid in the enthusiasm with which the ley-line filled him. Had he not dreamed of becoming one with beauty, and now achieved it? Was this curiosity, this desire to launch himself into something new, any different? After a hundred or a thousand thoughts, he followed the next sparkle to disappear into the material. He tried to make himself as sharp a point as the sparkle, to draw all himself together and push in through the layer of depression, disappointment, 'what am I bothering with this for' that afflicted him, and for a moment he seemed to be somewhere-heat, sound, ohohoh the world rocking, a shock, a shiver-and he was back.

Again and again he tried with no better results, always the same thing and no time to think about it or sort out what was happening, but each momentary experience gave him data. At length he rested, back in the comfort of the ley-line, and an explanation came to him as gently, as effortlessly, as a breeze on a summer day. The incubi flittered all around and through him; where they touched the material world it flared for an instant, and then they leapt back out into the plane where Warren lay.

***

"Some people would consider what you're thinking exploitative," the faux Teddy said, but Russell considered what he was thinking only natural. He was, after all, alone on a tropic isle with the good friend whom he had seen naked every morning for years. He was learning things about himself on this vacation, but by and large they weren't things that surprised or enlightened him. This disappointment, however, did not cause him to stop... He reached a hand out, investigating, and the faux Teddy did not bat it aside.

Pay attention, Russell told himself, *because this will never happen again!* It was like the time he had looked at the reef, though; the more attention he paid, the more he lost sensation. The sand under him, the tropic breezes wisping around his body, even Teddy's hands, all were washed away under the flow of his thoughts, and in the end sex with Teddy was exactly as he'd imagined it. Just the way it had been when he'd imagined it, alone, in his bedroom. Nothing more.

I didn't think I ever got depressed, Russell thought, *so at least I'm learning something new.* This gave him only limited satisfaction. He lay on the sand, doing nothing, because nothing was worth doing. Nothing was worth saying. When the faux Teddy tried to talk with him he turned away and dissolved her, he just made her disappear, and then he was all alone with nothing but himself, which was the way it was anyway, so he made the island and the sea disappear as well and just lay there. He wondered if he would ever be able to face Teddy again, but then realized that he could create a new one, who knew nothing of what had happened. She could be new every time. She could be more supportive, more understanding. She could do whatever he wanted her to. Russell felt sick at the thought. *I might be here a long time,* he thought. What would he learn about himself, as he grew more and more bored with the obvious?

**

Rho's day with the alchemist had given him a new perspective. Navanax asked good questions. *Why does the demon keep coming around? Why hasn't it offered the grimoire to some other, more cooperative magician? There's something special about me,* he thought, sometimes with elation and other times with disgust. *Special how? Specially powerful, or specially stupid?* Considering himself special was nice, but thinking about the grimoire gave Rho a nasty feeling as if he were caught in the edges of something tangled and dangerous. He didn't really have time to fuss over it, though. He had classes, and a department meeting in which they heard the IDA's formal report on the pentarium.

Rho could pick out emotions far better this time, perhaps because he already knew what Vinca was telling them and was free to look at faces. It was easy to tell, for instance, that Vinca enjoyed something about the bad news he was giving the demonologists and that he particularly wanted to see Teddy Whin's reaction; he emphasized any mention of the pentarium with a courtly inclination of his head in her direction, and she scowled in response.

"How d'you know this charm you found in the pentarium wasn't a side effect of the safety switch?" she asked sharply. "Demons can't cast charms."

"True," Vinca said. "Magicians can, however. In the charms of discourse, magicians and demons parley with one another at length. Could another demon present in the pentarium use your power to cast the same charms, in the arcane world?"

This didn't please Teddy at all, which was no surprise. Rho was a little prouder of noticing how much it did please certain other members of the department: Will, who steepled his fingers in front of a sly smile, Neil, who was watching with frank enjoyment, and Linus Ukadnian. Linus had looked up for the first time from the technical journals he read throughout every department meeting.

"Are you saying that's more likely with charms of discourse than with other charms?" Patsy Hoth fixed Vinca with a clear, bright gaze like a bird surveying a bug. Vinca gave her one of his blandest smiles.

"I am unfamiliar with modern charms of discourse," he answered. "When the pentarium was built, however, demonological invocations were quite different. You will not remember, but before charms of discourse were used invocation was done alone, through charms with a physical basis. Demons could not replicate charms which depended on the magician's body."

Regan stared at the table between his hands. "What else do you suppose the demons are listening to in there, and mimicking in their own realm? Who knows what we may have said in there, not knowing we were making a difference!"

Rho looked hard at Linus Ukadnian, who had gone back to his journals and appeared to feel nothing.

He's going to ignore all of it! Rho thought, and made his first contribution to the meeting. "That's why it says no shop talk in the pentarium," he said. "We never got demons from other ley-lines until Linus said we could."

Linus looked up with no trace of embarrassment. He glared at Rho. "I state facts," he said. "If you find them to be true, that simply means I am trustworthy in my statements. If believing facts has become a sin, rationality itself has departed from magic. This is highly likely, given that most magicians find logic even more difficult than mathematics."

Rho had no words to express what he thought of Linus. He spent the rest of the meeting searching for them instead of following the theoretical discussion, which Teddy Whin and Vinca dominated. It was a relief to get out of the building at last and onto the ley-line.

Rho walked along the line fuming, the things he might have said to Linus steaming off him into the calm afternoon air. The line ran straight west from the Magic Building, the little houses he had so often walked between set back at a discreet distance. Their backyards looked onto the line, betraying the fact in various arcane structures: shrines, scrying-pools, meditation platforms. The voice that hailed Rho, halfway along the row of houses, came from one of these.

"You look like the wicked magician in the book, dear," the voice said. "'He walked by the ley-line and laid his wicked plans'."

Turning to right and left Rho focused on Warren Oldham's mother, sitting in a deck chair under a gazebo hung with wards and wind chimes.

"Isn't it cold to sit out?" he asked, feeling combative.

"Oh, but it's sunny," Bosie said. "At my age, you don't waste a sunny afternoon. I watched everybody on this whole block get in their cars and drive away, looking as if they were going to accomplish great things, the sillies. And here you are, looking the same way. Very stern and intent. Tell me, have you seen any of the city's night life?"

"I went to a bar with one of the alchemists," Rho said.

Bosie shook her head and laughed. "I mean the nightclubs. Have that handsome young vampirologist take you out with him. He goes to all the stylish places, just to work of course, and wastes his time talking with those superior vampires until he depresses himself. On second thought, I suppose you would do better to meet a different group. There are really some quite lively people out if you find the right clubs. The Slap 'n Tickle is a lovely place if you don't mind incubi, but then of course you wouldn't being in demonology and all, would you? And they're your specialty. Did you find anything that could help you in Warren's grimoire?"

The sunny day turned a little colder.

"No," Rho said. "I gave it back to him on the morning-of the accident. Is he any better?"

"Why, there was never anything wrong with him," Bosie said. "Warren has always been a healthy boy, except for that one time-well, everybody has a little trouble some time. He's just ducky. Doesn't want a thing, and Warren has always known what he wanted, I'll say that for him. Goodness, just talking about it makes me think about that book I was telling you about-when he was a little boy, he wanted me to read that to him every minute of the day. Not that I minded, it was a most improving book. I can't imagine what made me think of it, except maybe that I bought it in Kasidora and you're from there. That was when I was carrying Warren, well of course he hadn't started to show then or I could hardly have been dancing, could I? People are a little prudish that way over there. And the book was actually written here in Osyth, but I bought it over there and brought it back with me, so pleased with myself and the cosmopolitan way I was going to raise my little magician, and there it was in the grocery stores for half the price." She sighed. "It just goes to show you that you should pay attention, doesn't it-but of course that's the moral of the book, so anything about it would make a person think that way, wouldn't it?"

Rho didn't answer these remarks. He kept quiet, like a bird watching a hawk circle overhead. Bosie took a deep breath.

"At any rate, dear, it's about this wicked magician who wants to curse everyone around him but he doesn't know anything about them so he ends up cursing them with things they really want." She paused. "Why were we talking about this?"

"We were just chatting," Rho said, stepping back. "I'm afraid I have to get back to work."

***

The cloud of incubi had moved, in a scattered and busy way, down along the ley-line. Warren could tell they had, because the texture of the material world below him had changed, from large grain to small. Where he had noticed its moods, as if they adhered to large chunks of it, he now felt little but its presence. The incubi still dipped into it, but for so short a time that they seemed only to flicker at its surface. The picture Warren made in his mind to explain this was that they had moved out of the area where humans lived along the ley-line and into the Westpark. He imagined all the trees and grasses of Westpark, its birds and squirrels, as they would appear in the summer. As he followed the incubi, though, the feeling of delight began to fade away. Warren's conviction of the world's goodness became less convincing; he began to wonder about the true worth of it all, and whether optimism were not just a convenient fiction, and from this he deduced the incubi were leaving the ley-line. Although he had grown fond of their company, he drew back.

The thought of parting with the incubi suddenly depressed him, as he hadn't been depressed since first leaving his body. He felt a mixture of sadness, anger and a dismal satisfaction, as if this were just another example of the uncaring world. He had been a fool to begin enjoying any of this. None of it cared for him. The incubi, the ley-line, the whole spiritual world, were as indifferent and meaningless as the material world. Hatred was the only response worthy of one's self-respect; only hurting them would make them care.

Warren had just enough objectivity left to wonder what he had stumbled into, and pulling himself to one side and another he found the mood did thin out. It was not some truth he had come upon in a moment of enlightenment, but another of the entities along the ley-line. He found the thinnest part of it and began to work his way in that direction, and as he did so other entities reappeared at the edges of his perception, all of them somewhat tinged with anger and discontentment. Even the single incubus he came upon, dancing up from the material world below, felt more like the professional gaiety of an abused whore than the bright delight he had been used to.

The incubus hesitated in its irregular path, unsure of which way to move in that enervating atmosphere, and the cloud of despair pounced onto it. Warren felt the incubus' busyness and energy go out. He felt it turn into-not pain precisely, but the feeling of knowing there was going to be pain, from now on; the feeling of knowing the world could allow it and revel in it, and that the basis of all being was not goodness but evil. Everything made, Warren saw clearly, was a plaything for the malignant universe; all lively sensations, that humans thought were designed for their pleasure, were only to allow more amusing tortures. Even he, himself, had been made in order to be destroyed, to be hurt as this sparkle was being hurt. He leapt away in the shock of uncovering such a secret, and in an instant he was back in the happy complacency of the ley-line.

***

It looks like a plan, Lilian thought, *but how would I know a magician's plan if I saw one? There could be all kinds of holes in this one.* She looked around the group, hoping for advice. They were all frowning in concentration, all except Teddy Whin, who had closed her eyes and fallen back into her meditative posture. Warren never needed any sort of posture like that, thought Lilian, and felt a sharp longing as she thought of him in his easy chair, with his ankles crossed and a vague look on his face. *If I get him back,* she thought, *I will never never snap at him for calming the house down when I'm trying to think. I'll go in there and sit with him. I'll never waste another minute of it...*

"This looks reasonable," Patsy Hoth said, laying the paper in her clipboard. "From the venery side, at least. I'm not expert in the rest."

Lilian looked at her copy of the paper again. On it, Teddy Whin had outlined steps for contacting Warren's spirit-that would be Susan and Will's job, using the seance-and for preparing the body for a spirit's possession, using some of the more obscure aphrodisiacs. The plan looked fine, but the demonologists seemed uninterested in it, except for Patsy Hoth. "Is something wrong with it?" Lilian asked.

"No," Susan said. "The plan seems fine. If we have a physical focus for each of them, we can take it under the hospital's shielding. That way we won't have to worry about keeping demons out of them." Teddy started to glare at her, and Susan raised her hands hastily. "No offense."

"What is going on?"

"We had a crappy department meeting," Will told Lilian in confidential tones. "The Alchemy Department is claiming that the demons have been casting our charms of discourse too, doing all the real magic for us through some kind of echo effect. They've cleared it all out of the pentarium."

363

"That's nonsense!" Teddy burst out. "Alchemists are so wedded to the idea that they shape the world! They can't imagine any other magicians being able to do real work."

"I don't know," Susan said. "We did start getting a whole new group of demons after Linus said the ley-lines were connected. What if he gave the demons the idea they could go between lines by saying it in the pentarium? It could have caused a catastrophe."

"Linus is a catastrophe," Teddy said. "We all know that. But charms of discourse only work if they're logical. If demons were providing the motive power behind them, why would they have to be logical to work?"

Patsy Hoth stood up. "It will be easily discovered," she said, "once we get Warren and Russell back, and are able to test the charms of discourse and see if they work." Her tone made it obvious that she neither thought they would still work, nor cared. "If we're done discussing Warren and Russell, I have work to do."

"I don't think we're done, at all. This plan's assuming the spirits will just flow back into their bodies as soon as they can," Will said. "It's still black magic if we push them in."

"Only if we do it," Teddy said. "Not if Warren and Russell do it themselves." Three mouths opened, but she forestalled them by swinging her fat rucksack around in an arc that almost pulled her off the bench. Balancing it on her knees, she dug within and pulled out two spiral-bound books. One was white, with a photograph of bison on the cover under large green letters reading *Nature First!* and

364

the other, a sober gray, bore the gold brick logo of the Bank of Mammon.

"Where did you get those?" Lilian asked, as Teddy opened the white book and revealed it to be a weekly planner, with a new nature photo for each week. She set it down on the benchtop.

"I broke into Warren's office for this one," Teddy said, and opened the second. "Russell's, I took away from him in the hospital. Now, when do we want to do this?"

"Tomorrow at nine o'clock," Will said, and looked around at the group. "What? Somebody has to choose a time."

"We won't have located the souls by then," Patsy Hoth said, "or cleared it with sorcery. Surely any date setting is premature?"

"We need to get moving," Teddy explained, "At some point, Salvation's going to weasel out of keeping them in the hospital, and move them into someplace where they're not shielded against demons. I work better with a deadline. But let's make it Sunday. Leap day. There's a lot of magic in leap day." She piled the two appointment books down on the bench and wrote in dark round letters, *return to body* at nine o'clock on Sunday, February 29th in the top one.

"I'm usually very busy on leap day. What reason do you have to think this will work?" Patsy Hoth asked.

"They do everything in the appointment books," Teddy said. "Don't they?"

"Yes, they do," Lilian said. "It's really quite eerie." She was filled with admiration. *How clever Teddy is!* The admiration might not last past the first flush of the idea-she could see that any Patsy Hoth had felt was already dissipated-but for a moment, it felt as if her problems were solved.

"But it's the body that reads the appointment book," Susan said, reading over Teddy's shoulder. "That memo is directed more toward the soul... "

"She's right," Will said. "Make it 'reunite with soul,' Teddy."

"We'll do an experiment. I'll put 'reunite with soul' in Warren's." She shut both the books firmly and stowed them back in the tie-dyed rucksack. "Now," she said, "all we have to do is schedule the pentarium for the seance, for Saturday."

***

Warren had a map. An incomplete map, probably a laughable one, but a map, nonetheless. The core of this map was the ley-line, and it had three zones; the first, Warren associated with the Academy. In this area there was much material activity, strong enough for even a spirit to perceive; the bits of grayness had individual moods about them. Warren took these to be magicians or the arcane artifacts in their offices and labs. In the second zone were fewer individual persons and more incubi, and this Warren associated with the neighborhood in which he and Lilian lived. In the last zone people were almost absent, and larger, more pessimistic spirits attacked the incubi. Warren imagined them swarming up the cliffs at the west end of Westpark, demons and banshees and things he could not name.

He could tell times, as well, by the goings-on in the west zone-for more demons swarmed up the cliffs at night-and the east zone, where morning brought a humming activity and midnight a few intense foci; he seemed able to be in all these places, and at all these times, at once, but it took an effort against concentration that was more than he could maintain. In the middle zone, there seemed to be no time difference. The incubi swarmed over these houses morning, noon, and night, and Warren thought about that quite a bit. If he returned to his body, he would investigate it. Having oriented himself, he began looking for individuals.

***

Lilian and Teddy's breaths came out in clouds of ice, it was so cold. Breath rimed their coat collars and froze into clanking masses in the interstices of Teddy's muffler. She walked faster. "Why is it that your boots only freeze solid if you stand still?" she asked rhetorically.

"I don't know," Lilian answered, as if she didn't really care. "I hear it's the same with your feet."

"I hope I never find that out," Teddy said, holding open the hospital's outer door. The door on the inner side of the vestibule, six feet ahead of her, was frosted half up its surface. *Ridiculous!* she thought, but didn't bother saying it. Instead, she unwound the stiff muffler and shook ice out of it as she followed Lilian down the hall. As soon as her hands and face started to warm up, she began to shiver. *Why?* Teddy thought. Winter was a mystery.

Lilian went into Warren's room without knocking, nodding to Sorcerer Pim, who was listening to his chest in what looked to Teddy like a perfunctory manner. Russell was in there as well-visiting, the nurse said cheerfully, but the two magicians did not seem to be discussing anything. Russell was doing the crossword, and Warren had a jigsaw puzzle. Teddy thought it was a pitiful thing to see two of the best minds in Osyth working on silly games. She dug Russell's calendar out of her backpack, and stood back to see what they would do.

Warren looked at the appointment book Lilian handed him. "'Reunite with soul,'" he read aloud. "Oh my! I must have forgotten about that."

"Are you serious?" Sorcerer Pim asked.

Teddy shrugged. She couldn't have stopped grinning if her life depended on it.

"He is the best magician in Osyth," she said, "unless Russell is better. Why not let them design the charm?"

"Go right ahead," the sorcerer said. "But if they figure anything out, I want to watch. If you're using magic to cure people, that's my turf." She went out shaking her head.

"Do you really know how to do this, Warren?" Lilian asked.

"Of course. It's in my grimoire. Reuniting soul and body is no trick at all. The difficulty," Warren said, "will be to catch their attention."

"Not with your soul," Russell contradicted him. "Mine yes, yours no. You'll be hanging around here in a state of angst. But actually, this isn't my issue.

My book says, 'return to body,' and here I am in my body."

"Don't be so literal," Warren said. "The note was obviously written by your soul, to your soul. You know how souls are. Self-absorbed."

"So the soul didn't think the body it was leaving behind mattered. Bodies are literal." Russell shrugged. "Payback's a bitch." He leaned back in his chair and looked at Warren with a benign smile.

"Let me look at that," Teddy said, and he handed her the book. "Well, I'll be," she said buoyantly, erasing and writing in it anew. "Now it says, 'reunite with soul.'"

"You just wrote that!" Russell protested.

"That's true, but look. That's what it says in your book."

"Damn," Russell said, looking.

"I guess we're on the same page," Warren said.

"Damn," Russell said again.

Lilian didn't seem as happy as she should have been. *People never appreciate genius properly,* Teddy thought, but at this moment it didn't matter. She had that surfing feeling, as if no wave could overcome her and she could balance on the top of life.

***

Lilian sat heavily in the chair in the waiting room. The charm Warren needed was in his grimoire, and Rho had the grimoire. "And I can't prove it," she said aloud. "It all depends on his deciding to give it back-" She closed her fingers like claws around the end of the chair arm. 'Are you

369

calling me a liar?' he had said, and she had backed down. She could hear that nasty, self-satisfied voice as if it were echoing through the hospital. *Liar!* she thought. *Lying like a mattress!* But she had backed down, and by now he might have done anything with the grimoire, he or his smoking friend... and at the thought of his smoking friend, Lilian let go of the chair and pulled her arms in to her body, as if to keep them safe. Teddy came out and sat beside her, looking delighted with herself.

"What's wrong?" she asked. "It's working just the way we hoped it would."

"Didn't you hear him?" Lilian said bitterly.

"I heard him say it was no problem."

"I heard him say the charm was in his grimoire," Lilian said, and stared at Teddy as if her eyes could push this phrase through the woman's self-satisfaction into her brain.

"So wha- oh," said Teddy. "The lost grimoire?"

"Maybe not," Lilian said, feeling as if the bottom had suddenly dropped out of her indignation. "He has three." She was pleased to see Teddy's jaw drop.

"Three!"

"And Rho only has one of them," Lilian went on, as if she astounded magicians every day.

"You don't mean three copies of one," Teddy said hopefully.

"No, I mean three grimoires. Full," Lilian added, a little spitefully. She got up a little more lightly than she had sat down. "I'll go ask him."

***

370

Teddy Whin gnawed at the edge of a fingernail when she thought about Warren having three grimoires. And that was on top of a distinguished career in wizardry before he had even taken up magic! (Not that wizardry was that much, just building stuff...) *Even if I save his life,* she thought, *he'll always be a better magician than I am. Hell, without a soul he's still a better magician than I am. What was it he said? No problem. After we all beat our brains out about it, just ask him and he says no problem.* Thinking about the other colleagues who had beaten their brains out with her helped a little. *At least I'm the one who thought to ask him,* Teddy told herself, but it was small comfort. She had chewed down two nails when Lilian came back, looking sour.

"Well?"

Lilian didn't sit down. She stood behind one of the chairs, holding her purse tightly by the strap. "It's in the one he loaned Rho," she said. "And Rho never gave it back to him. That was a lie. And I'm going to go tell him so!" She turned and started down the hall, her sneakers thumping at each step.

"Whoa," Teddy said, jumping up and hurrying after her. "Work it through a little first. If he lied to you before, he's not likely to admit it now."

Lilian stopped. "It's such a stupid lie! Did he think I couldn't just ask Warren?"

"He probably did think that. He hasn't been over to visit; for all he knows, Warren is still chanting that charm of discourse. But if he has Warren's grimoire and lied to keep it, he's maybe not the safest person for you to go insult."

"I don't see anybody else ready to do it for me."

"Andy Regan has to do it," Teddy said. "That's what we're paying him the big bucks for. He took over Warren's job... " *Regan!* she thought. *Regan would be hopeless at confronting a recalcitrant black magician.* "It's Warren's job to do that sort of thing," she said firmly. "We could write it in his book and have him do it himself."

"He doesn't have any magic!" Lilian said, glaring at Teddy. "You people over at the Academy think you're so clever when you've figured out how to make Warren do your work for you. I'm in charge of him now, and I say no more. Pick up your own messes. You hired this Rho, now you straighten him up and leave Warren out of it!"

"All right," Teddy said, taking a step back. "But let Andy try before you go charging up there again."

"All right, but no sitting on this. That grimoire's been in Warren's family for three generations. It's worth more than the whole department put together."

"I'll talk to him first thing tomorrow," Teddy promised. But she felt much better as she walked back to her apartment just inside the city walls. Of course Warren had outstanding powers! How could she have expected anything else? He had two generations of magicians behind him, passing things down to the eldest son, and each of them cared for by a full-time wife. None of Warren's male ancestors had ever so much as had to sew on a button. They could put in twenty-hour days and count on a hot meal when they got home... *It's the sort of thing that has to stop.* She opened the door to her apartment, shoving it against the mass of

372

satchels, coats and scarves hung over the inside doorknob. The thought of three generations of Oldhams and Oldham wives (traitors to their sex!) arrayed against the few single women, or even worse off, married women with their families perched on their shoulders, trying to make a mark in the field... well! Regan would never get the grimoire back from Rho, and maybe that was a good thing.

***

Lilian and Bosie set the home ward together, without much success. "Well, dear, that's not our best work," Bosie said, looking at the lopsided web of light. "It looks like nothing more than the antimacassars Warren's great-aunt Cecelia used to make. Poor dear, she was blind as a bat and never would ask directions, not that directions help much with crocheting, either you can do it or you can't. That was what killed her, she didn't ask for directions and went up the off-ramp of a highway. She couldn't read the signs by then, of course."

Lilian relaxed. She put her head back and sighed, and let Bosie wash over her unanswered.

"Why don't I get you a drink?" Bosie went on. "You look done in. Thank goodness that Mr. Grayson is doing his share of watching Warren, we never used to get that kind of service from funeral parlors in my day. Whatever they say," she continued from the kitchen, "I say the world is getting better. I don't see how anybody who's been around long enough to make comparisons could say anything else." She brought Lilian a glass of white wine, and Lilian sipped at it gratefully.

"This is good," she said. "Where did you get it?"

"I walked into town and did some shopping. I was always the one in the family who knew about wine, and incubi, and music. Warren's father was good for flowers, demons, and home repair. And scrubbing floors. He had such a talent for scrubbing floors, now you wouldn't think that was attractive, would you? But to see him scrubbing a floor in his undershirt, with his suspenders and his pants legs rolled up and his hair all up in spikes... " She sighed. "That's what I miss most, the silly things. Because whatever he might be doing in the spirit world, I can't even pretend he's scrubbing floors. It seems such an unspiritual thing to do."

Lilian cried. Without warning and without any gradual onset, as if she were a well uncapped or a faucet turned on. She looked blindly for someplace to put the glass, and Bosie took it out of her hand just as she was about to give up and drop it.

"Oh, poor baby," the older woman said, putting her arms around Lilian's shoulders. "Move over. Move over, poor baby."

Lilian felt her snuggling into the chair, and that was ridiculous. *A woman my age, sitting on my mother-in-law's lap like an overgrown baby!* she thought, but she was doing it anyway, feeling those hard thin arms tight around her and letting everything go in tears.

Chapter Eighteen

"Oh dear," Anders Regan said. His long nose glistened. "Oh dear-let me think about this a minute."

Teddy spent the minute swiveling around in Regan's guest chair. She liked Andy's office more than she liked Andy. It looked like so many of the faculty offices at her alma mater, the University of Selanto. Faculty there favored the maze effect, and arranged bookshelves to subdivide their quarters. She and Andy sat in the 'talk and office' section of his lab, hedged around by head-high shelves overflowing with books, bound journals, and pale gray cardboard filing boxes, their edges reinforced with metal ribs. The space barely held Andy's desk and chair, so Teddy, the guest, protruded between bookcases and could view some other parts of his maze. She could see the 'food and washing-up' part, with its sink and coffeepot, and the 'microscopic observations' part near the window. Both of these were outlined by waist-high shelving so as to provide convenient countertop space, on which plant specimens, dried or pickled or embedded in wax, cohabited with once-used tea bags and sugar cubes. The rest of the room was walled off from her by more of the high bookcases, with various degrees of light or darkness coming over their tops.

"You know, anybody in the lab could hear us in here," she said. "We shouldn't be talking about confidential matters."

"What? Nobody else is in yet," Andy said.

375

"The lights are on in the back." While Andy squeezed past her to investigate, Teddy amused herself by recalling things she had overheard in just such a lab as this. Observing faculty, she reflected, was much more informative than being taught by them. It was, in fact, part of a faculty member's duty to provide object lessons of some sort. That was why she disapproved of Andy, she decided as he squeezed back over her knees. He was too good. There was nothing to learn from observing him.

"I'll have to talk to him," he said now, looking very unhappy. He began looking through the file folders on his desk, shifting each of them three inches to the right.

"If you'd rather I did it... "

"No, you two might have to work together. I'll tell him Lilian spoke to me about it. That's true enough, she had me open up Warren's office for her on Monday."

"I don't care if you tell him I know about it," Teddy said. "It'll be better to tell him upfront than have him find out later. But if you need me, I'm only in till ten thirty."

"We're probably making too big a deal out of this." Regan shifted the folders back again. "I'm sure he'll have a perfectly simple explanation."

***

Rho was walking down the hall fast when Regan called his name in a nervous tenor voice. He stiffened when he heard it. It was the kind of voice that made him want to ignore it, that would only say petty things, either vacuous compliments or know-

376

nothing criticisms. Rho mentally hunched his shoulders as he turned around, prepared to let anything that voice said roll off them.

"We need to talk." Regan gestured toward his office.

"I was on my way to something," Rho said.

"It'll just be a minute."

It was more than that, Rho realized as he saw Regan's graduate students look up and leave the lab.

"Teddy Whin came to see me this morning," Regan said. "You know she's been over at the hospital a lot with Russell, so she's spoken with Lilian Oldham a good deal. Lilian complained to her about Warren's grimoire being lost. You remember that."

"Of course I remember it." Rho tried to remember what an innocent expression felt like from the inside, and to arrange his face into one. "She came up to my rooms in the middle of the night, demanding it. I thought the department's wards were supposed to keep unauthorized people out." A hostile expression was much easier, he decided. His heart beat faster, but that was because he was rightfully indignant.

"Since that's also the night a demon got in, we can take the condition of the wards as a given," Regan shot back. "You told Lilian that you'd given the grimoire back to Warren. But yesterday Warren told her that wasn't true, and she's pretty upset. I'm sure there's a simple explanation for it, of course."

"And she told Teddy, and Teddy told you? How far was this going to go before somebody had the decency to approach me in person?" Rho felt stronger, more in control, with every word. His tongue had been tied with Hoth, with the demon, but not now! Regan looked seriously off-balance.

"I just heard about it this morning," he said. "I hardly see how I could have told you sooner, without pulling you out of class."

"Sorry, I didn't mean you. But Teddy should have come to me."

"What would you have told her?"

"I'd have told her Mrs. Oldham ought to make these accusations officially or not at all."

"Well, that simplifies things," Regan said. "I can send that message back to her, if you'd sign this event report verifying that I asked you about the incident. Or we could discuss it as colleagues, and try to deal with it in-house rather than sending her to the authorities."

The printed form he pushed over his desktop made the whole thing horribly real. Rho got up and backed toward the door.

"I'm not signing anything until I've talked with a lawyer," he said. "If people are going to make accusations against me without cause based on the word of a body without a soul, and my own department members are more interested in covering their own butts than in supporting me, you can forget any kind of cooperation." His steps beat out the tempo of the declaration as he marched toward the exit and took the stairs two at a time up to his tower. His blood flowed hotter, his heart beat more fiercely as he replayed the conversation in his mind. He had been magnificent!

Rho couldn't settle to work. He looked at a page for five minutes at a time, running through his battle with Regan again in his mind, muttering phrases from it, and jumping up from his seat to stride around the room, gesturing to the air. But whenever he stopped for a minute, out of breath, papers looked at him reproachfully from their piles. Stacks of open books seemed to wilt in neglected depression. His computer whirred, as plaintive as an unpatted puppy... in short, he had work to do.

"Oh, crap." Rho sat down again, but in a moment he had thrown the book aside and was reliving the argument once more. He felt himself in the right, for the first time since the demon had taken Warren's grimoire. This was how Osyth dealt with problems! With blaming and legalities-and it wasn't a problem he had caused. It was the demons' fault, or Linus', or even Warren and Russell's, for running a pentarium they didn't understand. The more he thought about it, the more he saw that all of Osyth had worked in concert to cause his problems. *They didn't hire me for this crap!* he thought. *I'm supposed to talk with animals! If they pile all this stuff on me, they can't complain when I take care of myself.* He was so pleased with this phrase that he looked around for someone to share it with. He actually wished the demon were there, because only it would understand.

***

An abandoned cubicle was a sad-looking place, Lilian thought as she set her purse down on her desk at Salvation Insurance. After only a few days, it got that uninhabited air. Neglect and dismay filled up an empty cubicle. The mouse lay forlorn on its pad, the in basket looked an untidy reproach at her. Family

379

photographss that were better not looked at stared up at her from the desk. When she switched the computer on it whirred in reproach, and the 'you have mail' icon blinked like a mad thing, but Lilian ignored it. She opened a new document and began to fill out an insurance application with her husband's current data. There was nothing on the form about the state of his soul-a foolish omission, the professional part of her told the client part, which did not agree. Lilian printed out the form, feeling absurdly guilty, and tore it into strips. She put them into the little velvet bag, hoping to pour out anything but that dead pile of bones and paper strips, but it was the same as the day before, the same as the day before that. Lilian cast the bones three times before she gave up.

She propped her head on her hand and sighed, as old and tired as the building around her. A list of email stared at her from the computer screen, and as she reached to switch the program off she scanned it automatically. Green markers showed the unread messages, screens of them as she scrolled upward... and finally the first one, and the old messages before it. The applications that had already been dead, before anything happened to Warren. Lilian looked at them for a moment of indecision and clicked on *print*.

***

"Hard to believe," Teddy Whin said. "Hard to believe." She was lying in her hammock-chair at an unnatural angle with her feet propped up against one rope and her head against another, proofreading

380

the upcoming issue of *Crone* and marveling at triple-decker footnotes in one of the articles. "Three lines of text and forty-two of footnotes," she said aloud. "At this rate we'll have to start putting the papers in eight-point and the notes in ten, or our readership will go blind." She nodded, repeating the phrase to herself. It was a good one, but who would she share it with? Teddy sighed and went back to the article. It didn't seem half as funny, or as worth printing.

"There's a concept," she said. "The subjective element in academic merit." What if merit itself-not just her determination of it-varied with the mood of the reader? Which of course it did. Merit was a totally relative term. Teddy scowled. It was a well-known side effect of bereavement, but in her opinion a very bad sign, when one began rediscovering platitudes. "Bad enough to lose a friend, without losing my intellectual edge," she said, and put the offending article down on the floor. The telephone rang, and she looked at it balefully. It rang again, undaunted, and she disentangled herself from the chair.

"Yeah?" she said into it.

"Uh-Theodora Whin, please."

"This is."

"This is Lilian."

"Oh! Um, I thought you were a telemarketer," Teddy said.

"No, I'm at work. Can we meet somewhere?"

"Sure. You want to get lunch someplace?"

"Yes," Lilian said. "I'm right downtown. Where are you?"

"In the north end. I'll come down there."

381

"Well, I'm right next to the Downtown Club. Would you like to have lunch there?"

"Whoo!" said Teddy. "Well, yeah-how much is it?"

"My treat," Lilian said.

Well! Teddy Whin thought as she put on her best boots. *This is a treat. Observing the patriarchy in its natural habitat.* The thought sustained her through downtown Osyth's traffic and parking challenges, and she walked bright-eyed through crowds of people dressed like grown-ups, eyeing businessmen with an evaluative air. *I don't know,* she thought. *Maybe I'd like men better if I hung around with this kind.* They looked solid and effective, these men in suits. Too many men around the Academy looked as if they were still trying to figure out how to survive adolescence, a project in which Teddy had no desire to assist.

Business dress reduced the women, though. Even Susan Teale in her drab draperies looked more independent and enabled than these dollybirds. Teddy abandoned the business world as a possible utopia with little regret. She had really known better all along, but it was fun to dream. And it was fun to go up in a glass-fronted elevator and sit in a room with windows all around it, at a table with heavy linen and silver. The men up here were polished, white-haired CEOs and their obsequious juniors. Teddy sat bolt upright, looking around and noting every detail, until she came to herself and realized that a blase air would be more dignified. She had just achieved one when Lilian sat down across the table, wearing a navy suit that made her look like one more of the dollybirds.

382

"I'm sorry, am I late?"

"No, I got here early," Teddy said, and they discussed the menu, the weather, and the club for a few minutes. When the waitress left with their orders, Lilian leaned forward and scrabbled in her bag. Teddy almost held her breath, but all that came out was a book of matches. Lilian struck one without tearing it out of the book.

Cool, Teddy thought, planning to learn the trick.

Then Lilian lit the candle in the center of their table. Looking around, Teddy noticed for the first time that many of the tables had their candles lit, probably by the same attentive waiters who were producing silver cigarette lighters for the elderly businessmen's cigars, and that there was no perceptible smoke. This club was more than it seemed. She turned back to catch the tail end of movement as Lilian traced something on the tablecloth.

"Now, we can really talk," Lilian said. "Tell me what happened with Rho."

"I don't know," Teddy said. "Regan must have talked to him by now."

"You don't know?"

"I had stuff to do! We're getting a journal out."

"I read his runes," Lilian said. "It's absolutely illegal, what I'm about to tell you. Swear you won't tell."

"Blood oath," Teddy said. She held a finger out into the candle flame. Lilian nodded, a lot sooner than Teddy would have herself.

"All right," she said.

Teddy pulled her finger back and dunked it in her water glass. A waiter appeared, almost immediately, with a new glass and a finger bowl.

"The first time I threw Rho's runes, the cast fell dead," Lilian said. "Now Warren's are doing that. But Rho's have changed. It was what we call a black cast."

"That metaphor really troubles me," Teddy said. "Though I suppose I should say the same about 'falling dead,' to be consistent. There are all sorts of dead people who deserve more respect than to be made into a figure of speech."

"We're not politically correct in insurance," Lilian snapped. "Do you want to know what it means, or not?"

"I didn't come all the way down here just for the food," Teddy said.

"It's when the papers tie all the bones together," Lilian said. "They cover all the life marks on the bones. It all comes out as a bundle, and you can't get it apart. You can't imagine how spooky that is."

"Yeah, but what does it mean?" Teddy was trying to visualize what Lilian had described. She thought of beef bones, and soon realized that could not be right. No amount of paper strips would cover up beef bones.

"It means some kind of catastrophe. You can't tell what kind, because all the life marks are covered."

"But does that mean the person is going to die?" Teddy thought of human bones, this time. Fingerbones and foot bones, the little creepy ones.

384

"No. Where the papers touch the life marks is where the person's circumstances impinge on their nature. That's how you analyze a cast."

"So Rho's circumstances are-what? Wiping out his nature? Destroying it? Defining it-as if they don't already?"

"They aren't yet," Lilian said. "They're going to."

"But what's the news in that? Everyone's circumstances define their nature. But not all the casts indicate that, so this must mean something more." Teddy frowned at her plate as the waitress set it down. "Perhaps the cast distinguishes between past circumstances, which formed the current nature, and future ones, which might affect it? But then wouldn't insurance policies select against people who allow themselves to change?"

"The bones are more basic than that," Lilian said. "They don't vary with the person. They're about good and evil."

"As determined by?"

"Blood sacrifice," Lilian said.

Teddy, still thinking of fingerbones, started.

"Basically, by the chicken that used to own them. It's a nasty process, showing the bones the difference between good and evil. Not lunchtime conversation."

"I bet," Teddy said. She made a note to look it up later. The prospect was exciting; a new field with unexplored assumptions and significant practical consequences! In her mind's eye, she saw a theme issue of *Crone* on the topic, with at least one article of her own. And an introductory editorial, and maybe a summing up at the end. Perhaps a conference. She speared a scallop. "This food is great."

"Warren and I came here for our anniversary," Lilian said, and turned for just a second back into the woman Teddy had known at the hospital. "Anyway, the bones say bad things are going to happen to this Rho. Worse than what's happened to Warren. And if anybody finds out I told you, I'm out of a job. What do we do about it?"

***

Rho would not have said they needed to do anything about it at all. He took big bites of his burger and washed them down with gulps of beer, and when his glass was empty just one look brought the waitress hustling over with a fresh one. Rho liked this bar. He could see students react when they saw him-faculty! They steered respectfully away. Navanax leaned back from the table, still talking, and Rho listened a little bit, just to be a good sport.

"Half the consultants say the thing isn't any good unless it corrodes, because without planned obsolescence the economy goes to hell. The other half say it's no good if it does corrode, because it'll be used for vital functions. So I say, what are you using for those vital functions now, and does it corrode? I mean, I can make the damn metal do whatever they want, if they'll make up their fucking minds-but they say sometimes it corrodes and sometimes it doesn't. That doesn't upset them. They think it's just nature. People let nature get away with murder, but as soon as they realize a person is

386

designing it, they start to think he ought to be able to please everyone."

Navanax drank half his beer in one long, exasperated draft. A roar of student voices rose around them from the crowd at The King's. Rho could see past student heads to the front window and the College of Sorcery across the street. He saw the splintered bottom of the tavern's sign, broken off by sorcery students in an ever-repeated ritual. Nobody knew which of the King's possessions the tavern had originally been named for; its sign, usually scatological, was hung up whenever a student cared enough to make one, and smashed by the first subsequent comers.

"Why people think I can make two opposite facts be true, any more than nature can, I'll never know," Navanax said. He waved to the waitress for more beer. "So that's my day, how was yours?"

Rho reviewed his day. Accused of black magic. Job in question. No more pretending to respect the assholes in his department. "Pretty good," he said. "Considering."

Navanax raised his eyebrows. "Have you figured out what it wants?" he asked.

"I know what it wants. It wants power."

Navanax tucked the corners of his mouth in as if he were exasperated. "What for?"

"I don't know," Rho said, sulking. "What does a demon want?"

Navanax spread his hands. "You're the demonologist," he said. "D'you need to stay in my lab again tonight?"

Rho checked the sunlight. "I guess so," he said. "I'll come over around five." He walked back to his own building filled with ill will toward all he passed, from stodgy-looking administrators to effete arcane arts' students to the sorcerers' apprentices shivering in their scrubs.

It was easy for Navanax to talk, as if he expected Rho to just ask the demon what it wanted-but then, Navanax didn't know why Rho couldn't talk to it. He didn't know that Rho already knew what it wanted. *It never cared about me at all,* Rho thought. *Not after it found out it could use me to get Warren.* He sat in front of his computer staring at the Demonological Congress' internet archives and brooding, until someone knocked on his door in an official manner.

"Campus security," a voice from outside said. "Open up, please." Rho stood up, shocked.

"What's this about?" he asked, opening the door a crack. "I was just about to cast a rather dangerous charm."

"We're trying to find one of the magicians' grimoires," the guard said. "Do you mind if we come in and talk with you about it?"

"Yes, I do," Rho said. "I'll be at your service during my office hours, but right now you're interfering with my research." He sounded just right. Professional. Dignified. Unfortunately the guard was unimpressed, and pushed harder against the door.

"I'm afraid I must come in," he said.

Rho pushed back, until he realized how suspicious that must look.

"All right," he said, giving way suddenly so the guard almost fell into the room. He stood back and watched as the man regained his balance. "You're

doing this over my protests, and against my advice."
Frustration, deep inside him, jumped up and down
and gibbered as he answered an endless series of
inane questions. But Rho knew how to answer
questions. He knew how to stick to one lie, refusing
to be drawn off into speculation and attacking any
offered. He knew how to protest ignorance, and
when to indignantly rebut attempts to trap him. The
game became fun, as it went along-a sour sort of
fun, where all the points scored would eventually
count against oneself and spawn endless rematches,
but Rho had not begun it. He was the innocent
victim of this persecution. Sitting with his back
blocking off his computer from view, he parried
every attempt the guard made to implicate him.
Eventually the man stood up, and Rho thought he
would go, but he had only risen to begin a search of
Rho's quarters.

"This is unconscionable!" Rho said. "You have
no warrant."

"I do," the guard said. "It's in the waivers you
signed when you took the rooms."

"It is not," Rho said. The guard faltered, and
Rho drove into the weak spot. The man didn't have
a copy, and could not until working hours of the
next morning. Rho did, as the guard pointed out, but
then, as Rho pointed out, the guard couldn't search
for it. What was sweeter than victory over the forces
of persnickety order and petty suspicion? Rho stood
dignified by the door as his beaten adversary
withdrew, but as soon as he closed it something
began an annoying buzzing sound. Rho had to
search a few minutes before he located the sound in
his computer's alarm clock, telling him it was ten

minutes to five. He swore, cursing the guard and school impartially. Every mindless rule and every mindless person who thought professionalism was a matter of memorizing rules had a share in Rho's curses. As he turned the computer off, threw on his coat and grabbed the few papers he could find for his evening work, he called down maledictions on his colleagues, his employers, and his employers' employers, on all that sustained them and on all they cherished, and he ran down the stairs as fearless as if the tower were filled with solid anger to catch him if he fell.

Chapter Nineteen

This was loneliness. Not an empty void, not silence, not solitude. Lonely was a busy place, where every passing thought looked into Russell's face and made sport of him, and nothing was to be learned from any of them. An endless crowd of thoughts surrounded him, pushing in on every side, the detritus of a life's idle fancies, and Russell had no eyes to shut against them, no ears to stop. The mental chatter he had kept up all his life filled him now. It took its revenge; it asserted itself as primary, the one thing he had never forsaken or set aside. *This is loneliness,* Russell thought. *This is madness.* Lonely madness danced around him, making faces.

Russell blamed himself. He had long ago given up the disciplines of his graduate-school days, the attempts to quiet his mind and let the outside world in. It had been too much fun to work with the other magicians, concentrating on just one aspect of reality; Teddy and James would provide the others, but now Teddy and James weren't here to help him. Only his pictures of them, the simulacra of his fancy, spoke his parodies of their arguments. They paraded past him and he hated them without meaning to, destroyed them in a thousand ways, and was appalled at his mind's casual viciousness.

If I ever get out of here, Russell vowed, *I'll do all my thinking for myself. I'll go back to observation, disciplined observation without words.* He remembered the early years when he had made up, all alone, the charms used in the pentarium, when he had walked along the ley-line and through Osyth in a meditative haze, seeking out details he could enlarge, build upon until he had a structure of reality to trap a demon in. Every walk had been a new test of the structure... but collaborative work, the fun of writing down and arguing over theories, had charmed him, gradually taking over the time allotted to observation. With James' advent, bringing his reports of observations from field stations Russell had never visited, and then Teddy's appearance with her reinterpretations of everything, Russell had stopped walking the ley-line. What mattered for the team was a notion they could agree upon, something fruitful for generating new charms, whether they all had seen it or not; whether it existed or not. And he had forgotten how to silence his mind and look into the brilliant chaos of the world.

He tried to remember what it had felt like. The ley-line in high summer, buzzing with insects, he could conjure up, but that was not what he meant. What he needed to recapture was the focused yet relaxed wonder of simply walking through it. Russell imagined himself in that state he had once known so well. He had sometimes, back then, felt he was using new senses he could barely perceive. He had believed he felt the ley-line under him, sometimes, and thought this must be what Warren was talking about-for Warren had been a young and touchy-feely person in those long-ago days, a man prone to poetic effusions and long vanishings into the woods along the ley-line. How long ago had that been? How long ago had Warren turned, overnight it seemed, into the stolid fatty who talked of nothing but his department's needs? About the same time Russell's own hair had stopped being yellow and turned the dirty undies color he had finally bleached white out of sheer exasperated vanity. And no one had noticed. *By then,* Russell thought, *we had stopped seeing one another.* Alone among his crowd of fancies, Russell mourned a vanished world. The images around him faded away unnoticed, as he lost himself in grieving.

***

Rho sat on Navanax's cot and took out his papers. He found it easier to read every time he came to the alchemy lab. The first time he had tried it, the letters had rearranged themselves before his eyes into whatever he happened to be thinking, but they could be prevented from doing this by a sort of disciplined vagueness. That vagueness was impossible for him to attain this evening. The words he was reading turned from his notes on incubi into the conversation with Regan, the things he should have said, the things he would say next time, and the things he was thinking about Regan, Teddy Whin and Warren's wife. He hastily put the student essays back into his briefcase before he could turn them into something their authors should never see.

"If I made something in here, could it exist outside?" he asked Navanax.

"Not unless the guild approved it," Navanax answered. He was bending over a piece of apparatus, focusing it without touching it just by changing the shape of the lenses. Rho watched with admiration and resentment. For all his fierce talk,

393

Navanax was part of the status quo. He would never take a real risk. There was something pitiful about alchemists, so powerful and so bound to a system that did nothing for them. Not that they had any choice. The guild had them all, by blood oath. He imagined the guild as a black-robed tribunal; their prisoner, hauled before them in chains, bursting into flame as they pronounced judgment.

That was how the magicians of Osyth wanted their field to be. Professionalized, along the pattern of the alchemists. Everybody walking in lockstep toward one goal, with nobody trying anything new. Nobody standing out. He reviewed his argument with Regan in that light, and it made a horrible sense. And what had Neil Torecki said? *Osyth gives us the good life,* thought Rho. *They steal our souls, and give us the good life in return. I'm the only one who can see it, because I haven't accepted the good life. But they won't stop until they've made me into one of them.*

The theory enthralled and infuriated him, all at the same time. It made so much sense and it was so horrible, a plot without grandeur. A bunch of mediocrities, determined to make the world forget it had ever seen anything better than themselves. They hired good magicians, he was sure of that-there would be no challenge in corrupting the already corrupted. The challenge was to take good magicians, the ones who could have brought magic ahead, and turn them into agents to destroy their own kind. *I'll never do that,* Rho thought. *I won't run away, either. I'll face this system, expose it for what it is. They'll all be despised by the world, when*

I'm through showing the rest of the magicians what Osyth is really about.

He couldn't sit still, full to the brim with revelation, so he stood up and paced a few steps. Navanax barely glanced at him before turning back to the instrument. Rho glared at his back for a minute. There had to be someone he could tell. Some true friend, not enslaved to a guild or seduced by the comforts of Osyth. Navanax, he saw now, was just another part of the system. A safety valve, where disaffected junior faculty could let off steam without threatening the lords of Osyth. Before anybody took action, Navanax's oath would have made him betray them. *But who,* Rho thought, *are the lords of Osyth? Who stands to gain from the subversion of academic magic?* Staring at Navanax's back, he squinted as if it might make him able to see something he had been missing in plain view. Something was there. Something dark and cold, growing darker and larger by the second, something horribly familiar, and Rho lost his concentration. He gasped and lurched a step backwards, knocking something behind him to the floor with a crash. The demon looked around, and so did Navanax.

***

Rho gasped, there was a crash of glassware, and Bill Navanax turned to find himself almost within arm's length of a demon. *I've never seen a demon,* he thought, sardonic by reflex. *So this is one.* It was about his own height, variable in aspect. At one moment it was covered with fine black hair

395

and had a pig's snout, at another, it looked almost human. It always had multiple rows of jagged teeth and black wings. *On the whole,* Bill told himself, *a frightening creature.*

He kept his mind on those words, on the surface level, and tried to ignore what his heart and lungs were doing as the *grue* hit him. He took a big, stealthy step backwards, as if stealth mattered when the predator was looking directly at him, and the demon took an identical step forward. *This doesn't exist,* Bill told himself, and the demon should have disappeared at the thought. Instead, it took another step forward, and now it was almost touching him. He groped behind himself on the lab bench, thinking of a weapon, any weapon, and raised the first thing he could grab. It proved to be a wooden club with large knobs on its head, an item he had often admired in his grandfather's house. *Crap!* Bill thought, and hit the demon over the head. As he had feared, this only irritated it. "Rho, get rid of your damn demon!" he shouted.

The demon stopped in the middle of reaching for Bill's throat, and they both looked at Rho. He was sitting on the cot, squeezing his eyes shut with an expression of concentration. When Bill looked back at the demon, it had shrunk, was more piggy in appearance, and had shorter arms. He was able to dodge to the left, out of its reach. The demon stood still, panting, and glared at him through little hot eyes.

"And what are you?" it asked, giving him a start. "What rules do you want him to follow, to gain your favor? Whenever I see him, he has found a new master to obey." With every word, it stood taller.

"Hell, Rho," Bill bawled, "are you going to listen to a demon? Roaches aren't bad enough?" The demon developed a shinier skin and additional joints to its legs, and Bill was sorry he had mentioned roaches. "Not to mention fish," he yelled, but the moment for influencing Rho had apparently passed. The demon retained all its legs and joints, and looked at Bill through what were now definitely compound eyes. It moved from side to side, quite fast. "Dammit to hell." Bill turned the first thing he could reach into a fire extinguisher; it was his computer, and that was irritating in itself. He would certainly lose his unsaved work. "You're making this thing," he said to Rho, viciously. "Who told you you could make a demon in my lab? Do I make demons in your lab? Do I?" The thing wavered.

"You've never been in my lab," Rho said. The demon was definitely transparent now. It spoke in a squeak and a mumble, but its words could not be heard, and in a moment it had faded away.

Bill lowered his fire extinguisher and took a deep breath, but it didn't help. He had been able to joke in the demon's grasp but now, faced with someone who had to be jollied out of creating demons, he found himself too angry to speak. It was all he could do to keep the fire extinguisher pointed down. He put it on the desk, carefully. When he spoke again, it was in a tone that didn't hide his disgust. "Do you think you can keep it from coming back?" he asked. "Or should I leave this for you?"

397

"That wouldn't work on a demon," Rho said. He sounded unsure, not clear whether Bill was mad or joking. "I guess if I could make a demon, I could make my own weapons, anyway. Why couldn't you get rid of it?"

"It wasn't real," Bill said. "If it had been anything on its own, I could have changed it."

"I didn't make it up! You saw what it did to me in your house. Would I make up something like that?"

"You guys make up all your demons. Charms of discourse, remember? You tell 'em what to be."

"I don't tell things to rip me apart! I don't tell them to attack my friends."

When Bill looked at him, Rho's expression changed. He looked shifty.

"I don't see what I've done to deserve this kind of accusation," he said. "If you don't want me here, I'm sure I don't need to stay."

"You want attitude? I'll show you attitude," Bill said. Heat shimmered at the edges of his vision and the cot burst into flame.

Rho jumped up, his face pale, but there was nowhere for either of them to go. Fire filled every corner of the room, popping and crackling as bottles exploded. Flames drove Rho over toward Bill.

"You're fucking crazy!" he shouted.

"Yeh, but I'm only as crazy as I want to be." The fire was harder to stop than it had been to start. Bill made it die out in the back of the lab first, concentrating on rebuilding his equipment. He felt much better. It didn't hurt that Rho was looking at him with awe-at him, and then at the blaze that

398

blocked the doorway. "Don't just stand there," said Bill. "Fix the cot."

Rho looked at the blackened metal and it began to shift back into position. He crouched beside it, smoothing it into shape, and stood by his handiwork for a minute before cautiously sitting down on it. Then he looked at Bill and at the doorway again, frowned in concentration, and glared at the flames.

"Forget it," Bill said. "You're not getting out of here until you can tell me why you made a demon, when you could have made anything you wanted. What's it do for you?"

Rho scowled. "It doesn't give me any of this crap," he said. "I didn't come here to be psychoanalyzed."

"It gave you plenty of crap over at my place. If something tore me up like that, I wouldn't call it up again."

"I was mad," Rho said, sullen. "I was thinking about what a fascist state this place is. Can you believe Regan sent some goon to search my rooms?"

"What for?"

Bill didn't like this kind of quiet. The choosing-a-lie kind of quiet. The Oops-I've-said-too-much kind. The fire in his doorway disappeared as if it had never been, and he saw Rho looking that way as if planning an escape. "What did Regan think he was going to find?" he asked Rho. "A demon under the bed?"

"They know about the demon," Rho said, too easily. Too relieved.

"So what were they thinking they'd find in your rooms?" Bill stood up straight with a light feeling,

399

as if something inside of him was letting go of another, heavier part. The solid part was falling to the ground, and the rest was about to fly loose, to say, 'the hell with it' and soar away. "There's a big hole in this story," he said, but he didn't expect an answer and didn't care. He'd care later.

"Fuck you." Rho stood up.

"Likewise, I'm sure."

***

Warren knew he was in some part of the Academy. Moods hovered around the things below him like smells, but they were muffled, with a metallic tang to them that made him think of sorcery's protective wards. Beings so warded turned the spiritual world from a zone of edgeless, flowing motion into an obstacle track; the few incubi he could perceive were staying far away from them, congregating in just a few places. *Patient's rooms?* Warren wondered. *Surreptitious trysts in the broom closet, as shown on TV? Or places in only the spiritual sense, places every person entered when lost in lust?* He felt around, spreading himself through the complicated surroundings, and a familiar feeling shocked him. It was the springtime forest feeling, and with it the trumpets and glory that he believed was Bosie and something else he didn't know, but that felt balanced on a giddy height. Warren focused all of himself on drawing nearer to those feelings, and he was there-the metallic sensation all around him, blocking out the ley-line and all its denizens except one errant

400

incubus. Only Bosie would be able to lure an incubus into such a warded area.

The incubus dove toward them and was rebuffed, again and again, without losing its enthusiasm. It reminded Warren of a puppy with a ball it wanted someone to throw. He sympathized but, immaterial, could do nothing for it. As he watched, though, it found a spot it could get through. It sparkled more brightly and jigged as it came out again, as if it were wagging a tail.

The incubus swooped in and out again, without a moment's delay. This one spot seemed no barrier to it. Warren drifted closer, and ambition filled him. He had gone too long just looking and thinking. He wanted adventure, as much as he had ever wanted food or water when in his body. He gathered himself together and dove into the same spot, with a fanfare, and in the heart of it he stopped.

He had entered a crowded place. Every bit of space was filled with something-blood, bones, muscle. Familiarity with the physical returned only gradually, as if Warren had plunged himself into this body head downwards and had to reorient himself. Painstakingly, he turned himself about. The world around him came into focus... *Wonderful world!* For it contained the person he most wished to see, out of all people. Lilian was sitting across from him, worried, talking with someone this body would not look at directly.

Warren leapt in delight, and the body put a hand to its chest and belched. "Sorry, dear," it said. "I don't know what I can have eaten. You were saying?"

401

"I was saying we had to get that grimoire back. Warren can't remember the charm."

"Did you try writing 'remember charm' in his appointment book?" The voice was Teddy Whin's, as was the face Bosie turned to glance at. Warren thought this was a very strange suggestion from Teddy and so did Lilian, from her glare.

"Yes," she said, which was even odder. "He just can't remember, all right?"

Teddy put up her hands in a conciliatory gesture. "All right," she said.

Warren could not understand any of this; it was like watching one of those soap operas his daughters favored, coming in on the middle of a relationship without knowing who had done what to whom. The grimoire, though, he could understand. He could even feel it, like a part of himself tugging at him from further down the ley-line. He tried to speak, and nothing happened. After a while, though, the body he was in pointed west.

"It's that way," Bosie said. Teddy and Lilian looked at her.

"What?"

"I'm not sure, dear," Bosie said. "I just know it's that way."

"The grimoire? How would you know where the grimoire is?"

"Where that way? In the Magic Building? On what floor?"

"Way up," Bosie said.

Lilian jumped to her feet. "I knew it!" she cried.

"Hold on," Teddy said. "How could Bosie suddenly know where the grimoire is?"

"I don't know how I know it," Bosie said. "I just do."

Teddy and Lilian looked at one another, and Lilian grabbed her coat.

"I'm going over there," she said.

"Call security."

"I've already tried that. Can't you see I've had enough of this? Warren's spent his life at this Academy, and when he gets hurt all they want to do is cover their asses. I'm going over there and get the grimoire back from that little bastard, and if he gives me any lip he'll be sorry."

Teddy picked up her coat. "All right," she said, putting it on.

"Bosie, you wait here."

"But I'm the one who knows where it is," Bosie said.

"Tell us."

"Sweetie, I don't know anything about that building. I'll just have to smell it out as we go."

Every step on the pavement astonished Warren. Dull sidewalks and half-decomposed heaps of snow delighted him. He felt the pull of the ley-line and the sparkles of incubi above it, with stronger, more complex creatures wafting against him like the wind.

"My goodness," Bosie said, "Another windy night. It was a night like this when Warren's father solved some problem or other he'd been working on for years, I really can't remember what, but he stayed ever so late at work and I got worried enough to come out to the ley-line and wait for him. I'll never forget it, I might have blown away standing there. That was when we lived in the old Grimbgarn house, you know, the one five blocks down from you, Lilian. Anyway, there I was in the wind, and it had even started to snow like nothing you ever saw before-a regular blizzard-and then the stars came out. Just over my head, nowhere else. All that snow and the stars at once, and there he was coming up the ley-line with a bottle of champagne and his coat hung over his shoulders." She stopped just a moment, hugging herself and looking up as if to see remembered stars, but Lilian was impatient and put a hand on her arm. "Warren is so much like him," Bosie said. "Sometimes I almost mix them up. So silly, because he wasn't bald." The moment passed, and they walked on.

***

Rho wiped his forehead. His hand shook, and he scowled at it. *It's nothing but exhaustion,* he thought, but that was a lie; he didn't own furniture heavy enough for him to be exhausted from moving it to the corners of the room. He bent over to draw another line of the pentacle on the floor, thinking about nothing except the feel of the soft chalk and the importance of making a thick, solid line. It was a good big pentacle, if lopsided, nothing like the one Vivien had drawn in Selanto, but large enough for Rho to stretch out in if he were careful. He left a few feet open on one side while he assembled various articles to take into it with him. All the amulets he owned. Bittersmoke, and a dish to burn it in. His backpack, filled with magic supplies and serving double duty as a pillow, and the sleeping bag, with a supply of candy bars and three cans of

404

caffeinated soda tucked among its coils. Thus supplied, Rho entered the pentacle and closed it behind himself. This proved to be a mistake, as he had to unroll the sleeping bag without pushing himself through the pentacle. He stood on the unrolled half of the bag, trying to decide how to move it to the pentacle's end when there was no place else for him to stand, and felt frustration boiling up inside him. When he looked up from the bag, it was to see his demon peering in through the pentacle's clear walls.

"You seem to have a problem," it said gaily.

"Two," Rho said, glaring at it.

"The solution is to get into the bag, and move it along as if you were a caterpillar," the demon said. "The only thing more enlightening than seeing the level of problems posed at this establishment is observing how quickly your own intellect has declined to match your peers'. Perhaps the caterpillar analogy is accurate."

"Say what you like," Rho said, getting into the sleeping bag which could indeed, he found, be moved caterpillar-like across the floor. "You can't get through the pentacle."

"Indeed, so I shall say what I like," the demon said. "I see you have made your decision in favor of the civilized life here in Osyth. It looks cozy." It tossed Rho's coat onto his easy chair and sat down on it, stretching long legs out in front of itself, and sighed. "I could scarcely credit, had it not happened before my eyes, how quickly you have degenerated. I rarely misjudge a magician so, but I have never experienced a depth of mediocrity quite like this. The commonplace is usually neutral. I was not prepared to find it malignant. It is odd, is it not, that magicians of great talent would turn their strength toward destroying their own world? You can explain this to me, as I see you have made the same decision. Tell me what has enticed you into self-immolation on the altar of respectability."

"You have," Rho said. "I didn't like your alternative."

"Oh, please." The demon waved its hand. "We know better than to wax dramatic about a little thing like that. An animal moment, five minutes give and take; it is but an instant, compared to the life of slavery you propose to submit to, bending your mind to fit every new rule your masters can devise. How long will it take you to love the rules? To write rules of your own, and break those who flout them? You will have to find safe friends, and distance yourself from any who would question the rules. Instead of the annals of magicians, you will read the minutes of meetings; what the dean or the president said last will exercise you more than any wonders of the arcane world, and you will be proud of having learned to manipulate others and turn them away from their work into such slaves of the system as yourself."

Rho covered his ears and hummed, muffling his head in the sleeping bag, but the demon's voice cut through.

"Other magicians will still meet to share the wonders of the arcane world, but they will not interest you, those meetings. You will have nothing to say to them, unless they can be brought to care for the rules of Osyth. You will feel uneasy at such meetings, and grow to hate all who enjoy them and

406

ignore your precious rules. You will call them immature or reactionary, but something inside you will know they are really free and alive, until you manage to kill that little part of yourself and offer it up as the last sacrifice to your owners. I know this," the demon said, and its voice changed as if it were leaning forward. "We taste souls. We know when they have given up so much that the last spark becomes a torment, a memory of what could have been and now can never be. We know when the creature's only desire becomes to destroy that last hope."

"Oh, I'm sure you do." Rho stuck his fingers in his ears. The demon didn't bother to say anything more, though, and after a while lying with his head in the sleeping bag began to bother him. What was it doing out there? He poked his nose out and opened his eyes for a peek, and jumped to find the demon's own face only a few inches away. It was sitting on the floor, drawing a line of white sparks as it ran one of its claws idly along the outer rim of the pentacle. Rho watched as it went all around the lines, doing the same thing, and flicked chalk off its claw. He didn't like this. Shutting his eyes, he thought hard about the charm that had raised the pentacle and the demon, bent over to resume its task, jumped back in a cloud of smoke.

"Impressive," it said. "A charm of intent? What will happen to it when you sleep?"

Rho didn't answer. He was thinking about what to do next. The demon made itself comfortable. It closed the windows, turned the lights down, and sat down again in Rho's chair, on top of his coat. It sprawled, humming. The result was not conducive to deep thought, and the thing seemed settled for the night, without having touched any of the surfaces Rho had baited.

He had spat on all the chairs, smeared sweat and dripped urine around the room until it was marked all over with Rho. Why hadn't the demon sat on one of those chairs? Why hadn't it stood on any of those spots? It had walked around them, covered them with his coat, as if they were visible. Rho lay on his side, though he knew it was a bad idea. He went over the binding charm again and again, watching the demon. All it had to do was move to where it would be in contact with a part of Rho... Something banged on the door.

The demon sat up, its eyes gleaming, and stopped its hum, but this time it neither hid nor vanished. It rose, instead, and padded toward the door. Its claws clicked on the stone floor.

"Go away!" Rho yelled. "It's not safe in here!"

"It's not safe for you, if you don't give me back that grimoire," shouted a voice he hardly recognized.

The demon stopped just inside the door and grinned.

"The housewife!" it said to Rho. "We do need blood." It pulled the door open.

***

I hate this, Teddy thought, the minute she heard Lilian start a slanging match with Rho through the door. This was no way to start a negotiation. She shouldered her way past Lilian and had just opened her mouth to make a more tactful appeal when the

408

door opened. A demon was standing within four feet of her, holding the door open courteously, and Teddy heard herself gasp with shock as the *grue* hit her.

"Oh," she said, standing frozen. She started to take a step backward but one of the demon's taloned hands grabbed at her wrist, setting off a shower of sparks from her ward. Teddy's bones stuck together. She opened her mouth, trying to remember a charm, but none came to mind. "Run!" she yelled instead, pushing Bosie and Lilian back toward the stairwell.

"No, I'm through running." Lilian stuck her head under Teddy's arm. The demon gave her an appreciative look.

"Courage," it said, in a deep, seductive voice. "Nothing is more admirable in a mortal. Do come in."

Bosie poked Teddy from behind. "That was a courteous invitation, dear," she said. "Never begin by believing the worst of someone."

"You're crazy," Teddy said, standing fast. "This is a major demon." The demon took this as a compliment, nodding and smiling.

"Perhaps I can make my point clearer," it said, and disappeared. When Teddy looked around, it had reconstituted itself below them and was advancing up the stairs with its teeth bared in a grin. "Allow me to repeat my invitation," it said, patting Bosie's shoulder. "No wards, ladies? Please do come in."

Teddy groaned and marched into Rho's tower lair. The owner was sitting hunched in a sleeping bag in the middle of a lopsided pentacle drawn in chalk. He glared at her with a hatred she felt like returning.

"I told you to go away," he said.

Teddy shrugged. She didn't like the smell in here, or the feel of the room. There wasn't enough light. Rho looked like some kind of wizened imp trapped in his pentacle with cans and candy bars scattered around him. *Sloppy, unprofessional work,* thought Teddy. *No incense, no blood-what sort of amateurs are we hiring these days?* The demon had come around her as she made this inventory, and was smiling quite sweetly at Rho.

"Which one of them do you prefer?" it asked. "The short one is warded, but the others have ample blood."

Teddy heard Rho groan.

"I prefer using my own," he said, in a resigned voice. "If I cast the charm, will you let them go?"

"I swear," the demon said.

The least believable remark Teddy had ever heard.

It chuckled, and it did have a nice laugh. "Come out."

"I don't think so," Rho said, darkly suspicious. "Let's try it my way." He gestured at the floor in front of his pentacle, between the bases of two of its points, and then looked at Teddy. "We have lots of time," he said. "All night."

"True enough," the demon said. "I can afford to humor you. Ladies, would you prefer to sit?" It gestured toward two chairs, which none of the ladies were inclined to use. "As you please," it said, and shrugged its wings. Holding its hands out with a wringing motion, it produced a large book from thin air.

Teddy heard Lilian exclaim, put out a warning hand to keep her back, and felt a bit of excitement as the demon put the book down where Rho had indicated. It wasn't as all-powerful as her nerves were trying to tell her; it had made the first mistake a magician counted on the arcana to make. It had forgotten that the pentacle walls, a barrier to it, meant nothing to the magician inside them.

This opens up options, she thought, but they were options the presence of Lilian and Bosie interfered with. Still, if she could distract the demon long enough for Rho to grab the book and reset his pentacle, perhaps the other two could crowd inside with him.

"That's an elegant body you've created there," she told the demon. "Very aesthetically pleasing. Does it work as well as it looks?"

The demon was surprised by this compliment. It looked unsettled, then seemed to decide that none of the women was a threat. "It works quite well," it admitted. "I was originally motivated by aesthetics merely, but I find that this traditional design wears better for long-term use than the more fanciful creations I designed in the past. The alimentary canal was particularly gratifying to research and construct," it added in a tone of appreciative reminiscence, and rubbed its abdomen with a proprietary air.

Teddy concealed her reaction and nodded. "Might I examine you more closely?" she asked.

This made the demon suspicious. It looked at her through slitted yellow eyes and picked up the grimoire. But temptation was always too much for demons; it ended by setting the book down again

411

between two points on the far side of the pentacle, well out of Teddy's reach. Then it came back to the near side and beckoned Teddy forward. It turned around before her admiring gaze, and while its back was turned she made vigorous but silent gestures to the two other women and to Rho. They all looked at her in willing confusion, which was highly frustrating. That never happened on TV shows.

"I see you've included ectoparasites," she said to the demon, as it revolved back to face her. "I've often wondered why so many demons do that. It seems something that a creature making its own body would opt out of."

"Are they not part of the mortal body?" the demon asked. and Teddy realized that it was a serious question. "Is it not the body's nature to prey upon itself? Death and torment are built into the fleshly world, as its ends and goals."

"But if that were the case, why would the actual design work better than any variant? Doesn't the actual design minimize death and torment? You'd know this better than I," Teddy said, "since you've experienced alternatives."

"Indeed I have," the demon said. "There is something interesting in what you say. It accords with certain recent observations of my own." It squatted, suddenly, and seemed to plunge deep into thought. Teddy hoped it had good knees. Knees, she reckoned, were the weakest point in any argument for the innate goodness of natural design.

"There's quite a debate among humans as to whether design maximizes the goodness of mortal life, or merely ensures a level of pleasure adequate for the continuance of the species," she said, squatting to speak at the demon's level. "Your experience puts you in a unique position to contribute to this debate, the results of which are significant for our evaluation of nature's essential goodness."

"And if my experience were to indicate that all variants are inferior?"

"It would indicate an essentially benign nature, concerned to maximize the pleasure of all its inhabitants, would it not?" Teddy herself had always argued the 'minimally adequate' side of this debate, though, and her mind was putting up all kinds of unwanted second-guessing refutations of her own discourse. Usually Russell or James would be taking this side of the argument, leaving her with the luxury of criticism; tonight, that was a luxury she could not afford. "If nature is benign, it will have designed all things to maximize one another's pleasure, and to live in mutual goodwill and amity," she suggested, getting to the point a little too abruptly, but her knees were giving her hell. She flapped a hand behind her back, trying to indicate to Lilian and Bosie that they should stand nearer the pentacle, but the only person who paid attention to it was Rho. He moved back over toward the grimoire, distracting the demon.

"Very intriguing," it said absently, watching him with sharp eyes. "That would imply that all creatures' goods are essentially compatible, so if I pursue my own desires, the rest of you will find it to your benefit in the long run." It stood up and stretched. "Let us leave this question for later, after Magister Rho has performed the incantation which I currently desire."

413

"He doesn't seem to desire it," Teddy said, making a last effort. "Isn't it against nature to force someone to do what doesn't give them pleasure?"

The demon laughed. "I know what Rho enjoys better than you do," it said, and turned away from her.

Teddy struggled up from her crouching posture. Rho, watching her, looked downcast.

"Nice try," he said dolefully. "I guess you better keep your distance. I'm not sure what this book will do."

"What's the charm?" she asked him.

Rho opened his mouth to answer, but the demon snarled at him and he shut it again.

"I grow impatient," it said, and Rho hunched up at the side of the pentacle nearest the book.

"I need a light," he said.

The demon obliged by making one of its hands burst into flame, with a nasty smell of singed hair. It crouched again, this time near Rho, and Teddy made more hand gestures behind her back, waving Lilian and Bosie toward the stairwell, but they weren't even looking at her. She cursed all mundanes, all laywomen, all unprofessional fools. *You can't get good sidekicks anymore,* she thought, and a wave of missing Russell went over her.

Rho had begun his incantation in a weird droning language Teddy didn't know. As she watched, he pulled out a penknife and cut his left hand across the palm. The hair on the back of her neck began to stand up as the charm took shape. It felt as if she was catching just the edge of some storm in the arcane world.

***

Warren felt the grimoire, as well as seeing it through Bosie's eyes. He got a clearer perception of it, in fact, when Bosie shut her eyes. He could feel the strength of the book, all the hungry charms in it waiting to be cast. The ones that had been written in wizards' or demons' blood and had cried out ever since for their master's touch. The ones which had not been written at all but cast into the book whole, and as a result had spent years in the middle of their casting, unfinished and frustrated. An old grimoire was not a living thing but a thing greedy to live. It wanted a soul, a spirit with enough essence to let it move and think and cast the charms it contained. Warren felt his own grimoire's moods-the whirlwind of excitement that began as the charm Rho was speaking and the fresh blood woke it to its need, the shift as it decided to work with Rho instead of against him.

The book pulled at Warren, the person it was most familiar with, and he clung to Bosie in desperation, trying to make her run out of the room, scream, do anything that would stop this. Teddy had waved a similar message behind her back, but Bosie stood as if entranced. She had always loved to watch magic being done. *If I survive this, I'm going to kill her,* Warren thought, feeling himself drawn more into the book's desire. He could tell what it would be like to be trapped in there, unable to do anything except what the book's keeper allowed him to do, living the book's frustration until nothing remained of him but need. Warren had read of such books, and how they became more malignant over time as the souls trapped within them went mad with hate.

The next line of the charm dragged at him, and the things he was seeing with Bosie's vision stuttered out for a moment before he could get hold of her again. *Mama!* he cried without a voice, all his irritation with her swallowed up in panic. He thought of wholesome, milky things-sunny breakfasts, children's blocks, times when no ambition plagued him. Bosie seemed the antithesis of ambitions, and he clung to the thought of her and all her connections, the people without any achievements except enjoying life. The charm jerked and twisted around him, making those happy memories seem wrong, pointless and undirected. All accomplishment, all worthwhile focus of life, the charm said, led to the grimoire. In it he would work at the top of his ability, with no rules and customs to constrain him. In it he would live that intoxicating moment when the magic flowed out of him unhindered. He would share the wisdom of the ages, be part of something bigger than he had ever known. His power would be limitless, his knowledge unparalleled, and nobody would tell him how to interpret it, said the charm. Nobody else would have to be convinced.

But the book had misjudged Warren, and this didn't appeal to him. The more it spoke of power and autonomy, the more he remembered the feeling that had delighted him in the ley-line and his hopes of becoming part of the world around him. The grimoire told him about independence and traveling far, and with every argument it raised along these lines Warren's grasp on his mother grew stronger.

He pulled himself back into her busy body, and she hiccuped.

"Mercy," she said, patting her front, "I really don't know what's come over me lately, I used to be able to eat just anything. Why, when I was in Kasidora with Warren's father-" The demon gave her a glare that could hush even hiccups, and she relapsed into silence, but Warren was safe inside her. He heard the charm with her ears, incomprehensible, even as it spoke again of determination, accomplishment in spite of every attempt to hinder it, self-sufficiency and staunch, righteous alienation. He saw Lilian, her eyes wide, watching Rho and the demon. Teddy was holding on to her ward as if it were a life preserver, her eyes squeezed shut. The grimoire had made a mistake Warren could not fathom-it had chosen an appeal which spoke to none of them.

As he pondered this a motion caught his eye. Rho seemed to leap forward, through the pentacle walls, and the whirlpool of power snatched Warren out of Bosie. He could see nothing more, but he could feel them all around him, dwarfed by the ley-line that rose under him like confidence itself. The demon was there as well, a great cloud of sullen anger and the assurance of life's malignancy. Warren gathered himself up to meet it the way a wave gathers itself over shallow water, full of the joy of sunlight.

Chapter Twenty

Without knowing the charm's language, Rho understood it. The longer he chanted, the more sense it made. It was just what the demon had said—it spoke of friendship and respect, his superiority to the other intellects in Osyth and their jealousy, the need to stand up for himself and make his own way. He crouched, reading all this aloud in front of the people it was about, and at first he was ashamed. A heavy dry feeling took over his stomach, and he shrank. Then, strangely, the whole room shifted away from him until Lilian stood at its center and Rho was a peripheral nobody, only important because he had screwed up her life...

What crap! Rho thought. *Screw that!* He read the charm again. It was true, all of it. *I'm in the right,* he thought. *They're all idiots. I wasn't hired to put up with this sort of abuse!* He squinted at the third stanza and bent his head closer to the book. "All I want is to do my job," he read. "Just get out of my way and let me work. You leave me alone and I'll leave you alone." The demon leaned closer, its head just on the other side of the line from his, its lips moving in the same chant. It understood. It felt the same dream. "This is all that matters," Rho read to it. "Those others aren't worth thinking about."

The demon read something else in the charm, though. It spoke in a different rhythm than Rho's, and its voice rumbled on after his stopped. "Blood," it read. "Pain. Power... enslave them all." It swallowed, eyes fixed on the book.

Rho looked back at the page.

That's not what it says, he thought. The room started to shift again, away from him and the book. "That's not what it says!" he yelled. The demon chanted on, ignoring him. "Shut up!" He looked back at the book and for a second he saw the words the demon was reading printed on it, like a stain among the words he had just read. "Stop it," he cried. "You're ruining everything!" Before he knew it, he had reached through the pentacle walls. His hands were around the demon's throat, and he felt its laughter running up between them and bursting out over his head.

"Blood, pain, power," the demon chanted. Rho felt its hands on him, pushing him into the book. He clung to it, as much to save himself as to strangle an enemy, and it laughed again.

"This is my book now," it said, sneering. "Did you think I meant to share it? All your power will be mine. Yours and Oldham's."

It banged Rho's head against the book. He felt as if he were being pushed down into pure emotion, his skull filling up with it as his head went under. Fear, hatred... He roared and surfaced, heard women's voices, and as the demon tightened its grip and leaned over him, something hit Rho with the edge of a blow. The demon gasped and caved backwards. When Rho pulled himself up again, it was into something like a wind, the kind of air birds played in. Big and blustery, the wind knocked the demon backwards, tail over ears.

"Oldham," it snarled, righting itself, and glared at something to the left of Rho's head.

I'm not what it wants, he thought. *It's been about Warren all along-Warren and Lilian.*

"How well will you fight me alone?" the demon asked the air, and turned its gaze back toward the three women behind Rho. It leaped, without even a shift of weight to prepare.

Right over Rho's head it leapt, and he reached up for it as if he knew what to do, grabbed at its waist and fell backwards, onto the grimoire, babbling the binding charm. *I've got it all wrong,* he thought as his tongue missed one syllable, then another. *It's no good. I've killed all of them.*

***

Whatever Rho was chanting had power, Teddy could tell, but it was power in theory rather than in fact. She felt a spectator rather than a participant, as if the charm were simply flowing around her. The charm built, cajoled, argued, and finally grew desperate; there was a sparkle as Rho lunged through the walls of his pentacle, and Teddy saw him grab the demon by the throat. They grappled. *This is the time to leave,* thought Teddy. "Run!" she yelled, but something heavy fell onto her from the side. It was Bosie, and in disentangling herself, Teddy missed something. Whatever it was swirled around her like a hot storm, tugging at her every surface, and she gasped. A movement beside her made her heart jerk. *The demon!* But it was Lilian, leaping forward toward the book. She slammed it shut, caught it up and backed away from the pentacle until she was near the door.

"Hey!" Teddy yelled. "Give me a hand here!"

Lilian didn't stop for a second. When she reached the door she turned, and in a flash was gone. Her footsteps echoed in the stairwell, running down-and, Teddy reckoned, straight to the Academy hospital and Warren. That was love, and a damned nuisance it was too! Here she sat, abandoned, with an unconscious elderly lady draped over her, a demon somewhere in the room, and a black magician, thwarted in his evil plans, lying in front of them. She scrambled out from beneath Bosie and stood up, trying to remember protective charms she hadn't needed to think about for years. What she could remember seemed absurdly unsophisticated, and a real possibility that she might not be able to believe in the charms enough to cast them sprang to her mind. Rho, however, made no move to threaten her. He had not changed his position, sprawled on the floor, nor did he now as Teddy approached, except to look up at her with an expression of confused exhaustion. She stood at a prudent distance and watched him.

The room stood absurdly untouched, though with its furniture all pushed up against the walls it was easy to believe that some kind of whirlwind had been through. None of the papers and books were disordered. The demon was nowhere to be seen; perhaps it had gone out the open window, through which she could hear a throaty cooing. Over all of this lay a peaceful and vacant air, like that of a house yet to be moved into.

"Are you all right?" she asked, but Rho made no reply save a deep sigh. His eyes closed and he lay still. "Hey," Teddy said. "Wake up and tell me if that demon's coming back." Rho paid no attention.

She backed away from him to the phone, watchful against any tricks, and dialed security. The only other thing she could think to do was to put her ward around Bosie's neck, in case the demon came before the guards.

***

Lilian clutched the book to her chest and ran, her heart pounding and her feet quick and sure on the stairs. She felt sick with excitement and terror. Even when she had gotten down into the Magic Building proper, when she had started to think about Teddy and Bosie up there with the demon, she couldn't stop running, though with every step she grew more terrified about what might happen to them. They would be killed, maimed, and it would be all her fault. Warren would be lost forever, or if he did come back he'd divorce her for killing his mother. She'd lose him, the children, her home... The outside door of the building slammed behind her, and still Lilian was too afraid to stop running. Her breath came in gasps and tears streaked back from her eyes as she raced into the stiff wind blowing from the ley-line. When she began to stumble, terror caught up with her and grabbed at her aching chest. She knew every awful thing she had ever imagined was going to come true, and it was all deserved. She had left them... but she really wasn't thinking about Teddy and Bosie now. It was the chicken she couldn't stop thinking about, the one she had sacrificed for her degree in augury, the things she had done to that chicken to teach its bones the difference between good and evil. And

422

her daughter Joan, the nights she'd left her baby crying in the dark. The awful things she had done and thought, all the times she'd let people think she cared when all she wanted was for them to drop dead if that would make them go away. She was staggering now, almost out of the undeveloped land and into her own neighborhood, and she knew she had been running the wrong way, nothing good could come of this except getting the book to Warren and she had taken it the wrong way, thrown that hope away. She fell, and got up, and ran on. She held the book clutched against her, but it had gotten wet. It would be ruined, the way everything was ruined.

***

Three security guards and two ambulance crews filled the tower room and the stairwell to bursting. Claustrophobic, Teddy answered questions as quickly as she could and snaked her way out, down to the bottom of the stairs where a lone guard, unable to crush into the upper reaches, was standing beside a cruiser parked on the snow-covered grass. Teddy was turning to walk over to the ambulance and wait for the stretchers to come down when she just happened to look the other way, toward the west, and saw something dark on the ground. It looked like Lilian's scarf. She went over and picked it up, and the guard came as well.

"Look at this," Teddy said. The guard did, and swung her flashlight in a wide arc. Teddy saw Lilian's tracks heading straight west in the snow, their soles dark with melt water.

423

"They're pretty far apart," the guard said. "Looks like whoever it was, was running."

Teddy admired her matter-of-fact tone, and the way the guard holstered the flashlight and moved off along the ley-line. As she followed behind, she savored the experience. Woodsmanship. Tracking. But something that left no tracks must have herded Lilian this way, away from her destination, and Teddy knew a truly nice person would be worried to the exclusion of enjoying the adventure. That was what society would expect, anyway, and once again it was wrong.

"There she is," the guard said, and Teddy called out to the figure ahead. It shambled a few steps further and fell to its knees.

The guard had pulled her light out again, and its glare turned Lilian into planes of color against the night. Teddy saw her struggling to get up, unaccountably clumsy, and jerking another step away, trying to run like a hamstrung animal. Night blacked out everything except that staggering figure, its coat unbuttoned and its jeans soaked through from where it had fallen. A cold feeling went through Teddy, and she stopped.

"There's a demon out here," she said.

The guard swung her light from side to side, but it lit up only trees and bushes. Lilian had never stopped moving away, trotting a step or two and then falling again and painfully dragging herself upright. Watching it made Teddy feel sick. "Lilian!" she called and trotted forward herself, feeling around her neck and cursing. Bosie was still wearing her ward, and the *grue* around Lilian was the strongest Teddy had ever felt. She saw the guard

424

trotting toward them, an Academy ward bouncing on her chest. "Do you have another of those?"

"Yeah," the guard said, and slipped it over Lilian's head.

She paid them no attention at all. Her face was fixed and white, and she kept walking west until she ran into Teddy and the guard. They grabbed her arms, and she kicked Teddy in the shins. Teddy hopped and swore.

"We have to get her back to the hospital," the security guard said. "Can you walk?"

"Hell and damnation!" Teddy said in reply. They turned Lilian around and began to hustle her back along her own tracks. She fought, kicked, and dragged her feet, and would have beaten them off if she hadn't kept both arms wrapped around the book. Teddy's shins ached by the time they stepped back under campus lights, and she was depressed as hell. This was what she got for messing with things professionals should take care of. Nothing accomplished, everything made worse. Warren was still gone, and now Rho as well and Lilian under some sort of spell. What good were theorists, after all? Pompous, self-important fools who thought they knew better than anybody else! She damned herself for the most pompous of them all. With three magicians gone and three more involved in her asinine plotting, they'd close the program down. *And the last time they closed magic down,* she reminded herself, *they burnt all the magicians.* But that was just her being dramatic again. They only burned alchemists in this day and age. People like herself were too ineffectual to bother killing. The court of public opinion was good enough. Teddy

425

wondered if she could just drop her side of Lilian and run back into the darkness.

She cast a surreptitious look at the security guard, saw her fears echoed in the guard's face, and felt better immediately. "Are you as scared as I am?" she asked.

"Scared! I've never messed anything up this bad in my life," the guard said, as they struggled from one pool of lamplight to the next. "I'll get fired for sure, and sued, and we can't afford a lawyer. And this is the first job I've had in years that paid more than minimum wage. I'll have to leave him in that school, with the drugs and the gangs... " Her voice choked.

Teddy looked away toward the next lamp. *This is the sort of thing real people have to worry about,* she thought. *People who are involved with more than their own egos.* She wanted nothing more than to run back to the ley-line and let some demon eat her alive, anything to get away from her worthless self.

They were at the hospital by now, dragging Lilian along a maze of sidewalks and evergreen hedges that seemed designed to keep inconvenient patients from finding the emergency entrance, and then they were under a portico and into the light. An alarm made a nasty noise and Teddy saw people in the waiting room get up and back away from her as if she had the plague. *I may as well get used to it,* she thought. Official-looking people in scrubs rushed forward, fastening wards around their necks as they ran. They asked questions Teddy couldn't understand, though she heard the guard answering; they pulled Lilian's arm out of her grasp and sat

Teddy down hard on a chair, as if she were a naughty three-year-old (*and I may as well get used to that,* thought Teddy) and then they were gone. The waiting room lay still in shock for a moment, with only the alarms and equipment noises breaking its silence, and then all the people waiting in it began to talk at once. They put their heads together, looking at Teddy out of big eyes, and buzzed.

A scream of rage came down the hallway, and the waiting people all stopped talking for an instant; the scream sounded again, abruptly hushed, and they buzzed more than before. Someone in blue scrubs came down the hall, wearing three gold chains and carrying Warren's grimoire in a plastic bag held nervously at arm's length. The bag was sealed with yellow hazard tape, and had gold chains tied around it. Teddy looked at it for a second without identifying it, and then jumped up.

"What are you going to do with that?"

"Put it in the hazardous waste bin."

"No!" Teddy yelled, grabbed the bag, and despair came back down over her. She clasped it to her chest the way Lilian had, looking for a way to run out of the hospital, back to the darkness. She backed away from the person in scrubs and saw everybody else scrambling to back away from her, clearing a path to the door on her right. Just as she turned to run that way, someone with an official air stepped in to block her escape. When she turned back, baffled, a person in green scrubs was running down the hall toward her.

"Where's that book!"

"She took it," the person in blue said.

"He was going to throw it out," Teddy sobbed. "It's not yours! We need it to cure Warren and Russell."

"It's all right," the person in green said. "We're not throwing it out. You never throw away an arcane artifact," he told the person in blue. "It could hold all the secrets of its owner's illness. Wards, grimoires, amulets, potions-never throw out anything you find a client carrying. Got it?" He turned back to Teddy. "We'll put it in the alchemical safe in the morgue. That'll keep demons away from it. All right?"

"No, I won't let you. You'll throw it out."

"We'll give you a receipt. I'll let you watch me lock it up, if that helps." He was talking to Teddy as if she were an idiot.

I better get used to that, too, she thought. The person on her right took her arm gently. She tried to jerk it away.

"It's all right," this person said.

Teddy recognized her as the security guard, from her uniform. "It's the book that makes you so scared. Just the way it scared me. Here, let me take it." With professional skill, she got the thing out of Teddy's arms. The desperation began to ebb away, replaced by chagrin as Teddy watched the guard carry the book over to a desk and put it down while the person in green filled out a form. She walked over to join them, keeping well back when the person in green gave her a nervous look.

"I'm sorry, I don't know what came over me."

"We weren't wearing our wards," the guard said. "That's what happened."

"Oh," Teddy said, with great relief. She felt at her neck. "You're right! Oh! I was afraid I'd completely lost it!"

"I wouldn't want to fool with this without protection," the person in green said, pushing the form across the desk for Teddy to read and sign. "We haven't had anything this malignant in the hospital for a long time." He looked at her signature. "We'll be calling you folks in demonology to come over and run its aura through your database. Somebody over there has a camera arcana."

"That would be me," Teddy said. "Should I go get it?"

"No, I want to check both of you out." The person in green tore the form apart, taping one copy of it onto the grimoire, and handed another copy to Teddy. "Just take a seat, and we'll get to you as soon as we can."

***

Neil Torecki loved gossip, because it was the only way to find anything out. He had grown so convinced of this that when he actually saw the police tape across the doors to the west tower stairwell with his own two eyes on Saturday morning, and walked around to the base of the tower and stood in the footprints going every which way and smelled the bittersmoke, he thought of this not as personal experience but as some kind of particularly direct and immediate gossip, lacking the analytical commentary that made for real information. He wouldn't really know what this was

429

all about, Neil knew, until it had been discussed with someone. Fortunately for him, the vampire lab's lights were on.

"Hey, Susan!" Neil said, rapping on the doorway. "D'you know what's going on with Rho?"

"No!" Susan and Will said, which was gratifying.

Neil got to describe it all and they walked around the base of the tower together telling one another what they saw, what sort of things like it they had seen in their lives or read about, and what it might mean. Since none of them knew any more than they were looking at, though, the conversation stalled.

"I'm going to call security," Neil said. "Maybe they'll tell me what's going on. It might be important to those of us who work in the building. I'll bet anything that demon came back." He knew security wouldn't tell him anything, but he'd had a different idea he was not ready to share with anyone. The creatures in the live specimens' floor of the museum were always there, and when Neil thought of Rho, it gave him the idea that he might talk with other things than humans. Nobody ever tried asking the banshee what it had heard in the night.

It was a good idea, but difficult to execute. All the banshee spoke of was woe, the mourning women and the man full of old sorrows who had walked the stairs last night, the woman mad with grief who had run down again.

"Woe and sorrow," the banshee said. "Oh, grieve for the lost of the world."

***

430

"I hope nothing dreadful happened," Susan said to Will.

"I'm sure it did," Will answered. "I'm also sure Teddy knows about it. Some of those tracks were her boots."

"No! Really? I didn't know you could recognize them."

"You use a lot of tracking in my line of business," Will said complacently.

Susan looked at him with admiration. She did enjoy having a sweet, handsome lover, even one who knew he was handsome-and if he weren't a little insecure, a little needy, would he be interested in her?

"Another skill you never told me about," she said, and Will puffed up a little.

"Do we have everything for the séance?" he asked, changing the subject. They finished loading the cart with supplies and wheeled it to the elevator. They had the séance set up by the time Lilian and Teddy arrived from the hospital.

***

The pentarium made a good spot for a séance, quiet and dim. Lilian hadn't been inside it for years, and the room was inhabited for her by a younger Warren, proud and professional as he showed her his repairs. She looked around with a prickly feeling behind her eyes. It was awful, but she'd been crying ever since she picked up that horrible book that Warren must be trapped in. *I can't stand this,* she thought, and tears ran down her cheeks. She pressed

431

her hands against them hard. It was Susan who put warm arms around her and let her lean into a broad shoulder.

"I'm sorry," Lilian said, catching at her voice. She stood up, rubbing tears across her face, and felt in her bag for a tissue. "You should wear yellow," she said. "Pale yellow with flowers. Like a garden."

"I had a yellow dress when I was a girl," Susan said. "I loved it."

Teddy Whin had turned away from all this and was scanning the room with her hands linked behind her back, very tomboyish.

"Don't you need draperies?" she asked in a gruff voice.

"Not when there aren't any windows," Susan said.

"Or any tricks under the table," Will said.

The table was one of those glass-topped patio tables with a hole in the middle for an umbrella pole, obviously hauled downstairs just for the occasion. The matching chairs had lumpy white grapes all over them-most uncomfortable, in Lilian's opinion. When she sat in one she found the whole set was molded plastic, which made the grapes less troublesome than they looked.

"I like to use glass," Susan explained, "because so many mediums are charlatans. Everything has to be visible if you want your results to be trustworthy."

Lilian had never thought about that, and she didn't now. It was a big enough job to keep from crying.

432

"What do you want to happen?" she said, her voice shaking. "If Warren's in that book, how could we reach him, anyway?"

"We still have to do it, for Russell," Susan said gently.

Lilian put her head down on the cool glass. "Oh, I just can't stand any more of this," she wailed. Susan patted her shoulder.

Will sniffed, as well. "It's the banshee," he said, and once he mentioned it Lilian could hear a low, penetrating wail from the floor above. "Banshees make everybody cry."

Susan's warm hand closed around Lilian's and Lilian clung to it while she mopped her eyes. "Let's do it before I break down again," she said.

Will sat down on her other side, leaving the space opposite for Teddy. He lit the candles and they all sat back, not looking at one another in the dimness. Lilian put all her attention into the feel of Susan's warm hand and Will's cold one, and the pattern of candlelight on the ceiling. Susan's hand grew softer and softer until it seemed boneless, but then it started to life again and caught hers in a firm grasp. Teddy grunted from across the table. Susan had started upright, her head tipped back, and was breathing in long, heavy sighs. Will leaned forward, his amulets shining in the candlelight.

"Who do you seek?" Susan asked, in a low monotone something like the banshee's voice.

"Russell Cinea and Warren Oldham," Will said.

There followed a few moments of silence, during which Lilian could see Susan's eyes seeking around under her closed lids.

433

"They are not among the dead," the monotone answered at last.

"No, but they are in the spirit realms," Will answered.

Susan shuddered and bent her head further back, searching again, and her breathing grew thicker. The candlelight wavered, as if it were running through water.

Lilian looked at the candle and saw a stream of water pouring down onto the flame; yet the flame burned on, steady and clear. The water kept flowing, now in a wide column inside of which Lilian could see a jellyfish and startled-looking minnows. As she watched a pair of legs appeared, and a tall, thin body which took up more and more of the water's space until what stood on the table was a body with only a sheen of water running over it. The body was Russell Cinea's and it was completely naked, standing in what looked like an uncomfortable relationship to the candle flame. She heard Teddy gasp from across the table, stared through Russell's translucent legs at her, and looked away again. Will, on the other hand, was drinking in this reunion with his eyes wide open, and Lilian dared not kick him under the table for fear of disturbing Susan. She looked at the ghost's feet and saw them flushing a pretty pink.

"This isn't real," the ghost said, in a hopeless voice. "I'm making it all up."

"What nerve!" Teddy said, sniffing hard. "If anything, we're the ones making you up. As if we could, the way they've messed up our pentarium. Where the hell are you, anyway?"

"Wherever I think I am," Russell said. "I want to come back. There's nothing here except me. How can I come back?"

"Leave us something," Will said hastily, glancing at Susan. "Manifest something we can use to call you again. Something ectoplasmic. Think of it and put all of yourself into it. Anything-a scrap of fabric, a note, anything."

The ghost of Russell closed its eyes, screwing its face up in concentration, and began to shimmer and disappear. It wavered in and out of sight for a few minutes, then disappeared completely as Susan's hands fell limp. She bowed over, her head falling toward the table, and Lilian let go of Will's hand to catch her. She slipped her handbag under Susan's cheek and let the smooth head down on it, turning back to see what Will was picking up between his cupped hands from the base of the candle. He held a tiny crab, ivory and gold and ruby-striped, its black eyes swiveling from side to side. Teddy and Lilian leaned forward, their jaws ajar, as Will placed this ghostly artifact in a clear box and deposited the box in a cooler.

"Did he have an interest in crabs?" Lilian asked Teddy cautiously, and Teddy shook her head.

"Not that I know of," she said. "How's Susan?"

"Done for the day," Will said. He stroked Susan's hair, a possessive caress. "That was pretty spectacular, you know. Usually she gets a gauzy apparition or maybe a pair of hands. But that waterfall! And leaving a live crab! That's unheard of. I guess everything they say about Russell is true. Let's get her off the chair. She'll usually come round faster if you raise her feet."

435

This job took all three of them, and distracted Lilian for a while from her misery at not seeing Warren. She finished propping Susan's feet up on the chair, stood up dusting her hands, and sighed.

"At least you got to talk to Russell," she said to Teddy. That was a bad thing to think of, because she knew she'd be hearing what Russell had said all night. 'There's nothing here except me... how can I get back?' She heard it in Warren's voice and felt herself tearing up again. "Damn," she said, pressing her eyes. "Damn, damn, damn!"

Teddy didn't answer. She stood in an irritating theatrical pose, looking upward into the middle of the room, and Lilian wanted to shake her. This was Susan's area, not Teddy's, but Teddy could never let anybody else have the spotlight for long... She looked in spite of herself. Something above the candle was drawing its flame upward into a golden cone, a tornado of light, and through it she saw into a world made up of dark and scintillant patches. Sparks of light danced through it, up and down.

Lilian walked up to the table, not afraid and not weepy. She felt a clear, serene confidence, as on her wedding day when she walked down the aisle, in the hospital when they put Joan into her hands, on the day when Warren had proposed and she had said yes. She reached out a hand to the whirlpool and its color changed as she touched it. The patches within turned to fresh green and gold, the colors of a trembling spring, and the thing blazed up higher. It bent, as if in a stiff breeze, and brushed across her face, and it was gone. She felt on the brink of blazing up herself, into a fountain of light and glory, and when she faced Will and Teddy it was with a defiance that delighted in their open mouths and pale faces.

"That was Warren," she said, holding her purse strap tight and daring them to say a word. "That's what he's really like!"

***

Nothing. Nothing to see, nothing to hear or feel-or, perhaps, all sorts of things and no body to see or feel with. Rho could not define his situation, but he was sure of three things. First, he would dislike it even more when he figured out what it was; second, it would not count toward tenure; third, it was someone else's fault. He'd done the right thing, after all. He'd stopped the demon before it could kill any of them, or at least tried to. If he was in a mess now, it was someone else's fault! But the more he considered it, the more he questioned this point. More likely, his situation was everyone else's fault. Every person he could think of was at least partly to blame.

Rho was as angry with each person he listed as he ever had been with anyone. There seemed no limit to his rage, nothing to call it to an end, as his rages had so often ended, in hunger or physical action. This was what brought Rho back to considering his situation rather than its causes, because rage had always been linked to action before. Why not now? He searched around him for something to act with, or upon, and found nothing. Rage without the prospect of doing anything about it was unsatisfying. *Time enough for wrath,* Rho told himself, *when I've mastered my new habitat.*

Easier thought than done; every attempt he made to pay attention to his surroundings seemed to be turned back, as if one of the hundreds of people to blame for his problems stood in each pathway out of himself, barring the way. Not content with ruining his physical existence, they had messed with his mind-Regan and Hoth came to the fore in this new list of persecutors-and now Rho went over it all again in a new light, cataloguing the mental damages they had inflicted on him, and he began to suspect that the list of damages, like the list of damagers, might be infinite. Life itself might well be an endless catalogue of wrongs, a process of incurable injuries that ended only with one's total destruction.

This would have been a disheartening notion if it had not made him so vividly angry, so filled with righteous wrath and indignation, that he began his furious analyses all over again. He cycled through layers of anger-anger at his problems, at those who caused them, at those who made him the sort who got angry, at those who made him discontented with being the sort who got angry-he lost track of just what he was angry about, after a while, and that made him feel stupid, so he was angry at the people who made him feel stupid in the past, were making him feel stupid now, and had trained him to mind feeling stupid, to be afraid of their judgements and intimidated by their intellects, to care about their opinions. Why couldn't he have been born a nonsocial animal, something like an owl or a cat?

Rho thought of cats for just a minute before his mind slipped back into raging, but it left a contrast. He snatched at it again and again. The cat was a fancy, not the world around him that he longed to perceive, but it had found a corner of Rho's mind, where it stretched out in enviable calm. Thinking about how much he envied that silent peace was a change. Could he be getting bored with being angry? But that was what they all counted on. They knew nobody would make the sacrifice of inner peace required to oppose them. Rho wouldn't be fooled by that! Still, the cat lay in its quiet den, waiting for him whenever he wanted a rest, and he began to think more and more often that a man really had to have a refuge from the storm, if it were only to gasp a few breaths before he went back out to battle it again.

As if even the thought of shelter had taken him out of the whirlwind of emotions, he began to ask himself a new set of questions. Was the demon here with him? And odd to think of this, but why had he never included the demon itself in his list of people to blame? Setting that list aside, which was an almost impossible task, only accomplished after a few more rounds of re-remembering conflicts and cataloguing the scars they had left on his psyche-if Rho were in the grimoire and the demon outside, all his efforts to stop it had been for nothing. If it was inside the grimoire with him, where was it? It had always sympathized when he was angry. It had always understood.

This thought, strangely enough, did not throw him back into a review of his wrongs. It was a different kind of thought, an observational thought, as if Rho had two minds and had until this moment been using only one of them. How could the grimoire be a void? It had been almost alive, that

439

book. Pages had loved, hated, almost burst into flame. *Even if I'm inside it, I should be seeing all that,* Rho thought. *Something's trying to keep me from sensing what's around me.*

He began to watch the grimoire as if it were a bird he was learning to hear. Watching that way, listening to something not himself and scarcely heard, meant letting a combination of sensation and imagination overtake him. It meant not worrying about what was true, and his mind protested. *You're trapped in a book!* it said to him. *If you make up a dream world in here, you'll never get out!* Each thing that had happened to him in Osyth had been worse than the last, and he was taking refuge in fancies?

This is how I do my work when I'm not trapped in a book, Rho thought stubbornly. *If this isn't real, nothing I do is real.* He clenched his mind against self-criticism and listened, looked, felt as hard as he could. Something had to be out there.

The book appeared in his thoughts as a landscape. He found himself in a countryside that shifted under him from gentle to harsh, lit now by lava, now by long rays slanting between trees, or half-hidden in blizzard. *You're making all of this up,* said the critical part of his mind, and when it spoke the landscape began to fade away. *There's not a thing in here that you haven't already seen, some time. It's just a bunch of memories cobbled together, there's no meaning in it.* The landscape disappeared entirely, and something chuckled.

Rho's thoughts froze, as if a hawk's shadow had gone over him. But before he could tell what had chuckled, the landscape reappeared. Bits of it flashed into existence and out again-distorted images, tastes, feelings-as if someone were paging through Rho's mind, casually flipping from one notion to another.

***

"He's in there, all right," Teddy Whin said. "Look at this."

The grimoire shone neon green on the recording she had made with the camera arcana. "It matches his aura from this tape." She patted the tape Susan had given her, the one in which Rho fell out of a tree into a flock of incubus-ridden ducks.

That tape had pleased Teddy a great deal, and she had watched it more than was strictly necessary. It was amazing how much less angry she felt at someone after she had seen him fall out of a tree and land in duckshit.

"There's something else in it, though. I get a spike every now and then. See-there's one. That black flicker."

"It's probably the demon," Susan said.

"Yeah, I bet."

The demon must have caused Teddy's panic when she touched the book. She felt sorry for Rho, even though she suspected that a little panic, a little self-doubt, would do him good, especially when she thought about his awful room, messy and cold. Even the vampire lab, where she had come to share her findings with Susan, looked more professional than Rho's digs. "And," Teddy said to Susan, "it solves one problem we'd never even thought about. Warren and Russell might not have had enough

441

magic to make the thing work, if Rho hadn't trapped himself and the demon in it. A baby could cast those charms, now."

"But we can't leave Rho in there with a demon," Susan protested.

"Oh, yeah," Teddy said. "I'm with you there. But since we don't know how to get him out yet, let's do what we can. First thing tomorrow morning, we'll take the book up to Warren's room and fix that problem."

"What problem?" Neil Torecki was leaning against the doorjamb, his red hair flaming under the hallway's fluorescent lights. "Are you working on bringing Warren back to life? I should have known you'd be in on it, with the necromancy program."

"Well, sort of," Susan said.

"So how does the business last night fit in? All the traffic up and down Rho's stairs?"

"We're not sure yet," Teddy said, casting a warning glance at Susan.

"Oh, c'mon," Neil said. "No one tells me anything."

"We're not telling anybody anything, Neil," Teddy said. "It's Warren's business. I wouldn't discuss your medical problems with somebody who didn't know about them, either."

"I already know something was up last night. You two were probably the women who went up to Rho's lab. I suppose Will was the man?" Neil waited, but nobody took this bait. "Well, I guess my only role is to wish you luck." He heaved himself upright. "I'll get the juicy version of it, by the time it's filtered through the sorcery students. Just to show you how big I am, here's another piece for

442

your puzzle-I saw Rho having a drink in The King's yesterday afternoon with Bill Navanax."

"No!" Teddy said. "Are you sure?"

"Of course I'm sure. Everybody knows Navanax."

"Well, I'm glad," Susan said staunchly. "Bill Navanax needs a friend."

"Oh, please!" Teddy said.

"He does. That was terrible, what happened to him. It's bad enough losing someone, without being suspected yourself. And having to attend the execution! It was obscene."

"I signed as many petitions as you did for Gordon Weyerhauser," Teddy said, "but that doesn't mean I have to believe Bill was innocent. Nobody's that dumb. And he didn't have to attend the execution. He did it of his own free will. So now he's seeing Rho-he sure can pick 'em, can't he?" A sideways look at Neil, leaning into the lab with his eyes and ears wide open, reminded her to be cautious. She got off the benchtop. "Well, I've got to be going," she said. "I have half an issue of *Crone* on my dining room table and the other half on my bed. I don't get put to bed until it does."

"That's motivation," Susan said. "See you around. Neil."

Neil twisted his mouth in a good-humored moue and went back down to his office.

Teddy gave Susan a significant look as she left, but she knew it wasn't necessary. Susan would never say anything unwise. She had the instinct-which, Teddy freely admitted, she herself did not possess. She headed home, happy at the prospect of not having to talk to anybody about anything until

443

the next morning. But when she was walking through the city gates, something made her stop. Something about standing beside the stone side of the arch-somebody leaning against a doorway, saying something-Neil. Who was the man going up to Rho's tower last night?

***

Susan hadn't visited Warren or Russell in the hospital. She couldn't make herself face them and she'd felt guilty about it, but when she finally went in on Sunday morning it was an anticlimax. They were obviously not suffering. In fact, they both looked better than she was used to seeing them look. Warren, in particular, had a relaxed happy air. It almost made her wonder who she was trying to get their souls back for-the men themselves, or the people who had investments in them. If she hadn't had Russell's soul and its plea for help to remember, she would have backed out of the project. She would have said, wait a minute. These two placid old guys in the hospital room, they seemed to have all they needed; who were she and Teddy and Lilian to mess it up for them?

Warren and Russell made her welcome, but they didn't ask after anybody. That might have been because Teddy had already given them the news, before she went off to fetch the grimoire. Anyway, Warren's mother made all the conversation.

"Lilian told me what a lovely job you did at the séance," she told Susan. "Such a skilled trade, I used to know quite a few mediums and the respect we all held them in! Of course those were crooked

444

mediums, you know, the kind with little clicking boxes in their garters and acres of gauze and witchlights. So flattering, I always thought, for people to go to so much trouble. Nowadays people do so little for your money. Usually they just lie to you straight in your face and leave you to do all the work of believing them, so very rude and inconsiderate."

Susan supposed that was the case.

"Now in Selanto when we were there, they did a great sweep of all the false mediums and arrested a good many of them, and put them in the jail which happened to be actually haunted, isn't that poetic justice? But what was truly interesting was that it was supposed to be haunted by a medium, whether a true or false one I'm not sure. I suppose either kind could leave a ghost, couldn't they?"

Susan supposed they could.

"What I've always wondered," Bosie said, "is what a medium's ghost would call up. The ghosts of ghosts, I suppose. Is there any such thing?"

Susan was afraid not.

"That's a pity," Bosie said, and fell silent. She began doing the double acrostic from the Sunday paper. The room seemed big and empty when she stopped talking. Susan sat peacefully watching Bosie do the acrostic and Warren and Russell do a jigsaw and the crossword, until Teddy came back followed by someone in green scrubs, carrying Warren's grimoire in its warded bag.

Susan had never seen the grimoire and was curious to get a look at it, but she felt unimpressed by the actual thing. Of course it represented an impressive family history and it was a handsome book, but a malignant artifact? She looked at Teddy sideways and thought, *This is not that big a deal.* There was just a little bit of the *grue* around the grimoire when the bag was opened, and the book settled into the mattress of Warren's bed further than she would have expected from its size, but Susan had decided this was all more of Teddy's dramatics when Warren touched the book and it came to life.

What Susan always remembered later about the grimoire's effect was that everyone in the room seemed to be in a different world. Bosie, nodding and smiling as if whatever Warren did would make her pleased and proud. Lilian and Teddy, each backing away into something different in her own memories, and the sorcerer in green scrubs standing baffled between them, then Warren and Russell, looking at the book with bland appraisal.

Warren actually nodded as he picked it up (and it leapt into his hands, frantic), and said, "Hmm- very nice."

Russell nodded back and said, "Yes, the best I've seen-of course, I can't tell so well right now."

Warren said, "Neither can I, but it ought to do for what we want."

All the time the book was screaming for them to hurry up, help it, do something-and instead of paying attention to it, they were all looking at Susan as if she were the problem, patting her arm and hustling her out of the room, and she hated them for not seeing what they needed to do, hated them more than she had thought it possible to hate anybody, so much that they turned into a big red glare before her eyes and then into blackness and some maddening alarm noise and then nothing.

Patsy Hoth did not think, herself, that a professional should be dragged shrieking from the site of an experiment. She was willing to give Susan the benefit of the doubt, however, as she would have hoped to be excused herself in the event of some analogous occurrence in her own field. A lecher could not afford to be overcensorious. The grimoire was certainly a nasty bit of work, and nobody in the room displayed any notion of how to handle it. Warren was paging through the thing as if he were browsing, when any fool could see it was flipping its own pages up into his hands. Patsy Hoth set her teeth and pulled it away from him. "Put this on," she said, distracting him with the facilitating charm she had brought along. The old lady in the corner burst into uninvited speech at the sight of it.

"Well my goodness, if it hasn't been forever since I saw one of those. Why, we used to hang them up over the doors at wintertide, that made for a frisky holiday season."

At the look Patsy Hoth gave her, she trailed off into silence, which was a good thing because Patsy Hoth had had just about enough. She'd been here less than two minutes and had already had enough of all of them, and on page forty-two was just the charm to put all their tails between their legs-she looked down at the grimoire, which had made this unsolicited suggestion, and shook it.

"What page do you want, Warren?"

"Ninety-six," Warren said mildly. He was examining the charm with befuddled interest.

Patsy Hoth looked around the room and nobody was paying proper attention to business.

"How are we getting his soul in here?" she asked. "Was Susan going to help with that?"

"We're not worrying about it," Teddy said, standing by the bed with her arms folded. "We're assuming Warren can take care of himself."

That was just lovely.

"He's not done a good job of that so far."

"Just take my word for it," Teddy said. "We can always try it your way later."

"If this book doesn't kill us all." Patsy put the book down beside Warren, holding it open at page ninety-six with both hands. It kept suggesting page forty-two and she was tempted, but as a professional lecher she was used to temptation.

"Warren!" his wife said, in a sharp voice that was such a relief to Patsy Hoth. Somebody else knew how she felt. "Cast the charm, Warren."

"What? Oh, yes." Warren looked into the book. "Whose soul, dear?"

"Your own," his wife said.

"Yes, that's right," Warren said, as if to himself. "Always try it on yourself first." He began to read the charm.

It felt as if the book gave a cry of delight and a sigh of relief all at once, like something finally being let loose. The charm itself was nothing, a mundane-sounding string of syllables, and it ended too soon to suit the book. Brought up short, the thing began snarling in Patsy Hoth's mind again. She ignored it, being too interested in what was happening to Warren.

His features were changing, at first as if she saw them through swirling water or changing light, tightening up in some places and loosening in others so the round calm face she had been watching became longer, screwed up around the eyes and slack under the jaw. It was like watching intelligence come back into someone as an incubus left him. Patsy Hoth liked this Warren better, but the grimoire did not. It greeted the change with furious hatred, and the new Warren reciprocated. He pursed all of his face up in distaste and leapt backwards away from the book, into his wife's waiting grasp, and paused only long enough to wrap sheltering arms around her before retreating further.

"What the hell is that!" he cried. "Get away from it!"

"Like hell," Patsy Hoth said. "You can tell me what to do when you haven't been getting us almost killed. I'm the only person in this department who knows what I'm doing. We'd be better off with me in charge."

That would be page eighteen, the grimoire said.

It drowned out the other voices-Warren and Teddy and Lilian, all shrieking like idiots-and Patsy Hoth feared the racket might affect her own judgment. She hitched herself and the book over toward Russell. "What does he need to do?" she snapped. Her fingers were paging back along the corners of the book, searching of their own will for page eighteen.

"Wait," Teddy said, pulling out a plexi box and decanting something alive-a spider? a scorpion?-into Russell's hand. He peered at it. "Go ahead," Teddy said. "Don't drop it!" She held his hand closed over the wriggling thing and practically pushed his head into the book.

"All right, all right," he said, and began to read.

It took every ounce of professional ethics Patsy Hoth possessed to hold the book open, her fingers having found the page that would help her clear up all this nonsense. She didn't watch Russell's face as he read the charm; she was too tense, just waiting for the instant when he had finished, but when that instant came someone else snatched the book away from her. She looked up, furious, to see a spiky-haired sorcerer putting it into a warded bag. She felt as if she were being deflated.

Patsy Hoth stood up and straightened her skirt. Nobody was paying any attention to her. Warren had one arm around his wife and was holding the old lady's hand, and Russell and Teddy were sitting on the bed in a clinch neither would want publicized.

This was probably not the time to ask for her facilitating charms back. Patsy Hoth walked out into the hall. Nobody was in sight except a gaggle of nurses by the elevator. Even though she stopped and thought about it for a full minute, there was no reason not to go back to her lab and get some work done, so that was what she did.

Chapter Twenty-one

Being in a book should have been confining, Rho thought. *Boring. Monotonous.* Instead, it was an experience of constant upheaval. Fragmented images and feelings flickered through him; no sooner did he have an idea than it was snatched away. *Dammit to hell,* Rho thought, when he had an instant of clarity. *They're passing this fucking book around. They're just playing with it! Do they give a shit what's happening in here?*

He shut off everything except the familiar anger, and found stability in it. The world outside him settled into a hard-edged solidity. The grimoire became a place where something could be built, where thoughts could be set one on another to accomplish things and problems could be solved. Rho felt himself thinking more clearly than ever, using a kind of magic that needed nothing except his mind, as if he were an alchemist and whatever he wished for would build itself up at his bidding. *I don't have to stay here!* he thought, exultant. *I can do anything.* It stopped. Gone. Popped like a bubble, gone out like the little demon they had exorcised, and a voice from memory filling up the place where all that ambition had been.

"Do you really think they would let you escape?" the voice said sarcastically. "That is exactly what they want you to think. They use your power to cast their spells, and leave you here for use another day-but what else have you to do, except go mad from boredom?"

Rho hated whatever spoke, even if it were himself, almost as much as he hated whoever was holding the book. He felt rage welling up in him again, pulled out of him by something beyond his control; whether he would or not, he demanded release, fought toward it, grasped it, and felt the hope of it go out again, leaving him in an exhaustion past collapse. The book churned around him again and Rho could not even try to orient himself. He tumbled with it, fragmented and miserable, too tired even to hate.

***

I thought I couldn't feel worse, Susan thought as someone went by carrying the grimoire. She looked around for something to throw up in. Patsy Hoth came out of Warren's room, but didn't even look in Susan's direction; she stood very straight and stiff, as if disgusted by something, and walked away toward the elevator with an unapproachable air. Susan was too near throwing up to follow her and too close to tears to call out.

"So here you are," a voice with a bitter undertone said. "Were any of you ever going to tell me Rho was in the hospital?"

"What?" The hospital spun as Susan turned her head, trying to grasp what she had done or not done and how it was wrong. All that came to her was that Neil was angry, and he must be right. Everything was so horrible. "Oh, Neil, I'm sorry," she said vaguely, and began to cry.

"Hey!" Neil said, sounding nervous. "Hey, is it that bad? He's not dead, is he?"

452

Susan couldn't answer. She stood up, groping in her bag, but Neil, bless him, already had a handkerchief out. It was large and warm and smelled of oil paint. She held it over her face, breathing through it, and the fit began to pass.

"You'd better sit down," Neil said.

Susan sat down and blew her nose. "It wasn't me," she said. "It was the grimoire. They were using Warren's grimoire to try and cure him."

"Rho?"

"No, Warren and Russell."

Neil peered down the corridor. "Did it work?"

"I'm afraid not," she said sadly.

"Damn," he said, without much feeling. "What's with Rho? They won't even tell me where he is in this hospital. Some kind of warded exorcism suite. I can't believe you didn't tell me he was here. I'm his friend. I had to find out from Cham, of all people."

"I don't think any of us are his friends," Susan answered mournfully. "If he'd told anyone what was going on, he might not be here."

"It was that demon, wasn't it?" Neil said, looking older than she'd thought him-or, rather, looking like someone young playing at being old. "The one that killed its owner in Selanto." He looked down the corridor past Susan and sat up. "Hey! Speaking of devils-I thought you said it didn't work?"

Turning around, Susan saw Russell shuffling toward them, leaning on Teddy Whin's shoulder.

"Russell!" she cried, standing up. "You're back?" Russell looked at her as if seeing something inside or through her. He had an old man's face and watery eyes. He reached his arms forward, surprising Susan, and caught her in a hard embrace.

"Thank you," he said into the side of her head. "Thank you so much."

"Oh, Russell, we missed you," Susan said, blinking hard. She had to use Neil's handkerchief again, and that reminded her he was standing right there, sturdy and warm, grinning. Russell seemed sturdier himself as he reached a hand to Neil.

"I understand you're the hero," he said firmly.

"Yeah, well, that was last week," Neil said. Russell gave his hand a squeeze.

"We'll talk, when I get out of here," he said.

"Sure," Neil said. "Hey! If this treatment worked on you, did it fix up Warren too? And how about Rho? What's Cham coming over here for? Is someone getting exorcised?"

"Not so far as I know," Russell said, and shut his eyes. His face fell into long folds and grooves. He wobbled, and put his hand down heavily on Neil's shoulder.

"You better lie down," Teddy said. "Look, give me some help getting him back to bed."

They walked down the corridor at Russell's deliberate pace. Susan was left as alone as anyone could be in a busy hospital, the kind of place where all sorts of desperate operations might be going on behind closed doors, without anyone seeming to notice their horrific nature. Someone's soul might be being removed, or the structure of personality that gave them power torn apart by Cham's disbelief, and there would be no way to tell which door it was happening behind. She marched down to the nurse's station like an army with pennants.

454

"Where did they take that grimoire?"

*****

Rho felt himself coming back from wherever exhaustion sent the spirit. *Wonderful,* he thought bitterly. *I'll be strong again. All ready for someone to use.* He understood, now, the stories of djinns imprisoned so long that they killed the one who released them. He felt his future in one flash: an eternity of hatred, galling impotent hatred as he was used by whoever held the book, broken only when his masters' demands left him too exhausted to hate. If he could reach out of this book, he'd kill anything he could touch, rip it apart the way he had torn Ganeel to pieces. Or better yet, make them kill each other the way he had made that dupe kill the pigeon. Oh yes, that had been just right; misery for its own sake, but all that lovely anger for food. He'd make Oldham tear his nasty little wife's head off. Rho jerked himself away from this thought, horrified, and lost hold for a moment of everything except fear. While he was struggling with that emotion someone picked the book up again and the landscape he had glimpsed before came into existence all around him, solid and clear.

This person didn't change the shape of the landscape as the others had. Nothing heaved or twisted under Rho, but areas lit up, one after another, as if each one were being seriously considered. The light played over violent places that looked like hatred made solid, and over forests, rocky coastlines... it sparkled on frisky waves and glowed over vineyards, and Rho began to catch its

455

methodical tenor and to link parts of the landscape with charms he remembered reading in the book. The rough places were the curses and maledictions, the calm ones the meditative charms he had tried so hard to cast, the busy ones were charms with specific purposes. But what lit them? Not the external magician's intention, Rho had imagined light before anybody picked up the book. He had seen something in the book, at some time, that appeared to his spirit now as a source of light.

What nonsense, he thought, or the demon thought for him. *Or is there a difference, any longer?* Rho pushed that thought away and tried to look around it, but words popped up from it like bubbles from a swamp.

*There is no light for you, not any more,*it thought. *Not what you have become. What you will turn into, here in the dark with yourself?*

Rho howled at it. *What are you trying to keep me from seeing?* he thought, as loudly as he could, and got a moment's clear view of the landscape, but it wasn't until the magician looking through the book found it that he was able to tell where the slanting light came from. It was a little charm, one he had looked at and set aside, a charm for enlightenment or insight, such as one might find in any self-help book.

***

The grimoire's soft pages made no sound as Cham Ligalla flipped through them. They jumped in her hands. The first time she had gone through the book, it had wanted her to do dreadful things to

456

herself. Page eighty-three, in particular, had flipped open with a mindless, repetitive malice, though Cham would not read past the first line of that charm. She could tell trouble when she met it. The second time, the grimoire had suggested combustion. By her third reading, much of the fire had gone out of it and it had put up only a series of random charms, a what-does-it-matter-after-all assortment that added up to nothing. Now, on her fourth look through the book, she was getting even less. Whatever was inside the grimoire had realized it could expect nothing from her. More importantly, what should she expect from it?

She put the book down and leaned back away from it to consider it at a safe distance-not so much safe for her as for whatever was in the book. She could have thought about the book itself without damaging it, but the souls within it were more fragile, their access to power dependent on mental structures and self-images that Cham's questioning could disrupt. People never recovered from something like that. They were never the same. As Cham thought this, something pounded on the door.

"Come in," she said. It swung open and Susan Teale stood panting in its frame, the portrait of an emergency. "Is something wrong?"

"What are you doing to Rho?"

"Nothing," Cham said.

"You can't exorcise him!"

"I can, if necessary. I haven't made that determination yet."

Susan shut her eyes and took a deep breath, holding her fists down in front of her and relaxing them as she exhaled. Cham had seen her do this in

457

department meetings. Her eyes glittered when she reopened them.

"He hasn't done anything wrong. He doesn't deserve to lose his powers."

"He doesn't deserve to become part of a demon, either," Cham said. "Nobody deserves what happens to them in cases of possession. We don't resort to exorcism until it's the least of evils. This is better than most cases," she said, considering the book. "In bodily possession, we have to find a solution before the demon kills the body. Here, we have time. Though as time goes on, Rho will probably become more inextricably united with the demon. Do you know how many of our charms he can give it?"

"It's not about our charms. It's about a human soul."

"A human soul who might spend eternity as part of a demon, helping it destroy other human souls."

Susan closed her hands into fists again and took another deep breath. "I can't talk sense to you," she said, in tones of disgust. "We need to ask Warren about this."

"We do," Cham agreed. "It's his grimoire."

***

Warren had the most disconcerting feelings about his hospital room. On the one hand he had never seen it before, and looking at a new room could always occupy him for at least half an hour. The colors, scents, shapes and auras of a room were interesting, and this one was pleasant; while

458

convention would have deterred Warren from painting any room of his own pink, and expense would have ruled out the heavy shielding that bleached every aura in it to a pastel, he appreciated the combination. He also liked the painting in the corner, which depicted a woodland stream in spring.

His body, however, was bored with the room. It could not look at any of these items for more than a vague, unfocused moment. The bed felt old to it, every position worn and tiresome. The chair's idiosyncrasies grated on its bones, it had learned too well the few postures that made working at the wheeled table possible, and its fingers were tired of the feel of jigsaw puzzle pieces, pens, and book pages.

The body even wanted to skate its gaze over Lilian and Bosie, but here Warren refused to humor it. He insisted on looking at his wife, holding her hands, and telling her just what she was like in the spirit world.

"Of course I remember that," Lilian said. "We were sitting under a beech tree. You proposed and I said yes, and then we just sat there a lot like this."

"I remember the shadows were purple and cold," Warren said. "All the little leaves were new and soft, and it felt like the beginning of the world."

Lilian snuggled up into his arms and kissed him on the nose.

Bosie, who had been tactfully reading the back of the hospital's shampoo bottles, cleared her throat.

"Dearie, even though I hate to disturb the moment, I would like to know whether it was you who gave me those hiccups Friday night."

"Oh, were they hiccups?" Warren asked innocently. "I seem to remember-"

"Hiccups, dear," Bosie said firmly. "Because I really don't know a thing about that building. How I could know where that grimoire was, when it wasn't even in your office, I cannot imagine."

"It was me," Warren admitted. "Do you know incubi just jump in and out of you?"

"I've been told that," Bosie said. "So convenient for a dancer. Now, what was I like, dear?"

"You were like that book you always used to read me. The big one with knights on the cover. Trumpets and horses."

Bosie glowed. "Why, what a nice thing to say to an old lady!" she preened. "You'll be very popular if you go on this way, Warren. I must say I never taught you much, but you did pick up manners."

Warren felt absurdly proud, puffed up and significant; he knew before he looked up who was standing in the doorway. "Hello, Cham," he said. She stood with her briefcase held before her by both hands in a childlike pose and looked at him, seeing something that only her attention could call into existence. Susan Teale stood behind her, like an outline surrounding Cham on all sides, and it seemed entirely natural. Cham extended beyond herself.

"Hello, Warren," she said. "I'm glad to see you're back with us."

***

460

"This is exactly the sort of thing I wanted a vacation from," Russell said. "Have we been back five minutes, and already we're in a meeting?" He stuck his feet out, poked them into Teddy, who was sitting on his bed, and pulled them back in a hurry. "This bed is a bore," he said, and Warren understood completely.

Teddy had commandeered the hospital table and was making a list. "I see the following options," she said, and began ticking them off on her fingers. "Do nothing and keep the book as an artifact. Exorcise the book, before or after making a copy of it. Burn the book. Are there any others?"

"You've left out everything important!" Susan said. "It isn't about the damn book, it's about Rho."

"The book's what we have hold of."

Russell rubbed his eyes with the heels of his hands. "What happens to Rho in each of these cases?"

They all looked at Cham.

"In the first case, he would almost certainly become part of the demon. It would then have his powers and knowledge. On its eventual escape from the book, if any of Rho still remained, it would be able to cast magic charms, including some of those from the book. This isn't a legal option. You can't create something like that."

"So if you exorcise him?"

"The exorcism is always aimed at the demon. If the demon is sufficiently distinct from Rho, he might be able to save some of his powers. That's theory," Cham said. "In practice, it doesn't happen. Demons have too much control of the mind for the possessed to perceive their own magic as distinct

461

from the demon's. But if it were going to happen, this would be the case. Rho's a strong magician, and he's inside an artifact that can't control his nervous system. The demon has less to work with than it would in his body.

"Worst case, we'd destroy Rho's power along with the book's, but he and the demon would be driven out. It might be able to absorb him, in that case, but it wouldn't be able to use his powers. Best case, Rho might simply lose whatever part of him is most united with the demon. Then he'd remain in the book after it was driven out, and we'd have to burn the book to get his soul out of it and back into his body."

"And if we just burn the book, he and the demon will have to leave it."

"That's not legal either. The demon could have enough hold of him by now to use his powers."

"If we only had one option, why did you waste our time on this list?" Teddy asked, rather hot.

Cham didn't answer. She merely looked away, and Warren felt Teddy dwindle into insignificance.

"What does the demon want?" he asked. Everyone looked at him as if this were a new idea. "Has anybody asked it?"

"All we know about it is that it's from Selanto," Susan said. "It belonged to Ganeel."

"I met it," Teddy said.

"So did I," Bosie put in. "It was very well-mannered. Most courtly. I should have guessed it was from Selanto."

"But does anyone know what it wants with Rho?" Nobody answered. "If it's from Selanto, it won't have a territory here," Warren thought aloud.

462

"The local demons won't give it a moment's peace. It can't be taking prey here; they'll harry it away from any of the minor spirits. Probably all it has going for it is whatever it can steal of Rho's power."

"He was tired," Susan said. "I thought it was because he was charging crystals. He was falling-over tired. His readings on the ghostmeter went all over the map-from demonic right down to mundane."

"Why were you running a ghostmeter on Rho?"

"It doesn't matter," Susan said. "We have to find out about this demon. Are you saying we should talk to it, Warren? How?"

The discussion swirled around Warren like a windstorm. One person after another, bits of information blowing around. Would nobody else take responsibility for putting them together? "I don't think we should mess with the grimoire right now," he said, and Cham nodded. That was the only solid thing in the room. He shut his eyes and felt for the ley-line beneath him. The same feelings he had floated through in spirit were around him now, almost drowned out by his heart and lungs, his nerves, his blood. Commotion! He half-heard voices, tension and concern, and then hands took his shoulders and he had a moment's rush of the springtime feeling, a touch of strength and solidity. He leaned into them, and heard Lilian's voice cut through the chaos.

"How'd you all like to go do something else until tomorrow?"

***

463

The angriest man in all of Osyth was following a cowed security guard up the tower stairs of the Magic Building; a feat of intimidation, because an alchemist had no business in a magician's office and nobody had a right to cross the police tapes. It was simply hard to stand up against an alchemist in a rage, given that he could-if he wanted to brave the guild-make the world into a place the guard didn't exist in. This particular guard was sorry for Bill, as well, having been at Gordon's execution, and Bill took unfair advantage of the fact. People who had been at the execution, he knew, would always cut him slack. He might as well get something out of it. And there was a smell of burning on this stairwell.

"Crap," Bill said in awe, when he saw the furniture all pushed toward the wall, the broken pentacle and the blood. "What the fuck were they doing in here?"

"I don't know," the guard said. "We took one guy and a book over to the hospital about midnight on Friday."

Bill shut his eyes because he was too angry to look at the room any more. "Nobody tells me anything," he said in a tight voice. He could feel the guard stepping back. "Can I use your phone to call the hospital?"

"Sure," the guard said. "They were both in emergency when I left."

Which, if possible, made things worse. Bill Navanax picked his way down the stairs after her with furious care. He was not going to break his own neck before he had broken somebody else's. Whose, he wasn't sure, nor had he settled on exactly why.

When he had come by the Magic Building Friday night, nothing had seemed wrong in Rho's tower. He had heard a woman's voice coming from behind the door, an academic arguing voice that sounded a lot like Teddy Whin, who had taken his place on the faculty senate two years ago. That had decided him against going in; no problem was so bad that hearing Teddy talk it to death wouldn't be worse. Anyway, Rho had finally found help from his own department. Bill was off the hook. So when Rho didn't call him, Bill made excuses. The kid was busy. Whin had probably talked him to sleep. He'd call in the morning and let Bill know what she'd worked out.

But on Saturday Rho hadn't called. Bill had tried calling Rho himself, and gotten no answer, so he'd checked his own voice mail at the lab, and his office email, and then his home voice mail in case Rho had called while he was online. Nothing. Perhaps they were still working on it. He imagined Rho in meetings. Magicians had lots of meetings to decide how they ought to view the world, so as to make out that it supported their current agendas. Whin was probably still talking... Bill snorted and put Rho out of his mind. He started stripping wallpaper in his spare bedroom, trying to decide what color to paint it when he was done. Anything but brown, but invention palled and he found himself coming back to fawn and chocolate, as if he couldn't drum up a real interest. Besides, the room smelled of burning, more so as he moved the furniture around. The smell was in the carpet. That would have to come up too. It had blood on it, anyway. Bill went downstairs and called Rho again, then tried Regan's home number. It rang and rang, until Bill hung up and got himself a double whiskey. He sat beside the phone and tried Warren Oldham's house, the Demonology Department, and Regan again. He even looked up Teddy Whin's home number, but he hung up when he heard her answering machine. *It's not my problem,* he thought, and had another drink.

By afternoon, Bill Navanax was a dangerous man with a dangerous headache, and no one to vent it on but a security guard. He suspected this wasn't the right spirit in which to visit a friend in the hospital. It was the right frame of mind to deal with hospital receptionists, though, so he called. While the hospital operator searched Rho up in her files, Bill glared at the ranks of two-way radios recharging in the security office as if his gaze alone could charge them, and wondered how much that would amuse the guild. Not much. A voice came back on the telephone before he could do anything rash.

"I'm sorry," it said. "I don't have a current room assignment for any Mr. Rho."

"You mean he was released."

"We don't have any record for a patient of that name." Bill put his hand over the phone.

"They don't have a record."

"Have them check under campus security," the guard said.

"Check campus security admissions," Bill said into the phone. "Security brought him in Friday night."

"Let's see-oh yes, here he is. Admitted Friday night-but I don't have any other record of him."

466

"You lost a patient?" Bill could feel his eyebrows climbing up into his hair as he put the phone down over defensive protestations. The security guard looked at him with a similar expression. "Are we the only sane people on this campus?" Bill asked her.

"On a weekend? Probably."

"Can you tell me just what happened Friday night?"

"Not really. By the time I got there, everything was over except bringing back the lady who ran off with the book."

"Was the guy who went to hospital hurt bad?"

"Not from what I heard. He was out cold when the ambulance got there, but he woke up and was chatting away by the time they checked him in. They said he seemed fine. Cheerful."

Bill knew this should have relieved him, but it didn't. *Cheerful! Fine! Too fine and cheerful to call anybody, and now lost in the system. I hope they're giving him some horrible treatment,* Bill thought. *Debridement, or traction...* His imagination stuttered, for lack of sorcerous knowledge. *Intestinal lavage, perhaps.* He snarled as he walked toward the hospital, slipping in the snow, and when someone hailed him he answered with another snarl.

"Hey!" the person said, undaunted. He was a short man with red hair and an expression as if Bill were just the person he had been wanting to see. "Are you here to see Rho? They've got him in some sort of restricted access area, so you won't be able to get in."

"What do you know about it?"

467

The person beamed. "You're asking the right guy," he said. "Buy me a beer, and I'll bring you up to date."

***

Though it put him on bad terms with his sorcerer, and he didn't want to think about what his wife would say, Warren went to visit his grimoire in the warded storage room early on Sunday morning. He went out of a combination of sentiment and bone-deep boredom, the kind that burns inside, amusing itself by plucking at every nerve in turn. On the few occasions when Warren had been this bored in the past, he had endured agonies before giving in and doing something stupid. Now, having just gotten back into this body, he felt himself unwilling to endure agonies in it. *There's nothing much stupider than leaving your body and gallivanting around the ley-line as a naked soul, anyway,* he thought. *I hardly have to worry about doing anything stupider than that.*

When he got into the storeroom, after the energizing arguments with nurses and orderlies and Sorcerer Pim were all over, Warren hardly wanted to open the warded bag. It was like taking the lid off a coffin. When he touched the soft leather and softer pages his father seemed to reach up and hold him again, warm arms around either side of the little boy's body, a forefinger tracing words. His father's essence was in this book. His grandfather's as well, but Grandpa was a more remote and frightening figure. Grandpa had filled out page eighty-three. For good or ill, they lived in the grimoire. Warren could

468

meet them there, hear their voices, feel their embraces, discover them in these pages they had touched. A Xerox copy would never be the same.

Neither would the grimoire, though. He could tell it had changed, not into the sickening hatred he had felt in it before but into a tight sensation as if a spring were winding up inside it. The pages shifted and rustled in his hands, and Warren let them move to where they wanted to go. The book searched itself. With every page that turned, Warren saw another part of his father, as clearly as if for the last time. As if saying goodbye... the book paged onward, slower now and with effort, and a wad of pages flipped backwards suddenly, back to page eighty-three, as if whatever lived within it were having a serious difference of opinion. Warren turned the wad of pages back and leant on them, closing page eighty-three with all his weight.

The book seemed to shake itself and wind up even tighter, moving the pages slowly and with effort, which made no sense. The charms on these pages were minor charms Warren had written in when he was a boy. Charms cast by children. He had held his own daughters on his lap and read these charms to them, and he could feel their warm weight as he read the pages now. How soft children's flesh was, how creamy and gentle; how right he had felt, how good the world had seemed as he sat under the lamp, teaching his little girls the safe, warm things a child should learn. Warren's eyes prickled. The book turned one last page, as if it had no strength left, and laid itself out under his gaze.

There's no harm in casting this. Warren read the words over. He'd already cast one charm from the grimoire, and nothing had gone wrong. This charm was nothing that would release a trapped spirit. Cham would be furious if she knew. Lilian would scream at him... but Warren didn't want any good advice. He stopped pretending he needed any more reason than the thought of children, what they deserved, what their parents ought to teach them. He fished some stiff piece of medical waste out of the trash basket for a pen, bit his cuticle for blood, and on nothing but a whim or instinct he wrote the rune on the page itself, tore that corner off, and instead of swallowing the scrap of paper he slid it far in between the pages of the book and closed them tightly over it.

***

The light in the book solidified, turning from a mystery into an orb, spreading gold and pink around itself. Wherever the light touched, the landscape began to flow and rearrange itself, as if someone had taken hold of the book again, but there was none of the sickening feeling of being tumbled through someone else's plans. This reshaping felt like something out of Rho's own head. Everything around him crumbled and reformed, flattening and roughening until it was a hummocky meadow, bounded by hedgerows and lit by sunset. He watched the slanting gold rays, the clouds painted pink below and purple above, with one new star shining from behind them, and took a deep breath- not because he had lungs, but because it was the only thing to do when one stood in this peaceful glow. *This is what I like,* he thought, and something moved in the corner of his mind. Rho turned his attention and saw a rabbit sitting up on its haunches, the first animal he had seen in the landscape.

Hello, Rho thought, more in surprise than greeting. The rabbit thumped back down onto all four paws and lolloped forward to a tuft of grass, where it began to feed. Rho heard another stirring from behind him. The field rustled and whispered, coming alive with small creatures: hedgehogs, badgers and gophers, a harvest mouse climbing dry stalks to its nest and a vole's inquiring whiskery face looking out from its burrow. From the hedges he heard crows calling, blackbirds challenging each other, and the song of a thrush. Pigeons rose in a fluster from the next field, cooing to one another.

"Night, rest, safe, sleep," they said.

A pipit swayed on one of the stems near Rho; he held out a hand, not because he had one but because it was the only thing to do, and the bird hopped onto it.

"I had no idea you were so saccharine at heart," another part of him snorted. "What comes next, kitties with ribbons?"

The landscape froze, every little creature stopped in motion, suspended and bizarre. Rho felt himself freezing, crumbling with them, as if he had undressed in front of the demon and offered himself to it naked. Worse than naked-as if he had opened up every part of himself, slit open all his tender places and invited it to reach into them and pull out whatever it wanted. How had he been such a fool? He wanted nothing more than to curl up on himself, but he had no body to curl into. No shell. Nothing to keep the demon out of him, no part of him that could be protected. The meadow was a wavering mess of brown and gold now, like a world made of tears.

"How sweetly pretty," the demon said. "Twee."

Rho snarled inside himself. The wavering landscape turned into something hard and sharp, solid, armored, and where the bird had been there was only a mass of something that had been clenched into pulp.

Chapter Twenty-two

"I think I communicated with him," Warren said. "When I was going through the book, it wanted me to cast a charm of insight. Nothing that would interest a demon at all."

"And you did it?" Russell asked, raising his eyebrows. "What happened?"

"Nothing much. It seemed calmer-then it got angry again."

"Well, demons and insight usually don't mix," Neil said.

"You ought to cast it again, while we're scanning the book with the camera arcana," Teddy said. "We could check whether the two auras are more separate or not." She disappeared into her paper gown, and emerged looking at Warren with concern. "Are you sure you're up to this? You haven't even been out of the hospital for a day."

Warren shook himself and stood up. "None of the rest of you can do it," he said. "I'm the only one Nezumia talks to outside of the geas." He scowled at his feet. "You know it likes depression. I might as well take advantage of being tired."

"Why aren't there any demons that like confidence or good humor?" Teddy wondered aloud. "We're not all depressed or angry, after all. Some of us have the most energy when we're cheerful. If people can vary that much, demons ought to as well. Of course, if cheerful people are rare, demons might hang around them as familiar spirits, rather than roaming the ley-line."

"Whatever," Russell said, who had never cut off a theoretical conversation; he took Warren's arm, as if he had bigger problems, and didn't even look up when Teddy fell abruptly silent.

It was too much for Warren to deal with. He shut his eyes and let Russell steer him into the pentarium. It was too quiet in there, and he could feel the whole group worrying. He opened his eyes, hoping the feeling would go away, but that only showed him two rings of worried magicians, the real and the reflected. The pentacle drawn in blood, the gold chain between its posts, were both twice as thick as they needed to be.

"We're not entrapping a demon today," Warren said. "No charms of discourse. This is a specific summoning. We want Nezumia and nothing else. Is everybody ready?"

Heads nodded. Linus glared. Warren glared back and felt stronger.

"Let's do it, then," he said.

Summoning the demon by its name took only a few minutes, but waiting for it to appear took almost half an hour-time for the nervousness in the room to be replaced by impatience and boredom, and for Warren to become even more depressed. Nezumia had probably been waiting for a certain level of depression, as it appeared at the side of the pentacle nearest him, licking its chops.

The demon had chosen a vaguely feline form, mangy and bleary-eyed. It looked at Warren with appreciation and he felt the *grue* seize him in a new way, from the thoughts out. What did life hold but this-decrepitude, dismal inability. Dragging one's body from its foul nest into a hateful world and

474

back again. Every sensation, every motion, another meaningless unpleasantness.

"I saw you out on the ley-line," Nezumia said to him, ignoring all the other magicians. "You went adventuring."

Warren shivered, as every syllable scratched along his bones.

The demon laughed. "I see you know me better," it said.

Warren's hand closed tighter around Russell's on one side, Cham's on the other. He clung to them.

"I want to talk with you about the new demon," he said. "The demon from Selanto."

Nezumia stretched, showing raw spots in its fur, but its eyes were narrow. "The trespasser," it said. "The demon that tried to cast one of your charms on me. Did you think it could bind me, when you have failed?"

"I didn't know anything about the new demon," Warren said, exchanging a glance with Russell. "Haven't we been working well together? Why would I support another demon?"

"You have been supporting it," Nezumia said. "It runs to you magicians for help, whenever it weakens. You had best hope it wins. I can make as many stories about body and soul as you can. Did you like the one I told you a week ago? Did you enjoy believing what I told you to believe?"

"We're not supporting it!" Warren protested. "It's only done us harm. It stole power from one of my magicians, and now it's stolen him away entirely. I want him back. Tell us what you know about it, and we'll work with you to get rid of it."

"Getting rid of it is not my plan," Nezumia said, its voice filled with relish. "When I take it into myself, I will give it reason to despair. It will suffer for me. I will feed on its despair as it feeds on your magician's anger."

"But you can't do that until we get it out of the book," Teddy said.

The demon turned its head slowly, eyeing her.

"What can you tell us to help us get it out? It feeds on anger, but what else?"

Nezumia looked back at Warren, as if he had spoken. "Drive it out of the book," it said. "I will do the rest. This is my place." It leaned forward again, its head turning flat, reptilian. "Do you want to play in our games? Did they please you, out on the ley-line? Human souls do not fare well in the netherworld."

Warren clutched the hands on either side of him as tightly as he could, searching for some kind of warmth, some reality; he felt himself shaking apart, things inside him ripping loose, pains in places he hadn't known he could feel. He fought to look out of himself until he heard Teddy chanting the charm that would make it safe to break the circle, and then he let himself fall into his own innards.

***

"Damn, he's still cold. Turn that on hotter." Russell leaned his head out from under the shower and watched Neil adjust the temperature. Warren leant against him like a lump of putty. *Two naked old men sitting on the floor together,* Russell thought. *One too skinny and one too fat. Nothing dignified about any of this.* He ducked back under the water and held his friend, wishing some of his own warmth into Warren. For Russell was warm and comfortable. He hadn't felt any of the *grue* that seized Warren in the pentarium. *None of the miseries. I didn't see anything outside myself on the ley-line, either,* he thought. *I didn't meet any demons. Nothing worse than myself.*

Perhaps I am a demon, he thought, and held Warren tighter, as if by pressing against the other man he could make himself a better person. "This isn't working," he said. Neil turned the water off, and somebody else-Teddy, Russell thought-handed him down a towel, one of those luxurious bath sheets she used, thick enough to soak up the ocean. Russell didn't want to think about the ocean. He wrapped the thing around Warren, instead.

Feet shuffled away from them and Russell smelled herbal smoke as Cham Ligalla squatted in front of him, holding one of the candles from her exorcism kit.

"How is he?" she asked. Russell shook his head. Cham settled herself cross-legged on the floor and nodded at him. "Let me have a try," she said.

Russell leaned Warren against the shower wall, stood up, and moved out of her way. He felt himself disappearing. When Cham concentrated on Warren the rest of them didn't matter. Usually this would have irritated Russell, but now feeling that he didn't matter was a luxury. *Maybe I'm not a demon after all,* he thought. *I can at least conceive of myself not mattering.*

Cham took Warren's hands and spoke to him in that exorcist's language that Russell couldn't

477

understand, but as he listened it seemed to him that it spoke his own thoughts about Warren. Tubby, earnest Warren. A little dim and easily manipulated. Russell didn't like what he was hearing. *This is how I view my best friend,* he thought. *Maybe I am a demon, after all.* He looked up and saw Teddy scowling; her face was drawn up in unhappiness, and when he caught her gaze she blushed, scowled harder, and looked at the floor.

Russell looked around, happy for a distraction, and saw Linus glaring at Cham and Will Harding looking at her with an expression as if he were ashamed but secretly proud of himself at the same time. Patsy Hoth stood with her arms folded, defiant; she was hearing nothing she would not have said to Warren's face. Neil was looking at the floor with his face as red as his hair. Of the people in Russell's view, only Susan Teale and Isaac Graham seemed to be paying any attention to Warren, or wishing him well.

Warren moved; he leaned forward, into Cham's arms, and she stopped her chant. "Why don't you all just get out of here?" she said, her voice very cross. "Susan and Anders, you can stay."

Russell followed the rest back behind the second row of lockers, into the other end of the shower room.

"Crap!" Teddy said to him. "At least you got clean. My car keys are back there, and my clothes."

"Warren's only been out of hospital a day, and already I'm standing around watching him bust his hump," Russell said in disgust.

"Nezumia wouldn't have come for anybody else," Will said. "You saw it ignore Teddy."

"It was some use," Patsy Hoth said. "It gave us a little information. Russell is right, though. We're capable of dealing with a situation like this without making Warren do it. I have a proposal." This caught everybody's attention. "If the demon likes anger, to keep it from following Rho's spirit into his body we simply need to offer it someone angrier than Rho."

Russell felt his eyes bugging out, as if Patsy Hoth were pulling on strings attached to them. Then he felt them turn toward Linus, with just as little volition on his part.

"Go to hell!" Linus said, his face purple. "To hell with all of you! I knew you all hated me, but this is beyond any pretense of professionalism. I won't work in an environment where I'm subject to this kind of abuse!"

"You'd be warded," Patsy Hoth said. "We'd get you an alchemical ward."

"Yeah, from-" Neil stopped in mid-sentence. "We don't need Linus," he said.

***

Sitting in The King's P, waiting for a sinister alchemist, Neil Torecki thought he couldn't have been happier. He looked around the room and turned it into planes of color for a future painting, then into pen and ink for an architectural drawing, then into a gesture sketch. He made it into a sunny, jolly place, and thought out how a few brush strokes would turn the sunlit jollity into something hollow laid over the exhaustion of sorcerers just out of the operating room, having stepped away from the deathbed.

Neil saw a hundred pictures in The King's, but the most intriguing one was the man in brown who looked like a tired shopkeeper. *It would take skill to make him look like anything else,* Neil thought, until Navanax sat down and looked at him like something very different from a tired shopkeeper. It was in the eyes. To paint it, he'd have to do something with the pupils, and it couldn't be anything hackneyed like little flames... maybe a big blank highlight, as if the person were looking into something too bright and not squinting. While Neil was working this out, Navanax took off his overcoat.

"You're lucky I came at all," he said. "They might not warn you about this over in magic, but the young academic on the make usually doesn't call people up and tell them they're worse tempered than Linus Ukadnian."

Neil grinned. "Gosh, I guess I'm gauche," he said.

"How long have you been waiting to use that line?"

"Years and years."

"I can't believe you had to wait that long." Navanax waved to the waiter. When he turned his head, the folds in his face pulled into straight lines.

Neil's hand itched for a pencil.

"I know you're friends with Rho," he said. Duty.

"That's more than I know."

Yes! Neil thought. *Why did I think that?*

Navanax stared at him. "What did you want?"

480

"Um-well, Rho's got himself trapped inside a book with a demon that feeds off anger. We want to exorcise it, and we thought Linus could lure it out-"

Navanax laughed like a dog barking. "I wish I'd seen his face," he said. "I'll buy this round, just for that picture." Holding a beer, he seemed happier. For the first time, he smiled at Neil and lines curled round his jaws.

Neil grinned again. "He wasn't happy," he admitted. "Patsy Hoth told him we'd get him an alchemical ward, and that's when I thought about you instead. I mean, a demon can't touch an alchemist, right?"

"Maybe. Why should I take the risk for your department? Let Linus do it."

"I thought you liked Rho."

Navanax put his drink down and leaned over it, staring at Neil. "I don't like anybody who doesn't tell me what's really going on," he said. "You, for instance. This is a whole different story than you told me Saturday."

"It's a whole different story than I knew on Saturday," Neil protested. "Nobody tells me anything, either. I have to piece it all together. Look," he said, seeing an opportunity, "they really need you to help Rho. Linus won't do it. Let's share what we know, and write it down. Then we figure out where the holes are, and make them tell us before you'll help them. It all started with this demon that followed Rho home from Selanto."

"The pig he picked up," Navanax said.

Neil goggled at him. "What!" Something bright went off inside him, so strongly it must have shone out of his ears. *Gossip!* He'd found the mother lode.

481

"All right." Navanax looked at Neil as if he saw something he liked. "You tell me your part of the story, and I'll tell you mine. Then I'll consider it." He took notes while Neil talked, and then talked himself and filled in between the lines of his notes. "I knew he was leaving something out," he said. "This grimoire. How'd he get his hands on Warren's grimoire?"

"Nobody's told me that," Neil said.

Navanax looked at him with a stern face. "All we have here is bits and pieces," he said. "it doesn't answer any of the important questions."

"Like what?"

"Like whether Rho knew the demon was using his power against Nezumia in the pentarium. It could have stolen his power, or he could have helped it. And it's damned convenient for Rho that he has Warren's grimoire just when Warren's soul flies loose, ready to be trapped in it. Unless Warren's soul was already gone when Rho borrowed the book, which would explain why he did such a damn fool thing as loan it out. Warren's not supposed to be an idiot."

He pondered, doodling rows of little squares on the napkin. That was unimaginative, to Neil's point of view, but then Navanax began to fill the squares in with different penstrokes, like someone practicing his pen-and-ink skills.

"Worst case is that Rho's made an alliance with this demon and they planned the whole thing. Get Warren's soul, borrow the grimoire, trap Warren, then Rho becomes the most powerful magician in the city and the demon takes over from Nezumia. Allies."

482

"That doesn't make any sense," Neil protested. "Why would he be hiding in the pentarium, if they were allies? He would have just cast the charm and trapped Warren's soul."

"He could have had second thoughts," Navanax said, "or he could have failed to trap Warren, and the demon took it out on him."

Neil tried hard, but he couldn't fit this picture into the rest of what he'd seen of Rho. "It doesn't work," he said. "Anyone who's talked with Rho knows he didn't have some big ruthless plan. The only way he'd be involved in something like that is by being too unsettled to say no to it. He's moody. He probably liked the demon one day and hated it the next, the same way he treats all of us." He felt his voice turning sharp as he said this, and when he looked up, Navanax was staring back at him.

"You want him back?"

Neil almost said 'Of course!' or one of the other standard things people say to a question like that, but something about the way Navanax asked the question-flat, just dropping it onto the table between them-reminded him that he was talking to an alchemist. Alchemists didn't respect polite lies. He thought about Rho and whether having Rho back meant anything to him, and felt as if his answer might matter a great deal. It was a feeling Neil liked.

"Rho doesn't matter to me," he said finally. "I say I'm his friend, but he never liked me. It's just a habit I have, to be friendly with people who don't like me, because I'm darned if people with that poor taste get to decide who my friends are. If I never saw Rho again, it wouldn't matter. What would matter, though, is if I worked in a department that let a demon take one of its faculty. I mean, that demon would be hurting Rho forever, right? I'd have to get up every morning and think about that when I went in to work. Would you work with people who let that happen?"

"Maybe Rho would tell you all to mind your own business."

"He can't do that unless we get him back, right?"

"All right," Navanax said. "When do you want to do this?"

"Tomorrow morning at nine. We'll do it in the exorcism suite, over in the hospital."

***

"I cannot tell a lie," Teddy said, clasping her hands in front of her as she leaned back in Russell's easy chair. "I killed your plants."

"You sure did." Russell looked at the dried branches with dismay. "There's a little green left on this one."

"I can fix that."

"So can I," Russell said. "Watch." He touched the plant and pushed himself out into it, using his thoughts the same way he'd used them to make the crab in the pentarium. Green began to flush through the plant's stem and new branches pushed out under the dead leaves, knocking them off to flutter toward the floor. While he was at it, Russell sent them swirling into the wastebasket. He swept his attention through his office, whisking dust away from every scroll, setting every red and orange tassel asway.

Teddy's mouth fell open and she swiveled her head, watching the motion all around her. "Holy crap." She looked back at Russell. "Well? Spill it. What's happened to you? I knew something was up the minute I saw you in the pentarium with all that water. That was pretty showy."

"I don't know what's happened. I'll have to find out what charm Nezumia was trying to cast," Russell said. He sat down, suddenly downcast. "I suppose that's the next step, isn't it?"

"Well, yeah! It's a whole new field! Cooperative magic, human and demonic. And seeing what it's done for you, this could be the biggest thing any of us will ever run into. Plus it's all ours. Demons will never cooperate with other schools."

"We'll wreck it for ourselves, the way we wrecked the old charms," Russell said. "We'll deconstruct it until we don't believe in it anymore, and it'll stop working for us. It's the biggest thing we've ever run into and we're going to take it apart and publish the pieces." Teddy sat upright, frowning at nothing. He could hear a tassel tapping against the shelves. He could hear his plant growing, and every dry leaf that hit the floor behind him.

"I'm not sure I buy that," she said. "But I will buy that we ought to be careful until we know whether you're right or not. That sort of means leaving the demons in control, though."

Russell nodded. "In control of us."

"That's reconceptualizing the field with a vengeance." Teddy grinned. "What the hell. How

485

long has it been since we did any real groundbreaking? I can apply feminist theories in my sleep. It's time we tried something new."

Russell felt as if the sun behind him were shining right into him, filling him up with light and color. "Let's work on it, then," he said. The two of them sat in his office with their eyes shut, thinking, and the office rustled around them as if it were thinking too.

***

Bill Navanax spent the afternoon off-campus, listening to businessmen tell him why he ought to make metals do logically impossible things. When he thought about it, in snatched moments, Neil Torecki's request seemed reasonable by contrast. *I could attract all the demons in Osyth, if all they want is someone who's fed up,* Bill thought as he drove back to campus. He took his bad mood into the lab and his equipment responded, according to its kind, by swivelling toward or away from him or changing its settings. That was one of the frustrations of alchemy.

Bill sat on the desk and put his wet shoes on the chair, something he only did when feeling unusually rebellious or when pretending to feel rebellious to avoid feeling something else. "And to hell with this being honest with yourself crap, too," he said, lighting a cigarette. He only smoked when he was nervous.

The minute I saw that boy, I knew he was trouble, he thought. *Why do I let Vinca talk me into these things?* But Vinca hadn't driven Rho to Bill's house. Vinca hadn't let Rho spend his nights unsupervised in the alchemy labs. Bill hunched over his knees and glared at the wall, and all the equipment in the path of his glare cowered and shut itself off. He tried to convince himself that Neil Torecki was right about Rho. That Rho hadn't been calling up his demon in the lab every night, trying out alchemical spells to see what might be most useful for their power grab. Bill couldn't believe it. After all, nobody told Neil anything; he had said so himself. Bill sighed out a cloud of smoke. "Him and me." He looked at the wall again, but his mood had changed. His equipment began to cautiously turn itself back on.

The real laugh was that he'd done it to get in trouble. Helping Rho, that was just an excuse for getting up the guild's nose, for giving Vinca an ulcer when he found out about it. *For acting out,* Bill thought, insulting himself. He puffed harder. He'd been trying to bring it to open warfare between himself and the guild for two years, but he'd planned to be in the right when it finally blew. He'd been careful not to do anything that would give them a legitimate grievance. His would be the case that showed them up for what they were-arbitrary tyrants.

Nothing arbitrary, though, in not letting demons learn alchemy. Even Bill bought into that one. He stretched his legs out and reread his notes from the restaurant, and he was not pleased when Vinca came into the room unannounced. He stuffed the notes back into his coat pocket.

"I heard a disturbing rumor that you are participating in an exorcism tomorrow," Vinca said, without any of his normal courtly beating around the bush.

Bill raised his eyebrows.

"How the hell do you find things out, anyway?" he asked.

Vinca didn't answer this question, not even with a smug look or a smile. He turned and stared out the window, as if the lab itself were too insignificant to bother with. Vinca looked out toward his own research garden, where he set up experiments with time-what the world would be like without it-that could be seen by nobody who believed in time passing, in things happening and never being unhappened. That garden might be a way that Vinca found things out.

If a man were to do something about how angry he was, would Vinca know about it? Would he see it, in his garden, before the man knew himself? Would he come in, with his elegant authority, and fix that man before the poor fool could even guess what he was about to do? If it were a man Vinca cared about. A man he'd taken in hand. Other men could burn, for all Vinca cared. Bill thought about setting his lab on fire again, and decided against it. That wouldn't frighten Vinca or the guild; they'd look at a lab on fire with amused tolerance.

Vinca hadn't looked at Bill with amused tolerance yet today, and that in itself made playing at exorcism with the magicians worthwhile.

"You're the one who got me involved in all this, in the first place," Bill pointed out. Vinca didn't answer. He shifted his shoulders as if he couldn't decide what to say to get Bill back in line. "What did you expect me to get out of Rho? Wasn't I supposed to forget my troubles in remodelling someone else, the way you do? So, I'm doing it."

"Forgetting your troubles?"

"You wish!"

Vinca turned around and stood like a black cutout in front of the windows. Bill couldn't see out the windows of his own lab, unless he tried hard to disbelieve in all sorts of things. His eyes watered as he squinted at Vinca's silhouette.

"This demon is very dangerous," Vinca said.

"It was just as dangerous when we met Rho. Demons don't change."

"People do." Vinca stepped forward. "This demon is dangerous to you. You know it."

"It's no more dangerous to me than you are," Bill said. He knew he'd hit on a truth by how quiet things got inside him, as if some kind of white-noise machine had shut off. "Do you really think a demon is going to possess me in the middle of an exorcism, when I'm wearing my wards and Cham Ligalla's?" He leaned back in his chair and ticked off points on his fingers, because he knew it annoyed Vinca. "First it would have to materialize, then talk to me and convince me to take off all my wards and invite it in, then figure out how to keep Cham from exorcising it right there. And what are the other six or seven magicians supposed to be doing all this time, standing around with their mouths hanging open?"

"You're underestimating this demon," Vinca said. "It's already used the magicians' power to cast charms inside the pentarium. What could it do with yours?"

"Those magicians waltz around the pentarium without their wards on," Bill said scornfully. "Was Rho wearing wards when he slept down there? No. Anyone could grab their power, any day. I'll be wearing double wards. What would a demon do with alchemy in the arcane world, anyway? Demons already remake their world any time they want to. That's not what you're really worried about. Don't try to snow me."

"I should never have involved you with magicians," Vinca said, a little bitterly. "You're arguing like Magister Whin."

Bill thought that was meant as an olive branch, but he wanted none of it. "You haven't answered my question," he pointed out. "D'you really think I'm going to be taken in by a demon the way Rho was? You know I'm smarter than that. I know what I want, and I know I can't have it."

"I know."

"So why do you think I'll forget that the minute I'm in a room full of magicians?"

"Magicians don't want to believe in not being able to have things," Vinca said. "If they could accept that, they'd be alchemists. They'd rather stand back, instead, and pretend that if they only had the power they could build a world in which you can always have what you want. Especially Warren Oldham. That's the nature of middle managers. He has to believe he can make everybody happy, if he only tries hard enough, and Warren is a very strong magician."

"Well, maybe he's right," Bill said. "Maybe if we alchemists weren't so proud of accepting how bad things are, we could make them better. I ought

490

to pay attention to Warren, as long as I'm over there. D'you really want to know what made me decide to help them?"

"Of course," Vinca said.

"Torecki said he didn't give a fuck about Rho, but he wouldn't work in a department that let a demon take one of its own. He wouldn't come in every day and say hello to people who let that happen. He has more guts than I did. And higher standards."

Vinca didn't move, but his face stiffened as if he had taken a blow. The lab was more quiet than Bill had ever heard it. All his equipment was silent. It had shut itself off again. It was probably cowering toward the walls as well, or sneaking away, but he wouldn't look away from Vinca to check.

When Vinca spoke, he looked like a carving moving its mouth. "We shouldn't be having this conversation," he said, and walked away from the window.

"We should have had it two years ago," Bill said, standing up. He was surprised to find himself shaking. "It was cookware, dammit! They burned a man alive for making illegal cookware! You stood there and watched it happen. You could have stopped them. You could have asked the guild to pardon him, or lock him up somewhere."

"Yes, I could have."

"If you weren't my only friend, I'd kill you."

"I know." Vinca shut his eyes. When he opened them again, they were wet. "I love you very much, William. More than I love my own sons."

Bill felt a shaky triumph. He stuck his hands in his pockets and stared at the blank windows.

491

"You're really worried about this, aren't you?" he said, keeping his voice flat. "What are you afraid I'll figure out?"

"I don't want to see you burn." Bill thought of metals. He thought of sodium, stored under oil in his lab because contact with air would set it off in an orange blaze, and he stared at the window harder, as if he were looking for air himself.

"I'm doing this," he said. "It's the first thing I've done in two years that feels important, and I don't know why. I have to find out."

Chapter Twenty-three

Teddy Whin had to take a minute and look around the exorcism suite. It was the oddest hospital room she'd ever seen. The tiny bed Rho was lying in sat on a pentacle carved in the floor and the tiles were actually grooved to hold blood. Triple wards hung from the windows, and gold-plated fire extinguisher nozzles poked out of the ceiling. Set to the side in a corner was a gold post-and-chain setup like the pentarium's, and an alchemical safety switch was located on each side of the room. "Wow!" she said, cataloguing the safety measures and wondering which of them she could insist on having installed in her office. She looked at the grimoire sitting on one of those rollaway hospital tables, and it seemed no worse than any other book. *This is overkill...* Then Cham noticed her, or the camera arcana.

"Set the camera up over there," Cham said, nodding at a table under the wall-mounted television. "Patch it into the monitor." She turned back to the purification, setting up the posts and chain and fussing with bittersmoke while Teddy climbed, plugged, and focused. Rho's image appeared on the TV, looking placid and contented.

People are happier without their souls, Teddy thought. *Who says rescuing the soul is morally superior to leaving the body in peace? Why do we privilege the spiritual over the material?*

Rho looked at the camera, and his image smiled at her.

"Pretty neat, huh?" she said to it as she climbed down. "You're on TV." Without his suspicious expression, Rho looked years younger. Maybe he lied about his age. Too young to be a demonologist; too young to be anything. *This is where magicians end up when they're too young to know what they want,* thought Teddy. She felt tough, grown up. No flies on her.

Cham had set up the circle of gold chain with just one gap in it, beside one of the hospital's easy chairs. She climbed up on the foot of Rho's bed, the hospital table beside her set with a bundle of herbs, a brazier filled with glowing coals and a mirror on a silver stand. She leaned over, pouring blood into the grooved pentacle, and then sat up without a grunt, like someone made of muscle. "Warren, if you'll sit there. You'll cast the charm, and if it gets Rho away from the demon, pass the grimoire to Bill Navanax. When he passes it to me, you take out this block to close the pentacle and hook up the safety chains. Where's Russell? Where's Neil and Bill?"

"It's only five till," Teddy said.

Cham looked up at her and the television. "You want that on Warren and the book, not on Rho," she said.

"Oh yeah, duh," Teddy said, readjusting the camera, and that was why she missed seeing Russell, Neil and Navanax come in. When she looked up, everyone was watching Navanax watch Rho. Rho was smiling, but Navanax was not smiling back. *Whoa!* Teddy thought. *Not a happy couple. And look at little Neil, isn't he proud of what he brought in.* She looked sidewise at Russell, and found Russell looking sidewise at her. He cut his

494

eyes at the bed and made a soundless *Ooo* face, and Teddy *Oooed* back at him. This was getting better by the minute.

The door opened behind Russell and Magister Vinca stepped in. Teddy checked fast to make sure her *Ooo* face was gone, but Vinca wasn't looking at her. He was looking at Navanax, and Navanax glared back at him. Teddy began to feel uneasy. *I know we wanted someone angry,* she thought, *but Linus would at least have been controllable.* If it came to a magewar, alchemists would overpower magicians.

"Hello, Bill," Cham Ligalla said. "You sit here, on the chair beside Warren's. If this works, he's going to pass the grimoire to you and you hold it while I do the exorcism and drive the demon out of it. Then your job is to keep the demon occupied and pass me the grimoire. All we're trying to do is get the grimoire away from the demon and closed into this circle, then we can take our time getting Rho out of it."

"No problem," Navanax said.

"Then let's proceed," Cham said. "The rest of you take your places, please. I need to balance your wards." She shifted the magicians back and forth by inches, fractions of an inch, finally by nothing physical at all but with commands about their attention. "Focus," she said. "Think a little to the left."

It would have been one thing, Teddy thought, *if any of this were difficult.* If she needed telling.

"Concentrate, please," Cham said, and put her bundle of herbs onto the coals.

495

Warren opened the book and picked up a penknife from the table, and Teddy made herself stop thinking about anything except the charm they were about to cast. She forgot all about the alchemists, all about Neil, about Russell, about herself; she even almost forgot how irritating Cham was.

***

Rho was getting used to the harsh landscape around him. It had depth; it was more than a metaphor or a vision, it was a construct that extended down into one's thoughts and organized them. Everything fit into it. And it was labor-saving, for the demon could do most of the thinking about it. Rho could relax in this world. All he had to supply was the anger, a sort of comfortable simmering.

They're back, the demon thought.

Rho didn't wonder who. They were all malignant. Whatever they did with the book would be for their own benefit, not his, and when the soft light began to spread around him again, he knew it was true. They wanted to make him vulnerable-and he was. He couldn't stop the magicians holding the book from taking things out of the secret parts of his mind, spreading his most precious dreams out and poking in them.

Rage and terror replaced his comfortable anger, and he fought to pull himself out of the meadow forming around him, away from the footpath along its edge. Something lay behind the hedgerow and Rho wouldn't go there, wouldn't even go close enough to look at it. He wouldn't! *When people see what you want, they know how to hurt you; you mustn't ever think about what you really want. When you think about that sort of thing you turn soft.* Rho tugged away from the charm. *You start giving it away. I won't! They can't make me!*

The harsh landscape reappeared at the edges of his mind and he felt relief and safety. This pretty meadow was just another part of the hateful world. He could cope with it, as long as he never let anything fool him into thinking it could be real. He pulled anger back around him like a covering. *Fuck you,* he thought at the person holding the book, and flipped page eighty-three up at them.

***

The book was the only live thing in the room, or so Bill thought. He sat with his face turned away from Rho, or the complacent body that Rho had left behind, and thought about pushing Cham aside, turning and reaching down the bed in one movement and smashing its face in. He'd never gotten to smash Gordon. By the time Bill had found out-been told, he corrected himself-it had been too late for him to waste time being angry. He'd had to work at saving Gordon, instead.

Warren kept talking and writing, casting the charm from his green book. Something spread out from him, under the words Bill couldn't understand, and it was just what Vinca had told him to expect. It made a man think about what might happen if he decided what he wanted and went after it.

Hell, I know what I want, Bill thought. *I want to know why he did it. One question I've got. Just why. Not who, or when, or how much, or any of the six million questions people ask. But can I get an answer? Not fucking likely.*

"It's no use," Warren said, and put the book on the table. Bill didn't like the way he put it down. Too final, like closing the lid on something.

"What's no use?" he snapped. "Trying to fix things is always 'no use' around this Academy. It's cheaper just to burn them and buy new."

Teddy Whin glared at Bill. "There's no point taking it out on Warren," she said. "He can't get Rho away from the demon. You want to look at the auras yourself?"

"So now you just give up."

That shut Teddy up. She obviously hadn't thought of a plan B.

"I don't have all day to waste on this," Bill said.

Cham Ligalla blew out her candle. "How long do your bad moods usually last?" she asked, and Bill almost answered, 'two years so far,' when he saw the question was aimed at Rho.

"A few hours," Rho said cheerfully.

"It's ten now," Cham said. "Let's come back at two."

"No, let me try," Russell spoke up, from near the door. "I can cast that charm as well as you can," he said to Warren. "You've got to take a break some time." He sat down and put the book on his lap. For a long time he sat there, holding it as if it were something heavy and soft.

The room grew quieter and quieter, and Bill found it impossible to concentrate. He kept wandering away into his own thoughts. He listed all the 'why' questions he wanted answers to and all the people he wanted them from.

Russell read the charm as if he were thinking hard about each syllable. He cut his hand in the middle of the reading, not before it, and because he read so slowly there seemed to be plenty of time for the cutting and writing.

Bill didn't have any sense of options when Russell was reading the charm. He felt all his attention sucked into the syllables, as if they were a whirlpool leading into one point; it was like listening to a guild tribunal. Russell was leading him through something, to some specific point, but when Bill shut his eyes all he could see was Gordon's face, more sharply than he'd seen it for months. Time went away, until Russell shut the book and held it closed. Then the world began to rebuild itself, but it wasn't real enough to move in for a few minutes. Everyone in the room looked dazed. Then Teddy Whin looked away and picked up the camera arcana.

"Wow," she said, looking through it. "We have results. Two separate auras again. Your turn, Cham!"

***

All Rho's anger slipped away from him, as if he had slid out of it into something else, something hard to identify... *I'm bored,* he thought, and immediately snarled at himself. *Bored! Just because you are trapped in a book for all eternity? Poor baby! This is what it is supposed to be like. If you did not get bored, they would hardly be able to count on your doing whatever they wanted whenever they finally do you the favor of opening the book. Bored! Just wait until you have been in here a few hundred years! You will be begging for their attention...* All this commentary, while accurate, seemed beside the point, because Rho's first thought had been misleading. Bored was the wrong word. What he really felt was lonely.

I miss talking to animals, he thought, and the part of his mind that was abusing the magicians, the book, and the nature of life in general seemed not to hear him. He explored the notion in little thoughts, trying to escape his own notice.

For eighteen years Rho had listened to animals every day, even if it were only roaches or ants in the corner of a hotel room. Why that should make a difference, he didn't know, for roaches and ants had little to say. What was he really missing? An interesting puzzle. One that could become engrossing. One couldn't be bored with such an interesting puzzle at hand, but neither could one think about it hard. It had to be nibbled at so quietly, like a mouse or a roach; he had to sneak up on it, under its edges, pick bits off it while the other mind, the big complaining one, was thinking about something else.

Rho imagined himself picking at this problem and carrying bits of it back into the darkness under the kitchen cupboards, where he would build something out of it. A world of his own. What would he put into it? He felt oddly fearless as he began to construct what he wanted. It didn't matter if the demon saw it or not, because the demon would see it eventually no matter what Rho did.

I want that meadow, Rho thought, *and those hedgerows.* He knew what every clump of grass should be like, and how the aspen leaves flashed in the wind. He knew every creature, down to the slugs under leaves beside the path, and he knew what was behind the trees, at the center of the next field. He knew every inch of the house, the garden, the yard and barns. It hurt when he looked at them, like having something pulled out. *You're not doing this by yourself!* part of Rho's mind warned him. *They're not making you do this for your health. Somebody's trying to get control of you in a new way, to use your dreams against you. You're going to get hurt.* The buildings turned dim and foggy.

I always get hurt, Rho thought, and he should have become angry at the thought, but he didn't. It felt more like finding something out, or like starting to understand a new kind of animal. *I'll be in here forever with a demon. What's the point of trying not to get hurt? It has forever to hurt me in.*

That's only because they've left you in here, said the other part of his mind. *They know what's happening to you. They just don't care.* Rho didn't care either.

I have forever to be mad, he thought. The farmyard came back into focus. Rho thought he saw someone sitting on the porch, rocking, but he would have to get closer to make sure; he began to think up the path that would take him there.

***

501

When Warren cast the charm it was like looking into a clear space filled with potential. Neil would have painted it in layers of black and dark blue, with stars. What Russell cast out of the same charm was like one of those stars imploding.

Black holes, Neil thought. *How could I paint black holes?*

He was bullshitting and he knew it. He hadn't paid enough attention to paint either charm; he'd been too preoccupied with what Navanax and Vinca must be thinking. It was like taking someone to his favorite play, or bringing a date home to meet the family. Warren looked too fat and lazy, Russell sounded pompous and kept making faces at Teddy. Neil couldn't remember when he had been so anxious for his colleagues to act respectable, to just keep from embarrassing him for half an hour. If only it had been a different set of them, Patsy Hoth and Susan... *It could be worse,* he thought. *We could have had Will and Linus.*

It wasn't the other magicians' fault. *It's all me,* Neil thought. *Just me being stupid.* He mentally shook himself and thought about the charms again. Warren had cast a charm about going out into the world and finding what was there. Russell had cast one about looking inside yourself. Neil didn't know which one he liked better, but Rho must have known, because the second charm had worked. Russell was handing the book over to Bill, and Cham was beginning her part of the invocation, speaking directly to the book in Bill's lap. Neil knew Cham wouldn't embarrass him. He relaxed and focused on his part of the exorcism.

***

Bill took the grimoire without really looking at it. He was still thinking about how different the charm had been when Warren and Russell cast it. Then Cham began to speak to the book and her voice caught at him. She used a language Bill couldn't understand, but she was talking about anger. She was sympathizing, telling the demon she knew how it felt, and every syllable made Bill more furious than the last. A lot she knew! He looked at Cham's smooth head and calm face. She was an emotionless bitch. She had never felt anything not involved with her own superiority.

Now her voice was changing, turning more remote, shutting off that false empathy. Anger was really pointless, wasn't it? he heard her saying, and Bill thought he would love to show her how wrong she was. She could be the last person to ever tell him anger was pointless. He glanced up, and saw Vinca and Warren watching him.

Oh, calm down, Bill thought. *I'm not the sort who has psychotic flashbacks. I'm not suddenly going to think we're in the city square and you're all guild inquisitors. I know exactly where I am-but still,* he admitted, *I might hurt somebody.* It was an odd feeling, to surface for an instant and realize he was in deeper water than he had thought. Cham spoke again, and the moment's uncertainty ebbed away as something flowed out of the book and across Bill's chest.

I suppose I expected it to materialize, Bill thought, *but it probably doesn't have enough strength to do that.* He could feel the demon against

503

his wards, like a weak electric shock spreading out from the grimoire. There was something puzzled about it; it searched across him, and Bill imagined himself as a new quantity in its experience. *We belong to different worlds,* he thought. *Alchemists are really just glorified mundanes.*

He shut his eyes, and that closed off everything except the electric feeling and Cham Ligalla's voice telling him that anger was pointless. Bill found himself listening to Cham in reverse, as if her voice were one of those pictures that only spelled out words when he stopped looking at the black shapes and looked at the white between them. The space between Cham's syllables would tell him why anger did matter. It would tell him what a man could do with his anger, if he forgot about the rules. The feeling around him prickled, growing stronger. Cham Ligalla's voice went faster, and there was less space between the syllables, but Bill didn't want to be hurried on something this important. He wished she would be quiet.

Chapter Twenty-four

Warren stood beside the door, holding one of Cham's candles and keeping up the chant that had to be kept up around an exorcism. He felt as if he weren't really there. *I ought to be worrying,* he thought. *If I were here, I'd be worrying, wouldn't I?* But he wasn't, and that was all to say about that. Without that distraction, Warren found that Cham's charm was no challenge at all. He could do it without thinking. He could look around at Russell, at Teddy and Vinca, and read what was in their faces when they looked back at him. He could see the blue shimmer where something brushed up against Bill Navanax's wards, and how it snuggled closer with every word Cham Ligalla spoke.

"Will you be quiet?" Navanax said to her, and handed her the book.

Cham stopped speaking as if this was what she had expected. She nodded at Russell, and he pulled the block out of the grooved tiles so blood could flow together, closing Cham and the book inside the pentacle with Rho. Warren felt all the magicians relaxing as Russell hooked up the safety chain. Cham spoke a few words and the lines went up from the pentacle, shimmering where they were closest to Navanax and the demon.

"All right," she said. "You can stop chanting and let it go. Good work."

The magicians stopped chanting and grinned at each other. Neil was the only one who looked worried.

505

"It's not going," he said, pointing at the chair where Navanax sat, still surrounded by the blue glow.

Looking at him, Warren felt that middle manager feeling. The feeling that knowing what was going to happen would do nothing to avoid it. He could almost see ideas chasing each other through Navanax's mind, and why not? Demons, remaking the arcane world with a thought; alchemists, making this world by wanting it to change. This had been an alliance waiting to happen, but who would have believed Warren if he had told them?

"William!" Vinca said, in a sharp voice, and Warren could have told him that was a mistake. The blue light grew brighter.

"Cham, do you think you can finish in there?" Warren asked quietly.

Cham looked up from the book she was holding open in front of Rho.

"This isn't working," she said.

"Neither is this."

Cham's glance took in the magicians, frozen in their places, and the blue glow around Navanax. "I can't let it get at the book," she said.

"Burn the book, if you have to."

"Give it a minute," Cham said.

The glow around Navanax was pulling away into a familiar-looking column of smoke. *It's going to materialize!* Warren thought, and felt for his wards. He stepped back as far as he could, almost pressing himself out the window, and saw snatches of the others through the smoke-Teddy saying something, Neil looking sick, Navanax with his

506

eyes open and the white face of someone who had lost too much power. Then the smoke coalesced, and a new person stood in the room with them.

***

The room seemed bigger when the new guy stood in it. He was expansive. It was the way he stood, with his broad shoulders held out as if he were going to make one gesture and push the world open around him. He had a jock's face, broad and shiny, and a blond crew cut.

Neil liked him, except for the eyes. They were a demon's eyes-it looked at Neil as if it were looking in a mirror, and the eyes changed. They turned gray. It smiled at Neil and turned away.

"You wanted to talk with me?" it said to Navanax. It held its arms out toward him. "Here I am."

Everybody yelled at once, except Cham and Rho.

"Don't touch! It's the demon! That's how it got Rho! Look out for your wards, William!" they yelled.

Navanax stood up. He braced himself against the chair. Neil wondered if he had heard anything.

"Why are you-why did you... ?" he said.

The demon put its hands on its hips and laughed. "For money," it said. "I wanted enough money to have my own life. To do things the way I wanted to do them. To get away from you. I was tired of selling myself."

"Oh, bull," Teddy said, from behind Neil. "We don't make enough money to buy boy toys."

507

"This may not be the moment-" Russell said.

"Why not? We need a little reality check here. Of course," Teddy admitted, "they might do better over in alchemy."

Neil had missed whatever else the demon said to Navanax, but it had made Warren's face turn red. He was looking tactfully out the window.

"Get away from me," Navanax said, turning away from the demon. "You're not really Gordon."

"I am what you think he was," the demon said. "This is what you dream of bringing back. What you cry over at night. Is it my fault if it is pitiful?"

"Go to hell!" Navanax said, and tried to step forward, past the demon.

Its arm flared blue against his wards, but it stood its ground. Neil caught his breath. How little a difference there was between the demon touching Navanax and his touching the demon! As little as an intention. He couldn't push it aside.

The demon smiled in triumph, and then its expression changed. It looked past Navanax into the pentacle and snarled. Neil had barely enough time to see the gray mass of smoke trapped inside the pentacle, then it burst out, filling the room, and for a moment he couldn't see anything.

***

Something tugged at Rho, and he shook it off. *Later,* he thought. *Right now, I'm doing something else. Right now, I'm making dirt.*

He made perfect dirt, dirt with muddy patches and frostings of sand granules, where long-legged

508

beetles balanced until they saw Rho watching them, said "Yikes!" and flew away.

He made pebbles half-buried in the dirt. He made little frog-faced insects with red eyes, damselflies folding black wings over their iridescent bodies, and hurrying off the edges of the path he put this year's toads, black and nimble.

He did all this rather than look up at the house the dirt was taking him toward. He could feel himself building that house, somewhere back in his mind, and he didn't want to take control of it. He wanted it to be real, not something he could edit and revise the way he was revising the path, pushing elderberry bushes back from it and pulling buttercups closer in. He would have shut his eyes to keep the house a secret from himself, but he had no eyes to shut, so he made dirt instead, patches of moss, red-crested lichens on fallen branches.

As he drew nearer to the house he felt its glow, as if he were walking into a fire. At first that seemed part of the power of whatever his mind had built, but then it was too hot and Rho began to imagine flame and wonder why. Had the demon withdrawn itself in order to prepare a horrid surprise? Was it letting him imagine important things only so it could destroy them before him? The path began to lose its substance, to flicker and become flames itself, and Rho realized he had made a terrible mistake.

Common sense told him to give up now, before something worse happened. His feeling of reckless bravery had evaporated in the growing heat, and he couldn't imagine why he had thought it didn't matter if he got hurt. Here, in the place he had thought would hold comfort, he was feeling the first physical pain he'd felt since he entered the book. He was burning, scorching, breathing in air so hot it tore at his lungs.

Give it up! his common sense told him. *Pick up the anger you set aside, armor yourself with it, go back to the spiky landscape where nothing can change for the worse. Whatever you do, don't look up. Don't see what was on the porch the way it will be now. Don't see what fire is doing to it.*

But I want it, Rho cried out to himself. *It's what I really want! I need to know what it is. I have to see!* The path in front of him shimmered, silica crystals turning to colorless flames. One of the toads writhed between them and Rho thought it out of the way, into the grass, before he realized the grass itself was now an inferno. Little things were dying in it all around him. He heard their cries.

He wrenched his gaze upward before common sense could say anything more, to look at the bonfire of a house in front of him, flames outlining its door and windows. The porch railings and steps, the rocking chair, were made up of flame. Rho opened his mouth to say something, and choked on hot air. Then he saw a face, one that didn't belong there. It looked at him soberly from the middle of the flames, and he couldn't think it out of there to safety, even if there had been anywhere safe. He couldn't think at all, the fire hurt so, but he threw himself toward the face and into the flames, not certain whether he meant to save it or destroy it.

***

I saw it all, Teddy thought, even as it was happening. She knew she was going to be telling this story for the rest of her life. Nobody else had seen all of it. They'd all seen the demon get in Bill Navanax's face, and maybe some of them had seen Cham put the book into the brazier full of coals. Vinca had probably seen Warren pull the wards down from the window and jump back from it, gone white of a sudden the way he had in the pentarium. Maybe Neil had seen Russell cast a charm at the demon, one that made Teddy's hair stand on end but was just a casual gesture for Russell. And everyone had seen the pentacle come down in a tumble of bedding and hot coals, smoke and flame. *That part would even be on tape,* Teddy thought. *A record of inflammable bedding in the exorcism suite, and serve the hospital right.*

They'd all seen the demon roar, swat at something in front of it, and leap for the brazier, searching through coals for what might remain of Warren's grimoire, but nobody except Teddy had seen all of it.

***

Rho didn't have time to see any of it. The room was a blur of faces and flames, the person he had lunged for only another of the faces as he let go of her. He had been so close to knowing something. So close to being certain! Now it was all confusion, heat and smoke. Something loomed up beside him, brushing against him, and Rho seized it. It was the demon, something he knew. It was chanting words that seemed familiar, but it broke off the chant to snarl at Rho.

"Fool!" it said, pushing him aside. "You have lost everything."

It began the chant again, and Rho recognized it. It was the charm he'd thought of the most when he was in the book, the one he'd suggested to everyone who picked the thing up. The charm from page eighty-three.

Rho grabbed at the demon again. "This has to stop," he said. "It's gone on long enough." The demon kept chanting, and Rho felt the charm building itself around them. He tried to think of a countercharm, but his head was full of the demon's syllables. He mouthed them himself, spoke them; he pulled the charm away from the demon and cast it back.

He heard the demon howl and felt it trying to twist away, but he held on. Flames were rising all around him now, from the demon as well as the bedding. Something sharp ripped across his arm. The demon shrieked again, higher pitched and desperate. Some of the faces leapt toward him, grappled with one another, pulled back. There weren't as many of them in the room now. Page eighty-three destroyed things, but it had to be done. This had to be over with. He shut his eyes and hung on till there was nothing left to hang on to.

***

That's what it looks like when somebody burns, Neil thought. *What his face looks like in the flames. What his lover's face looks like, and his lover's*

512

friends, and all the witnesses. He knew he'd never paint it. He'd never paint Bill's expression when he saw the flames rise around the demon, or the way he looked when Warren and Vinca stopped him from jumping toward the bed. He'd never paint the way Vinca's face had looked, either, when Bill Navanax pushed him away and stumbled out the door. Neil wished he hadn't seen any of it.

He looked around the room for someone who could tell him it was all right to leave, but they were all watching Rho and the demon. For once, Neil was where the action was, and he couldn't have cared less. He blew out the candle he was holding and walked past Teddy to the door. He poked her as he passed. "I'm gonna check on Bill," he said, and Teddy nodded without looking at him.

The hospital corridor didn't look as if anything horrible were going on in one of the rooms. Neil found Bill in the closet around the corner, trying to get his coat out of a tangle of wire hangers.

"Are you all right?"

"I can't do this," Bill said. He put a hand on the closet rod and leaned his forehead against it. He was shaking.

Neil felt cold, just looking at him.

"You don't need to do anything," Neil said. "They've got it under control."

"I mean this," Bill said. "These hangers."

"Oh. Let me have a shot." Bill didn't move. Neil had to push him to one side to get the coat. He had to pull Bill out of the closet and drape the coat over his shoulders. "You can't go out like this," Neil said. "Sit here till I find a nurse."

"I don't want to stay in here," Bill said, but he sat down. "It's too cold." He crunched down in the chair, trying to get warm.

"No, you have to stay here," Neil said. "Something's really wrong with you. Do you have a sorcerer? Did you see anybody after Gordon died? Who should I call?"

"I don't have a sorcerer," Bill said. "I haven't been sick."

"I think you're coming down with something now," Neil said. It was like talking to a child. He felt Bill's hands, his forehead, as if he were reassuring a ten-year-old. "You're really cold," he said. "That's the way Warren was after Nezumia talked to him. Cham Ligalla did something to warm him up."

"Keep her away from me," Bill said, sounding more like himself.

"Then I have to get a nurse."

The nurse acted as if alchemists stumbled out of exorcisms every day. She cracked open a warming charm, plastered it on Bill's back, and heated up a potion for him in the microwave. Then she put them both in a room with three bunk beds and a row of lockers.

"So did they finish the exorcism?" Bill asked.

"I don't know. I came out to see how you were. I'm just not meant to know what's happening," Neil said. "I've accepted my fate."

"That's more than most of us can say."

"Look," Neil said, "I didn't hear everything that demon said, but you know it was lying. It was just trying to make you mad."

514

"How could you not hear what it said? It wasn't six feet away from you."

"Talent. No, really. I heard as far as selling itself, and then Teddy started bitching about how low our salaries were."

Bill put a hand over his face. "This is unreal."

"Sometimes Teddy is sort of thoughtful," Neil said. The nurse came back in.

"I told you we'd have a crowd in here," she said cheerfully, ushering Warren, Russell, and Teddy into the room. Warren looked almost as sick as Bill, and they made him lie down on one of the other bunks.

"What's wrong with Warren?" Neil asked.

"Oh, Nezumia got in when he took down the wards," Teddy said, sounding proud of herself for knowing. "It took a lot out of him."

"I didn't know you took the wards down," Russell said to Warren.

"We needed help. I didn't think Cham would get done in time. You all right, Bill?"

"Fine." Bill rolled over so all they could see was his back. Teddy looked at it doubtfully.

"That was one nasty demon," she said to all and sundry. "I hope Rho and Nezumia finished it off for good."

"Where is Rho?"

"He's still in the suite. He and Cham both got burned. Can you believe it? Inflammable bedding! That is so stupid," Teddy said.

"Hindsight," Russell said. He bent over and looked at Warren. "We ought to get out of here and let these two sleep. On second thought, I think I'll lie down for a while myself."

515

"You don't look so good," Teddy agreed. "I'll ask that nurse to have a look at you."

Neil looked at Bill's back, but it gave no sign whether he should stay or go. He felt embarrassed about asking. *After all,* he thought, *I just came out and shoved myself into all this. He didn't ask me to look after him.* When they got out in the hall, Neil wished he had stayed inside, but he knew if he had remained he would have wished he'd left. He was standing outside the door, waiting for Teddy to come back from the nurse's station, when Vinca came up.

"How is William?" he asked.

"I think he's sleeping. He didn't want to talk."

Vinca nodded. "Thank you for looking after him."

"That's okay. I didn't do anything."

Teddy came back, following the nurse. "You're sure this is normal?" she was saying.

"Mm-hm," the nurse said. "Don't worry. After a tough exorcism, sometimes Magister Ligalla sleeps for two or three days. Now you all ought to go eat something, as long as you're up. Get some protein."

"Come along with us," Teddy said to Vinca.

"No. No, I think I will wait here," Vinca said. "Thank you for the offer."

He sat down, a small figure in one of the plastic chairs, and Neil felt sorry for him. The magicians were quiet as they walked down to the elevators.

"I guess it's all over," Teddy said when the doors closed. She stretched her arms up toward the elevator's amber lights and sighed. "Something for Warren to put in his year-end report, between enrollment figures and grant revenues."

516

She's right, Neil thought. Things could happen and be over with in a flash just as he started to be a part of them, just the way people got on this elevator and then got off again and left it unchanged. The elevator doors opened on bustle, conversation, and the smell of soup. Teddy stepped out of the elevator, and the bustle parted and let her in. She looked back at Neil.

"Come on," she said. "I'll buy you lunch."

Epilogue

"I never thought I'd complain about invoking big demons," Teddy said, "but this is starting to make me nervous."

Warren hid his smile in the steam, turning his face into the shower spray.

"We shouldn't be able to trap these demons without all thirteen of us in the circle," she went on, drying her shoulders. "And have you heard the questions they're asking? Nezumia grilled me for half an hour yesterday on the nature of gender."

"They're up to something," Russell said. "What have they been asking the rest of you?"

"Nothing new with me," Warren said. "We've always talked geography."

"Um, I wasn't exactly talking to one of them Tuesday," Isaac Graham said, "that is, I was just reinforcing the lines after that visiting magician cast that charm-you remember-"

"Yeah," and "Sure," everybody said, encouraging Isaac.

"And this demon asked me if it was entitled to a library card. And to use the gym. As, ah, an Academy employee. I think it was just teasing," Isaac said. He twisted his beard into a point.

"What did you tell it?" Teddy asked.

"I, uh, said it would have to ask someone in charge. Probably Warren."

"It said 'entitled'?" Russell hung his towel over his shoulder. "Is that the exact word it used?"

"Oh, yes."

518

"James," Russell and Teddy said, almost in chorus.

James Kalin looked up with an air of staunch righteousness. He looked more like a working man than ever, his face windburned from two weeks in the field.

"You're trying to unionize demons!" Teddy accused.

"They seem interested," James said. "Just because you don't see the virtue in solidarity doesn't mean the demons can't."

"That is a reckless and irresponsible action," Linus said.

Warren saw Patsy Hoth shut her mouth on the beginnings of a similar protest. She opened it again to disagree with Linus.

"That's just what people said about the Society for Ethical Lechery," she said. "And the IDA, for that matter."

Warren grinned. "The dean's been wanting me to name someone to answer for independent demonic activity, ever since they got Vinca's report on the pentarium. You're it, James."

"I'll do it."

"Oh no, I want in on that too," Teddy said. "and Russell. Right, Russell?"

"Same old group," Russell said. "Maybe we should ask Rho, when he gets back."

Rho's name had a dampening effect on the magicians. Nobody wanted to talk about him in front of Cham, because she must have had some part in what happened to him. And they didn't want to talk in front of Warren, because it had been his grandfather's charm that finished the damage. The

519

pentarium shower room was not the right place to have the argument about renewing Rho's contract. Russell had been more than mischievous in suggesting he be part of a new project.

"We have enough questionable specialties represented in this department, without keeping mundanes on salary," Linus said, pointedly not looking at Patsy Hoth.

"We're not having this discussion," Warren said sharply. "If I were Rho, I wouldn't want anything more to do with demons or with this department. We haven't had a semester that inspires confidence. Have any of you visited him in the hospital?"

"I stopped in last night," Will said.

"How is he?"

"How would any of us be? He's depressed as hell. He misses hearing the animals. Not that he said any of that. He just talked about when they were letting him out."

"When?"

"Monday, I think. He's pushing for the weekend, though."

"There probably aren't any animals in that hospital, anyway," Teddy said. "We ought to drop in on him tonight."

"Rho says there always are. Animals in hospitals."

"I didn't need to know that," Teddy said. She tucked in her turtleneck and headed out the door, just behind Neil and just ahead of Warren. "So hey, Neil. Want to go over and see Rho?"

"I can't tonight," Neil said.

"Say what?" Teddy asked. She poked him. "What's going on here? How long does it take to paint a spare room, hey?"

"I thought you didn't like gossip." Neil grinned.

"Me? I love gossip. Dish!"

Warren cleared his throat and the two looked around with innocent faces. They stood aside, deferring to his rank and bulk, and let him precede them up the stairs. He heard them whispering and giggling below him, but they must have stopped on the second floor, because when Warren stood outside his office, unlocking it, Russell was the next person to come out of the stairwell. He looked a little abashed when he saw Warren looking at him.

"We didn't need to start that conversation just now," Warren said.

"Look," Russell said, pushing past into Warren's office. "Whatever those demons did, it brought back my power. Who's to say it can't do the same for Rho?"

"Well, if you think you can do something for him, I'll put you down as his mentor. Lilian will never forgive me if I do it myself."

"You're in a delegating mood today! I'll flee while I'm only wounded." Russell grinned.

"Flee over to the hospital and see Rho."

"I was there yesterday, and I'm going back tomorrow. What's your plan for the weekend?"

"We're going to Lilian's cousin's wedding. Our plane leaves in about three hours, if it can get out between snowstorms." Warren shuffled through the stack of mail on his desk. "What else can I delegate before I leave?"

"I'm gone!" Russell said, backing into the corridor. Warren heard him warning other faculty as he went.

Warren sat down, leaning his chair back into the silence that pushed in on the building after a snowstorm. All the department's noises were closed in, as if Warren were inside a living body listening to its cells. He shut his eyes and thought he could feel the shape of the body. If he paid attention long enough, he would know what it was meant to be and do. But long before he could pay that much attention, his phone was ringing and people were knocking on his door.

***

When Rho got into his tower room Saturday morning, after a cold walk from the hospital, it was clean. He hadn't thought about that. When he saw everything neat, his furniture in place and the floor scrubbed, then he thought about how awful it would have been to come back to the mess he had left. *I want to stay here,* he thought. *People are nice here.* But it was too late to think that.

White light filled the room. Rho saw white clouds, white snowflakes, piles of white mounting on his windowsill. The only splash of color was a red tent on the roof below his window. As he watched it, wondering, a door slammed outside. Isaac Graham came into view, walking carefully along the roof. He stopped outside the tent and looked into the sky, but didn't seem to notice Rho at the window. He bent and went into the tent.

Nothing more moved on the rooftops. Nothing flew past except snowflakes. Rho huddled in his chair and looked at the pile of wood someone had put beside his fireplace. He could have a fire. He could light up the room, make it warm, make himself feel as if it were home for two, maybe three more months, and then have to go. His breath felt thick.

I can't just sit here, he thought. *I have to know.* Without thinking about how nasty the trip up the stairs had been, he went back down them to the third floor. He took a deep breath before he pushed the door open onto the empty corridor. He went by the vampire lab, Warren's and Russell's offices, and almost on tiptoe past Patsy Hoth's door. He went to the far end of the hall, to Patsy Hoth's rabbit room, and before he got there he knew. It was hardly worth going all the way, but he did. He stood with his head pressed against the door, listening to a room full of rabbits with incubi. It should have sounded like a singles bar. Rho should have heard catcalls. He should have heard come-ons and wolf whistles. Instead, he heard a rustle, a thump, a squeal cut off in the middle. He heard a door sighing shut and footsteps, and he didn't care.

"The hospital said you'd checked yourself out," Russell said. "Did you walk over here? One of us would've given you a ride."

Rho nodded and let the noise wash over him. The door felt smooth against his forehead. Perhaps he could just stand here and not think-but no, Russell was steering him down the hall. Rho went where he was pushed and sat where Russell put him. It was just one of those things that happened to

523

him. They went on for a while and then they were over.

"I'll get you some water." Russell went away somewhere.

Rho looked around. The sun had come out, and sent light through three arrow slit windows to flash off plants with glossy leaves and off bright and shiny things hanging off the bookcases, all of them in motion. Crystal wards hung in every window, sending shattered bits of light around the room.

"Have you ever used crystal wards?" Russell said, coming back in and handing Rho a mug of water. "Susan said you were a dab hand with crystals."

"I was."

"Well, that's the issue, isn't it?"

Rho looked into the mug. "I'll be all right," he said. "I've been unemployed before." But then he'd been with the cats. The pigeons and rats and roaches. He'd never been on his own.

"Don't jump to conclusions," Russell said. "You're not the first person this has happened to. I lost most of my power last year, and got it back again when the demons cast me out of my body last month."

"How?" Rho asked, disbelieving. It was impossible to believe Russell, smug and confident behind his desk, had ever felt his power go, his life over.

"I don't know," Russell said firmly, and smiled. "I was thinking we might find out together. The first thing to do is categorize what's been lost. I think we both should sit down and describe our magic in as

524

much detail as possible. And what made it go away."

"I'm not sure what did that," Rho said cautiously. "I don't know everything that went on during the exorcism."

"You'll have to ask around. Talk to Cham."

"That charm I cast on the demon-it was a charm of destruction. What if I destroyed my power?"

"Nobody learns theory anymore," Russell said to the room at large. It glittered its agreement. "You can't create or destroy power. You can only mess with your connection to it. You can cut yourself off from it, but it's still out there. The question is, what kind of power did you connect to, and how? That's why I want a detailed description of every time you can remember gaining power. I didn't read that charm you cast," he said, writing on a scrap of paper, "but I remember the one I cast. Copy this one into your grimoire. Give it a try. It seemed important, at the time."

"All right," Rho said. He put the paper in his pocket. He stood up, feeling better, but Russell looked concerned.

"I can't make any promises for the department," he warned, standing up himself. "Who knows what's going to happen? It's just your first year."

"I know," Rho said. "Even if I had my powers, they might not want to keep me on. I might not want to stay."

"That's the spirit!" Russell said. "Have you got window wards up there? Take some of these until you can make your own." He walked around his office gathering crystals, as if he had to be doing something. When he handed them to Rho, his face

525

was sober. "I can't guarantee this will save your job here," he said. "But it's a great topic. It's the next big thing for demonology. I've always felt, if you have a project, you'll find the place to work on it. The project makes the job."

Rho nodded. "Thanks," he said. The crystals were warm in his hands as he climbed the stairs, and he found his room as full of sunlight as a bubble.

Rho lit a fire and hung the crystals in every window. There wasn't anything dangerous in liking his room. In enjoying it while he had it. *Nothing lasts forever.* He looked in his refrigerator for evidence. The larder was in better condition than he expected; he found cereal, an unopened box of milk, and some shriveled apples. The bread had fossilized; he pounded it into crumbs and scattered them on the windowsill. By the time he'd finished his cereal, the first pigeon had arrived.

Rho watched the birds for a while, but it was too depressing to see and not hear them. He turned around, instead, and began to make notes about when he had used his magic. When it had been strongest. The project grew, as a good project should, and before long he had spread old notebooks over the table, stacked folders of class notes beside his chair, and created a list of people to ask. Cham, Warren, Susan Teale.

The list was what slowed him down. On Monday, he'd have to face them all. They'd all be in the pentarium, and Rho wouldn't be in the circle doing his part. He'd have to ask Susan for her ghostmeter readings, after lying to her about the demon. He'd have to face Warren, after destroying his grimoire and lying to his wife. Patsy Hoth would be there, and Anders Regan. Rho pushed his notes away. The department wasn't just Russell Cinea and a new project.

"Maybe this isn't for me," he said aloud. The room disagreed; it glinted and crackled, warm, full of light. "There are nice rooms everywhere," Rho said. "Maybe magic isn't for me." He looked at his notes from the past month. Had his power come from the demon? From being angry? "Maybe I screw up with magic because my magic is screwed up," Rho said.

Something rapped on the window behind him. He turned around in his chair, and the pigeon rapped again. It held its head sideways and looked at Rho with one eye. "What?" he said, and the pigeon backed a step away. It pecked at something in front of it, picked up a snow-covered twig and dropped it. When Rho opened the window it hovered beside him for a moment, its wings blowing snow crystals up in a swirl.

"It's too early to nest," Rho said. "But don't take my advice." He blew and dusted as best he could, clearing snow off the messy nest. The pigeon landed as soon as he closed the window and began rearranging the twigs. Rho put his hands in his pockets, closing one of them on something that rustled.

"Well, hell," he said, and spread Russell's charm out on the table. Paper and blood were all it called for. But when he cast it, it left him with nothing but the taste of paper and a sore finger. He put his head down on the table, in the sunlight. *I had more magic in the book,* he thought, looking at the sun through his lashes and watching the rainbows

527

they made. This charm worked, in the book. It made a sunset. Rho shut his eyes and made a sunset in his mind, out of the orange glow on his eyelids. *It made a whole world,* he thought. *A meadow and a hedgerow, a path and a farm.*

Rho opened his eyes into dazzle. There was no sound except the crackle of his fire. He had to search through the room for the telephone book, for the overseas exchange numbers, and he didn't dare stop for a second. He didn't dare let himself think he could wait and think things over. He dialed out of the Academy and out of Osyth, and didn't dare let thought get in the way of the number his parents had made him memorize twenty years ago, in case he ever got lost... He heard crackling on the line, buzzing. A ring, another, and then a voice.

The Magic Building shone in the sunlight as if it were frosted, and on the west tower's windowsill a pigeon put its last stick in place and snuggled down into the nest, closing its eyes as if to enjoy a job well done.

THE END

528

www.ingramcontent.com/pod-product-compliance
Lightning Source LLC
Chambersburg PA
CBHW011359010726
47495CB00009B/2701